PRAISE FOR
NEW TOMORROW

"What could better suit history that refuses to confine itself to the past, than the present scenario? Starting in LA, a ragtag People and a few mil grunts fighting for the future of civilization? Where do you fit in this, and how do you cope? Do you doomscroll, escape, try to ignore? I say "try" because no one can escape.

Instead, I recommend a companion, New Tomorrow by Cody Goodfellow. I've been carrying it around for weeks like soldiers at the Front did, the book of poetry against the chest. New Tomorrow takes place in a past that is all so present, you can smell its blood. I don't know how long it took to write but I do know that he has to have transported himself and lived in this version of time and place, for every time I checked, he's as faithful to a parallel history and it's all so immediate and fresh, I couldn't help thinking he must have made it up or he was wrong, but he's more accurate than Movietone news. Yet fearless."

ANNA TAMBOUR
(DEATH GOES TO THE DOGS)

"New Tomorrow is punching above its weight class on almost every page. It is an epic worthy of the word... as strange as it is ambitious. An unbelievable triumph."

DAVID AGRANOFF
(author of PUNK ROCK GHOST STORY)

"Without giving too much away, Goodfellow once again manages to write something I fucking WISH I had written. His terrible new weird science impacts his world in ways that I BEGGED my fellow Delta Green writers to allow me to include in Arc Dream Publishing's re-release of Delta Green."

ADAM SCOTT GLANCY
(author of DELTA GREEN)

"NEW TOMORROW is a neo-pulp joyride through an alternate yesteryear populated with super-scientists, interdimensional aliens, insane technologies, plenty of rayguns, and one very lovable blob. An endlessly-inventive, gonzo retrofuturist take on the Great Depression, filtered through modern sensibilities. It's one wild time!"

BRIAN ASMAN
*(author of MAN, F*CK THIS HOUSE)*

PRAISE FOR
CODY GOODFELLOW

"Cody Goodfellow knows how to chill your blood."

STEPHEN KING
(author of IT, THE STAND)

"It doesn't matter if he's doing crime, Lovecraftian short stories, strange literary fiction disguised as madman narratives, horror, or something in between, you always get an explosive mixture of ideas and superb use of language when reading Cody Goodfellow."

GABINO IGLESIAS
(author of COYOTE SONGS)

"80s vintage horror with a contemporary edge. An exemplary wordsmith, his prose sticks a needle in your brain and gives it a twist. This stuff is Lovecraft on acid."

LAIRD BARRON
(author of THE IMAGO SEQUENCE & OTHER STORIES)

"Cody Goodfellow's imagination is a freeway flyer, and his prose is a ride on a rocket-sled. He's one of the two or three god-damned best writers in the genres today."

MICHAEL SHEA
(author of NIFFT THE LEAN AND COPPING SQUID)

NEW TOMORROW

written by
CODY GOODFELLOW

with illustrations by
MIKE DUBISCH

ODDNESS Presents
NEW TOMORROW
FIRST EDITION JULY 2025

Softback ISBN: 978-1-960213-45-7
Hardback ISBN: 978-1-960213-46-4
Electronic ISBN: 978-1-960213-47-1

To request permission, contact the
publisher at: info@oddness.us

All artwork by **Mike Dubisch**
Layout and edit by **Oddness**
with editoral input from
Anthony Trevino
& **Anna Tambour**

Ordering information:
info@oddness.us

www.oddness.us

NEW TOMORROW

written by
CODY GOODFELLOW

with illustrations by
MIKE DUBISCH

Never underestimate a man who overestimates himself.

—Franklin D. Roosevelt

"The war should be a tremendous opportunity for America."

—J.P. Morgan

Nesle, France | April 1918

Before they went to war, her big sister told Matilda Lynch that she must always make herself useful. Father always said you either were or you weren't, and nothing was worse than being useless. She'd built it up so that Matilda had expected to faint dead away when the moment came. Now up to her elbows in blood, the sight made her guts churn, but she couldn't stop staring because the horror kept her awake, and all that kept her on her feet was the fear that she might not be useful and someone would die.

"*Clamp, girl!*"

"Erm… which one?" The array of tools was a glittering blur.

"Ye gods, Til. The #3. The little one!" Minerva snatched the tool herself and slapped it in the surgeon's rubber palm.

"Steady on, nurse," Dr. Chichester gritted his teeth behind his mask, "both of you. *Cauterizing wand.*"

"Wand." He poked and dabbed at leaking blood vessels like a bored lawyer initialing a dull contract. Matilda gagged at the smoke, the stench of burning blood.

He carelessly dropped the cauterizing wand and held up his hands for fresh gloves. "*Suction…*"

"*Suction…*" Minerva swept the open abdominal cavity with the gurgling tube. "Is that satisfactory, sir?"

"One mustn't be so starved for praise. There's a girl. And *you*," Chichester arched an eyebrow at Matilda, "don't stare so. It's not the poor boy's fault he's got no face."

A throbbing detonation shook the operating theater. Minerva leaned over the steaming crevasse in the young soldier's belly as plaster dust and debris rained from the ceiling. The chapel's improvised second skeleton of spray-concrete buttresses promised to survive all but a direct hit, and the worst of the barrage had passed them by, which had everyone more frightened than the bombing itself.

It was easier when she remembered what her sister told her: "The body's just a machine, with all its plumbing and moving parts. A machine needs oil to make it go, doesn't it? That's all blood is." Automobiles didn't get sick at the sight of their own oil, nor did they cry for their mothers as the mechanic repaired them. They didn't leave behind weeping little cars when they broke down and got scrapped.

This was why Father called her the *imaginative* one with a click of his tongue and a great, soft sigh. They'd called Mother *imaginative*, and though she was an award-winning authoress of children's books, she was locked away at Saratoga Convalescence until she died, last year. Only then did Matilda see that it wasn't a compliment.

"You know so much," Matilda muttered under her breath, "you're going to waste here. They ought to make you a general." Matilda averted her gaze but still saw violet ghosts of obliterated limbs and exposed organs wherever she closed her eyes. They had been on duty for almost twenty hours. Minerva had pinched her cruelly for dozing off on her feet, but she looked more asleep than awake herself.

The suction tube nearly jumped out of her hand when Minerva handed it to her. Chichester shed his bloody, septic gloves and dunked his hands into sapphire antiseptic before donning a fresh pair and turning to the next patient. "Let's see about this gamy leg, hey?"

"Doctor," Minerva stage-whispered, "the abdominal wound..."

"What of it?"

"It's still open...?"

"So close it! One assumes even a Yank girl knows how to sew." To Matilda, he barked, "Tie it off just above the knee, won't take long."

Matilda might have gone away for a moment. Someone's fingers snapped in her face. She slapped herself with the back of her hand and hurried to apply the tourniquet. "Don't let's go all weepy over a foot, eh? Marvelous inventions, prosthetics. Better than the real thing, some say. Now, let's have the chopper..." It wasn't too heavy for Matilda to lift, but Matilda nearly dropped it on his foot.

"Another flower for the Spring bouquet," Chichester said as he worked the spring-loaded jaws through the boy's left femur. Matilda reached to sweep clear the debris, but Minerva nudged her aside and picked up the mutilated leg. Toes faintly phosphorescent with some exotic chemical. It quivered in her hand—had she tickled it? She seethed as she threw it into the bin.

"Bloody waste," the doctor working behind them muttered. "Poor bastard won't last the night, but he could do a lot of good for his mates."

His assistant, up to his elbows in the patient, replied. "Shame none of these boys could donate a clever pair of hands for Chichester, eh?"

In their desperation, the Germans had resorted to a ghoulish technique of repairing the wounded with hasty transplants grafted from the ranks of the dead. The technique was experimental at best, and the new limb often necrotized, taking the patient with it, but they died fighting. The story had given Matilda nightmares, but Minerva had told her, "They don't want girls' legs, fool. If it only worked a little better, our side would do it too."

She was only twelve when the war started, but she remembered how both sides had hailed it as if a healthy modern war would leave the world a better place.

Four years of trench warfare had forced both sides to resort to strange and awful innovations. To combat the German patchwork troops, some French vivisectionist tried surgically altering animals to carry rifles. The Italians deployed automata to man machine gun nests, but the clockwork killers mowed down anything that moved, especially each other. The Ottoman Empire was said to be fielding battalions of monsters that partook equally of all three awful options.

No less desperate, the Brits had even turned to creating some ladies' reserve infantry units. At least three of the unfortunate Tommies they'd had to work on, many no older than Matilda, had turned out to be girls.

Chichester abruptly stripped off his sodden smock and flung it into the bin. "Why isn't that belly closed yet? Tidy up here, nurse," he said. "Who's got a bloody flask?"

Minerva trembled with rage. She took the cauterizing wand herself and began applying it to a slew of pinprick hemorrhages in the bowel cavity. "Have the orderlies bring the next one."

"You're not a doctor, Nerva…"

"This bowel is leaking like a sieve, and that foot was as sound as either of yours. He only lopped it off to spare his drinking hour. Go tell Oglethorpe to have them bring the next course, won't you please?"

"Should I fetch Sir Algernon? He should be well enough to take over…"

"Why don't you go down the line and shove an ice pick into their ears and save them the agony? Be *useful*, Til."

Matilda degloved and bowed out of the operating theater. The sterile bubble-tent of clear rubber erected in the chapel had double doors, but the pressure fan had broken down, and smoke, mud, and blood tracked in and out of the theater. The trouble was, you wouldn't know if you'd been useful until you were through being used.

Sgt. Oglethorpe, the head orderly, cruised the rows of cots and stretchers that had replaced the pews in the nave.

"They're ready for another, sir," Matilda said.

"Glad to hear it, Miss," replied Oglethorpe. "You may tell them their watch is at an end. All who were unable to relocate to the battalion aid station have no need of further care."

"They're all…" She sighed, closing her eyes. "Oh, I'm sorry…"

Oglethorpe's rough red hand gently caged her tiny pale one. "No room for shame here, young Miss. Can't afford to be dead before we die." He patted her arm and gave her a weary smile. "Go on and remind Dr. Lark that we await his pleasure to evacuate this place, if his nibs can tear himself from his experiments."

The attack came before dawn with overwhelming ferocity. After a marathon bombardment that must've killed more of their own than the Allies did, the Second and Eighteenth armies were overrun by waves of berserkers who charged into machine gun fire and jumped with live grenades into the Allied trenches. They drove a wedge between the two armies, which parted like oil and water to let the Germans breach a front that hadn't moved more than a hundred yards in three years.

Just as Minerva had said, the French were committed to defending Paris at all costs, while the British only fretted at losing the Dunkirk ports and their escape back to England. General Ludendorff had astutely pushed here at just the right time and cut the front like a ribbon. Suddenly, the village where they had felt safe two miles from the front had been swallowed whole, and the news kept getting worse until it stopped coming at all.

The company commander had dithered as the collapsing front bled infantry and heavy artillery pieces before an underling gave the order to retreat. Everything that might serve the enemy was sabotaged, burned, or blown up. The rooftops of Nesle were ablaze; mines had been planted under the cobblestones of the main street to give a few of the Boche cause to regret their victory, and haphazard bombs fell from scattered French flying artillery circling over the routed battlefield.

When it came time to take the last ambulances out, the roads were aswarm with German infantry. The wires were all cut, but the wireless buzzed with terrified voices and desperate coded clicking. The Germans had annihilated the Fifth and Third armies. The French divisions were in full retreat. Valhalla dreadnoughts had trampled Petain's reserve forces and crossed the Somme, and the Red Baron's Flying Circus had turned the battlefield into a hunting ground. Big Bertha and the other ten-story-long guns rained poison gas and uranium shells on Notre Dame and made a blazing pyre of Montmartre. Regenwurm tanks had surfaced on the Champs-Elysee and claimed what remained of Paris for the Kaiser.

All or none of this might be true, but without doubt, the Boche had them surrounded. The few stragglers who returned from the aborted retreat had stripped the insignia off their uniforms. They were crucifying any Brits they found with gunners' patches. The Boche had an especial hatred for the Lynch Magneto-Cannon.

Oglethorpe blanched when she told them her family name. She thought the British soldiers would cherish the silent machine gun as much as the Germans hated it.

"Well, you see, Miss, it's not so simple as all that." Struggling for an excuse to drop the subject, he winced and shook out a stick of kola gum. Something came out with it, and he shoved it back into his pocket. "Y'see, it's not a very *kind* weapon… Once men see their mates get done over like that… all punched full of holes, and so quiet, like…"

Matilda asked him for a stick of gum and about the red bit of paper that'd come with it.

Reluctantly, he showed it to her. Creased and furry with wear, it was a sort of Christmas card. FRÖHLICHE WEIHNACHTEN! it said, beneath an engraving of a warlike Sankt Nikolaus. "See, the war, when it started… well, we were just soldiers, and we didn't feel about it as the men in charge. On Christmas Day in '14, there was a grand cease-fire, and we shared a case of cherry brandy with the fellows over the Siegfried Line. We weren't traitors, Miss, don't misunderstand. We just… didn't hate those poor young fellows any more than they hated us. Not then, at any rate…

"Oh, bigger bombs and the gas and all the tanks and blimps and infernal devices the boffins concocted put paid to our little tradition. But the one that made it easiest to mow down the enemy… not even like men or beasts, but like they were naught but grass… it was that gun.

"Before long, the Boche had them, as well. Not as many, but they drew us in at Bazancourt in '15 and minced whole companies of us with them, so they did…"

The blood rushed to her face so hard it might come out of her eyes. "Stands to reason they'd use any they captured to get back at you. It wouldn't surprise me if the Hun figured out how to copy them…" The shame she could weather, but the disgust she heaped upon herself for feeling she must defend her father.…

"Begging your pardon, Miss, but they didn't copy them. Everyone on the front talks about how they bought them from that concern in America what makes them. I'm sure you're no relation to *those* Lynches, Miss, but I'd call myself something else, if I was you…"

No one had proved so beastly as to call them out, but Minerva would tell them if someone didn't know. The doctors were generally pigs, doubly patronizing with American girls, and the French even worse. The wounded were unfailingly polite and kind, but she knew they didn't see her. That was the worst part—standing in for the face so many men dreamed of kissing just before they died.

In spite of the danger involved, she rather enjoyed the company of the man the others hated and feared most, the only one here who treated her as neither pet nor potential concubine.

She descended the steps into the chapel's crypt with a loud, warning tread. It wouldn't be wise to startle the Third Army's chief science marshal.

The only flag officer left behind, Col. Dr. Sir Algernon Lark-Hallidie was still dithering with his experiments when the line collapsed, and the others left. No one knew he was still down there until they had to find a place to store the dead.

Sir Algernon had the credit for their continued survival so far. When the shelling had abolished the surrounding village, the worst of it had caromed away from the chapel, owing to the Tesla towers that generated a magnetic field that repelled all but the most direct artillery. That it had also triggered the electrical fire that destroyed the motor pool, leaving them stranded, would probably not be included in his posthumous citation from the Royal Society. Still, it was all he was known for here.

"Dr. Lark—"

"I'm not hungry! Go away!"

"There's no food. We need to evacuate, or we'll be captured—"

The crypt door opened a crack. Dr. Lark's wild silver hair undulated on his head like some ghostly undersea weed. His enormously magnified eyes swam like fish behind his spectacles. "Oh, bother…" Removing his glasses, he polished them on the sleeve of his smock. His tiny, avid eyes seemed to vanish completely under his overgrown eyebrows. "I trust there's been no change?"

"We're still in the soup."

Dr. Lark perched his spectacles on the bony bridge of his nose and invited her in. "Not to worry, my child. I have only this morning perfected a device which, I remain cautiously hopeful, shall secure our deliverance."

"That's wonderful! I'll go tell them…"

"You mustn't! I won't be the bearer of false hope. But… Oh, come and see. I'll need a stouthearted adventurer to assist me, in any case." Matilda blushed.

Taking up a peculiar headset bristling with antennae and light-bulbs, he retraced its reticulated cable to a rat-king tangle he'd made of the aid station's switchboard and bowed as if to an applauding audience of his peers. "I hold in my hands an instrument for wireless transmission via the aether from one individual mind to another. After all, what is the human brain but an organic transceiver of subtle but unmeasured potential?"

She looked it over again but still couldn't see it. "You're going to use it to call for help, then…?"

"Oh, there're no allies left to save us. Far better and fortunate you are to have me here… for I aim to use the device to contact my counterpart on the German side."

"To *surrender*?"

"No, no, no. Such territorial scrimmages as these are of no concern to the man of science. No savant who receives such an extraordinary transmission could deny that something far more important than the outcome of this battle is in the offing."

"I don't… That is, I'm sure it will work, but…" If having an Englishman barge into his brain unannounced could win anyone over, she thought, he might as well try to establish a rapport with the Kaiser.

"I assure you; I'm hardly fumbling in the dark. No less a light than Lord Belphegor, President of our Royal Society, has declared that it is a question not of if but when. In fact, Doktor Zukunft and I were working closely at Heidelberg on a crude attempt at a cerebral transmitter when this idiotic conflagration first flared up. We came to share an extraordinary commingling of intellects insofar as one may comprehend the mechanistic bent of the Teutonic temperament, and I believe some vestige of it must persist. We sang together in choir, if you can imagine. I had a wretched voice… In any case, I wouldn't be surprised to find him still pursuing the same research in his idle hours when he's not presiding over the cavalcade of horrors out there… Zukunft is a reasonable man, and I'm quite certain if I can only get through, we can negotiate an amicable cease-fire… A hot bath, a proper meal, and clean sheets. Won't that be lovely?"

Far too lovely to believe. "What do you need me to do?"

"Only this, my dear." He held up an aerial like the skeleton of a box kite. A patchwork cable of copper strands trailed from it in long coils. The poor lunatic must've been up all last night scavenging and braiding it while the bombs fell. "My apparatus only wants an antenna, placed as high as you can hang it, to work. And outside the structure, that's imperative, and the good, solid stone of the chapel should insulate our side from the transmission…"

As the professor wound into another lecture, Matilda carefully bore the aerial up the stairs and then climbed the scaffolding on the inner wall of the chapel, past boarded-up stained glass windows and elongated wooden saints. Shored up and fortified until it looked more like a cavernous bunker than a church, the chapel had already become all too familiar, the dread of waiting and worrying made manifest in neo-Gothic stones.

She fretted that she might be caught doing Lark-Hallidie's bidding, that somehow, she would be accused of climbing the wall to wave a white flag. But the others were too preoccupied with the dead and doomed to look up.

There was a hole in the roof where the belltower had been knocked down so the Hun couldn't use it for a benchmark, and the bells had been carted away and melted down for ordnance long ago. An observer's post was still up there, but half a soldier sat in the chair, the remains so charred that he would not be removed. She swung out by one arm to hang the aerial on a shattered timber projecting from the steep shingled roof. She nearly fell when she saw the view.

Beyond the burst bubble dome huts of instant concrete and the toppled Tesla projectors of the aid station perimeter, past the shapeless ruins of the British forward trenches and dugouts, the narrow communication trenches running back towards the village, there were no men left, and perhaps no countries, either. The gray earth bubbled like a witch's cauldron, with forests of thermite fire and great slabs of blasted landscape hurtled skyward with the impacts of shells. Clouds of ball lightning played over the horizon, mile-long tendrils of plasma incinerating every last vestige of man's works.

Matilda thought her sister was the smartest and most beautiful girl in the world, but Minerva argued that her features were too symmetrical and that she was only as pretty as a mathematical proof. Their mother had been the real beauty, so much so that when he lost her, Father had all her pictures destroyed. As for her brain, she freely admitted she was smart about everything but Father.

He raged and fulminated when Minerva announced her plan to go overseas and support the war effort. Father impugned her motives—couldn't she find a suitable man in America? She let fly with the muckrakers' articles about the shameful profiteers who'd made a killing off both sides of a war they militated against America entering. She'd be hard enough to marry off without a wooden leg or a hook for a hand, he said into his morning paper, digging Minerva deeper.

Matilda couldn't resist rubbing her sister's nose in the encounter. Of course, Father *said* he didn't want her to go. Father had abandoned his honeymoon in the Sandwich Isles for the Philippines to jaunt in Mr. Hearst's war. He had no boys to send off to war himself, no other blood to spill for the family name. Clearly, he wanted to be rebelled against. Even when Minerva saw how she'd miscalculated, she would not be denied her prize goat. So, she took Matilda with her.

They had to finance a Red Cross ambulance unit to be considered. Minerva sponsored seven and leveraged her father's influence to let them follow the first American reserves sent to the front. The 12th and 32nd regiments were folded into General Gough's forces, while the Lynch sisters were diverted to *Les Invalides* in Paris to change dressings and read to young American men blinded by gas because of some fusty British convention that forbade women at the front.

The shelling from Big Max and Bertha and the new rockets had wrought a new wave of irrational fear upon the Parisians who roamed their ashen ghost capitol, vast tracts of which glowed radium green at night. The whole city stank of death and exhausted terror, and there seemed to be no men over fifteen or under sixty left.

Feeling the need for beauty, they visited the Louvre. It was one of the only places that had lights on after dark. Minerva despised the antiquities collection, especially the Egyptian stuff, which she called a pirate hoard. Still, she loved the late Romantics and the Orientalists, those vast, florid canvases of tormented beauty crowding every wall and even the ceilings. They were arguing in the stairwell beneath the Nike of Samothrace about what to see next when a bomb came whistling out of the ruddy clouds to smash into the gallery of French Romantic masterpieces.

The air wardens evacuated the museum, herding them through catacombs with carbide torches. Matilda understood enough French to know that the missile was a "dirty bomb." Minerva told her rather testily that this meant it had uranium slag in it. They were lucky not only to have survived, but they might be the last to see the inside of the Louvre for a century.

Flying in the face of every faceless bureaucratic adversary she could find, Minerva pressed to go to the front, and finally, last week, they had relented. Matilda attributed it to the indomitable Lynch will, which could be turned into charitable acts as easily as to the industrialization of death. Only when they arrived at the aid station had they found that the policy had changed because there were no men left and precious little of anything else. By then, Matilda already thought she had seen the elephant her father always talked about and wanted to go home.

They tended the wounded deep into the night and listened to the radio. She was thankful for the music, for it kept her awake, but then, like a goldfish going round and round to rediscover it's in a bowl, she remembered what it was.

Nobody would tell her, so she had to eavesdrop. The cannon-fodder in the German's suicidal wave attacks were British and French soldiers who'd been taken prisoner, and their unthinkable betrayal had something to do with the music.

"Tilda, mind your work. This poor boy's bleeding out." Matilda ran to help her sister. With four doctors, two nurses, three orderlies, and no medicine left, there was no end of it and little to do but apologize for what couldn't be fixed.

Out of twenty-four patients, only a handful were ambulatory, and half were expected to slip away by morning without better care than they could manage. Men with no limbs, with eyes burned out, men whose wounds glowed in the dark and would never heal, men slowly melting, disintegrating, or, worst of all, growing because of the bold scientific wonders they'd faced out there.

The worst were the survivors of the antiaircraft crews who'd manned the big Tesla projectors. While their support artillery peppered the sky with aerosolized silver nitrate clouds, the projectors lashed them with raw electricity to turn the clouds into superconductive storm cells. They had blown out of the sky wave after wave of Hun fighters and harmlessly detonated waves of shells in midair. Still, when Lark-Hallidie's modifications overloaded the generator, the whole crew was electrocuted. The few who weren't killed outright seemed alright at first, but all the iron and such in their blood began to align into crystalline spikes that sprouted from their bones, ripped them up inside and burst through the skin.

British Central Command went off the air sometime in the night, or someone was jamming them off the airwaves. The French and British armies had retreated out of range and lost their transmitters.

Fitz scanned the frequencies, but all he found among the unearthly warbling of empty airwaves was the garbled goblin drone of encoded German transmissions and the harsh French of an officer barking commands, as if to a slow child.

"Why does he shout at them like that?" Matilda asked.

"He's not talking to men, Miss," Fitz said. "The French left the field to fortify Paris, but they've got dogs wired up to hear their masters' orders over the radio…"

"But what can dogs do out there? Are they going out to rescue the other soldiers?"

"No, Miss. They carry bombs to the enemy."

"But how do they drop them without, you know, hands—?"

"They don't."

She started to cry, but then she felt all kinds of foolish. Crying for dogs, when she hadn't wept for all the boys her age destroyed in this stupid war, or the heartbroken ghost town of London or the luminous ruin of Paris… but those tragic things had seemed somehow removed from her world, even when their stink soaked into her hair.

Suddenly, a patient stood up from his cot and hobbled towards them down the nave. "Right! This has gone far enough!"

Oglethorpe gently took Stokes's arm but was shaken off. Dr. Chichester's piercing nasal shout echoed in the chapel. "Now see here, Sergeant Major. You had your chance. You'll do no one any good with this display…"

Sergeant Major Stokes of the 3rd Bangalore Velocipede Cavaliers had been treated for grievous chemical burns and was to be evacuated in the last ambulance, but refused to leave his men. "You lot are welcome to stay behind," he said. "The bombings only stopped because they've moved so far past us. We're falling further into the Hun's gullet every minute we fiddle."

"I say," Chichester bristled, "this isn't a French unit. We don't just scarper at the first sign of trouble…"

Stokes grimaced so hard, the grafts on the right side of his face split at his jaw, leaking straw-colored fluid. "First sign, hell…! Nobody's coming to save us."

"We'll beat them back," Oglethorpe said. "We've done it before, and we'll do it again, with or without the Americans' help."

"As ranking surgeon," Chichester blustered, "I'd give you leave to toddle off to glory on your bloody unicycle, but as an officer, need I remind you that this kind of insubordination…"

Stokes growled and went for the doctor. Oglethorpe caught him. Several of the wounded tried to get off their cots and take sides.

Matilda felt her sister tugging her arm. "Come away, Til. Let the fools fight."

"We should go, shouldn't we? I mean… If Pershing's not coming…"

Minerva pushed Matilda back against an empty dressing station. Matilda tensed in anticipation of a lecture. "We came here to help, Til. Not for an adventure or to meet boys. We came to render service to the ones who're giving their lives for a cause, no matter that the men in charge will waste all of them. We can't just light out when it stops being fun…"

"When was it ever *fun*?" Matilda indulged a girlish pout, but then she bit her tongue and met her sister's eyes. "You're doing this to hurt him. You'd be just about satisfied if we both died, if you could see the look on his face when he read the news…"

Minerva slapped her, then trapped her in a hug that left her no breath.

A melancholy tune seeped out of the speakers. "It's like another flavor of nerve gas," Minerva grumbled.

"It's Schubert," Matilda said. "*Death And The Maiden*. He wrote it shortly after he learned he was about to—"

"Turn it off, please," Minerva said to Fitz, which he did. Matilda squirmed free and went towards the crypt just as Sir Algernon emerged.

"I can't seem to raise Zukunft. I fear someone else is commanding our opposition. Do you hear music?" he asked.

She nodded and then she froze, jaw dropping. Though the radio was tuned to soft, seashell static, *Death And The Maiden* persisted, and only seemed to get louder.

It wasn't coming from the speakers, but from off across the lunar ruin of no man's land.

"Oh heavens, no," Sir Algernon said. "This won't do at all." Where he'd barely taken note of the bombing, now he quivered with commingled terror and fury. "They said, when he demonstrated his abominations in Utrecht, that they'd surely have him committed. They couldn't, they wouldn't…" He scurried back to the crypt.

"Sir Algernon, you're wanted here," Chichester called out. "Someone must make a showing to bolster morale…"

"Bugger morale, man! The Devil's at the door!" The savant scuttled back to his crypt. "I must intensify my signal!"

As they all stood frozen, the music grew ever louder. Matilda ran for the scaffolding and clambered up to the nearest window, pried away a loose board.

A mob filled the triage yard, silent except for the ones who played violins and horns and drums. A marching band here, playing that song—

She could make out no faces in the pallid light from a German armored troop transport shaped like a giant woodlouse parked in the road, and the fitful flashes of distant lightning. She could see flared steel infantry helmets among the convex disks of the British and American units, and even a few of the crested firefighter's affairs the French favored. No one was anyone's prisoner. No one spoke. They were one army. And they were knocking on the door.

"Don't open it!" Matilda shouted from the scaffolding. "Don't let them in!"

Sgt. Stokes lurched down the row of cots. Half a dozen men rose and followed him. "We need weapons."

A burly man with his face completely bandaged seized Chichester by the collar. "Hand over your sidearm, you useless…"

The sentries at the door peered through the grate and asked for the password. Thunder rocked the chapel. The doors flew into the atrium, smashing one sentry flat and clipping the other so he flew into a column.

They came in two abreast with tommy guns. Oglethorpe charged them with a raised fist and was cut in half. They poured fire down the nave, strafing the rows of cots and stretchers, wounded, doctors, orderlies. Two of them were felled by the bandaged soldier who'd taken Chichester's revolver.

Half were British, a few were French or American, the rest German. They looked straight ahead and did mass murder without any of the hesitation Matilda had observed in even the cruelest men she'd seen in this war.

The radio squealed until the speaker blew out. The lights dimmed. Matilda screamed. A sound so loud it made a bell of her skull knocked her off the scaffolding. The loudest sound she'd ever heard was inside her head.

God was singing.

AND DID THOSE FEET—

The murderers in the nave stood transfixed, looking about as if surprised to find themselves in a battle.

IN ANCIENT TIMES—

In that gap, Fitz the radio operator flung a grenade into their midst and shouted, "Down!" Dull thunder obliterated the sleepwalking mob in the nave and flung steel sleet at the ones in the doorway.

Matilda rolled off a mound of wrecked cots and corpses and vomited on the first clear patch of floor she found. A few pistols and another grenade went off, barely penetrating the ringing in her ears. She crawled blindly, choking on dusty tears, calling for Minerva.

Someone stepped on her hand. "Right! Fall out, you lot!" Stokes shouted, hauling her to her feet. "If you can, carry a man who can't…"

Matilda tried to help, but they pushed her out with the others. The silence outside was like deafness. The mob of nearly a hundred men was still here. Every one of them lay on the ground like they wanted to make snow angels in the mud. Not a wound on them, but here and there, blood trickled from nostrils, ears, tear ducts, and some bare heads shed plumes of steam.

Only eight wounded survivors were carried out of the chapel. Stokes shouted, "Round up enough greatcoats and cookpots for the lot." Matilda just stared, waiting for Minerva to come out, She saw others taking German helmets from the dead and moved to help.

Dr. Chichester shouted for Oglethorpe. Someone else said he was dead. "Right! Worst cases in the troop van, the rest in the ambulances. If there's trouble, everyone shifts for themselves." He looked around, then pointed at Matilda. "You."

"What?"

He waved in the direction of the chapel. "See to your sister!"

Heart in her mouth, Matilda pushed upstream through the doors. The flagstones were slippery with blood. Minerva sat up on a stretcher with a compress against her chest. "Don't look at me like that. It went clean through me."

Matilda pushed her sister's hands away. Blood welled up through the soaked dressing. "Ye gods, it went through a lung."

"In His wisdom, God gave me two. Go and help someone who need it."

Matilda stepped over bodies and body parts up the outside aisle of the chapel, which Cpl. Fitz was dousing with kerosene.

The door to the crypt was partly open, but she had to shove something aside to get in. The stench of ozone, scorched plastic and burnt hair threatened to make her sick again. Lights flickered on the instrument panels arrayed atop the rows of sarcophagi. Sir Algernon lay behind the door. The charred headset he wore was fused to his brow. Black smoke still wafted off the burst pressure-cooker of his skull.

"You were wrong, sir," Matilda said, her voice breaking like glass in her throat. "You sing beautifully..."

Ten minutes later, they rolled out in the German half-track transport and two hastily salvaged Red Cross ambulances—three doctors, the radio operator, an orderly, the Lynch sisters and seven wounded. Stokes drove the transport while Matilda and Dr. Chichester tried to keep the four worst-off patients from dying. Minerva rode with a bad burn case in an ambulance driven by a gruff Scots Color Sergeant with a broom strapped to the stump of his right leg. Fitz drove the other ambulance, with Dr. Stanlow and the orderly and the other two wounded.

There was no plan, and little point in making one. The unstable new front would be utterly unpredictable. All they could hope for, as Stokes told them, was to press on and pray that no one noticed they weren't German.

Be brave, she told herself. *Be useful, be brave,* until the words meant nothing at all.

Tortured clouds writhed in the howling wind, while some prowled among it—streamlined, manmade thunderheads that lashed the earth with arcs of superheated plasma, forking tongues of blue-white lightning that augured their targets into vapor.

Sturminsels, the Germans called their gigantic war-dirigibles. *Storm-islands.* One hove into view over the red-orange clouds from a blazing chemical munitions depot to the south. Alarmingly low to the ground, the observation cameras, aerials and radomes dangling from its triple gondola eagerly seeking out pockets of Allied resistance.

From the roof of the chapel, she had thought the land denuded of humanity. Now, peering out the gun-slits of the half-track, she realized how wrong she'd been.

The landscape was *made of* men.

Mountains and smoldering pyres of bodies. Limbs stuck out like gnarled roots from blasted earthworks, collapsed dugouts and flooded bomb shelters. Bomb craters cut into clay palisades revealed a monstrous layer cake of carnage, the putrid strata of successive campaigns plowed under and buried in an endless, nameless grave.

The ragged convoy crawled out of no man's land like a procession of beetles, straggling up the face of one crater and down the next. The stench was unspeakable. Matilda clutched at her churning belly as if to massage the knots out of it. She'd long since run out of things to sick up, but her guts stubbornly revolted at even the prospect of water. A dark-skinned soldier with thick, lustrous black hair and no eyes reached out and grabbed her hand. He tried to say something into her ear, and then he died.

Chichester injected his charges in the neck with something, then took a dose for himself as he tunelessly belted out his alma mater's fight song. "Come on, lads, don't pretend you don't know the words…"

She could barely see from under the heavy steel helmet and was lost in the bulky, mildewy woolen greatcoat, but it couldn't be helped.

They turned onto an unpaved road and drove alongside a river of dead-eyed German infantry shambling through the nightmarish spoils of their victory like damned souls overlooked by Hell. Burning troop trucks, tanks, and artillery pieces littered the roadside where they'd been hit by errant French flying artillery or run over landmines in the road.

She found a pipe and tobacco pouch in the coat pockets, a flat flask half-filled with cherry schnapps, a few letters, and racy French postcards. Wearing a dead soldier's coat she could bear, but it made her feel horrible to touch his personal effects like she'd stolen his life.

Chichester offered her a spike of stimulant, but her heart was racing enough, already. The road abruptly become smoother, the empty wasteland to show symptoms of natural terrain, the charcoal sticks of forests, chimneys, ruins and sometimes miraculously untouched farmhouses.

They went over a shell-pocked hill and passed through a meadow dotted with trees and a vineyard, then a small French village. After the front, it seemed impossibly fragile and strange, the lights and the houses with windows and flower boxes and people.

A milk delivery wagon rolled into the Y-intersection at the village's heart to block their path. A gang with torches crossed in front of the half-track, pounding the hood. More spilled out of a café to crowd the ambulances. They had balaclavas or scarves over their faces. One of them rushed the first ambulance, held up a magnum of champagne, shouted something about a toast to Germany, lit a wick jutting out the neck, and christened the ambulance.

A curtain of fire engulfed the windshield. The burning Scotsman toppled out into the road. The second ambulance swerved around its mate, only to smash into the café.

"Minerva!" Matilda lunged for the loading doors.

Rocks and bottles buffeted the walls. "Someone man the bloody turret!" Stokes roared as he shot into the dark.

Chichester caught her by the arm. "Can you work a gun, girl?" Matilda struggled in his arms. "You can do no good out there. If you want to help your sister, lay down some bloody cover fire!"

Numbly, she looked out the slot. The blazing ambulance's back doors sprang open. A soldier with his arm in a sling held the crowd at bay with a revolver. Then he clutched his chest and fell to his knees, shooting into the serried windows above the café.

Matilda climbed into the gunner's seat that hung from the roof and stuck her head up out of the hole. Her feet rested on pedals that rotated the turret. Her hands had nowhere to rest but the grubby grips of the gun. Amidst all this, it should have been a comfort to touch something familiar.

It's not exactly a kind weapon....

Her father gave her a Lynch Hoplite .22 Magneto-Rifle for her ninth birthday to infuriate Minerva, who was staging a hunger strike over a massacre in Nicaragua. Matilda had to shoot down balloons hanging over a field to bring her other presents to earth. All the children took turns firing at a gallery of fanciful targets. Jolly fun. Later, her big sister showed her pictures of what the gun was really for, and she never touched it again. Still, she had seen the Magneto-Cannon in use more than enough times to find the safety, wind up the galvanizer to charge the barrel, and spin the drum of projectiles under her seat into the belt-feed.

The only thing she couldn't do was pull the trigger.

The partisans evaporated into the dark before a wall of approaching German infantry. Clad in raincoats and wearing gas masks, they looked less than human, and they marched with their rifles shouldered, but it didn't make it any easier.

One of the few really useful things her father had told her, or at least said in her presence, had naturally seemed useless at the time, but it came hammering home now.

"A coward doesn't run away, or there'd never be any armies. No, a coward stands his ground and aims his rifle, and sometimes he fires, but he doesn't kill anything on purpose. Too frightened even to run away, so he holds to his last orders like one of those Italian automatons, emptying his rifle over the enemy's head and sleepwalking towards the objective. But his heart's not in it, and the fear takes his head. Most men, when the chips are down, couldn't kill to save their own lives."

Now she understood what he'd meant. When she looked down the steeplejack sight of the gauss gun, she saw a host of targets against the smoky black night. She saw the muzzle flashes as they fired into the village. She saw all this, and she mastered the fear that told her to curl up into a ball and let a man save them, but she found, to her towering dismay, that even in war, a chasm lay between looking down the sights of a gun and actually using it.

Calling out in muffled gutturals, the Germans approached the half-track with rifles poised. She closed her eyes when she pulled the trigger, and she aimed high. She had to open them to see if there was a safety catch. It made no noise beyond a flurry of clicks and clinks and the *fwoosh* of each recoilless discharge. But when she opened her eyes, it was still firing, chopping the heads off Germans like red dandelions.

A grenade bounced off the roof and exploded, peppering her shield with shrapnel. Matilda slid out of the turret and crashed into the tightly packed stretchers as the half-track leaped forward.

"Stop!" Matilda clawed her way to the cab. "You've got to go back… My sister…."

"There's no going back, Miss," Stokes said. They plowed an abandoned ox-cart off the narrow village road and sent a courier's motorcycle into a ditch. The village ended at a small bridge that had been blown up, but the Germans had inflated a rubber pontoon bridge in its place. "She's either alive or she's not. It's not up to you, is it? See to the gun, lass. There's another roadblock ahead."

Outside, fallow fields rolled away, pastures overrun with wildflowers picked out by stray moonlight shining through unnatural clouds. Less than a mile ahead, their unpaved two-lane track crossed a high road on which an unbroken column of German trucks, tanks, and captured French vehicles stretched over the horizon to the old front. Blackened hulks filled the ditches. Here and there, she heard boisterous, drunken singing, but every face she saw was ashen and empty.

An icy, ozone-charged wind blew out of the west, driving stinging rain into her face. Lightning speared down from thunderheads a few miles off, ominously silhouetting a Sturminsel headed for Paris.

An officer stepped into the road and raised a hand. A squad of fusiliers with gyro-rifles backed him up. Stokes braked and coasted to within a few yards of the human wall arrayed between tank traps and sandbag ramparts with recoilless rifles on tripods and klieg lights atop them. A sort of tank oversaw the flow of traffic on the main road—a gawky gun platform on huge chicken legs, which the Germans called Baba Yagas.

Chichester donned a captain's white peaked cap. "Here's hoping I remember my *Hochdeutsch*. If it goes pear-shaped, push through and stop for nothing."

The officer approached Chichester as he climbed out the loading doors. Matilda hunched down in her greatcoat, then took out the pipe and stuck it in her mouth so she'd look like half the German infantry she saw on the road.

Chichester fired off a salvo of crisp German, at which the dour Prussian lieutenant could only frown in distaste, then disbelief. As the spiel built to a frantic crescendo, panic welled up in his tiny, ice-blue eyes. Finally, he spat a terse comment and waved an arm to disperse the firing squad. Stokes pressed on through the gap, crossing in front of the tanks and a line of fuel trucks.

The Baba Yaga lurched into the crossroads to block them. Stokes cursed and hit the brakes.

As he stiffly climbed back into the half-track, Chichester lost his hat when the wind changed, now howling into the west as if some great vacuum had opened over Paris. Matilda's ears popped.

"What'd you tell them?" Stokes demanded.

"I'm a medical officer and we're delivering wounded prisoners to the front, and that I'd infected you all with a dashing new strain of experimental plague…"

Matilda saw it first.

The Red Cross ambulance sped towards them from the burning village.

It was her sister. It had to be. She had never lived in such a world, but even with all that had passed, if Nerva was gone, she would feel it—

The fusiliers came back. The officer ordered Stokes out into the road. Two gunners sat behind heavy shields atop the chicken-legged tank. Their guns were bigger than hers.

The ambulance slid sideways on the road less than fifty yards away. The Baba Yaga fired a shell and knocked it on its side.

Matilda shrieked and took the grips of the magneto-cannon. With her eyes wide open, she strafed the tank. The stream of silent 70-mm shells bounced harmlessly off its shielding before she tilted down and shot its knees off.

The tank tilted, firing into the ground between its severed legs, and collapsed. The fusiliers opened up, the rocket-propelled shells punched through the windshield and made a flaming scarecrow of Dr. Chichester.

Matilda spun round and round in the turret, spraying everything in sight. Fuel trucks ruptured and sent white-hot light hundreds of feet into the air. Hunkering down against the wheel, Stokes geared up and charged the firing squad, parting them and shooting out the murder-hole with his revolver as he passed.

Matilda watched the flaming wreck of the last ambulance dwindle smaller in the wind and the rain. Lightning struck on the horizon and backlit a stormcloud a hundred miles high, putting down tornado fingers up and down the plain. It was impossibly huge, the kind of storm the dime-novel science heroes whipped up to foil sky-pirate cattle-rustlers on the Great Plains.

It was so impossibly grand and wantonly destructive that it had to be American. Stokes knew it, too, and drove across the field into it.

Matilda fired at the lights, pursuing them until the cannon went empty; then she turned for another drum, and something hit her and ripped her arm off like a petal from a flower.

They were flying through the air upside down and she was flung from the turret and dashed into the mud.

She lay there, in the cold and wet and dark. When a faceless thing came to her saying something with no mouth, she cried out for her sister, and the thing was saying her name, but it sounded all wrong—

And then nothing.

Someone carried her in the dark, and then she lay in a bed, and it was warm and soft and dry, and it was so lovely, she couldn't remember what she'd dreamt about. She and Minerva were in a war, and they were running, but they got separated, and she knew Father would be angry with them because they ran away—

She screamed at the touch of cold steel fingers on her face and screamed even louder when she realized they were her own.

"You're all right, Miss," said a kindly older British man's voice. "Steady on, there's a good girl. You've had a rough time, but you're alright now…"

"Where… what's wrong with my hand?"

The nurse tucked her arm out of sight and turned up the flow on the IV drip hanging above the bed. "You'll get used to it, Miss. You were lucky not to have bled out. It's not much, but we thought it'd be more of a comfort than nothing at all. I suppose when you get home to America, you can have a fine bespoke one made…"

Matilda wanted to ask him to take the horrid thing off her and ask about her sister, but her lids fell, and she sank into a deep, dreamless sleep.

New York City | October 1928

Tonight, it looked as if all of New York had turned out to celebrate Spider McGowan busting out of jail.

He knew in his head that it was really all for Columbus Day. The Knights had outdone themselves; the show dwarfed the festivities for the Fourth, which he'd watched from the window of his cell. Fireworks in green, white, and red blasted from barges along the East River and spiraled down from dirigibles soaring above the spires of the city, so the entire sky was a fiery Italian flag. Speakers on the same barges carried Caruso's voice, bellowing "Ave Maria," so loud that it almost drowned out the chattering of circling autogyros and their machine guns.

Spider hung out the open door of the hijacked Coast Guard blimp and contemplated the wavelets below like endless rows of black teeth, growing ever sharper as they lost altitude.

He clutched his rosary, St. Christopher medal, rabbit's foot and a little leather pouch with all his baby teeth in it. "Lord," he said as solemnly as he could manage, "if you could see giving me just one more chance, I promise, I'll never pick another pocket. This time, I mean it… So help me…"

He might've been praying to the city itself. Its glittering canyons dished out more miracles than free meals. But nothing about it was any help to the man running for his life.

Only an hour ago, just after chow, he lay on his bunk in Black-well Prison on Welfare Island, puffing a Lucky Strike and listening to Ribeye Reuss at the end of the block play "Beautiful Dreamer" on his pocket theremin and dying inside, when Cockrum told him the news. "We're busting out, kid. You're coming with us."

Never occurred to him to say no. He had another year on his sentence, and if his cellmates weren't giving him a choice, neither was his blood. At nineteen, Spider McGowan had tried hop, coke, gorilla glue, pluto, horse, and every kind of booze you could find in a saloon, blind pig, or hobo jungle, but there was no drug like free air. He only got moved into this cell a month before. Right away, he didn't like Elmer Minky or Aloysius Cockrum. Strongarm mob, they ran raw-jaw, rip-tear grifts on immigrants and worked the muzzle shake on twists in public restrooms. But they mostly left him alone until tonight. Cockrum, vicious widow's peak that almost connected with his eyebrows, breath reeking of crushed gardenias, had pulled the fix to land a soft job as night nurse in the infirmary. Minky worked in the sail shop, making the nacelles and skins for the city's airship fleet.

Their block had been through a shakedown only a week before and Spider never saw nothing like an escape plan being hatched, so he took it for a joke, which rubbed them the wrong way. Minky was too simple to know he was simple, and prone to take offense at anything. Twice Cockrum's size, the littler man used him like a club. Completely hairless from getting struck by lightning as a boy and completely toothless from too many bare-knuckle fights. He could magnetize small metallic objects with a touch and was impervious to pain, but he yowled like a cat every time he used the can.

"Dummy up and play along," Cockrum muttered out the corner of his mouth, "or I'll let Minky have you before we go. It's been hell keeping him off you all this time—"

Half an hour after lights out and the screws had done the first bed-check. Cockrum and Minky took the stuffing out of their pillows and shook them out into long, wrinkled balloons they inflated to look like resting human bodies. They gave Spider his own balloon. He gave himself a dizzy spell, filling it. He tucked his twin under the paper blankets on his bunk and followed them through the hole they must've chiseled in the wall before he moved in, artfully disguised with plaster and paint.

They shinnied up the sewage pipes to the top of the tier and then through another hole onto the roof. Blackwells was built just after the Civil War and was due to shut down soon. They'd all be moved to the new prison on Rikers. Word was the place was impenetrable.

But they used to say that about Blackwells.

From the roof, there was nowhere to go. Six towers overlooked the outer courtyards below their block with klieg lights and Lynch guns. Then the fireworks started up, painting the sky red. The guards shut off the searchlights to watch the show, just as they had in July. The clear October sky was obscured by a canopy of silver smoke and gunpowder stench from a fireworks battery on the center span of the Queensboro Bridge, which passed almost directly over the prison.

Cockrum dragged three rucksacks out of the hole in the roof and strapped one on, then helped Minky with his. Spider was left to shift for himself, but he was a quick study.

When they were all wearing the cumbersome bags, Cockrum waited for a spectacular salvo to go off overhead, pulled a cord, and a giant helium balloon swelled up out of his rucksack. When he ditched the tank, he was able to kick off the roof and float over the courtyard and the outer wall. Minky and Spider hurried after him. All the seconds and minutes he dangled in the harness, canvas straps gouging his armpits, he felt the piercing needles of eyes crawling over him and heard the terrible silent magnetic cannons charging up to punch fifty new mouths in him.

Cockrum floated over the wall in a blind spot where the water tower and the peaked roof of the workhouse blocked the nearest guard towers, drifted like an overgrown bumblebee over the greensward and the fences around the Blackwell Lighthouse blimp station. A patrol blimp was tethered there, her gondola unlit.

Cockrum dropped on the hapless screw watching the top of the lighthouse, dropped him over the railing without making a sound. Cockrum floated up to the blimp and landed Minky and Spider as they came swimming after him.

Spider risked asking a stupid question. "D'you know how to fly one of these things?"

"We ain't flying it," Cockrum said and towed Minky up along the underbelly of the blimp. Cockrum found the slit in the skin of the dirigible and swam up into the crawlspace between the helium nacelles. Spider floated past Minky and tried to flatter Cockrum into elaborating on his plans for the rest of the evening. He was nervous; when he was nervous, he needed to talk, but Cockrum was not in a talking mood. If Spider was a better judge of people, he might suspect Cockrum was feeling guilty about something he hadn't done yet.

He didn't need his cellmate to explain the rest of the plan. The blimp pilots would have to call the coppers to request clearance for takeoff and read some password, or they'd be shot down. And the pilots would not make the call if the blimp was an ounce heavier than when it came in. Floating suspended inside the superstructure, they would pass unnoticed, so long as nobody noticed the dead screw at the foot of the mooring tower.

The next signal light on their patrol was across the river in Bayonne. Cockrum told him they would hitch a ride across the river, then steal off the airship in the yard and go to ground. Cockrum knew places in Jersey they could hide out until the heat blew over. Spider was too exhilarated to object but figured he'd go off alone as soon as they touched down.

They hid and held their breath as the trapdoor was opened, and someone peeked inside the balloon. A few tense minutes later, they got underway. Cockrum and Minky slipped out of their harnesses and dropped to the catwalk, and Spider followed them.

He came down the ladder just as Cockrum entered the gondola. A pilot and copilot in heavy gabardine coats and peaked caps stood at the wheel with their hands in the air. A guard turned and leveled a Thompson. Cockrum shot him in the neck with the dead screw's gauss pistol. Minky took the dead man's trench gun and a bandolier of ammo drums.

Cockrum approached the pilots. "We only need one," he said. To the younger one, he asked, "Can you swim?"

Too terrified to speak, the copilot only shook his head as if trying to unscrew himself from his neck.

"Then I'm doing you a favor," Cockrum said and shot him in the chest.

Minky dragged the bodies to the hatch and tossed them out. Spider watched them tumble into the black river, watched the slim clipper ship of Welfare Island recede behind them as the pilot strained the engines to take them south. They passed under the gray cantilever fortress of the Williamsburg Bridge, so low they could hear the cheers from the sailboats and tugs arrayed on the river.

Spider took in deep breaths of air so as not to be sick. In all his misspent years, he'd never pointed a real, loaded gun at another human being. He was halfway through a two-year jolt for picking the pocket of a swell too square to let the system fix it. It didn't matter now. They wouldn't be caught. They'd be hunted down like rabid dogs.

Through the curtains of tricolor sparks shooting up from and raining down from the Brooklyn Bridge, he saw clusters of harsher lights darting around over the river like fireflies, far too fast to be blimps, heading for them and spreading out. Spider tried to keep the quaver out of his voice as he said, "Looks like they're wise to us."

Cockrum sat down on the chart table and rummaged in a coat hanging on a stool, produced a flask, and tipped half of it down his throat. "We're going to Jersey. If they want a fight, we'll give 'em hell." He made a vague gesture like a canoe capsizing. "What d'you want from me? Do I look like Houdini to you, kid?"

Cockrum didn't even look like Hardeen, but now wasn't the time. "Sure, Jersey is fine, but if it's all the same to you, Brooklyn's just over there. Drop onto a rooftop somewhere and go to ground in the parades."

The pilot said, "You'll never get away, you know. They'll catch you wherever you go."

"This punk tipped them off," Cockrum snarled. Waving his gun in the pilot's face, he nudged the pilot towards the open hatch. "Blinking the running lights, or something..."

"I'm tired of him," Minky said.

"Me too," Cockrum said. He shot the pilot through the eye and took his captain's cap as he fell to the deck.

Minky sprayed the dead man with the Thompson. "*You never let me have one!*"

Spider hunkered down behind the chart table. The spray of bullets smashed out the windscreen.

"As I was saying," Spider said, "if it's all the same to you—"

"It *isn't*," Cockrum said, poking Spider in the belly with the gun. "Take the wheel."

"Regrettably, I never had so much as a balloon on my birthday. The orphanage was too poor, so I've never handled one, you understand—?"

"I understand I wasted a lot of work bringing you along," Cockrum said. "Are you a bright boy? Is that your problem?"

"I most assuredly am not." Spider took the wheel.

Minky went to the hatch and shot at a harbor patrol cutter that seemed to be popping off signal flares at them. An autogyro dropped out of their blind spot and stitched the flank of their balloon with tracer fire. The whole airship lurched and seemed to droop nose-down towards the river as it approached the Brooklyn Bridge.

"Over or under?" Spider shouted. His hand twitched on the lever that seemed to control their altitude.

"Over!" Cockrum hung out the shattered windscreen. Minky cackled as he shot up the airborne whirligig and whooped when it spun off to crash into the river.

Spider pulled back on the lever, cranked up the propellers, clung to the wheel, and prayed through gritted teeth. The belly of the gondola barely cleared the bridge railing and passed within spitting distance of a Columbus Day parade.

"Balls," Spider said.

A mob of revelers armed with red and green sparklers capered across the bridge amid a procession of parade floats and giant inflated cartoon characters anchored by guy wires. A huge, goofy Christopher Columbus hove into their path and seemed to try to wrestle the blimp. The motors whined as they stalled out, entangled in the masts of a Spanish galleon float.

"Everybody out!" Cockrum shoved Minky out the hatch. Spider saw them drop onto the galleon's deck. He started to follow them, but the bridge was swarming with coppers, and the traffic backed up solidly from Brooklyn to Battery Park.

The itch in the back of his head that so seldom steered him wrong told him to cling to the wheel and name every saint he could remember. Saint Nicholas was the patron saint of repentant thieves, but good or bad, Spider never got anything for Xmas, so he left him out of his prayers until tonight. *Deliver me, and it's the straight-and-narrow from here on—*

Someone else out there must have been praying even harder. Another police autogyro swooped down like a dragonfly to hover in front of him and open fire. Red and blue tracers scissored the nose of the blimp. The canvas peeled back in blazing sheets.

Spider looked down at the crowds racing in panic from a pitched gun battle between the coppers and Minky, shooting from behind the figurehead on the galleon. More fake pirate ships towing gigantic balloons lined the bridge, and more cops poured out of the crowd like ants out of sugar.

Suddenly, the burning blimp ripped free of the galleon and floated out over the river, dragging the floundering Columbus balloon in its wake but losing lift and speed.

The autogyro moved in closer, and blue lightning arced around it as it charged up its Jacob's ladder cannon. Spider spun the wheel counterclockwise and closed his eyes.

When he opened them, the autogyro fell, screaming out of the sky. One of its rotors must have clipped a trailing wire, for the drifting Columbus was ripped out of the air and wound around the autogyro, which seemed to vanish in a blue fireball that nosedived into the black water.

Spider pulled back on the wheel and pushed all available thrust to clear the approaching airship gantries of the Brooklyn waterfront. The blimp's forward nacelles were gone. Smoke and sparks trailed from the starboard motor, so the airship limped along with its tattered nose tilted to the river. Spider had to fight the wheel to keep it from lagging back towards the bridge.

He looked at the canyons of Brooklyn with melancholy longing and felt tender envy for the teeming millions below, all of them gawping at him as an army of punks like himself picked their pockets.

He'd come to New York because it was the world capitol of grifting. Ads and peddlers, scalpers, and pushers everywhere put the touch on you. Brokers hyped and dumped stocks. A bucket brigade of graft from the lowest beat cops to the politicians and judges who sold law and order by the pound. Everyone stole from everyone, and almost everyone was in on the fix. Spider had come from nothing and swiped and grifted his way to a level of some respectability to the ones who knew the score. For just a moment, he felt an acute longing to be a regular citizen down there, getting drunk to forget work tomorrow. *What wouldn't you give?*

Nothing, that's what. Thinking like that had undone better thieves than he. Wages of sobriety. He regretted most that Cockrum must've taken the flask when he ditched.

Even with scant minutes of aeronautical experience under his belt, Spider knew he wouldn't make it. The bastards were everywhere, in the air above and the water below, and they'd never stop looking for him unless they thought he was dead—

Spider took his rosary beads in his teeth and brought the airship around, so it crossed over a floating barge with a fireworks battery on it. The steady barrage of rockets lit up the airship's flaccid prow in a shower of green sparks.

Spider leapt out the hatch headfirst, but it was such a long way down, he somersaulted ass over teakettle and only slammed into the water with his toes pointed by pure Irish luck. Even so, the impact knocked his breath out of him. He drifted stunned in chill water and watched green sparks dapple and die on the surface. It was as if the sun set in the river when the blazing blimp came down.

Struggling against the drag of his sodden clothes, he broke the surface, sucking in air and coughing up brackish water. Boats were already converging on the blazing wreck of the airship. The tide was sluggish, but Spider's legs felt like concertinas. It was a miracle he hadn't broken anything. He swam like a man who'd just lost a boxing match. He tried to reach the outthrust docks, weary arms flailing on the water, but was swept past them, gasping for breath.

The tide was going out, but he'd drown long before he was swept out to sea. He was barely afloat when his arm caught on a jumble of slimy rocks below a storm drain. He crawled out of the river, shivering gratefully, kissing the stones and all his charms as a searchlight stabbed at him, and a harbor patrol cutter passed close enough for him to hear the captain yelling at his crew to watch for survivors.

When they were gone, he scaled the spill of rocks to the storm drain. He'd lost his shoes swimming. His hands and feet were numb rubber. The bars were rusted through and already broken off to admit someone larger than Spider, who was of average height but greyhound-skinny and double-jointed enough to work in a carnival sideshow. He used to dislocate his shoulder and climb through an unstrung tennis racquet to win bar bets. He had no fat to burn, but his nerve and will to beat the rap lifted him like puppeteer's strings. He slithered through the broken grille and staggered up the cylindrical pipe to a junction with a wider tunnel at the limit of the light's reach. He leaned against the wall on a ledge to catch his breath.

"Saint Christopher, you're a wanker, but I love ye," he said, crossing spectacles to testicles, dip to duke. "So, I promise I'll lift the first drink I can find in your name and never pick another pocket so long as I live. It's strictly the heel, second-story work, and some short cons on ungodly Protestant swells who've got it coming, so help me…"

The tunnel was summertime-dry and overripe with a vile miasma he could taste vividly down the back of his throat.

He peeled off his denim jailbird shirt and wrung it out, then did the same with his trousers. He was as parched on the inside as he was soaked outside. Blackwells was a tight house and notoriously inhospitable to the freelance professional thief. He hadn't had anything finer than toilet punch since he went in. It only remained to find his way out of the sewer and into some easily burgled haberdashery, and he'd be free, barring some sort of citywide dragnet, in which case he might as well never come up.

So… no more working the cannon, no more fanning the duke and executing his flawless lift. He'd sworn it off after he got pinched, though he doubted the saints would hold it against him if he didn't backslide a bit. If anyone was owed, it was he.

He'd been striving to better himself when it happened, anyway—prowling the library, reading beyond the racing section of the paper, eavesdropping on better classes of conversation in choicer eateries that were also easier to skip out on. He knew he couldn't straggle along dipping pedestrians all his life if he wanted to have more than a poke of fall money to retire on. He had to acquire the veneer of a gentleman of quality if he was ever to graduate to the long con. The real money cruised the streets in long chauffeured limousines and wafted through the air carelessly in luxury blimps, but if you spoke their language, they were dumb as dodoes and even easier to pluck.

If he'd stayed true to his bootstrap aspirations, he might not be in this mess at all. It was the temptation of a pocketbook lifted outside a theater that had undone him. The egg was roaring drunk, and the fat billfold all but sprang out of his hip pocket. He'd lifted it cleanly only to find his hand trapped by its owner, who'd just won a bet with his friends.

Like any journeyman thief, Spider had fall money stashed away. Still, his local fixer had been unable to shake the victim, who dogged him through four continuances, two recusals, three changes of venue, and six bogus summonses with misleading dates or venue changes. Son of a bitch laid out six times what he'd had in his wallet to put Spider inside, but he still got a bargain. Spider threw away nearly twice that to beat the rap. He got the maximum, two years, the first pick-pocket to actually be convicted in New York in over a decade.

At his sentencing, the victim had come over to blow champagne fumes in his face, but he seemed contrite now the game was done and offered Spider some advice.

"You played well with a bad hand, Paddy. I like your spirit, but you're going to waste. Stop stealing pennies, son. Use your time inside to study the stock market. That's where the big ones get skinned…"

Writing's on the wall, he thought. *New York's got a line on you. Now, you'll never work the swells in the Circle. Fuck off to the frozen tundra, they've got suckers in the sticks, too. Maybe someday, Spider McGowan out of New York could be S.P. Gower, Consigliere of Kenosha, Fixer of Frog's Ass Falls—*

Someone shouted, "Did you hear that? I think he's down here!"

Spider choked on his next breath and crushed himself against the scum-encrusted wall. Muddled echoes of shouts seemed to come from up and down the tunnel to close in on him.

Was it possible? After all, they must have seen him crawl out of the river, the bastards. A growl of frustration became a most unbecoming whine before he could stifle it.

The nearest junction was only a few feet away from him. He started to slide towards it but then froze with his hand over his mouth.

Harsh green-white light splashed the gutter and the ledge he rested on—scores of cockroaches scattered away from it, over the tops of his feet.

He kicked and cursed into his fist.

They were right around the corner.

Saint Christopher, you prick, Spider thought, *the deal's off.* He dropped the rosary beads and squeezed the pouch until the tiny teeth inside it were ground to powder. *Anybody out there, just give me a sign—*

Suddenly, the mush of voices came as clear as if they were in his pocket. He could smell the Beemans gum on the breath of one of them over the stink of the sewer.

"He's close. I can feel it..."

"What's the use? He skunked us again, damn it." Scratchy Texan drawl, veteran lawman swagger.

"We drilled him, but good. He's not getting away this time. We're not going back to Washington without his head." Clipped midwestern accent.

Spider shivered. His mouth was dry, and it felt like ants marched up the back of his throat. They might fry him for all the people Cockrum and Minky killed, but what could he have done to have the Bureau of Investigation trawl the sewers for him? He wasn't so notorious already, was he? He heard the rasp of a match and smelled a Lucky Strike and sulfur.

"Put it out. You know I'll have to put you on report..."

"Hell with the Director and his blue-haired rules, and hell with you too, if you squeal."

A long, pregnant pause. "Have it your way..."

"I've talked to birds who say they dropped him before you or I had teeth. They say he's cursed so he can't die, even if he wants to..."

"Nuts. He's just a goddam man..."

Spider pushed away from the wall. All a case of mistaken identity. Sure, and they'd let him go, for they had bigger fish on the hook.

The other Bureau agent chuckled. "I saw you shoot him. I didn't see you *stop* him... Quiet! Hear that?"

It was almost silent, except for the purl and slosh of the sewage. Spider eased off his haunches, winced at the blood prickling back into his feet. He braced himself against the wall. He could run if he had to, but they'd hear him instantly. He could try to go past them, or back into the river.

Before he could choose, his hand slipped into something when he pushed away from the wall. It was cold and sticky, and it wasn't water.

He looked up. In the reflected light off their flashlights, he saw a drainpipe protruding from the wall at his back, just three feet above his head.

Blood dripped in Spider's eye.

"*Ssshhh… I heard it, too.*"

What could they hear? Could they hear his *heart*?

Balls to this, Spider thought. He reached up to climb into the drainpipe when he saw a pair of fiery eyes glaring down at him out of the dark.

He fell back into the water. No percentage in being between a dog and his meat. He scrambled on all fours back down the storm drain. Flashlight beams fell on him, sending his doubled shadow scuttling ahead of him like a crazed tarantula. His bare feet slapped scummy brickwork, breath whickering into his chest like hot knives, but he got his feet under him and ran, then threw himself flat on the floor when he heard a shot and the scream of a ricochet.

"It's not him!"

He crawled and grabbed the bars of the grate. His legs refused to lift him through the gap. Flaming agony ripped his belly open when he tried to stand.

"Hey jailbird, freeze!"

"Don't shoot me, I didn't do any of it, I swear!" The storm drain was like the barrel of an enormous gun. The bullet when it came would be larger than he was, and would reduce him to a cloud of red Irish mist.

"We don't have time for this, Glen. Just clip him and let's get on with it…"

"What gives?" Spider cried. "You have to arrest me—"

"Shut up! Just do it," the Texan snapped at his partner.

"Why can't *you* do it for a change?"

"Oh, don't start…"

Spider clung to the bars and tried to pray. His answer came in a barrage of bullets.

He lay there for a long time, listening to the stillness. They said in stir that your head lived for a minute after they chopped it off with the old French guillotine. They said their new one sent you to a nowhere of frozen time, so you were dying forever, but never dead.

He'd been shot in the belly. He marveled at how little it hurt for something that bled so heavily, but the shock would wear off soon enough, if he lived that long.

The two government men were face down in the gutter. Something blacker than the shadows climbed down out of the drainpipe, stepped over the corpses, and came staggering into the light of the fallen flashlights.

Spider raised his hands to shade his eyes but couldn't believe what he saw.

"Don't try to move." The voice came from a cavern deeper than any sewer—a hollow, brimstone voice.

Spider held his hands out in front of him. "I'm only a thief, sir—"

"Be silent." The phantom came to stand over him. "I know what you are."

Spider literally bit his tongue. There hadn't been a situation he couldn't talk his way out of until last year.

"You're running from the law," said the terrible voice. "You have blood on your hands."

Icy dread clutched at Spider's vitals. He had a sinking feeling he'd have been better off with the Bureau dicks. "Not to dispute your keen perception, but you've got me wrong, sir. I never killed anyone—"

"You know you're a liar."

"I didn't hurt anyone! It was the others—"

"Did you stop them?"

"How the hell could I do that?"

"Did you try?"

"No—"

"Then you are guilty."

Hands lifted him by his collar and threw him against the concave wall of the storm drain. Spider sank to the filthy bricks and kept his eyes down, his hands up to ward off blows. "The hell with you, whoever you are! Only God can judge me—"

"Listen to your voice." An arm like an iron rod pinned him to the wall. "You judge yourself."

Spider stopped struggling, but he kept his eyes tightly closed. His head swam, and his honeymoon with his new belly button was just about over.

"Look at me."

Spider shook his head. "I won't tell a soul what I saw, please, just let me go home to my family—"

"You have no home and no family. Nowhere to go."

Spider opened his eyes and cleared his throat to spit in the bastard's eye, but the impulse died, and he just hung there.

"You know who I am."

Spider had some idea, yes indeed. Not who, certainly, but *what*, oh yes, and it was worse than he could ever have feared. *I didn't summon you—did I?*

The coppers could be bought off. If they couldn't, then the prosecutors or the judge. Rival mobs, likewise, weren't in the undertaker business and could be reasoned with, no matter the size of the difficulty.

But then there were the vigilantes.

Why they did what they did, nobody really knew, but they couldn't be bargained with. Some, like the Corsair of Queens or the Barnstormer, played by some Hollywood matinee standard of fair play, delivering their victims to the coppers like catered supper. Some who were known by the gruesome names the papers gave them never left their enemies alive, at all.

Even Satan could be bargained with, but they said you'd have better chances with Death Himself than with the White Devil.

The face staring into his was a mask of pale, gleaming gold inlaid with rubies and fire opals that gave the illusion of cold, lambent flames playing over the ghastly features.

A demonic leering skull regarded him with lidless, goggling eyes bulging out of their sockets. A phalanx of fangs long as fingers curled out from the gaping grimace.

The various newspapers called him the Yellow Death and the Headhunter. The pulps and the dime novels called him the Golden Ghost. But his true name followed him out of Asia, where he was known as *Gweilo, Quiloc,* or *Gaijin*—the White Devil.

According to the pulps, Lionel Fanning was an unscrupulous fortune hunter in Asia who uncovered the grotesque but powerful mask and donned it to repent of his crimes and fight evil. They said he cut thumbs off thieves and fingers off pimps; the hands off men of violence and the privates off men of vice, and only beheaded the ringleaders, the bosses and moguls who all too often passed among polite society until they went missing north of their bowties.

But Spider had heard jailhouse ghost stories that insisted the legend was real, weirder, and worse than the wildest dime novel he had ever swiped from a newsstand. In his long and storied career, the White Devil had executed more crooks than every gallows, electric chair, firing squad, and gas chamber east of the Mississippi put together.

The bastard had to be at least seventy years old…but his grip was still as sure and unbreakable as a nun holding him down when he was a boy. It made his skin crawl, but there was fuck-all he could do about it.

Spider felt his feet lose touch with the floor. He looked away from the piercing stare, blinking through tears, down at the antique white tuxedo and seemingly boundless ebony Inverness cape, down at the pair of twin automatics in a cross-draw rig on his hips alongside a short, wickedly curved sword. The rivers of gore bubbled out from the holes in the Devil's starched white shirtfront.

"The law pursues me, as well."

"I shouldn't wonder," Spider said, looking past the hideous apparition at his victims. "Looks like…they caught you…a bit…"

"I am not…dying," the White Devil insisted. "Would that I could. But there is a darkness deeper than death…colder than Hell…that has a prior claim upon me."

Nothing could have caught Spider more by surprise, saving a hasty acquittal. "Then perhaps…a last…act of mercy…? Nothing trumps a good deathbed conversion, right? I'll mend my ways, and you…"

"You'll die here. More men will come. They will kill you for what you've seen."

"Then I'll take my chances with the river. Please, sir…I've never done much good…but I never gave back half as bad as I got."

Blood oozed from the White Devil's chest in a weary sigh. "A poor excuse for evil acts."

"Nuts to you, and your Evil Eye too," Spider snapped. "I just did what I could with a bum hand in a rigged game, so I guess that makes me a bad man. So go on and plug me so kids can read about it in your damned funny books. Make out like I was a mad dog who had to be put down, yeah? You wouldn't want to look like some screwy bastard who kills shoeless penny-ante thugs in cold blood, would you? Wouldn't want the bastards who run the Great Big Grifts to think you weren't holding your end up…"

The White Devil paused, lambent eyes guttering like lamps in a high wind. "If you could punish them…the ones who commit their crimes in plain sight…the ones who rig the game… Would you?"

Spider quivered with rage because he was all out of fear. He thought of the drunken stockbroker who hounded him to jail to amuse his swell friends, the coppers who raked in the bribes to look the other way and took the fall money to let crooks skate, only to shake them down again and call it justice; the grifters of officialdom who got fat skimming the money that should've gone to decent food, clothes and board for the orphans, creating a brutal hothouse where those who couldn't fight or steal starved. He thought of the politicians and papers who called New York the light of the world, who preached the gospel of the jungle to sheep waiting to be sheared, selling insurance to cows in a slaughterhouse.

"I don't," Spider started. "I don't understand."

He heard men shouting and water splashing from somewhere down in the sewer.

"Then I must leave you—" The vigilante dropped Spider and drew his guns. His step faltered, and he rebounded off a wall and staggered away. "This is not mercy," he said over his shoulder.

Spider reached out and caught the Devil's cape. "Not a bit of it. You wronged my getaway, you bastard. Now, what were you offering?"

The White Devil turned back to Spider, holstering his pistols. "If you had this power," he asked again, "would you punish them?"

"I'd make them pay and pay," Spider said.

A wind wafted out of the darkness within the cape, a chill so deep it turned the sweat streaming down Spider's brow to icicles. Spider fumbled, took a step backwards and sucked in breath for a prayer.

"Then…take this." The White Devil lifted his gloved hands to his face and removed his mask. He stumbled and seemed to shrink. Behind him, Spider saw sweeping carbide lamp beams and heard men approaching.

The mask was held out to him, and before he could refuse, his hands took it and placed it over his face just as the tunnel was bathed in blinding light.

Spider's last wordless gasp was abruptly cut off in a whisper of fabric. Between the first bursts of gunfire and the sound of the slugs hitting stone, the White Devil collapsed upon himself so that the bullets passed through a shadow. What fell onto the slimy bricks at Spider's feet was a bundle of bones swaddled in rotten rags, an effigy of decay that might've died years ago.

He was pinned in the light, battered by threats and commands. Spider stumbled, tripping on bunched fabric—a cape?

He tumbled backwards into its folds, into moonless, starless night.

Into the dark, whipped by fierce winds that threatened to strip clothing from flesh and skin from bone. But when he felt the ground, it was as if he'd only tripped and fallen on the pavement.

He clung to the rough-hewn flagstones like a castaway on a desert isle.

All was frigid darkness, but when he reached out, he discovered he lay under the blanket of a silk-lined cape of fuliginous fabric, softer than velvet, tougher than chainmail. He heard the roaring wind and his own labored breathing. The air was thinner than flophouse steak. He barely felt the hole in his belly, but he felt himself dying in his fingers and toes, felt his lungs bursting and bleeding for want of oxygen.

It's no more nor less a stretch than anything else that's happened since supper, he told himself and whipped away the cape.

He sat in a courtyard of gray, unmortared stones open to the sky on two sides and altars or shrines in the shadowy recesses of the other two walls. Above a low, wide double door, a bas-relief carving of a bug-eyed, fanged demon—like the face of his savior—leered down at him with eyes of gleaming rubies bigger than his fists.

His hands went to his face, and he could not find it.

The mask, so cold his fingers turned black with frostbite wherever they touched its, covered his face. It had delivered him and healed his wounds, but at what price? Still not sure he hadn't made a deal with the Devil and slid straight to Hell, he stood up and forced himself to take a deep, burning breath.

Before him, the doors slowly opened. Beyond them, a waterfall of steep stairs spilled down the sheer face of a pyramid. Far below, lesser pyramids, domes, and towers loomed out of a blue-white mist that covered the earth beneath a starless sky more black than blue.

Well, this was a fine fix.

He felt rather than heard them, but he knew when they came, and they had the drop on him.

"Alright, officers…" He turned and tried to remove the mask, but it wouldn't come off. Something cut his legs out from under him and laid him out on the stones.

For just a moment, he looked up at a figure in white robes and a mask of bone with glittering crystal eyes. Hands with nails like talons brandished a short, curved sword. Before he could plead for his life, the flat of the blade came down on his head, and he was hurled into the deepest darkness of all.

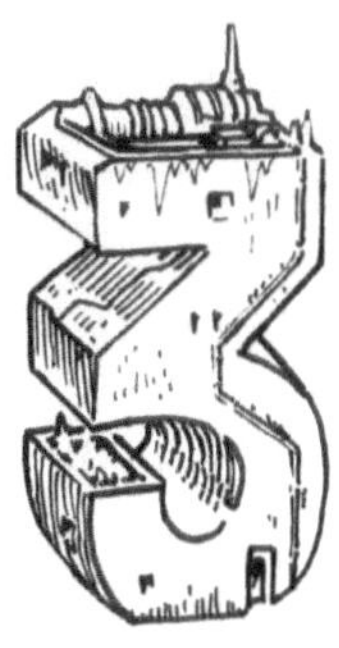

Get the news. Get it first. Make a great and continuous noise to attract readers; denounce crooked wealth and promise better conditions for the poor to keep readers. INCREASE CIRCULATION.

—William Randolph Hearst

Eureka, CA | September 29, 1929

"**I**t's a kiss-off," Busby Aaronson snapped his gum and sailed the paper plane he'd made of the telegram from the Examiner's city desk out over Eureka Bay. "Something big is gonna happen in the City, so you can bet somebody with more pull got us sent on this fly-ropin' trip."

"But Busby...the editor likes you," Millard Crabtree said, "and the press release said it's gonna be a major event—"

"So why isn't *he* here? Sure, he likes me. He just likes everybody else more." Waving his cigar at the frowning scribblers waiting on the railroad platform. "D'you recognize any of these ham-and-eggers? Nobody else from a real paper tramped up here on this bum tip. And don't get me started on why he hung *you* around my neck." He cocked an overgrown eyebrow at Crabtree's crestfallen look, and the dogeared issue of *Top Notch* wadded in his side pocket and tried to soften the blow. "Don't trust nobody, hunkie, and nothin' but your own nose. And I've told you a thousand times that pulp crap'll rot your brains."

Crabtree threw *Top Notch* in the trash—he'd already read the good story with the sky-pirates twice, anyway—and tried to adopt a suitably mistrustful expression whenever the veteran reporter chanced to look up from his racing form.

Working with the great Busby Aronson was an education that left Crabtree torn. Day by day, the less imbecilic he was in word and deed, the more irritable Mr. Aronson got. He'd just about doped out the rudimentary of the reportage game, but every so often, he had to throw a shoe in the works and stage some sort of pratfall to keep his mentor happy.

He sounded pretty happy right now. "Look at this place. God, it's the land time tried to forget. It's more ass-backward than wherever *you* come from." The coastal town of Eureka was but an outgrowth of its port, a clearinghouse for timber coming out of the redwood forests. Still, Crabtree welcomed the break from the noise and chaos of the city until Busby started in.

He still held out hope this trip might make Busby eat his words. It'd all been rather cloak-and-dagger, with the secret invitation to witness "a practical demonstration of antediluvian super-science applied to modern innovation that will revolutionize Man's place in the World, nay, the Universe!" The "super-scientist" in question was an archaeologist and ethnologist and something of a crackpot. Still, Mr. Dodd had been adamant that they would make the flight up the coast on an amphibious turboprop, as Eureka had no proper aerodrome that was not the property of the Navy.

Crabtree waited for the air to clear before he tried to talk. "I hear there might be a bridge from Fort Point to the Marin Headlands before too long, even finer than the old pontoon bridge to Oakland."

"Aw, you're nuts. Nothing's faster than the aeroferry."

"Well, I play tennis with this fellow at the YMCA, and he says the Norton Foundation's going to sponsor one of their engineering contests to get a design—"

"Applesauce. Everything they throw across the Gate gets knocked down by the first tidal wave or steam-powered juggernaut that comes out of the Pacific before it's finished. It's not happening anytime soon. Did your tennis partner let slip how he's gonna pay for it?"

Crabtree let the question go flat. The Norton Foundation had done a lot of good for the City. Old "Emperor" Norton made his fortune when he cornered the domestic market on rice back in the silver boom days, and any number of his crazy ideas had since come to fruition.

"The fellow we're going to see says he's thought up something that could make all bridges, trains, and even ships obsolete. Says we could use it to put men on the Moon."

"He's nuts, too."

"Well, what's so all-fired important in the City that they wouldn't let you cover it?"

It took Aaronson a moment to admit, "I don't know…but half the fat cats in town are sitting at the Palace Hotel waiting to hear some egghead give a speech, and there won't be room for anything else in the paper tomorrow, that's what I heard."

"Who's the egghead?"

"Some big noise back east. Sylvester Chalice. Everybody's saying he's going to drop a bomb in our backyard today, and we're the only ones who'll miss it."

"Well, that shows what you know," Crabtree blurted, snapping up the copy of the *Examiner* he'd been pretending to read. "That Chalice fella just talked to Congress yesterday, and he's in Manhattan today, talking to the…uh, the New York Explorer's Club."

Aaronson blew a raspberry. "This is exciting to you, isn't it? You're so dumb. This feels like news."

Crabtree shrugged his big, sloping shoulders. If he had his druthers, he'd be out east right now, covering the roving gangs of bank robbers who'd captured the public imagination. The Tape Bandits had been rounded up only last winter after their leader, "Baby Face" Nelson, brazenly stripped the jewels off the wife of Chicago's mayor, and Pretty Boy Floyd and the Barker-Karpis gang were still at large. That was where the action was.

At last, the train arrived, giving Aaronson fresh fodder for his keen sensibilities. "This is it, kid. Next stop, the glue factory."

It was an antique steam locomotive used for hauling timber, with two passenger cars, a flatcar piled with cargo covered in canvas, and a caboose. A short, buxom redhead in a leather aviatrix getup stepped down from the locomotive. "Good morning, ladies and gentlemen of the press," she said, trying to keep the disappointment out of her voice as she surveyed the pitiful company. Only sixteen reporters and photographers, and a junior professor and a handful of graduate students from the University of California.

"My name is Zelda Kurtzberg," she said. "My uncle regrets that he can't meet you himself this morning, but he is preparing our demonstration, and while we're certain that what we've discovered will astound you…"

A hand shot up. "Ms. Kurtzberg? Ms. Kurtzberg, if I may?"

Flushed until her freckles disappeared, Zelda yielded to Crabtree's question. "Isn't Dr. Kurtzberg a student of ancient pre-Columbian and Amerind civilizations, Ms. Kurtzberg?"

Exasperated, she nodded. "My uncle's areas of expertise are many and varied, and we've brought together the finest minds in several disciplines. All questions will be answered after the demonstration, and I'm sure you'll have a lot of them."

Crabtree was still stuttering out his follow-on question when someone else cut in. "He means, will there be Indian rain-dancing, and will it be co-ed?"

A few chuckles and disgusted *well-I-never* erupted from the group. Zelda flushed as red as her hair and marked Aaronson and Crabtree in her mind with a knitted brow and wrinkled nose. "My uncle will explain everything, including why we couldn't be more forthcoming. I assure you; your dedication will be rewarded." She turned and climbed back into the locomotive, leaving them to file up the mounting block to the first passenger car.

Aaronson took a seat on a bare wood bench scarred by cigars and flicked his butt out the window. "We are the damned," he said.

In the year since he somehow found his way out of the *Examiner's* mailroom, Crabtree had never been to the soirees put on to lubricate the press. Still, he'd heard stories of champagne fountains and dancing girls to promote movies, politicians, and even reform campaigns. Aaronson always said the ritzier the spread, the smaller the scoop. By his lights, this ought to be the discovery of the age.

The train wheezed to a stop in the middle of the woods and disgorged the party beside an abandoned sawmill. A leathery, balding man with blue, blurry tattoos on his robust forearms led them up a path to a picnic area beside a handsome three-story lodge of redwood logs and expressed the hope that they enjoyed a good barbecue. An autogyro from the *Times* touched down, and a few more jaded reporters joined the group. Nothing wins over the press like free food, but the goodwill turned sour when the group was introduced to the buffet and noticed the distinctly bloodless aroma of the smoke wafting from the huge open-air grill. Kurtzberg's camp was strictly vegetarian. The fare consisted of salads and roasted ears of sweet corn, butternut squash, baked potatoes, chilled honeydew melon, and rhubarb pie for dessert. Aaronson cursed this Kurtzberg clown with every breath he took between plates, of which he finished three.

"Never turn down free food, kid," he gasped between gulps, "and you just might survive this business."

When they'd tucked into the disappointing luncheon, a short, stoopshouldered man with a remarkable beard and crown of unkempt white hair climbed up onto a rough-hewn table and clapped his chafed, blackened hands nervously to get their attention.

Once they gave it to him, it nearly knocked him down. "Good morning, all… Is it still…? Ah, good afternoon, then… I, uh…" Looking over at Zelda, the man tucked his hands guiltily into the pockets of his dirty green mechanic's smock. "Where was I…? Yes! I am Professor Jacob Kurtzberg, of, ah…formerly of Cornell University. I thank you for coming and will strive not to waste any more of your time than I must to help you understand what you are about to witness.

"Since the dawn of human civilization, humankind has dedicated its highest aspirations, its obsessive energy, to escaping this world and joining the gods in their heaven, or at least, to finding a less painful path than the one we all know.

"Everywhere in the world, we see parallel traditions that propel the living spirit to a higher plane of existence that brings knowledge impossible to acquire otherwise, as witness the medicine men of the Amazon, the Dogon tribes of Africa and the—"

"Get to the point!" someone snapped.

The professor looked around, lost his place, then reshuffled his notes with a befuddled sigh. "Everywhere, we find evidence that primitive peoples erected standing stones on hilltops and at crossroads, which served both as sacred ritual centers and early observatories, until their priests were scattered, their secrets forgotten… But we maintain that the commonalities from Stonehenge to the monoliths of Lake Titicaca was no coincidence, but something much more wondrous at work."

The lecture had so thoroughly bored its audience that only a few among them were alert enough to chuckle at the word "Titicaca."

"Even today, so-called modern science can only hurl conjecture at the true purpose of the megaliths scattered throughout the

British Isles, Europe, Asia, Africa, and yes, even in the New World. The Anasazi and Chaco Canyon civilizations and the Moundbuilders of Cahokia showed similar aspirations. However, their ruins are often overlooked where they were not summarily wiped away by American manifest destiny… But I digress…"

"I'll say you do, Doc," shouted a stocky reporter in a straw hat to widespread laughter. Several flasks had been passed around to fortify the weak lemonade on offer, but one could almost hear nerves fraying in the stifling heat.

"So, to the point… In my research, I discovered that many stone circles were aligned according to a principle of subtle magnetic energy. Namely, they harnessed that magnetism, which is generated by the Earth's rotation but also subject to cosmic rhythms, even as the tides and seasons, to open portals to the Otherworld, to visit the realm of spirit and commune with entities they mistook for gods. Today, we will endeavor to reproduce their efforts with science substituted for superstition."

If he was boring them before, now he was beginning to drive them to outrage. "Blasphemer!" an older woman hissed, and others grumbled.

"Buncha crap," Aaronson said, sliding off his bench. "I'm gonna try to get the dope down south." Aaronson strolled away, and he wasn't alone. A few others ducked out to gather around a parked automobile and listen to the radio, and some looked antsy to leave at the earliest opportunity, as if they weren't trapped up here…

"Please don't leave!" Kurtzberg looked stricken. "I assure you, all that I've said will be borne out by empirical evidence. If my assistants have prepared the space…"

Dr. Kutrzberg turned and impatiently waved for them to follow. The whole sweaty, half-drunk press junket followed him up a stone path to a fairly new red gambrel-roof barn that appeared to have trees growing through its roof.

He went over to the double doors and threw them open for the group, which filed into the shadowy barn, rubbing their eyes mistrustfully. Crabtree was in the front, hoping to make a good showing before Miss Kurtzberg.

Stepping through the doors, Crabtree was surprised to find himself standing simultaneously in a laboratory and a forest. Enclosed in a great glasshouse inside the barn, a tight circle of seven sentinel redwoods reared up from the bare earth and pierced the incomplete roof. A mountain range of exotic electrical devices lined the walls of the barn. Banks of meters, gauges, and water valves ticked and buzzed and spewed ticker tape. Tesla coils traded crackling licks of lightning and sparkling filigreed arcs of energy climbed Jacob's ladder. Unsettling noises and unhealthy odors emitted from devices to which he could put no name.

The sweltering air was so charged with static that the hairs on his arms and the back of his neck seemed to rise and fall in time with the pulse of the machines.

"The Indians in this part of the country did not rely on megaliths, but these trees you see before you were planted and nurtured in this carefully chosen spot to capture the flow of earth energy along what the inspired amateur Mr. Watkins first referred to as ley lines, and focus it on such days as this… Surely some of you are familiar with the French Beltane, the German Walpurgisnacht…"

"Witch's Sabbath!" said the disapproving woman.

"Indeed!" Kurtzberg was jubilant. "But rather than dancing and animal sacrifice, we have devised a more precise and civilized means of activating the circle."

"He's mad!" cried the woman. "Someone should stop him. One of you men should—"

"He's just a crackpot," another reporter said. "Let him ramble. What's the worst that could happen?"

Nothing, Crabtree thought. *Nothing is the worst thing that can happen.* And when he was around, it never failed.

Zelda Kurtzberg went to her uncle and tugged his arm. "It's nearly noon," she said.

Kurtzberg looked startled. "Now, you've already met my niece, who has insisted, yes, on accompanying today's expedition. Now, she will introduce her cohorts in this mad venture."

Zelda came forward again. While she talked, a reed-thin boy with cropped blond hair connected hoses to plugs and sockets in her odd flying jacket and strapped a steel tank to her back. "As I'm sure you gathered, my uncle taught me everything I know about ancient cultures and their lesser-known scientific attainments, so I will lead our expedition force today. We fully expect to find ruins older and yet more advanced than any in pre-Columbian America…perhaps older than humanity itself."

She touched the shoulder of a grizzled Negro in a smock stuffed with gadgets who nodded to the group and went back to plugging patch cords into a switchboard. "This is Otis Dutton, our resident physics and electronics wizard. He's had to accept more impossible things before breakfast around here than most of you will face your entire lives, so please excuse his bluff demeanor.

"And this," she strolled around the ring of trees to tug on the hoses dangling from the rubber deep sea diving suit of a young Asian man with thick spectacles, "is Dr. John Akiyama, a professor of natural history at the University of California—" Zelda paused to let the Cal contingent give a cheer, and she wasn't disappointed. "And also was an ambulance driver in the Great War, so if anyone gets hurt, knock on wood, we'll be prepared."

Someone behind Crabtree puffed a cigar and grumbled, "Well, I'll be. A Jew, a Jap, and a ni—" before someone with more sense shushed him.

"And for protection—not that we'll need it—we've pressed into service our friend, Sgt. Butch Billings, United States Marine Corps, whom you've already met."

The cook from the unpopular barbecue stood up from where he'd been kneeling, apparently in silent prayer. "I'm here," he said, "so if you end up eyeball to eyeball with Saint Peter, someone can put in a good word for you heathens."

"And this," Zelda stepped away from the shy, towheaded boy hiding behind her. She pushed him towards the crowd, "our invaluable assistant, Mr. Trevor Ringquist, without whom my esteemed but absentminded uncle might forget to bring us back."

Nobody laughed.—A swarm of hands shot up immediately while the rest simply started braying.

"Again, please hold your questions. We hope to have one more join us on our expedition, but we require a volunteer. You'll be back before the ice melts in your lemonade, and I assure you it's much safer than my uncle made it sound."

Crabtree's hand waved even before some wag shoved him out into the open.

Zelda called out, "Yes, you, the impatient one with the quizzical hair. Again." Crabtree was startled to find she was pointing at him. He looked around for Aaronson, who must've stayed outside.

Flattening his cowlick, Crabtree said, "Well, uh…I suppose, as far as what you've explained, ah, goes…it sounds, uh…sound as a dollar, but…where are we going? How do you propose we get there? When we get there…will there be…Indians?"

Someone in the back guffawed into his fist.

"All…well, mostly good questions, which we will attempt to answer, but we must be brief, and seeing is believing, no?" She motioned for Crabtree to come over to where Dutton helped him climb into a rubber and canvas suit like the one Zelda wore.

Dutton said, "Show them Ambrose!"

"Amelia!" Zelda shouted back, then cleared her throat and brushed her copper bangs out of her eyes. Crabtree choked his heart back down out of his throat. "Dr. Akiyama, if you please."

The reserved scientist stood beside a covered cage on wheels that came up to his shoulder. "To illustrate just how very different is the place we've begun to explore, I think it's better if we just show you." He lifted the cover off a glass enclosure large enough to cage a monkey.

Inside, a shapeless, liver-tinted blob resembling a beached octopus contracted and rose up in a shoulder-high pillar that looked like an overgrown human tongue.

The audience recoiled and choked on the rising rhubarb. A few flashbulbs detonated, causing the thing to pale to near-translucence, clench into a wad like a fist, and flail at the walls of its cage. Crabtree's head swam. He looked around again for Aaronson.

"As you can see, this is a very simple organism. Indeed, it is unicellular, like amoebae and other microscopic organisms that inhabit the unseen world all around us…only much larger, of course, and highly reactive, as you've seen. This ability to mimic and camouflage made its capture quite interesting, I can tell you."

"If memory serves," Dutton cut in, "Butch tracked it back into the greenhouse on his boot the first time we went through. And then he fed it."

"Is that thing dangerous?" A stout reporter in a houndstooth suit and a green derby hat barged through the crowd to approach the glass and tap it with a tarnished cigarette lighter. "Is everything over there that ugly?"

He jerked away and choked on his cigar smoke when the thing tapped back. His cigar stuck to his lip, so his fat fingers slid down the stogie and grabbed the coal at the end. He shouted and made a rude gesture at the thing under the glass, then went back into the crowd, sucking his fingers.

"While we haven't established whether or not Ambrose or Amelia has true intelligence, it's shown uncanny prowess in parroting every behavior it witnesses through thousands of tiny light-sensitive organelles we've observed within its membrane. I think the question may be less how intelligent it is, but how intelligent are we, that a single-celled organism from this other world might learn to ape us so easily?"

Akiyama covered the cage just as the blob reformed and surged up against the glass. Its membrane was distorted into a crude imitation of a human hand, with the middle finger extended towards the reporter who'd taught him the gesture.

Someone shouted, "What's to stop more of those things coming through with you?"

"This glasshouse and other measures are in place to prevent any contamination between worlds. We've taken every precaution and made several jaunts without incident. Thank you, please."

Akiyama retired from the stage as Zelda took his place, holding a diving helmet, but the air hoses fed into a cumbersome tank strapped to her back. "Now, as to where we're going.... It's not so much a question of where, but to a different *here*...another earth that coexists with our own. It's all around us right now, but it is only by altering our molecular vibrations at places like this that the translation may occur. In a very literal sense, we will not be leaving this circle, but in a theoretical sense, we will travel further than any human being has ever traveled before...or at least, not in a very long time.

"I assure you, it'll come clear soon enough. Are we ready?" Billings, Crabtree, Akiyama, and Zelda Kurtzberg stood just outside the circle of sentinel redwoods, donning their helmets as Dutton went down the row, checking gauges and winching down seals.

"You gonna faint?" Dutton asked. "You puke in this thing, you drown. Got that?"

Crabtree nodded, closed his eyes, and held his breath as the other man entombed him in the helmet.

Zelda came close enough for him to see her through the tinted glass of their respective helmets. "Breathe," she said, and he jumped as the sound of her voice came out of a speaker inside the helmet with him.

Dutton sprayed them with a foamy business he said would keep them from tracking foreign biological material to the other side, then he and the young intern busied themselves throwing knife switches and turning massive dials on the banks of machinery.

After reassuring her nervous uncle, Zelda returned to the crowd but kept her eyes pinned to the displays. Everyone jumped as her voice boomed from a loudspeaker hanging above the doors. "We will only stage a brief demonstration today of the extraordinary claims we've made, with the hope that further research may take place. We hope that you will observe skeptically but honestly report back what you have witnessed so that the world may share in this discovery for the benefit of all her people."

Ignoring the storm of questions and demands, Zelda Kurtzberg took her place at the head of the small expeditionary party. Trevor opened a glass door, and they filed into the greenhouse.

Once he got over the confinement, Crabtree felt more than a little ridiculous, standing in a grove of trees dressed up like Jules Verne's lunar explorers, but he also felt giddy. The crackle and whine of the machines had reached a crescendo impenetrable to human voices. Zelda gave her uncle an A-OK sign.

Crabtree looked from one to the next, waiting to see what he should do and what would happen. The lights from the laboratory equipment seemed to spin around them, the bars of light flying faster and faster as if the whole world were spinning around the circle of trees. The green-shaded grove tingled with brilliant colors he could not name. Everything around it was drained of color and seemed to dissolve in an acid of pure white light. The trees turned like the spokes of a wheel, the four faceless bodies standing within the circle flickering like ghostly images in a hand-cranked movieola until Crabtree felt dizzy and had to close his eyes. When he did, he gave a gasp of surprise that coursed through the crowd as everyone witnessed and gradually, in their own time, came to realize what had happened.

They were gone.

Busby Aaronson had an infallible nose for news, and it was itchier than a fleabite with hay fever. He caught the *Times* reporters outside and prevailed on them to let him use the wireless set in their auto-gyro to contact the *Examiner* city desk before they returned to Los Angeles.

Cyrus Gassaway answered. "Say, Buzz, what's the rumpus?"

"You tell me. Winning a snoring contest in Eureka, Cy. What'd I miss?"

"Magic, to hear Beanie tell it." Rustling as Cy rummaged through a blizzard of photostat dispatches and typed copy in the hopper for the evening edition. "Fella name of Chalice pulled one for the ages. 'Inventor Travels From New York to San Francisco Instantly! And Back Even Faster! Sylvester Chalice Demonstrates Revolutionary Teleportal!'"

"With exclamations yet," Aaronson sighed. The publisher hated punctuation of any kind in their headlines.

"Can you beat it?"

"Not with a bat. We'll have a pratfall piece for Page Twelve if we're lucky." He looked around, realizing he was shouting into the wireless headset to be heard above an unearthly racket coming from Kurtz-berg's barn. "See ya, Cy."

He hung up and jumped down from the wing to let the bored reporters take off. Holding his fedora on his head against the wind from the rotors, he ran to the barn just as the sound wound down. *Cripes, I even missed the big payoff here.* His belly churned to pro-test the rabbit-feed lunch. The barn doors were shut but swung open when he pushed. The crowd was flummoxed, crowding up against the glass. About half seemed convinced they'd just witnessed some kind of conjurer's trick. The rest were unable to find words at all. Old nutty Kurtzberg stood before the greenhouse, waiting for them to come to their senses. And where was Crabtree?

Aaronson elbowed a fat reporter in a derby who looked to be sucking his thumb. "Hey bud, you seen the big dope who was shadowing me?"

The reporter took his blistered thumb out and replaced it with a cigar. "What's he look like?"

"Like an orangutan walking on his hands, with a hat on his ass." Aaronson pushed towards the front; if the lummox were here, he'd be impossible to miss.

The storm of electrical noise had subsided, but a weird flickering persisted in the circle. Aaronson felt as if he was watching moving pictures of an eclipse, yet every tenth frame was not a Northern California forest at all, but someplace utterly *other*—

"Please contain yourselves," Kurtzberg shouted, "or we'll be forced to clear the room!" Wringing his bony hands, he went back to a monolithic console with dozens of glass gauges and bulbs that blinked with incandescent gas. "A crossing between realities is potentially very volatile. If anything goes wrong, cascading effects on causality can result, opening the doorway to infinite parallel universes… or potentially destroying our own. Theoretically, of course…"

Even if nobody understood it, he had confused and terrified them into silence. "In two minutes, our expedition will return with further samples for you to examine, and then we will retire to the terrace, where your questions will be answered in rigorous detail. We welcome your scrutiny, I promise you! But be patient…"

Kurtzberg, Dutton and the kid turned to do things to their machines. Aaronson lit a cigarette and scratched the back of his neck. It was a hell of a coincidence, two crackpots pulling the same trick on the same day. But a few years before, Aaronson was present at the first demonstration of a new kind of radio that also showed pictures.

The inventor, a Mormon farm boy from Idaho, dreamed up the idea and got Crocker and some other local moguls to finance it. The kid seemed to think his new invention would change the world, so everyone got a free college education and quoted Shakespeare, but last Aaronson heard, RCA had the last laugh. Radio was still king, and television was going nowhere.

"Now we shall return our brave voyagers safely to Earth," Kurtzberg announced. The murmuring died down. "I am sure our brave volunteer, Mr. Crabtree, will be a far more credible witness than ourselves."

Crabtree! Aaronson dropped his cigarette on the ground and tugged the brim of his hat. That hammerhead found a new way to screw up everything he touched. Aaronson turned his back for one minute and the big dope committed the cardinal journalistic sin. He was part of the story. Whatever the payoff to this little charade turned out to be, Crabtree would be its dupe. With arms crossed, he waited for his junior associate to return from the camera obscura they were hiding in, so they could get the hell out of here.

Dutton and the professor shouted at each other, but the roaring machinery drowned them out. The kid's voice was higher and somehow cut through, or maybe he was just screaming at the top of his lungs in abject terror.

"Must be interference from another crossing!"

A weird glow shone through the trees and seemed to rotate like the lamp in a lighthouse, and the sickening feeling of seeing split-second frames from another movie cut into the one he was watching.

The trees seemed to stand still and to spin at the same time, until they were washed in a strobing blast of light, and then four figures stood in the circle.

"Don't that beat all," someone beside him said. Kurtzberg faced the crowd. "I assure you that what you have witnessed is no trick! We have successfully penetrated the veil between worlds!"

Trevor and Dutton came rushing towards them to help them out of their gear, the only ones who didn't seem to see that it wasn't the same group.

Their helmets were different, for one—more like gas masks. For another, they were heavily armed, with belt-fed submachine guns and elephant guns that drooled blue sparks. For a third, they immediately began shooting everyone.

The glasshouse shattered everywhere at once. Bullets and lightning swept the crowd of reporters. Kurtzberg was thrown backward and knocked Aaronson flat on his ass. He pushed and squirmed out from under the smoking corpse but then realized he was safer where he was.

The invaders came out of the trees, flanking the crowd and catching them at the barn doors in a monstrous crossfire. Not one of the gentlemen and ladies of the fourth estate got three steps closer to the door before they were raked with gunfire or burned halfway to ashes.

One of the masked murderers stood almost on top of Aaronson when the padded leather armor on his chest stopped a bullet. He blasted Dutton, who held a snubnosed .38 in one hand. The lightning arced from Dutton to Trevor and the machines behind him. A control panel ignited and all the display lights around them flashed red or died out entirely.

"You mugs spread out and toss the place," one of them said. For an invader from another world, his Bronx accent sounded just like the East Coast torpedoes who routinely came out to California for easy pickings and ended up catching the gas at San Quentin.

Now, there was no one else and nowhere to go. They were between him and the door. One peeked outside, leaving the door open just wide enough for a bar of blessed sunlight to spill across the earthen floor, then disappeared among the banks of machinery. The other two began splashing gasoline around the barn and breaking things.

Just play dead. Wait for your chance. In his head, he was already puzzling out how to sell this story to the chief. He couldn't see the torpedoes and couldn't risk moving to look, but he could hear them. One kicked over a bunch of glass, then shouted, "Christ, lookit this thing! It's like a giant slug." An ugly, childish giggle. "Hey, Lenny, got a match?"

"Sure, Skeezix…your face and my ass. Quit fooling around."

Through slitted eyes, Aaronson saw the weird witch lights in the circle of trees flickering like a neon sign on the fritz. Standing in the middle of it was a hulking oaf in a spacesuit, waving his arms and silently screaming.

Aaronson stared longer than he should have. He silently urged the gormless lummox to hide, but Crabtree just stood there. The image got burned into Aaronson's eyeballs, doubled, then trebled. As if one of the maroons wasn't one too many…

Crabtree came bumbling out of the weird light. "Hey buddy," he shouted, "what's the rumpus? Where am I?"

"Dummy up, dummy!" Aaronson stage-whispered, pointing at the barn door. "Beat your feet and get help!"

"How'd I get here, buddy? Where am I? Who…?"

"Just get lost, imbecile!"

The rube had never looked so utterly at sea. His eyes darted uncomprehendingly from Aaronson to the piles of corpses to the pulsing witch-light. He pressed his gloved hands against the glasshouse frame and screamed. The witchy light from out of the trees winked out, and Crabtree was gone, hopefully to a better place.

"Nuts!" the torpedo banged a wrench on a generator. "This whole screwy apparatus is bassackwards, but I can lick it."

Just play dead. Someone would come…

Skeezix ran back into the barn and rolled in the dirt, tugging on a dollop of strawberry jam stuck to his leg like taffy. "Get it off, Lenny. It burns!"

"Hold still, ya dope…" Lenny aimed a funny kind of rifle at the blob and painted it with fire. The whole barn shivered with a weird, keening scream.

"Watch it with that thing!" the third torpedo shouted. "Don't get killed yet, you dopes! Our ride's here…" The lab equipment spat sparks, and a dynamo rattled and howled. The lights went out, and the weird glow came back. And so did Crabtree. The banks of machinery coughed out a fireworks display, and everything fell still.

"Goddamnit!" the third torpedo roared.

"Do something, Lenny, it's eating me!" Skeezix screamed.

The lunkhead smashed through the last unbroken glass and ripped off his helmet.

"Good gravy, we got a live one!" Lenny turned his torch on Crabtree, who flung his helmet in the torpedo's face, knocking him cold. An arc of wildfire splashed Skeezix and the butt of the big dope's spacesuit. The burning blob leapt off and skipped across the barn like butter on a hot skillet.

"Hey buddy, where am I?" Crabtree looked like a lost infant. It seemed to have escaped his notice that his ass was on fire.

"I told you to beat it! Can't you do anything right?"

Crabtree blinked and rubbed his eyes. "Mister, I ain't never seen you before. I just wanna wake up from this crazy dream…"

How dumb could one dummy be? "What'd I tell you? Beat your feet!"

"Alright, fall out, you mutts," the third torpedo shouted as he emerged from the machinery holding an armload of science junk. "We're taking the train after all… Hey! Who the hell're you?"

Crabtree looked around the barn as if for the first time, then ducked as the third torpedo dropped his loot and covered him with a pistol.

God hates a coward. Aaronson rolled Kurtzberg's alarmingly light body off him and sat up. "Drop your gun, or I'll libel you to smithereens!"

The startled torpedo turned and shot Aaronson in the chest. Crabtree finally got the message and ran for the door, bullets chopping wood all around him.

The torpedo came over and stepped on his neck. Aaronson had only a moment to ponder who would write this mess up for the *Examiner*. *Please, Lord…anyone but Crabtree.*

"This is gonna hurt me more than it'll hurt you, bud," said his killer.

"So, let's trade," Aaronson replied.

The man who builds a factory builds a temple. The man who works there worships there.

—President Calvin Coolidge

New York, New York | January 15, 1931

Father disapproved of the outing. Buffalo Bill's Wild West Revival at Madison Square Garden was not just a lowbrow dumb show for the ungrateful unwashed, he fulminated. It was a symptom of America's decadence and corruption, for "whenever the adversities of the present day become too much for a weakened nation, it seeks succor in illusory reenactments of a bygone or purely imaginary past."

He paused theatrically, defying her to observe that he had one finger in Toynbee, that the smoke from his pipe tonight was not tobacco, or that his disgruntlement with the Wild West Show stemmed from its use and commercial endorsement of the Winchester Gyro-Rifle, but she generously conceded the field. "You're right, Daddy. I'll be happy to relay your condemnation."

"Come into the light, dear," he said in a somewhat gentler voice. "Let me see you."

Stepping out of the shadowy doorway, Matilda curtsied to reveal her dress for the evening, which provoked a smoky snort from his nostrils. But she saw his good eye twinkle behind its monocle as it registered the splendid sapphire brooch at her throat, a recent gift for her thirty-third birthday. It was a splendid piece with its own name, like a racehorse or somesuch, and probably a curse. "So, you're forbidding me to go?"

"Haven't you read the papers? Labor's on the warpath again. Bethlehem Steel, can you believe it? That bastard Ochlocrat is calling for a general strike, egging the mob to drag us out of our homes. I merely fear for your safety, but I know if I forbade you to go…"

"I'd make you come with me," Matilda said, tipping a wink and pulling the saloon doors shut as she backed out on her perilously high heels.

Mrs. Hildebrandt presented her purse and draped silver fox fur around her shoulders. She complimented her perfume but tutted her intention of attending the show alone.

"I'll be safe as a piggy bank at a policeman's ball, Mabel. Safer. You be sure Father has no excuse to stay up past supper, or he'll become convinced I've come to some sordid end and make trouble."

Mrs. Hildebrandt searched her overtaxed memory and reminded Matilda that she had an appointment tomorrow at 9:30 a.m. with her psychoanalyst. "No concern of mine, but it does irk your father, your sharing family secrets with a Hun."

"Dr. Frauenwahl is Swiss and safer than a confessional." She arched her eyebrows at her lapsed Catholic warder, who followed her to the self-service express elevator, reminding her to top off her batteries in the box seats and to stay vigilant. There'd been an anarchist bomb threat in Times Square only this morning, and someone like Matilda presented a juicy target for treasonous miscreants.

Matilda sighed and nodded as she checked herself one last time in the mirror beside the elevator. Her austerely cut midnight blue serge gown clove to her form in a way Father might find unbecoming, but it was reassuringly out of fashion. Opera gloves and mid-calf underskirt concealed her prosthetic arm and leg, and with her dark auburn hair swept up in a conservative braid, she could easily pass for a dowager half-again her age.

The brooch threw off wheels of azure light just from the hooded lamps set into the ceiling of the apartment, obscuring all but the barest outlines of her face. Perfect.

Lastly, she ran the fingers of her prosthetic arm through her hair and cycled the digits through some of her old piano lessons. It would've sounded like a startled cat running across the keys, but at least the agonizing needles conveyed the nervous impulses properly without the maddening lag that cropped up when she'd last used it for shooting. Two weeks at a Swiss clinic to be fitted and trained with the abominable thing, and she probably could have found something more reliable from a black-market machinist in Chinatown. She reminded herself to leave it with Aurora and trade it for something a bit more imperative.

Donning a cloche hat and taking her cane, Matilda stepped into the elevator, bowing her head so Mrs. Hildebrandt could throw a shoulder into the sliding door, kiss her brow, and whisper one last time to watch herself.

Mrs. Hildebrandt had cared for her since before she could walk. She was closer to Matilda than her mother; God rest her soul. But did she know?

Dr. Frauenwahl never pressed her about her secret life, though he warned her that omitting any detail blinded him to her reality and rendered his analysis useless. She sometimes suspected that he knew more than he let on.

At their last session, he'd warned her against looking to her "shadow self" for validation, lest she lose her essential self.

She'd retorted that perhaps that wouldn't be such a bad thing, leaving him smiling bemusedly at her, his eyes hidden behind the burnished coins of his spectacles. "That could lead to the most disastrous of all possible outcomes," he said. "You might decide to stop seeing me."

The elevator was too fast, dropping fifteen stories from the Lynchs' penthouse apartment to the flight deck in less time than it took to reapply her lipstick; Matilda thought that the proper way to leave home would be a hyperbaric chamber and several hours' decompression.

She smiled and nodded at Bruno, the sullen carpenter sanding the decorative baseboards in the hall outside their suite. Though the apartment stubbornly concealed any feature that wasn't old hat by the Civil War, it was a thoroughly modern dwelling, with oscillating dust-magnets, electro-static precipotron and an ultrasonic laundry system. The building was so new it was not, strictly speaking, completed. Only a glimmer in the eye of its architect when the market crashed, the Majestic Apartments would've been reworked into a mere thirty-two-story hotel or even abandoned, had Father not rushed in and funded the skyscraper, claiming the forty-fifth-story penthouse and installing a rare peacetime application of the Lynch Magneto-Cannon's patented gauss launch system. The flight deck, a short runway on the thirtieth floor, caught incoming aeroplanes, brought them to a halt, or flung them silently out over Strawberry Fields and the Central Park Lake before their turboprops kicked in.

Father fulminated, and Mabel Hildebrandt fretted, but they were glad to see her go out these last few years. She dreaded it almost as much as staying in, but she'd had to go to the trouble of showing the family's hand in the society pages and providing cover for how she preferred to spend her evenings.

The mag-lev elevator did not brake, so much as it stopped as if it had never moved, which always made her rock seasickishly on her "good" leg, which was still meat. The door opened on a service worker's floor, and another woman stepped in. Matilda looked her over approvingly as if appraising herself in a mirror—which, after a fashion, she was.

Wearing the same dress and the same hairstyle, down to the silver fox on her shoulders, the woman could be Matilda's reflection, set free from the mirror. Matilda nodded to her and reminded her not to smile for the photographers at the El Morocco and the Rainbow Room. The women doffed and traded overcoats, Matilda tucking her double's under her arm. As she moved to leave, she remembered one more detail. Removing the brooch from her collar, she pinned it to her double and reminded her that it bore a Hindoo curse and was not to be carried off at evening's end.

Her double smiled at the joke. Elvira Seaton was a chorus girl with a promising future until one night in '28 when a masher she'd told to go to hell shoved her off a subway platform. Losing an arm and her career to the train, she was lucky to find work as a counter girl at a department store until she answered a personal ad. She had come to depend on the regular booking and become something of an expert in her role, and she could be trusted as much as anyone. The elevator stopped. Matilda placed a metallic hand on her twin's shoulder as she stepped out through the open door.

"Break a leg," Matilda said.

"You too," Elvira replied as the elevator shut and descended to the flight deck.

Matilda hurried down the service corridor to the door that opened only for her. She stepped inside, kicked out of her heels, peeled off her gloves, unbuttoned her gown, and flung it all into a laundry chute. Underneath, she wore only a rubberized union suit. She was struggling into her quilted flight leathers when she heard the other door open and smelled a rumor of magnolias. She said, "I can't do a damned thing with this arm."

Aurora Benoit wiped the lenses of her telescoping glasses on the lapel of her coveralls. "You want the Peacekeeper, the Lumberjack or the Diplomat?"

Matilda zipped the suit up to her solar plexus, loosening the straps on her prosthetic arm. "The Diplomat, I suppose. Does it still discharge when the middle digit is extended?"

"It'd be an easy fix," Aurora said, taking a torque wrench out of one of her pockets.

"Never mind that." Shucking off the fancy bespoke prosthetic, she watched in the mirror as Aurora limbered up the Diplomat.

Aurora Benoit helped her into the combat prosthetic's web harness and slid the needles into the nerve transmitter sockets in the stump of her shoulder. She ran through the manual checklist until she could snap her fingers and cinch the straps without electrocuting herself. "So… Is it ready?"

Aurora rolled her eyes at Matilda's impatience as she opened the armory. "Hasn't been tested outside the wind tunnel, and I'm worried about the weight."

"It'll swim, Aurora," Matilda said. "Scratch the reserve parachute. I never use it, anyway."

Aurora patted the reserve chute pouch strapped down taut under her breastplate. "You will if the new design doesn't hold up. It's all new. It won't tangle you up. You never need it until you don't have it. Keep cutting it close, and you'll make me install an inflatable life raft up in there."

She felt weighed down enough already, even in the new, lighter armor of aluminum coated with a new "kinetic retardant" emulsion, which gave it a vaguely sinister cobalt luster that may or may not deflect bullets. "Is that any way for a mad scientist to talk?"

Aurora shook her head exasperatedly, but her smile could give you a sunburn. "I'm just a mad engineer. The only experimenting we get to do down here is on you."

Donning her chrome-plated helmet and checking the oxygen mask, she couldn't express her confidence with an arched eyebrow, so she gave Benoit a thumbs-up as her mad engineer did up the straps and seals on her armor. A bit of relief once the power couplings were closed, but she still felt as if she were in a deep-sea diver's suit and knew she looked like a second-place bowling trophy.

"Don't ditch the oxygen tanks when you land this time," Aurora reminded her, pointing out a vent on the intake nozzle. "Refill as soon as you get a chance, in case the bulls are using blackout or tear gas."

Though she had trained as a pilot and a soldier and overseen the armor's design herself, if not for Aurora Benoit, Matilda would probably have satisfied herself with a life of seclusion and philanthropy.

For five years after she returned from Europe, Matilda bitterly resisted every attempt to draw her out. The doctors called it shellshock, but few veterans who fought in the trenches lost what she lost—her sister, as well as an arm and a leg. Father had resigned himself to having lost both daughters to the war when she finally showed some sign of interest in the outside world, even if it did drive him to distraction.

After reading about a legless veteran arrested for vagrancy in Morningside Park, she emerged from her private room at Bellevue to push her father to provide for New York veterans, especially the wounded and surviving families of the 369th Infantry Regiment, also known as the Harlem Hellfighters.

The 369th served longer and lost more men than any other American unit. Matilda denied her father a moment's peace until he'd endowed a scholarship for sons and daughters of the Hellfighters to attend any university that would admit them. Aurora Benoit, only a year older than Matilda, graduated from Cornell in 1924 with an engineering degree. However, she couldn't find a job, even at Lynch Munitions, where her father had long since tired of indulging his daughter's charitable whims. In a fit of pique, Matilda, only just coming to dream after too many matinee serials of becoming a costumed vigilante, remembered Aurora Benoit and hired her as a secretary, then put her in charge of perfecting a death trap of a personal jet engine that killed its last daredevil owner at a flying circus in France.

Following Aurora out of the armory, Matilda was surrounded by the other girls in her retinue. They busied themselves with checklists and weather conditions and strapped the latest gimmick onto her back. The whole mess weighed almost sixty pounds, and the armor groused with every step toward the chimney. As if she wasn't weighed down enough, two more attendants stepped in to help her into her wingsuit. The densely woven plastic and oiled canvas suit clung seamlessly to her armored form, making her look like something born to the sky; however, she hobbled on the ground.

After a last radio check, Matilda clomped into the chimney and stood by as the attendants cinched her legs together. Finally, the flue was slammed and locked behind her.

Through the scorched glass porthole, Aurora gave her a thumbs-up. Matilda depressed a stud on the back of her left gauntlet to activate the miniature pulsejet strapped to her back and was slingshotted up the smokestack on a pillar of white fire.

Feeling her brain smashed against the back of her skull and her guts compressing into her pelvis, she fought to remain conscious while straining to thread the needle of the narrowing shaft, emerging from the chimney of a decommissioned incinerator on the roof of the building and climbing at over 300 miles per hour until she was clear of the municipal flight path.

Looking down on Manhattan with its firefly swarms of airborne commuter traffic and herds of dirigibles docked atop Grand Central Station, she felt a spark of that old delight that had galvanized her to do this in the first place, a sense that this was where she belonged. Even the unsightly green stalagmite that had toadstooled up out of the Lower West Side just this year, a bulbous monstrosity designed by a mad Spaniard and reared up by an upstart outfit calling itself Chalice Electric, only enlivened the harmonious chaos of her city.

A burning bird, she ascended until the cyclopean ziggurats and skyscrapers flattened into a glittering grid girded on both sides by black rivers bedecked with flitting lights that shamed the stars.

It was a marvelous night for flying, with low cloud cover but very little wind. She didn't activate the heater in her flight suit, letting the chill quicken her breath. She cut a slaloming course west over midtown to 59th Street, where the half-mile Victory Bridge spanned the dark waters of the Hudson to the Jersey Shore.

Almost universally reviled as a pox on the skyline and a colossal engineering mistake, the double-decker bridge pumped cars and trains into the heart of midtown like a firehose filling a shot glass. Its railroads were already rendered redundant by the airship freighters and the pneumatic vacuum-tube tunnel out of Penn Station, and the knives were out for it to be demolished as soon as the George Washington Bridge was opened in a few months. One plan gaining traction called for offices and luxury apartments to be added to the span and for what remained of the throughway to become a toll road.

She loved it all the more for its impracticality, but she was sure she'd feel differently if she was stuck in its traffic and not flying over it. She couldn't resist threading the Gothic needles of the twin towers, dropping low enough to hear the horns and thunder of the double-decker bridge's bustling auto and rail traffic over the helmet-muffled roar of her rocket.

Over New Jersey, where the air traffic was blessedly lighter, and the lights dwindled to pearl strands laid on barren black velvet, she throttled up and climbed until she felt lightheaded. She chinned the suit heater and oxygen mask when she leveled off at 20,000 feet, where the pummeling wind was forty degrees below zero, then turned the rudders projecting from her legs until her ballistic course took her west towards Pennsylvania.

A last look over her shoulder at Manhattan showed the island as a colossal glittering tugboat, towing the benighted hulk of North America into a foggy future.

This was what she lived for. The difference between it and everything else was, as Mr. Twain once said, as the lightning to the lightning bug. She had come to it in fits and starts, only admitting to herself what she had become when the newspapers branded her one.

Hearst's syndicate called them masked vigilantes and a worse threat than the new and extraordinary stripe of crook they fought. The *World*, reflexively taking the opposing view as it struggled to stay afloat, almost obsequiously called them *super-heroes*.

Many of her peers were little more than publicity stunts to sell toys and newspapers. Others were exploited precisely because they were unwilling or without the means to fend off commercial use of their name and likeness. She'd learned this the hard way when she crossed paths with the Electrocutioner, a celebrated superhero with a popular radio serial in national syndication, from which he saw not a penny. His backstory described him as a red-blooded American inventor wracked by suicidal anguish when common hoodlums murdered his family. Turning his crackpot broadcast free-energy experiment upon himself in his grief, he was imbued with the power to spray murderous lightning bolts from his fingertips, exacting ultimate justice upon similarly costumed crooks.

The real Electrocutioner was a Russian immigrant named Perchik Zorich. As a child, he was struck by a plasma arc from a disastrous Soviet broadcast power transmitter. All his hair fell out, and he suffered epileptic seizures if he didn't release the voltage, but channeling it was like riding Old Sparky in the death-house. Among other things, the solute in his sweat and urine crystalized inside him, making every secreted drop of fluid an exercise in agony. Even so, he was tortured to the edge of insanity with guilt over the murderers, rapists, and racketeers he'd incinerated when he lost control of his power.

All this she'd learned when the real Electrocutioner died in her arms after saving the city from Dr. Gift, another suicidal lunatic who couldn't just hang himself. And still, the comics, the radio serial, the Electrocutioner™ Shock-Mittens, kept coming, as if their hero hadn't died before he was old enough to vote.

So much for superheroes. She didn't know if she would ever be worthy of the pretentious title, nor it worthy of her. She only knew she loved it.

The mask craze first struck New York four years ago when a gang in rakish pirate costumes and a bullet-proof flying coupe began knocking over jewelry stores and banks under the colorful sobriquet, the Red Hook Wreckers. A rogue mobster calling himself El Pulpo donned an octopus mask and gunned down crime boss Guiseppe Masseria in Coney Island and eluded police for six months before he was served equally rough justice by the Corsair, who was later unmasked as a former cop drummed out of the force for being Sicilian. That so many on both sides of this weird civil war were frustrated inventors, scientists, and engineers whose bright ideas had been suppressed by the patent office only added fuel to the controversy.

From the summer of '26, the craze had spread across the nation like every other fad, and the FBI's Most Wanted list had begun to look like a masquerade ball at an insane asylum. It had just begun to fade from the front pages when it resumed with a terrifying new urgency after the Crash.

Dozens of masked vigilantes operated in the city now, and few played with any respect for the law. The Dogcatcher left street hoods chained to fire hydrants for the cops, but gangs of angry citizens often beat or even set them afire before they could be arrested. The Hangman, as the name implied, denied his unlucky foes even that much of a chance, sentencing rapists, robbers, and petty pursesnatchers alike to twist at the end of his speargun-nooses. She'd heard that regular citizens had intervened to prevent police from arresting the Hangman and the Dogcatcher, which only deepened their public appeal. The Mayor's office had backed off their order to the NYPD to shoot any masked miscreants on sight, instead taking a de facto policy of letting the costume party take care of itself.

Matilda set out on this path three years before, when her father urged her to take an interest in the family business. She felt sick when she reviewed the assembly lines and product catalogs of ingenious killing machines. If they were going to profit from death, she should give something back. Already an absentee member of the Daughters of the American Revolution, the Circle of 400, and sundry other charitable organizations and ladies' auxiliaries, she resolved to do something good with the evil they'd created. The impulse might have found its outlet in more charity work, if not for Aurora Benoit and the anarchists.

A splinter faction of the of the International Workers of the World known as the Levelers proclaimed themselves "radical pacifists" in '27 and so declared war on American businesses that profited from war. When an attempt to coerce factory workers to walk off the job came to nothing, they embarked on a campaign of sabotage and terror. Though most of their threats were idle monomania, they urged anyone who sympathized with their cause to kidnap or simply assassinate the presidents and governing boards of such companies, as well as their families.

After an anarchist's plot turned a monorail car into a deadly mustard gas bomb that took twenty-seven lives at the New Jersey Lynch factory, she began taking boxing lessons and practicing with the full line of Lynch products, from the ladylike needle pistols to the tripod-mounted Magneto-Cannon. She took flying lessons and mastered parachuting. When the training was lagging because of her prostheses, she went to Ms. Benoit, who helped turn her crutches into weapons and wings, and her obsession into a crusade.

Aurora probably thought it was just a crazy white woman's hobby when she was tasked to improve on Matilda's electro-hydraulic limbs. Still, she was more than game and came to serve as Matilda's chief of a small, discreet team of women engineers who'd been denied more respectable work. They made her almost invulnerable, and they kept her secret. Even the amplified voice of her helmet was stripped of its higher registers, so she sounded like a man.

That was, perhaps, the sweetest plum in the pie of Matilda's little pastime. Naturally, when they saw an armored vigilante who could fly and trade machine gun salvos with crooks, they assumed they were looking at a man. It didn't restore the foolish girl's confidence she'd enjoyed before the War, but it gave her something better. Instead of looking at her with pity or contempt, they regarded her with awe, even the ones who tried to arrest her.

She had christened her alter ego the Silver Sentry but didn't actively chase press clippings, and she'd come to regret it. Her chosen sobriquet hadn't caught on, but others had. The *World*, inspired by her erratic early rocket flights, called her the Buzzbomb. One wag at the *Times* called her the Doodlebug. But Hearst's syndicate seemed to have the last word when they picked on an unfortunate incident in which a street thug had tackled her in the air. She shook him off, trying to drop him in a tree but she missed, and he was impaled on a wrought iron gate outside Central Park. Though he survived, the *American* made the gory image her front-page debut and called her the Butcher Bird.

She figured it was only a matter of time before she was caught and unmasked and would have to explain it all to Father. She knew he would rage at her for taking such risks, but she couldn't believe he would be anything but proud of her. Certainly, with the same blood running in their veins, he couldn't be surprised and should be gratified, for it was as close as he'd ever get to having a son.

There was more precedent for eccentricity and instability among the Lynches than most wealthy American families, but only the female cases were marked, for the particular madness that gripped every male Lynch who won through to adulthood made them excellent captains of industry and fiends for firearms. Any deviation from this bellicose mania was seen as a failing of heredity.

Matilda's mother, Mildred, had achieved a sort of fame writing and illustrating very popular children's books under the pseudonym Millie Hilyard. Titles like *Yuk For The Duck*, *The Piano Clam*, and *The Hippocricket* had delighted Matilda's generation in childhood, but how could any mother read lines like, "*You must, oh you must, shake hands with the Man in the boat/Or your trust will be mussed with dusty rust and rusty dust/and you'll wear the horns of a goat,*" and not hear a sexually frustrated wife crying for help? Her fictitious biography omitted that Millie only turned to writing after she was committed to the most luxuriant insane asylum in the nation for attempting to poison herself.

A buzzer sounded in Matilda's ear. She was ten minutes out of New York City and fast approaching the target area. Thick cloud cover swaddled the sparsely lit land below, and it was easy to imagine this was the first night of creation, the land not yet separated from the sea, only the darkness above separated from the lightness below, without form and void. Touching a stud in her helmet with her chin, she activated a map overlay in her goggles, imposing a radium-green grid over the invisible terrain six miles below.

Matilda cut off her thrusters. After a delicious moment of weightlessness, with her arms at her sides and legs bound into a rigid rudder, she plummeted like a diving eagle at 120 miles per hour.

The clouds rushed up to meet her, seeming to spread out and flourish with captivating detail all at once, and then she was among them. Buffeted by updrafts in the primordial sky-soup, the green lines of the superimposed map burned her retinas. She watched her altimeter closely, waiting for the alert, hoping she would be able to see the target before she crashed into it.

She tumbled out of the clouds, and the lights and smokestacks of Bethlehem, Pennsylvania, blazed up beneath her. Fighting the battering wind trying to flip her on her back, Matilda hit the switch on her harness.

Forward-swept batwings burst out from under her arms and caught the wind to inflate to semi-rigidity. They extended only a foot beyond her fingertips and attached to the outside of her calves with a rudder stretched between her legs down to her ankles. Still, the thermoplastic fabric caught the wind and drastically arrested her descent, the glide-ratio converting terminal velocity into forward thrust so quickly that she saw glowing silverfish dot her vision before she leveled off. Extending her right arm, she dipped into a spiraling descent over the target.

Long before the invention of the aeroplane, men had attached wings to their bodies and leapt from great heights, betting their lives on a cautionary myth and a few sketches by DaVinci. At once the most mercilessly exacting and shaggiest of sciences, the pursuit of winged flight had claimed all its failures and wrapped its few fleeting successes in lies. Still, Ms. Benoit's team had extensively tested the wingsuit on a dressmaker's dummy in a wind tunnel at the Lynch factory in New Jersey. It had come through with flying colors once they removed the old reserve chute, which tended to stall in the vacuum backwash just behind the rudder or snarl around the mannequin's head and snap its neck. Even with Aurora's promise, she was more afraid of deploying it than of falling out of the sky.

The wings were uncannily stable as long as she kept her legs extended, but their strain became unbearable. Lucky for her, she was almost over the target.

The Bethlehem Steel mill was no stranger to strikes, but this was something else again. They'd capitulated to a violent strike only a year ago, agreeing to dissolve their sham union and let the Steelworker's Organizing Committee set up a real shop amid a host of other concessions. The price of steel went up fifty percent overnight, but none of the profit found its way to the workers. Last week, the company dropped the other shoe and locked the entire workforce out of the mill.

The 2,000 liquidated workers had been picketing in shifts round the clock, and nearly all of them were camped outside the front gate tonight, bearing signs, sterno torches, bats, crowbars, and other improvised weapons. With near-military discipline, they had ensured that not a lump of coal, not a palette of pig iron, and not a single scab had entered the mill. That no trains or trucks had tried to approach or leave since the lockout began only reassured them that they were winning.

The mill had nearly two hundred armed security guards and an undisclosed number of Pinkertons, alongside a hundred local policemen. The company president, Eugene Brace, had refused the governor's offer to send in the National Guard and promised to resume production at full capacity by the following Monday, despite refusing to meet with the union.

Matilda was surely not the only one who realized what the steel mill was trying to do. But she had also learned through a well-cultivated and expensive grapevine that the Levelers had endorsed the locked-out workers and promised support in their struggle. They were not told in what form such support would come, only to be prepared to storm the factory tonight.

Circling over the mill, a walled city between the Conrail tracks and the Lehigh River, she saw a picket line of torches from the 2nd Street gate to Bessemer Street, clashing against the searchlights of the guard towers at each gate. Blast Furnace Row was in shadow, and she noticed little sign of human activity within the jumble of sheet-metal sheds and mills, no smoke pouring from the towering stacks. Knots of armed men patrolled the twelve-foot fence or gathered around a bivouac in the shipping yard, smoking and waiting for orders.

Matilda circled once more before igniting her pulsejet rocket to arrest her glide. Touching down on the sloping corrugated tin roof of the steel foundry overlooking the picket line, she stepped out of the scorched remnants of her tail assembly and shucked off the wings before she noticed she was not alone.

Startled, she raised her gauntlets and charged the Diplomat's lightning projector. "I didn't see you there," she blurted to the cloaked silhouette crouching on the corner of the roof. Even the flinty basso growl the helmet made of her voice couldn't mask her diffidence.

She could make out no details but somehow knew he was no Pinkerton. She'd just flown eighty miles, landed without a parachute, and lightning came from her fingers. Let *them* explain themselves—

"Well, blow me down," said a sepulchral voice, "if it isn't the Butcher Bird."

She hadn't expected to run into another vigilante so far from the city. One could assume nothing about another mask except that they were more than a little mad. "Perhaps you already know, but something rotten's in the offing tonight…I've come to stop it."

Still turned away from her, the shadow rose to its full height. "Yes, men are being denied the right to work, beaten, killed… Are you here to stop *that*?"

Matilda took a step back, nervous fingers dancing on triggers. A Red, or even an anarchist! For all she knew, she had the drop on the very agent of chaos she had been sent to stop. "These men are flouting the law, impeding vital industry, and conspiring with a cabal of anarchists—"

He cut her short with a theatrical wave of his gloved hand. "These workers were egged on to strike by a twenty percent cut in wages, and when they demanded arbitration, they were locked out. Their own union deserted them, the government they voted for is threatening to mow them down, and they've got scab vigilantes running around spreading conspiracy theories. So, the only question is… Which side are *you* on?"

His cavernous voice seemed to come from just behind her ear, even as she cautiously approached him, still itching to use her lightning projector. "I sympathize with the workers' plight, but I'm on the side of law and order," she said.

"So, you stand with the factory owners, the Pinkerton mercenaries, the hastily sworn-in deputies, and soon, the Army. They don't need you. You'll have to find your fun somewhere else."

"I don't do this for sport…"

"To protect your investments, then?"

"You don't know the first thing about me…"

He threw back his head and laughed. "Oh, I know all about you. I can see right through your mask, but I don't need to. All that shiny gear didn't come on a worker's salary, and it makes one wonder if you'd have taken up this game at all if America had foxhunting. But it's just more fun, isn't it, to hunt men?"

At last, he turned to face her. Matilda bit back a gasp of recognition that sounded utterly fatuous coming out of her helmet.

It was putting it too broadly to say the masked vigilante craze had started a few years back. Some were around long before, whose exploits in dime novels nurtured the dream in those who patrolled the streets tonight. Chief among them was the one standing before her.

"The Golden Ghost," she said, turning the disbelieving remark into an accusation.

"That's not my name," he said, "Butcher Bird." Above the black cowl hovered that ghastly white-gold mask that haunted her early childhood—a hideous skull with curving tusks in a glittering rictus, its leering glee utterly refuted by the cold stare of its spiraling, ruby eyes, which she could feel prying at every seam in her armor. She averted her gaze, remembering the hoary warning: *Beware the Evil*

Eye that masters men's minds! Beware the White Devil! "I couldn't care less what your name is," she said. "If you are who you pretend to be, you're older than Methuselah. And with all due respect to your hoodoo, if it looks like magic, it just means your gear cost more than mine. And I still haven't heard which side *you're* on—"

"You have no idea what it cost me." The White Devil planted gloved hands on his hips, throwing wide the cape to reveal the deathly white tuxedo he wore underneath. A short, curved blade was in its sheath at his hip, and the notorious automatic pistols were in quick-draw shoulder rigs under his arms. "I'm on the side of justice. And thus, I am always alone." The ghastly apparition threw up a gloved hand to cut off her retort and returned to the confrontation below.

The mob gathered around a platform erected just inside the main gate, behind a magnetic deflector screen. A compact man with a vulpine aspect took up a microphone and cleared his throat, which resounded from speakers posted all along the fence. She recognized the company president, Eugene Brace, from his long patrician nose and bulging bald head. Before she could credit him with the guts to show his face, the snowballs, bottles, rocks, and other missiles flung by the strikers bounced off a small rear-projection screen playing a visual recording of the embattled steel tycoon.

"For far too long," the speakers brayed, "the owners of this mill have bowed to the dictates of trade and labor unions regarding every aspect of its management. We have tried to negotiate in good faith to accommodate their ever-increasing demands…but in vain."

The crowd tried to shout him down, but the amplified voice, cold as ice and dry as chalk, only grew louder.

"And so, we have been left with no choice but to take the bold step towards total efficiency you shall witness tonight. I regret to inform you that, as of this moment, Bethlehem Steel Works has no need for your services…"

Brace's speech trailed off under the mob's ferocious response. He had said his piece and pointed to a gilded knife switch on the podium. Beaming in spite of the hailstorm hurled at the platform, he made a show of throwing the switch as if he were actually present and as if it were the most strenuous work he'd been called upon to perform in many moons, as a helpful Pinkerton came over and moved it into the ON position.

All over the mill, warning klaxons sounded. Amber lights flashed on each of the buildings within the walled complex. Dynamos began to hum, blast furnaces to roar, and smoke to belch from chimneys. The catcalls from the mob of steelworkers faltered in a collective gasp as they realized that the steel mill was swinging back to life without anyone running it.

Brace saluted the crowd and then vanished as the film ran out. Strikers tried to climb the fence even as the loudspeakers warned that they would be fired upon if they did not desist. Firehoses sprayed icy water on the already freezing crowd, sweeping them off the company's doorstep like so many dead leaves.

"Looks like the forces of law-and-order triumph again," said the White Devil, "without your help."

Matilda's tongue twitched with a pithy rejoinder, but she followed the caped vigilante as he crossed the rooftop to peer in the windows of the neighboring foundry.

It reminded Matilda of *The Sorcerer's Apprentice*—the endless bucket brigade of animate brooms toiling away at a lazy child's task. A legion of dull gray automatons, like water heaters with segmented hydraulic limbs, shuttled iron ore, fed the furnaces, and ferried the molds once they were filled from the cauldron, which was cradled by a gigantic variation on their utilitarian form. They moved about like bees in a hive, a model of productivity unimaginable with mere flesh and bone.

The Lynch plants had gone big on automation but kept a contingent of skilled machinists and gunsmiths whose trade union secured their generous wages and hours. As long as the government contracts kept coming, they could afford not to chisel their workforce.

But they'd looked into the full automation programs on offer. The new Vulcan industrial automatons were controlled by a central electronic brain that read its orders from hundreds of punchcards as they bumbled through their rote tasks, guided by cameras in their rudimentary heads. A handful of operators watched over every component of the machine on banks of consoles and televisors.

So far, no one had used them in such a large operation and attempts to implement fully automated assembly lines had met with more colorful misfires than the first attempts at winged flight. But she couldn't deny that everything seemed to be in order.

The strikers outside couldn't see into the foundry, but word seemed to spread through the crowd, bringing their rage to a boil. The last hope of going back to work had been brutally snuffed out. They began in deadly earnest to attack the fence. From the far perimeter of the mill came the echoes of gunfire.

If the Levelers were going to make good on their threat, it would come now. Bracing herself for anything, she checked her fuel reserve and kicked off the safety catches on her heavier armaments.

"You should go try to pacify the crowd," said the White Devil. "Maybe your fancy kit will inspire them to reevaluate their wasted lives."

"Do it yourself," she snapped, but she remained torn. If she flew out over the crowd, they'd attack her, and the situation was unlikely to be resolved without escalating violence.

"I'm going to cut the head off this thing before it gets out of control." He stepped off the edge with his arms outstretched, and then he simply wasn't there.

Damn him, she thought. No more useful than any other man with his union suit on outside his pants, but the way he talked tied her brain in knots. He'd made a lot of noise about seeing behind her mask, and he'd never called her a man, had he?

The strikers were boosting each other over the fence while the Pinkertons began firing into the mass of men through their gun-slits. Cursing, Matilda fired up her rocket. Hovering in place over the gate, she boosted her voice to its loudest setting. "Cease and disperse immediately!"

Soaring out over the skirmish line, she dialed her lightning projector to its widest dispersal and blasted the fence. Men on both sides were jolted away and sent scurrying, but the gunfire only intensified. A few wild shots pinged off her armor. The strikers retreated behind barricades and a delivery van they'd outfitted with steel plates and a battering ram. The few who noticed her cursed her as a stooge and threw bricks, which did nothing for her mood.

She blasted the delivery van with the Diplomat, stopping it in its tracks. Tires burst and men collapsed in seizures or were flung head over heels into the crowd, but more rushed to take their places. She dropped a salvo of tear-gas grenades and repeated her plea for them to disperse, but the conflict had spiraled beyond anyone's control.

A wireless alert tone crackled in her ear. "Your assistance is appreciated but unnecessary," Eugene Brace said. "Please vacate the premises immediately…"

Matilda hated talking on the wireless because it relayed her unaltered voice. Clearing her throat and speaking in her deepest baritone, she replied, "You're not in control of anything that I can see… Stop shooting into that crowd, or you'll leave me no choice!"

The infuriatingly unflustered voice cut her off, "The situation is… Christ, what's that music?" The line went dead.

In the nearest foundry, the roar and clang of industry gave way to a resounding crash that froze the sea of combatants. Matilda goosed her attitude jets and swooped to a nearby rooftop for a better look.

A gigantic four-armed automaton staggered out of the mold-pouring station, spinning like a top cradling a cauldron of molten steel with its upper arms and an iron ore cart in each lower claw.

Trampling the smaller robots that blindly stepped in its path, it seemed to have gone haywire, but then they all had, as if they were reeling to some insane, silent music.

This is it, she thought—the invitation to dance.

The whole facade of the foundry smashed wide open, sheet-metal walls shredding like flimsy fabric. The mold-pouring automaton lumbered out into the night, swinging the cauldron so that white-hot molten steel slopped on the pavement like wine from a drunkard's goblet. The Pinkertons and uniformed security deserted the battlements of the main gate. The strikers surged over the fence, oblivious to the catastrophe headed their way.

The giant automaton stomped fleeing Pinkertons and clumsily kicked down the fence, arms pitched to dump the bubbling cauldron on the mill's front office.

Matilda armed her gyro-rockets and fired them all at the robot—two connected with its upper right shoulder, shearing off an arm. The cauldron tipped and dumped its glowing contents onto its legs, fusing it to the pavement, an instant monument. Wreathed in a curtain of steam, the automaton shuddered to a halt, looming over the panicked crowd of strikers pouring through the gap in the fence into the steel mill, but there was nothing they could do to it that the robots were not already doing.

Everywhere she looked, the automatons were smashing the means of production, each other, and themselves. Fires engulfed half the buildings while the power plants gushed arcs of white lightning into the sky. The Pinkertons fell back to the rail yard and attempted to get a locomotive working to beat a retreat while the uniformed security clambered onto barges and set off downriver.

Both sides were shooting at her. There was nothing more she could do here. Kicking off the roof, Matilda climbed to five hundred feet and activated her map, then flew over the company town, homing in on the modest office tower of Bethlehem Steel's headquarters.

Brace's autogyro was parked on the roof and the lights were burning on the top floor, where the board of directors were no doubt choking on their champagne, so she took the liberty of crashing through the window.

"I hope you're proud of yourselves," she said to the half-dozen well-heeled older men sitting at the long chestnut table with their heads bowed as if saying grace. Cigars smoldered in ashtrays and champagne bottles glistened in ice buckets stationed up and down the table, but no one moved as she stepped on crackling glass shards to stand behind the company president.

"Will your balance sheet record this as a greater expense than paying a fair wage? In the end, untold hundreds dead and your mill in flames, and for what?"

No one moved, no one spoke.

She only then noticed the deep crimson cravat each man wore, the bloodstains spilling down their otherwise spotless dickies from cleanly slit throats.

Matilda stepped back from the table, her hand going out to touch Mr. Brace's shoulder. For a moment, it looked as if the company president was about to speak, but then his head tumbled from his shoulders and thudded onto the incomplete speech scribbled in front of him and rolled down the length of the table to rest against a bucket of champagne.

Matilda gasped, and the last words of the White Devil echoed in her brain.

I'm going to cut the head off this thing—

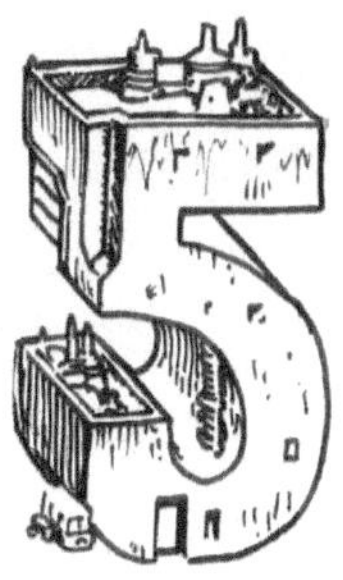

The Russians have shown you the way out. What are you going to do about it? You are doomed to wage slavery until you die unless you wake up and realize that you and the boss have not one thing in common: that the employing class must be overthrown and that you, the workers, must take over the control of your jobs, and through them, the control of your lives, instead of offering yourself as a sacrifice to the masters six days a week, so that they may coin profits out of your sweat and toil.

—Harvey O'Connor, "Russia Did It" pamphlet, 1919

January 17, 1931 | Allentown, Pennsylvania & points north

The Keystone Express out of Allentown highballed for Chicago under an icy hunter's moon. The train was a double-header, with diesel magnetic repulsor locomotives at either end hauling a mix of freight and Pullman sleeper cars. Out of fear that the ongoing steel and coal protests could metastasize into a general strike, the railroads had federal troops onboard. Still, once the train had pulled out of the station and began climbing to its cruising speed of 125 miles per hour, they retired to their barracks cars to play poker and smoke.

Many of the freight cars running lately were barely loaded or even empty, and thus, many ended up more densely packed with humanity than the Pullman cars up front.

But not on Shackleton's train.

The old-time jungle buzzards, scissor bills, gay cats, bindle-stiffs, dingbats, whangs, D.D. mimes, and the veteran Johnsons all knew that if you were caught on Shack's train, you could expect a free flying lesson. Always an irritant, these parasites, but since the market crashed, the bums' numbers were multiplied tenfold by greenhorn kids, ill-prepared for the dangers of riding the rails. But even they knew better than to ride the Keystone.

Cursing the frigid wind ripping at his canvas overcoat and leather mask, Shackleton climbed off the baggage car, decoupling his harness ropes from the safety bars running the length of each car. Spurning the ladder, he leapt from the baggage car to the top of the first boxcar, one hand over his chest to hold the various tools of his trade in his pockets.

They were still in city limits for another seven minutes, but if he didn't shake a leg, he wouldn't make it to the caboose before they spun up to cruising speed. His blood was up, and he could handle it better than the bunch of yeggs he saw jump the train as they pulled out of the Allentown yard. Saw them with his own eyes, but he had to help the damned passengers into the sleeper cars, and the yard-ape baggage handlers couldn't put shit in a toilet without two supervisors.

He was a train man, and this was *his* train.

How he hated them, the ones who hopped it. He'd been a conductor for almost twenty years—worked his way up from porter, and when he rode, he bought a goddamn ticket like everybody else. When he came across a gaggle of them drinking and roasting a plucked chicken on a shaky stewpot stove like lords of the goddamn land, what was he supposed to do with them? Bow and offer to fetch some sparkling champagne and a side of succotash from the dining car? *If you please, your Majesty, don't burn my goddam train down to the wheels.* Tramps met bad ends every day riding the rails, and nobody blinked. Out on the Rio Grande line, they threw so many off, the vultures and coyotes followed the trains and waited on the bluffs outside of Gallup, Phoenix and Ogden, tramp meat being the easiest game in the Southwest.

The boxcar was a bust. He sprawled on the roof and opened the peephole, shining a penlight into every corner of the car, which was less than half-full of lumber. Veteran bos knew such berths were a death-trap, because loose cargo was prone to shift.

Shackleton didn't try to understand the machinations of the higher powers that shipped freight, but it almost felt like there was some other railroad carrying most of the goods lately. He'd heard rumors that the new Big Boy locomotives would be fully automated and flying so fast on magnetic tracks there'd be no need for flesh and blood conductors or railroad dicks at all.

Shutting the peep, Shackleton got up and let the battering wind blow him down to the next car. He didn't miss the cinders and coal smoke too much since they replaced the old locomotive with these new magnet jobs, but the speed made it harder to do his job. Did it have to go so goddamn fast?

Flatbed car next, with a load of Bethlehem steel and pontoons for a bridge or something out west. The landscape beyond was a white blur, with only fleeting glimpses of isolated farmhouses and one-horse towns that didn't rate a stop.

Shack's eyes were blurred with tears from the wind, but through the slits in his mask, he could see a dim glimmer of light shining from the top of one of the pontoons, and his mood brightened. In spite of being upwind on a racing train, his wolverine's nose could already smell charcoal and tobacco, sterno and roasted chicken, coffee, and unwashed bodies.

Limbering up the shock-rod and the lag-chain from his pockets, he clambered across the steel palettes and shinnied up the wall of the pontoon. Sure enough, when he pressed his ear to the plastic he could hear them—the bastards.

"When we struck in Seattle in '19, we didn't dream it'd go so far, but the owners backed off, and we wound up running every-thing—"

Shackleton smiled grimly as the old tramp ran his Red mouth. He was going to learn. Rutherford Herbert Shackleton would teach them all.

A hand fell on his shoulder. Colder than the wind. He turned to face the man who'd dared touch him and stared into Hell. Coldly blazing eyes that spun and flashed hypnotically, drawing him out of his body, leaving him helpless when those iron hands seized him by his lapels and flung him bodily off his own goddamn train.

He soared through the icy emptiness like a scarecrow, turning away from the wind and the oncoming trees. He flew over a frozen stream that the train crossed on a sturdy bridge, unlike the gimcrack pontoon job those yeggs were jugged in.

He hit the ice on his left side hard enough to break every bone in his arm and half his ribs, as well as the ice. As he sank, paralyzed with shock and agony, he had but a moment to reflect.

I did this to I don't know how many yeggs, I don't know how many times. I did it for a company that won't piss in my hand the day I retire.

Was it like this for all the ones he tossed and forgot? How could he hate anyone so much, just strangers trying to get away from their own problems? How could he take pride in killing them, leaving them graveless and nameless on the side of the tracks?

How could he have turned into this?

There were things you never did, the orphanage nuns knew, things that brought bad spirits. You never left an incomplete letter out, or you'd damn the addressee to a horrible fate. If you set a plate out for someone who didn't come to supper, you didn't touch it until they came home, or you might be signing their death warrant.

But nothing was more irresistible to the dark outside than a nameless newborn.

His mother died in the vestibule of the Sisters of Mercy Hospital as a result of injuries incurred in a sweatshop fire. She was a young lady of close counsel and modest virtue with few friends among the other seamstresses, who knew only her given name and that she'd recently come from New Orleans. Nobody knew she was pregnant.

The nurses had already moved on to other patients when the dead girl's water broke. The baby lay wailing between his mother's legs on the cold steel trolley until almost dawn when he was discovered by an orderly. Loud as the debate over what to do with the foundling, between those moved by their Catholic faith and vow of charity and those moved by superstition to give a more permanent form of baptism to the unruly and clearly miscegenated newborn with milk teeth like finishing nails and a full head of black hair who had, the old Irish nuns asserted, already been named in Hell.

They named him after St. Thomas, on whose feast day he was born, but not even the nuns called him that. From the moment he climbed out of his crib to steal bottles of formula, they called him Spider.

As a boy, Spider got all he needed in the way of an official education at one of the more progressive orphanages in Utica. To inculcate in the children "the tonic of responsibility, the pride of ownership," the warden saw fit to grant each child a small plot of land in the shadowy courtyard of the county home to grow vegetables, and they would succeed in yielding edible comestibles, they were told, if they meant to eat.

Right away, Spider had begun to take a different lesson.

The hard gray soil seemed to have no use for the crumbling old seeds they were given, but it seemed to have some almost magical property for nourishing weeds. Every gust of wind heralded a fresh wave of dandelions, ragweed, wild cucumber, or some new mutant weed species that the warders accused them of inventing out of a perverse desire to starve. The stews and steamed puddings concocted by the kitchen out of said weeds made them more desperate, if not more successful, gardeners. Tillers of the soil they would never be, but Spider figured the lesson was that if they owned even a patch of dirt, they would come to hate the weeds, come to crave digging them out of the ground until their fingers bled the soil pink out of pure crazy spite.

And in their infinite, ugly variety, he began to see all sorts of tricks. Weeds blew in and took over, disguised as useful sprouts until they grew stickers and barbs to hitch a ride in pelts or socks; they thrived on neglect and made grazing animals mad with intoxication until they threw up seeds, thus perpetuating the cycle. Far from hating them, Spider not only gave up ripping them out of his patch, he nurtured and studied them and learned much.

Weeds expected nothing from the world. Every trick that a weed could employ, an orphan—a human weed in a cruel garden—could use to invade their own plot of earth and own it. And if one were not to be uprooted and tossed away, one would have to think up more clever tricks than getting oneself eaten to get somewhere in this world.

Armed with such bitter wisdom, Spider ran away to the Big City as soon as he was tall enough to hop a freight train. He was better prepared to don the mask of the White Devil than any of the mercenary playboys or repentant pirates who came before him.

If you shave off a couple hours of sleep each night, you can learn a language or a trade in a year. If you only sleep a few hours every night, you could master the sciences, create art, and dream up inventions. Just think of all you could learn if you never had to sleep again. He didn't see it as a curse but as a gift, for the first year.

He held onto the hard lessons of the orphanage as to a mother's love. He had been given nothing else in this world and feared when even those might fade away. For every time he played at being what the dime novels called the Golden Ghost, used its diabolic powers to fight evil, he forgot a little more of who he used to be.

All told it was a sweet deal. He could do almost anything and never fear death or jail again, so long as he never took off the mask.

The White Devil shrouded his true form in the shape and seeming of a simple knight of the road as he climbed down the rope ladder into the pontoon. Four bums sat around a portable stove that was heating coffee. Three men, two of them at least in their fifties and one eighteen, maybe, and a fourth, as rawboned and cherry-cheeked as the others, but was clearly a woman.

He'd known many women and girls who rode the rails dressed as men because they thought they'd be safer, but for many, it was just what they were. More than a few hit the road because tramps were the only class of people outside of some islands of bohemians on either coast, where they could freely wear drag and live as they were inside. Many green bums had trifled with sisters of the road like Mother Mustache or Fishfinger LaRue to their everlasting regret.

"Can I beg a cup of coffee?" asked Spider.

"Depends on who the hell you are, youngster," said the older and grayer of the old men. He had a cast in one eye and crisscrossing scars over what little of his face wasn't covered in greasy silver whiskers. "These are uncertain times, and a man likes to know—"

"Pipe down, Silky," said the sister in a smoky drawl. Sturdy and plain with a mischievous glint in her eye and taller than all but himself, she might've been twenty- or forty-five. "Montana Black," she introduced herself and waved a hand across the camp stove at the suspicious party. "That ugly yegg there is Silky McFadden, so mind your watch and wallet. This old Wobbly is Joe the Germ, and the Kid…is Jasper. So, like the man said, who the hell are you? Are you a real bum?"

He had to admire how sharply she'd set him a trap. Regular folks with memories of jobs and folding money took the word "bum" hard, but a real knight of the road knew it was a hard-won title to be proud of. Spider kept his eye on the kid. He wore a decent overcoat with the labels still in it, so he wasn't a real bum and hadn't apprenticed under one. "Spider McGowan out of New York and points south… Eighty-three trains."

The Kid whistled. "Ain't never heard of him," said the Germ, waving his arms impatiently like a man with a great notion he was about to forget.

"I have," Silky put in. "He did a stretch in the skookum-house with a tillicum of mine up Minnesota. Said he was a klose yegg for a sitkum-man." The old tramp spiked his speech with Chinook *wawa* jargon, the pidgin Indian cant spread by the Hudson Bay Company in the frontier days to simplify negotiations with various Northwest tribes and adopted by bums and yeggs everywhere. But he also called Spider a "half man," a blunt knock on his mixed heritage.

Spider tensed up, dreading that the old tramp would name Minky and Cockrum. "If you're talking about me," he said, not unkindly, "I'm right here."

"I heard he busted out and went down in the East River, couple years back."

"You heard nothing," Spider replied, "unless you heard it from me."

"I heard of you, too." Montana tipped him a wink and filled a rusty soup can with coffee. "Come sit a spell, Spider. The coffee is bad, and we ain't got anything else, but it'll keep the chuck horrors at bay."

Spider took the can and sipped it, the coarse grounds sticking in his teeth. "I interrupted a conversation. Don't stop jawing on my account…"

"Oh, we was just solving the world situation," Montana said. "Joe thinks the revolution has come at last, and the workers are rising up, but Silk here says it's already past, the machines are taking all the jobs…"

"Sure," Silky put in. "Everybody is obsolete. We were pioneers. Now, we're native guides to the new frontier. Everybody wants to be a bum. So, we should open up a trade college."

"I don't know whether to laugh or cry," Joe the Germ grumbled.

"What do you say, Spider?" Montana asked.

"I think," Spider said, eyes on the kid, "that nobody in this country has the sand for that kind of fight quite yet. The revolution won't come until the machines rise up and walk the picket line."

Jasper blinked nervously at that. Spider discovered a couple clods of Jamaica ginger in a forgotten pocket of his coat and offered it around in a corncob pipe by way of changing the subject.

Joe the Germ became furiously silent after a rip on the crooked pipe. Silky smiled like a Brahmin, finding and forgetting tidbits of cosmic wisdom. Montana Black became affably fuzzy, if still fixated in a more than motherly way on Jasper, who wisely declined.

Spider took it and seemed to suck a big hit but kept it in his mouth and throat. When he expelled it, the cloud enveloped each of the three bums in turn as he stared into their eyes, one by one, until they sat upright, yet fast asleep.

"What'd you do?" Jasper sputtered.

"Hypnosis," Spider said. "Gets the job done better than grass." Banging dottle out of the pipe, he cracked his knuckles and stood up from the circle.

"I ain't a real bum," Jasper said. He looked scared.

"Is that a fact?" Spider fixed the kid in his gaze and tried to pick him like a lock. Since the crash, with schools closing and companies going under, a million kids had taken to riding the rails. Some set out on a lark, while others were ejected from homes that could not afford to feed them. You could tell at a glance how long they'd been on the bum. The giddy flying-carpet glee of adventure lasted until the first bad accident, yard-bull rousting, or spell on a chain gang. After a bad break or just a few months on the circuit chasing seasonal crops and running from the law, they hardened up, doggedly looking for work that was always just beyond the next state line, until they'd give up and go home if they could, or they just rode on in a fatalistic fugue, stealing or worse just to get by. This kid was a puzzler, green as grass but starched with sterner stuff than the typical runaway.

"I could tell you're new to this game. So, what I'm wondering is why a bunch of wise old birds like these are running Shackleton's train. Anyone who's been on the bum more than a day knows it's a ticket to the boneyard."

Jasper looked for help from the glassy-eyed stiffs and saw none forthcoming.

"Relax, kid. I know what you did back at the mill."

Jasper's eyes went wide, his face white. "I didn't do nothing. I was nowhere near Bethlehem—"

Spider smiled wearily. "I didn't say which mill. Who put you up to it? The Wobblies are a ghost these days. Museum exhibits like Joe, here." When Jasper stalled, he leaned across the stove. "Come on, out with it. If they put you on this train, they either don't care enough about you to save your bacon, or they want you dead."

"I…I don't know who they are, honest. They're called the Levelers. We hopped the train shipping the robots to Indiana, and I swapped their cards for the ones they gave us. We still had to go to the mill to manage the strike once they threw off their chains… But I wasn't…I didn't make them do what they did. The other guys, they brought me into it, but Izzy got pinched, and Olaf got shot, so I had to give these bums the last of our folding money to take me along on the first train out…"

"You must feel pretty strongly about the plight of the worker."

Jasper's thin-lipped mouth became a scar. "I ain't got any other family. My pop died in a cannery accident, and my mother…she gave me up so she could go find work…"

"Some of your brother workers got killed back there. A lot of kids will wake up orphans tomorrow because of what you did."

Jasper's face went dead white as he seemed to choke on something. "I didn't mean to! They just wanted 'em to put on a show… Everybody's scared, saying the machines will replace us all and something else's coming that's gonna put a lot more out of work. There's already millions of us in breadlines, making soup out of shoes. Somebody's gotta strike back…"

"Sure, and if a bunch of striking workers get trampled underfoot, it just throws sympathy to the cause, but with your skills, you could join a fancy trade union and bag a plush office job someday."

"I would never turn my back on my brothers."

"How'd you learn to run those punchcards?"

"What do you mean?"

"I mean, that's pretty highbrow stuff, and I don't figure you for a college boy…"

"At the state home… The warden got some company to donate an auto-mower, but the gardener was too thick to script it, and it kept running over the flower beds. I took to it and doped out how to cut a script to make it go where they wanted the grass cut, and from there, I just started lifting machines, taking them apart, and making my programs for them… Electronic brains are the coming thing. Once they get them down to size, they'll run everything, you'll see."

"With a background like yours, you could easily have gone into the service…"

"I won't be a cog in their machine, killing other workers to expand their empire."

"Spoken like a true science-pirate…"

"I just want to earn an honest living," Jasper said, "same as everyone else."

"What's your name, kid?"

"They said I shouldn't—"

"They haven't done you any favors yet, kid."

"Jasper Zwick," Jasper said.

"Really?"

Gritting his teeth, the kid looked ready to knock his teeth down his throat. "You calling me a liar?"

"Kid, the dopes you threw in with tossed you away like a dud card. The system you tried to smash; you didn't even knock its hat off."

"We won't be stopped. Once the working man is unified…"

"You really want to strike a blow? Against the *real* enemy?"

"I do, but what do you know about it?"

Spider turned away and seemed to vanish in his own shadow. When he turned back to Jasper, the terrified kid faced the naked golden mask, flowing black cape, and deathly white tuxedo.

"Holy cats, you're the G-g-g—!" Jasper jumped up from the crate he'd been sitting on and made for the rope ladder. Spider laid a hand on his shoulder, and the kid twisted, against every impulse racing through his nerves, to face his accuser.

"That's not my name. It's the name of a character in the pulps. Say my true name."

"You…" Jasper struggled for the nerve to say it. "You're the White Devil."

"You have the heart and the brain of a player in this war, but you don't know who your friends are, let alone your enemies. If I showed you the truth, what would you do with it?"

"Show me…show me the truth."

The White Devil threw a wing of his cape over the kid's head and brought him close as if in an embrace. The cape fell flat against his chest. Jasper vanished as if through a trapdoor.

And not a moment too soon… The train was braking for its first stop. Spider climbed the rope ladder and pushed the plug out of the manhole. Emerging on top of the bridge pontoon as the ripping wind subsided to a mere bone-chilling gust, he climbed down to stand over the body wedged between the pontoon and the wall of the flatcar.

He laid a kid-skin glove on the conductor's leather mask and pried it off his face. Shack's bloodshot eyes blinked open and stared emptily at the ghastly, glittering visage hovering above him.

"These folks are gonna ride through to Detroit, and you won't put a hand on them. Live and let live... understand?"

Still lost in the fuzzy reverie of one dreaming, the conductor nodded absently, but his mind was elsewhere, perhaps considering what he'd done with his life and what it had cost him. "Sure, it's no skin off my ass if they do…I'm cold…so cold…"

"So are they, Shack. Let 'em alone. They're doing their best, just like you."

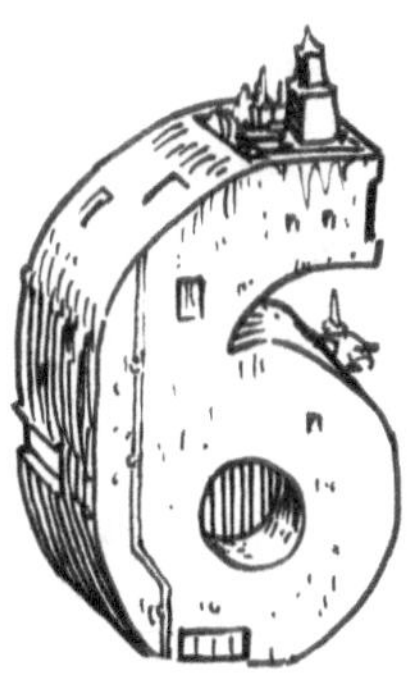

There is something addictive about secrets.

— J. Edgar Hoover

New York City | April 1931

Hoover waited for the elevator on the ninth-floor mezzanine helipad of Chalice Pavilion, cursing volubly under his breath, and grew three inches taller.

He had not always been a vain man, but he was not just a man anymore. The Press, with their infantile penchant for cheap theater and easy symbolism, would conflate the Bureau with the man who ran it, paint whatever faults they found in him on its face. If *he* was small, the Bureau would be small, which would never suffice.

And he could scarcely recall a time when he'd been made to feel so small as he did right now.

Relieved to find no operator at the controls, Hoover jabbed the button for the 113th floor. He'd been in taller buildings but was profoundly unnerved by this one. Perhaps because this skyscraper had been assembled in less than six months, or something about it felt unAmerican, if not unholy.

The cluster of vaguely organic cones was somewhat like a coral reef, a cathedral, a termite mound, and a rocket ship while evoking something else that stirred Hoover's guts with a hot poker. The

Spaniard Antoni Gaudi had taken up the commission to design what would have been the Hotel Attraction back in 1908 before his radical leanings were discovered. Saner heads prevailed, but Chalice had purchased the entire block between West and Greenwich Streets, dusted off the blueprints and erected this obscenity overlooking the Battery as if nothing meant anything, anymore.

The lower floors were sealed, and the adjoining hotels and restaurants were not yet open for business. However, the glass elevator whisked him up through cavernous galleries, theaters, and exhibition halls embellished with frescoes depicting astronomical scenes with a reverence better reserved for religious subjects.

For all its youth and modest size, Hoover took pride in his Bureau's ability to learn anything about anyone upon whom they cast their eye, and yet just one glance at the mysterious Mr. Chalice and Hoover found that what little they did know was probably wrong.

Sylvester NMI Chalice, a.k.a. Sylvester Skolnic; born on 16 May or 17 April 1896 to Juris and Inga Skolnic. United States citizen as of 1911. No criminal record. Education unknown. No known political affiliation. No trade or fraternal association memberships. Contributed to Republican Presidential and Senatorial candidates in the last election.

He had never communicated with Sylvester Chalice, a naturalized immigrant. He would never have deigned to visit Chalice Electrical in person if the upstart had not made himself so instantly inevitable. His company had not existed at all, except as a legal fiction, until about fourteen months ago. Hoover watched closely but had deemed it politic to wait until the company had been served with a notice that several of their employees were known Trotskyites. Still, he'd ruled out sending agents immediately and opted to see for himself whether this Sylvester Chalice was not an elaborate confidence trickster.

He deeply regretted the decision.

If it worked, this pipe-dream Chalice promised would uproot the entire American economic system, and he was not susceptible to the hooks by which such threats to stability were commonly brought to heel, such as withdrawal of capital, immigrant status or ruin of reputation. Hoover thought of that anarchic Balkan monster Tesla and indulged a chuckle. This one would be harder to get a handle on. How he'd gotten this far was anyone's guess, but this morning would see him get no further without judicious neutering, which he had taken pains to keep secret from the very reporters he'd trained to dog his footsteps.

The elevator braked abruptly as it approached the apex of the tower. Hoover stumbled on his extended platform shoes. A confidential product of the Bureau's forensic laboratory, they could subtly but effectively rise as much as much as five inches to give one the psychological edge in public situations where he could not command the high ground from his elevated desk at the capitol. He despised them but appreciated the effect they conveyed upon the unsuspecting.

At last, the doors opened. Hoover's ears popped painfully, and he felt his close-cropped hair squirm on his scalp; the telegraph key in his cuff twitched, and one of his shoes deflated like a failed soufflé.

He lurched lopsidedly out of the elevator car, turning his ankle and nearly falling flat on his ass. Looking down, he nearly wet his pants.

There was no floor. There were no walls. He stood on thin air.

Between his misaligned toes, the view plunged unobstructed to the lobby almost a quarter mile straight down. The laborers scurrying across the marble floor so far below were like aphids on a rose petal.

He realized with a rush of relief and then rage that he stood on a floor of bulletproof glass, the office a spherical bubble perched atop the tower's spire.

It was magnificently effective and made the engineering of his own office look like a petty child's trick. For just a moment, it had utterly unmanned the chief of the nation's police force, leaving him panting, red as a beet, veins throbbing in his temples.

From the wide, low Bauhaus desk across the remarkable room rose a tall, gaunt stork of a man, with stilts for legs and massive snow-shovel hands and a grin that somehow gave Hoover the fleeting instinctive reflex to protect his throat and genitalia.

"Mr. Hoover! So delighted you could make the journey in the flesh! I've been of a mind to come see you myself, but I felt it would be too presumptuous. I'm an ardent admirer of your work, sir. Please, make yourself comfortable."

Hoover had to bite his lip and recite the alphabet backward in his head before he spoke. This infuriating man gave him no room to pin the last few minutes of psychological warfare on a sense of malice. Still, his appearance and mellifluous, fruity radio announcer's voice dared the Director to stamp his absurdly shod foot and demand an end to this charade.

"Mr. Chalice, I hope you recognize that this is not a social call. The United States Department of Justice is not in the habit of taking tea with potential suspects of investigation."

According to his records, Chalice was five foot seven, but the man pumping Hoover's hand like priming a well stood nearly a foot taller than him. He found himself looking from the man's maddeningly cleft chin to his…slippers?

Chalice's hand still hung between them, his smile only half an apology. "Nonetheless, I deeply appreciate your taking the time."

Hoover hesitated and stomped his foot in a vain attempt to reactivate the failed left shoe; then he stumbled into Chalice's steadying hand, his mortification complete.

The pile of heads that would roll for this humiliation would stack nearly high enough for him to stand upon it and see over an undoctored podium… Good Lord, now he was doing it to himself.

"Allow me, sir," Chalice knelt before him and took hold of the malfunctioning shoe. Just as Hoover stepped back to kick the interloper's hands away from his person, the right shoe deflated a reasonable two inches while its mate rose an inch to give him a modicum of height without sacrificing his dignity.

Hoover barely managed a strangled "Thank you," already plotting swift revenge for this maddening treatment.

"Think nothing of it, sir," Chalice said, slick as greased mink. "I fully recognize, as I know you do, the importance of maintaining a proper public image in these superficial times. I've only just come into the public eye and have already suffered much injury from the fickle whims of the press. I know well, too, the paradox that such intelligent creatures as humans must continually be manipulated and sometimes misled to persuade them to choose that which obviously serves the greatest good."

Hoover merely nodded, following Chalice warily across the harrowing glass floor to where a pair of brutalist chrome and leather chairs seemed to bow in supplication to Chalice's ziggurat-shaped desk. Hoover gratefully took one and focused his stare on Chalice as he circled to his own chair and offered the Director a drink.

"I have no fondness for alcohol, particularly at this hour," he began, but Chalice assured him he had no such spirits on the premises. "I prefer a rejuvenating tonic of pineapple and other tropical juices combined with vitamins and additives that sharpen the mind and bolster the constitution. Sure I can't persuade you to try one, sir?"

The tonic sounded marvelous and almost tailored to his innermost desires in a beverage, so he acquiesced as he tried to recollect the notes he'd mentally prepared for this interview. "Now see here, Chalice—"

Chalice ambled over and set a tall, frosty glass before Hoover. "You're still sore about the shoes."

Hoover's ears reddened. He broiled in sheer disbelief that this nobody, this *citizen*, would bring up such a narrowly averted personal disaster so soon. "Just before the doors opened, there was a…static charge…"

"Sir, I do apologize if that went off…I tell them to turn it off for special appointments, but this one was a secret, I wasn't to tell anyone, and in any case, it's only a security measure. It disables or disrupts any troublesome personal transmitters or recording devices. I've actually had people—some employees, some claiming to represent local, state, and even federal government—attempting to learn more than we're prepared to tell at present. Trade secrets. Not that I'd ever accuse you of such perfidy, but… Anyway, I was assured you don't wear a pacemaker, so no harm done, hopefully…?"

Hoover kicked his platform shoe against the clear glass floor. Spitefully, the damned things grew another inch taller again. "I am disinclined to explore the topic…but to the point…"

"Try the tonic, Mr. Hoover. Its properties are best absorbed while cold." Hoover obliged, more to busy his nervous hands than to please this oily cipher. The flavor was bland, with coconut and pineapple extract masking a slight alkaloid taint. Still, after the unpleasant cranial ache of cold, it settled his stomach and instilled a wash of warmth and…clarity. There was no other word for it.

"Better?" Chalice rubbed his hands together like a sharp shuffling cards. Hoover recognized it as a smoker's tic, but mercifully, he did not indulge it. "Now… Naturally, you're upset about the press junket downstairs. I apologize for that, as well, sir. Every attempt was made to keep your visit private, but the papers and radio networks keep stringers posted at our door in the event we decide to tell them what we're going to do next…"

"And this is exactly why I'm here, Mr. Chalice," Hoover finally managed. "Your company has filed 217 patent applications in the last thirteen months. All sealed and confidential, pending public announcements. Yet all we've seen so far is…"

"Magic tricks, yes. Conjurer's illusions. Ballyhoo headlines. You might well believe what Wall Street is saying about us…many still weighed down with railroad and oil stocks that will, I assure you, be tomorrow's toilet paper. Well might they worry, yes? That we're a flim-flam racket, or worse, the kind of reckless science-pirates who ruined Europe. Who wouldn't be concerned after seeing what unchecked hubris wrought upon that sad continent? Who wouldn't take a strong hand in regulating progress to insure it doesn't happen here? But American know-how is restless, sir. It won't be constrained from remaking the world.

"You have every right to be concerned, and as the head of the nation's police force, you are entitled to answers. If you will follow me, I relish the opportunity to demonstrate what we're about…"

Chalice launched from his chair and came around the desk, vibrating with a sunny energy Hoover could not help but reciprocate. He beckoned the Director to an ostentatious door in an alcove behind his desk. The control panel set into the wall had seven numbered mother-of-pearl buttons. Beside it, on a long row of coatracks was draped an assortment of coats, overcoats, anoraks, slickers, hats of all descriptions and even a gas mask and air recycler oversuit.

Jabbing a button, he continued talking as Hoover observed a humming of machinery in the wall and (still deeply disturbing) floor.

"Now, our name is a bit of a red herring, I'm afraid, dating back to my college days…"

"Where *did* you attend college, Mr. Chalice? Your records are frustratingly incomplete." Hoover's neck prickled. In his gawky body, lantern-jawed features, and unstoppable clipped Yankee accent, Chalice reminded the Director of the blue-nosed Boston aristocrats who never missed a chance to rub his nose in his own humble alma mater, George Washington University.

"I must confess," Chalice blushed, "I had neither the means nor the temperament to attend a big school… My poor widowed mother could only afford correspondence courses, for I couldn't be spared from the family business… Father died in the Great War, you see…"

The doors emitted with a crisp, bell-like tone. "But enough about me! This is my private vestibule…"

Chalice opened the door and held it wide for the Director, who somehow felt foolish and hastened through it.

He found himself in a dimly lit salon with low, overstuffed couches arranged in a circle around a grand piano. "I like to come here to think when it all gets too much." Chalice ambled over to the piano and tickled out a few bars of "Beautiful Dreamer," but Hoover barely noticed for looking out the windows.

From floor to ceiling on every side of the octagonal salon, they provided the only light. There were no doors aside from the one by which they'd entered. Outside, a desert panorama of pitted silvery-white rock was painted in stark naked sunlight under a sackcloth sky with one visible feature: a blue globe whorled with white clouds and specks of brown earth.

Earth—

Hoover stood at the window, one palm on the double-paned crystal window, absorbing its uncanny chill. "It isn't possible," he muttered. "We've just… You… *teleported* us?"

"Ah, I understand your concern. Let me alleviate them, sir. My teleportals are nothing like Dr. Roi's Electric Guillotine. There is none of that disintegration and reassembly…and there will be no Greta's, I assure you."

Still, Hoover wiped his sweaty palms on his trousers, shuffling from the windows mistrustfully back to the door. The teleportal stood half-open, the dishwater light of a New York spring still warm on his face.

But then he remembered the kinetoscope newsreels.

Six years ago, Dr. Roi claimed that his teleportation projector would send men and materiel through the wires like telegraph messages. Due to an adding-machine breakdown, the projector became misaligned during a demonstration with a French bulldog.

Greta was disintegrated at a laboratory in Caen but never emerged from the crystal dome in Paris. The French had since converted the projector into an arguably more humane means of execution than the old mechanical guillotine, sending the worst criminals into nothingness…though some amateur radio operators claimed that an eerie phantom, whining like a lost dog, haunts the shortwave frequencies to this day.

"The simplest explanation I can give is that when one steps through a teleportal, he emerges out the other side, wherever it may be, instantaneously, because it is not two identical doors, but the same door, occupying two different spaces. The office we just left is both ten feet and 243,000 miles away… And I must warn you to make no abrupt movements, for we weigh only one-sixth of our mass on Earth."

Hoover stared out at the lunar landscape as Chalice prattled on, but the moment his back was turned, the Director bent his knees and jumped just a little. To his delight, he floated up towards the ceiling and was still gently descending to the floor when Chalice caught him.

"Watch your step, Director. You see? Irresistible, isn't it? Now, our first order of business has been cargo, working with a handful of trustworthy industry partners, and we're already making great strides in changing the nature of the freight game. No fuel costs, no ships, no Panama Canal, no railroad strikes… Of course, the flow of goods will be stiffly regulated, and tariffs leveraged to bring costs closer to current prices, and diligent customs and immigration officers would ensure that contraband and undesirable foreigners stay out."

"This will wreak untold havoc upon every facet of the shipping and transportation industries," Hoover mused, "particularly labor."

"Very true," Chalice crowed, striding over to stand beside Hoover, "and long overdue, says I. The brigands will no longer be able to hold the nation's business hostage for their own fell ends."

Hoover allowed himself a sour smile. The anarchists and Bolsheviks he'd made his bones deporting had burrowed into the fatty heart of the "labor movement," those parasitic ticks on the blood of industry. He would gleefully see them perish.

Chalice strolled along the windows with his hands clasped behind his back. "Obviously, the big noise would be travel…we're not rushing into that phase, and I have anticipated your concerns unto the most minute detail. But for now, suffice to say that the price would initially be double that of air travel, to limit access to those who present relatively little risk, and build a cachet about the process. And, of course, we would initially limit travelers to domestic destinations until such time as treaties with friendly nations could be amended to insure that the benefits of this miraculous boon flow to the right people of our great nation."

Hoover struggled with his warring emotions. The moon! A child's fantasy come true. Nothing was outside their reach. But who was this glib cipher who controlled it? Could he be trusted? Of course not. No man could be trusted with even a fraction of the power these miraculous doors presented. "I have…quantifiable reservations."

"No doubt," Chalice admitted, laying a careless hand on the Director's shoulder. "And that is why I open my books to you. I did not summon you here to ask permission but to offer you the opportunity to put my discovery to the service of the nation."

Hoover turned away from the hand, feeling stirred by sensations better left unexamined. "You've already taken too many liberties, Mr. Chalice. Don't presume to dictate government policy, too."

Throwing his hands up, Chalice cried, "I wouldn't dream of it, sir! But suppose I could endow the Bureau of Investigation with the ability to travel instantly across this vast nation to combat lawlessness and to observe potential criminal and seditious activities, and did not do so. What kind of patriot…nay, what kind of citizen would I be?"

Hoover felt his skin tighten and his bowels clench with excitement and apprehension. He moved across the salon, averting his face from Chalice, to sink into the nearest couch, feeling considerably more than a sixth of his terrestrial weight bearing down upon him.

Chalice kept coming at him. "Sir, I know you'll recognize that this country has been mired in systemic stagnation since long before the market crashed. Government has kept a heavy hand on the brakes of progress, and with good reason. Nobody recognizes that more keenly than I.

"That's why I reach out to you now. Imagine what America could become in ten years, or even two, with the right hands at the wheel and a weather eye on the horizon if she seized her destiny at the forefront of the new age. Europe is all but dead, but it wasn't scientific innovation that destroyed them. It was the retention of old thinking about new ideas."

This last remark raised a tiny alarm in Hoover's brain, but there was no time to do more than flag it for later reflection.

"Imagine what *you* could do if you could go from Washington, D.C. to New York to San Francisco as easily as moving from one room to the next. Imagine what injustices you could stop if your agents could instantly step onto the scene of any crime anywhere in the land. Think of what you could learn if they could look or listen to anyone, anywhere… One could acquire the secrets of every public life that could make them levers, reliable cutout spies for criminal enterprises, foreign agents, or the Bureau. Why, anyone's hidden or repressed sexual peccadilloes could become fodder for exploitation by the right kind of agent if one were weak enough to succumb to his innermost… deviant leanings."

Bullets of sweat popped out of his brow. Chalice was looking at him like the sun looks at an iceberg, letting the promises fester in his ear.

Too far.

"All of this sounds…far too dangerous to rest in the hands of any one man. Your company isn't even publicly held, Mr. Chalice. My recommendation—"

Chalice shook his head and mopped sweat off his brow. "Let me be clear, Mr. Hoover. The access, the authority, the power I am offering is not and will never be yours to take. This is not just another invention the government can commandeer and give to a reliable corporate partner to reverse-engineer and reintroduce from their own labs on some bureaucrat's timetable. This is not something I invented or even discovered. It was *revealed* to me. Do you understand the difference? Do you have enough of a religious education to understand the difference between an earthly work and a Revealed Truth?

"I do not claim to understand it, Mr. Hoover, but I know that it works, for I have used it literally hundreds of times myself. And it will make America not only the heart and mind of all humankind, but it will also extend our hegemony to the planets in the night sky… and beyond them. And yet I assure you, if you were to take possession of my humble company's assets, you would doom yourself and perhaps all life on this earth within the hour."

Hoover looked searchingly at Chalice, then out the windows. Could he trust the man? Of course not. But he could trust him to be what he was. Standing up to his full height, Hoover adjusted his suit and felt his silver-plated automatic in its custom-fitted shoulder holster. "I appreciate your candor, Mr. Chalice. If your commitment to supporting the Bureau's fight against crime is sincere…I believe we may be able to assist each other in achieving our respective goals."

Chalice's hand hovered over a control panel for a moment, but now he wiped sweat off his palm and rose to offer it for the Director to shake. "I wish everyone in government were so shrewd in seeing and seizing the future."

Hoover declined the handshake, instead covering his mouth to stifle a wet, weighty cough. "Begging your pardon, I seem to be coming down with something. You will hear from us presently."

Pushing through the revolving door, Hoover braced himself for the ordeal of escaping Chalice's bizarre tower and New York City, but he emerged from the door to find himself outside, in an alley off K Street, directly across from the Denrike Building, current headquarters of the Department of Justice, in Washington, DC, in the pouring rain.

Both his shoes went flat.

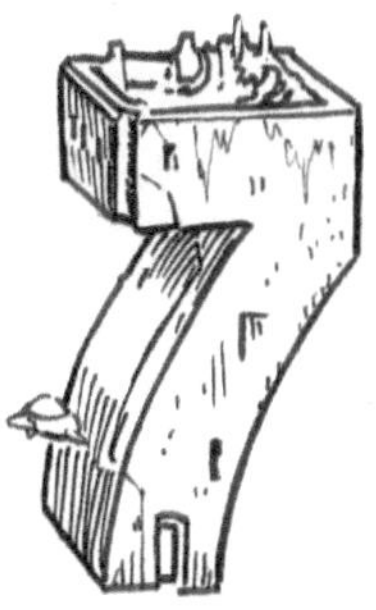

Seventy-five percent of all crimes now are perpetrated with the automobile. Automobiles and good roads have done much to increase certain kinds of banditry. We now have a definitely established type called an automobile bandit who operates exclusively in motor vehicles, whether it is to perpetrate a holdup on a bank or merely to stick up pedestrians or rob homes.

—unknown crime writer, 1924.

May 12, 1931 | Delos, Indiana

The town was not unlike any of the other suburban islands that had sprung up downwind of Chicago with the new craze in commuter airplanes, but for a few critical details one might easily miss, if just passing through. Delos had its own handsomely appointed private aerodrome so residents could easily pilot their private airborne conveyances to and from Chicago or Fort Wayne, though the majority of residents worked the Vulcan factory at the end of Main Street. The upstart robotics company had built the company town from scratch, only two years before.

The town itself was exceptionally clean and fresh, having been designed from a central plan that won a nationwide competition. It had a cinema, a verdant park with a bandstand, and a comprehensive shopper's arcade off its wide Main Street, which was of a green-gray iridescent rubber rather than asphalt or tar. Cars approved for use in Delos did not require gas or carbide batteries but drew their power from the road itself. Soon, the colorful brochures promised that the road would be able to steer and pilot your car as well, so you could finish shaving or watch the ballgame while cruising safely to your programmed destination.

Life recently featured Delos as the *City of Tomorrow—Today,* stressing the town's cleanliness, safety, and security from the epidemic of crime raging in the big cities.

Most importantly, at a time when hundreds of banks across the nation had folded and taken customers' life savings into the abyss, the First Engineers' Bank of Delos was flush and doing brisk business on Friday morning. Payroll for the robot factory had been delivered at dawn, but with news of Vulcan's sabotaged robots causing the Bethlehem riot, a small panic had set in. The line to cash payroll checks spilled out onto the sidewalk when the big green Pontiac roadster screeched to a halt out front, boxing in several electric flivvers and winged sedans slant-parked along Main Street.

By 8 a.m., the morning was already gravid with moist, stifling heat. To one side of the bank, there was a post office and a dry cleaner; on the other, a barber shop, and directly across from it, a Wright Bros. airplane dealership with a service department.

Three men got out of the Pontiac and moved towards the line, while a fourth remained behind the wheel. Their faces were hidden behind handkerchiefs and sweat-stained hats, but the guns in their hands and the dynamite sticks strapped to their chests eloquently proclaimed their resolve.

"Everybody in," barked the leader, a short, acne-scarred party in a snappy sharkskin suit, while two barrel-chested, younger men in shirtsleeves herded them into the bank.

They pulled the door shut behind the last customer, a bespectacled engineer who puffed up with a clueless, "What's all this?"

"I guess you all know what this is," said the leader. "We don't want your money, just the bank's."

The two gunsels in shirtsleeves bumped shoulders as they crossed the room to the counter. The frosted light globes surged with brightness, then burned out. Two bulbs burst, showering the crowd with sparks.

The leader fired his automatic into the ceiling. "Down on the floor! Nobody move, or you'll wish you never heard of the Haywire Gang!"

The crowd rushed to obey, and the cashiers behind the bars and bulletproof glass stood with their hands up. At his desk in a corner office, the bank manager pushed a recessed button and immediately jolted upright in his chair as all the voltage powering the bank's various fixtures and modern security measures ramrodded through his uninsulated body. Finger frozen to the button, the bank manager died in his chair.

"What'd I tell you hayseeds?" The leader stalked the room, closing the blinds on the windows. "These guns are to make a point, but we don't need 'em, see?" Pulling back his lapel to emphasize the sticks of TNT strapped across his chest, he added, "This here dynamite is on a dead man's switch. If any of us goes cold, we all get hot, get me?"

The leader, Otto-Matic Osborne, had only linked up with the other three last month at the notorious Green Lantern Tavern in St. Paul, but they'd already staked out a niche in regional infamy with a tri-state rampage, knocking over four grocers and eight banks and kidnapping an Indianapolis millionaire, even if the ransom ended up burned to ash.

To hear him tell it, Otto was a triggerman for the Capone mob and one of the perpetrators of the St. Valentine's Day Massacre, but none of the other yeggs who haunted the Green Lantern trusted him. When he came across the identical Haywire triplets, they'd already robbed their way across the Midwest, taking down filling stations for folding money, cigarettes, and Moon Pies. Green as they came, they'd somehow escaped capture by a chain of incredibly unlikely breaks, but anyone with sense wrote Tom, Dick, and Harry Haywire off as a spooky catastrophe in the making.

Banks like the First Engineers were a fool's errand for robbers, with their electric security measures that locked down the bank until the well-armed constabulary opened it up. Still, Otto saw something more than a quirk in their wild luck, maybe a weapon more effective than their silent gyro rifles.

While Otto covered the customers, Tom and Dick prowled the cashiers, emptying the drawers into canvas laundry sacks. Tom called out, "Something's wrong with this money."

Dick shot back, "Aw, what do you know?"

"I know what money looks like—"

"Shut up, both of you!" Otto snapped.

Tom held up a wrapped, neat stack of freshly minted blue bills. "It's the wrong color."

"God damn it, what's wrong with you people? What damn country is this?"

"It's Technocracy scrip, Mister," said a housepainter in white denim overalls, hunkered at Otto's feet. "Spends a lot longer than greenbacks around here. Take all you want, but you won't get a plug of tobacco with a wheelbarrow of it outside of Delos."

"Ain't there any real money back there?"

Tom opened the last drawers and threw fistfuls of blue bills up in disgust.

"Where's the green stuff?" Dick prodded a terrified teller.

"Folks've been cashing out all day. They think the company's gonna go bust because of what happened in Bethlehem."

"The company's not going anywhere!" the housepainter cried. "It was Bolshevik saboteurs, but the G-Men will find them, you'll see—"

Otto kicked the bigmouth in the gut. "Take it all," he barked. "Of all the dumb, dirty double-crosses… One of you birds better open up that vault."

"Only Mr. Horbiger knows the combination," the teller said. She pointed to the manager, slumped across his desk, his thinning silver hair mellowly burning on his Moroccan leather blotter.

Outside, Harry honked the Pontiac's horn twice, the signal that trouble was coming. Otto went to a window and peeked through the blinds. "What the hell…"

A Brinks armored car was parked outside, nose to nose with the Pontiac. A uniformed driver kicked the bank's front door open and blasted the ceiling with a shotgun. "Everybody on the floor, this is a goddamn holdup! Play nice, and you can tell your grandkids you got robbed by the Ramrods—"

"Harley, you blamed fool, this is our score," Otto shouted, "but you're welcome to it…"

"Otto Osborne? You gotta be the unluckiest sonsofbitches I ever—"

Harlan Rodman's next words were cut off when he tripped on the outstretched leg of a bank customer. He fell on his own cut-down shotgun and blew off the upper half of his skull.

The other Ramrod said, "Nuts to this," and turned to retreat. Otto shot him in the back. He fell across the threshold, propping the door open.

The crowd panicked and went for the exit. The phony Brinks driver opened fire on the front of the bank with a Browning automatic rifle, sending them stampeding back into the bank.

Tom and Dick came out of the cash pit with sacks of worthless cash clutched to their barrel-chests. Otto cracked an ampule of Grit under his nose and inhaled deeply, and with a shrill war-whoop, charged out onto the sidewalk with his gun blazing.

The Ramrods' driver was hunched down behind the armored car's engine block. He clipped Otto as soon as he came into view, the .50-caliber bullets tearing his left arm off at the shoulder. Otto stumbled backwards into the open mouth of a tele-visor booth, eyes glazing over, but raised his .45 and returned fire.

The Pontiac reversed and smashed the Ramrods' driver into the armored car. Otto staggered into the street, blood sloshing out of him like a lawn sprinkler. The police had blocked off Main Street at either end of the block and cleared it of pedestrians and traffic.

Tom and Dick lugged the sacks toward the Pontiac. Otto crawled in the open rear door of the armored car. He rolled in sacks overflowing with good old-fashioned greenbacks. "Let's take this one, boys!" he cried, voice thready from blood loss but giddy with the bathtub speed coursing through his veins. Tucking his gun in his shoulder holster, he picked up a ream of 100-dollar bills and kissed it. "I think our luck is finally fixin' to change—"

Shooting over their shoulders at the cops, the rest of the Haywire Gang converged on the armored car just as Otto exploded. The dynamite had ignited from contact with the hot barrel of his automatic. A blizzard of bloody green confetti blasted across Main Street as if shot from a cannon.

From behind the line of squad cars, the entire Delos Police force opened fire. The Pontiac was riddled. Tom shoved Harry towards it. Harry swung his laundry sack and hit Tom over the head. An arc of feral electricity swam up the space between them at the moment of contact and poured into the street.

The distributed electrical system of Delos shorted out. Batteries in every car on the street exploded. The jack-booted policemen were sent leaping into the air like fleas. Grounded in rubber-soled sneakers, the three surviving members of the Haywire Gang somehow found themselves the only ones standing.

A handful of cops climbed out of their smoking squad cars and opened fire on the Haywire gang, but they were shell-shocked and demoralized and ducked under the withering barrage of silent projectiles punching holes in their cars like so much wet tissue.

The Haywire triplets crossed the street, firing in both directions, to the open doors of the Wright dealership's service department.

They rousted a grease monkey who lay prone beneath a yellow Kitty Hawk aerocoupe. Climbing in with two sacks of money, the brothers kept a gun trained on the mechanic until he unfolded their wings and spun up their propellers.

Dick sat behind the wheel. Tom boxed his ear. "You don't know how to fly."

"Neither do you," Harry said from the back seat. Pulling down his handkerchief, he vomited on the floor of the plane.

Dick taxied out into the street. The controls mimicked a car well enough, except the steering column swiveled. Dick floored the gas and charged the line of cop cars. Buckshot skated off their windshield as they approached.

"You're gonna crash us!" Tom shouted, cocking his arm to hit his brother.

"Don't touch him, moron!" Harry roared.

Dick pulled back on the steering wheel, and they hopped over the roadblock before dropping back to earth, bouncing hard on their front wheels.

Dick downshifted and accelerated again. Tom hung out the window, hosing down the police cars, the storefront windows, and the sky with his gyro rifle. The plane bobbed and jerked at the end of Main Street but took to the air, just grazing the roof of the first of an armada of state police just arriving on the scene.

Banking and catching the jet stream headed west, the flying car began to buzz with alerts from the local aerodrome. Dick cut them off and turned on the radio. Radar Royce & His Theremin Rangers played "It's My Night To Howl" from the Maenad Ballroom in Fort Wayne's Concordia Hotel. A moment later, the music was interrupted by a special bulletin.

"Delos, Indiana: The First Engineers' Bank was held up at gunpoint by the Haywire and Ramrod Gangs at 8:00 a.m. this morning. Eleven peace officers and two civilians were shot or electrocuted to death, as well as all three members of the Ramrod gang, which had embarked on a statewide crime spree after hijacking an armored car early yesterday. One unidentified member of the Haywire gang was killed at the scene, but the other three are at large in a late-model canary yellow Kitty Hawk flying coupe and are to be considered armed and extremely dangerous. Bank officials estimate that the thieves took more than $200,000…"

"That's a nice pack of lies," Tom said. "We didn't kill nobody on purpose…"

Dick switched off the radio. "Ain't more than fifty thousand in company scrip… those chiseling bastards…"

Harry emptied both bags out the window. The cloud of bluebacks rained out of the clear blue sky on a county fair, inciting a stampede.

Dick nodded off at the wheel with his face against the windscreen. It never failed. After every robbery, the adrenaline receded, and he slipped into an infantile slumber. Harry, in the back, seemed to be asleep too, but he was probably faking, waiting to catch Tom out.

Tom kept the plane about a hundred feet off the ground, skimming treetops and watching out for patrol planes and observation balloons. He wore his fedora pulled down to his eyebrows and chain-smoked cigarettes like a man sucking venom out of a snakebite.

"Tom," "Dick," and "Harry" were just a convenience Otto thought up to tell his partners apart. In truth, they all shared a single given name, though none spoke it because it started them fighting, and things went wrong when they fought.

If you got them alone, each of them would tell you that his name was not Haywire at all, but one got confused, one got angry, and one just laughed when you asked what their real name was. Even if he couldn't remember his last name, where he came from, or anything else of his life before the accident, he'd insist that the other two were doppelgangers from some other Earth.

They had reasons for this that were their own secret, like the re-curring dream where they saw a magician perform, and there was a blob of jelly that shadow-boxed and a magic door, and the magician picked him as a volunteer to go through it, and everything went away. There was also the way things broke or shorted out or otherwise went wrong when they were together, and the closer they got, the wronger things went—

It wasn't so bad when they were asleep, so he didn't mind driving.

They'd land at a rooftop airstrip run by the Syndicate in Cicero, and they'd go out and tie one on with a vengeance while Tom hid in a dingy hotel room. Those little differences became more exaggerated every day. Harry wore his hair long, with a spit curl corkscrewing down to the tip of his nose and a straw-boater jauntily tipped back on his head. Dick obsessively trimmed his with a pocket clipper, so he looked like he just got drummed out of Parris Island. Tom never took off his fedora and tried to grow a mustache.

When they got tight and argued, each of them had a theory. Harry thought they must've been condemned men who got such a jolt from Old Sparky that their memories were wiped away. Dick was sure he got struck by lightning, and the other two were copies made by the mysteries of electricity. Tom didn't have to have an answer so long as they kept moving.

But then he learned about the door to nowhere.

It made no sense since they weren't French, but he read about how they executed folks in France in *Popular Mechanics* when they were laying low in a cabin outside St. Paul. The magazine talked about how soon they could zap you from one place to another in no time flat. All your atoms shoot down a wire and come together on the other side, just like a voice on the telephone. But it didn't work, and folks who went in went nowhere. Maybe something like that happened to them. It made as much sense as anything else.

It fascinated Tom and then began to eat at him when he watched his brothers sleep: the idea of being turned into electricity and put back together. If they could send you anywhere or nowhere, maybe they could foul up and send you to three places at once. But which one was the original?

Tom's earliest memory was laying in long grass on a hill in a circle of stones or petrified trees like broken teeth sticking out of the ground, shivering in a cloud of fog. Some Indians found him and brought him to the reservation police, who locked him up for vagrancy in what turned out to be the Black Hills of South Dakota.

He was sentenced to a month's hard labor, but it wasn't so bad. They told him what to do and he did it, until he got the call.

He was breaking rocks on a chain-gang when it came like lightning out of a clear blue sky. To ignore it was to stop breathing. In a frenzy, he used his shovel to chop through the chain and ran away. He stopped the first truck he came across and stole it. The call pulled him across eight states to a snake-pit asylum in Rhode Island, where he beat up an orderly and took his uniform to enter the isolation ward without any idea what he was doing there.

It was a shock to find his identical twin strapped to a table with 10,000 volts of electricity shooting through him, and another when he clubbed the doctor overseeing the shock treatment, and the lights went out. Fumbling in the dark, he got his twin off the table and helped him out of the asylum.

A freezing rain fell on them as they stumbled across fallow cornfields towards a glowing beacon brighter than the sun at noon, a light only they could see. Snowblind and drunk on the warmth of imminent death by exposure, they found themselves kneeling in the headlights of a stolen Cadillac. A man in a raccoon coat who looked exactly like them offered them half a wheel of cheese and his last cigarette. He was a bouncer at a speakeasy in California when he got the brainwave. When Tom and Dick got in the car, the engine seized up and wouldn't start, so they huddled in the back while the third one told them his plans.

While Tom was in jail, he'd met a bird who told him how to rob a bank. With a good car, a couple of guns, and a solid getaway map, the world was yours.

When the ice storm let up, they hobbled across the field to the nearest farm, stole a truck, and drove to St. Paul, where all the torpedoes and wheelmen operated. Nothing worked out as they had planned, but any plan was as good as another for the other two.

The dance music on the radio turned into a legless dog's howl, then a sizzling roar like it was raining bacon grease, out of which came a buzzing, seductive voice that felt like bumblebees crawling into his ears. "Hello, you people…Daddy Long-Legs has been trying to reach you, but they chase me up and down the dial. New frequency every day, but you'll find me if you search for the truth…and what *is* the truth?"

Tom snapped the radio off, wiping sweat from his brow, knocking his hat back.

What is the truth?

The voice on the radio didn't know the truth. Who did? *Don't trust nobody, and nothing but your nose…*

Dick abruptly sat up, rubbed his eyes, turned the radio back on, and twiddled the dial until he found music. He turned it all the way up, laughing deeply from his belly.

"What are you laughing at?" Tom snarled. He pointed a snubnose .38 revolver at Dick's head. The flying car nosed towards the ground, the collision klaxon chirping on the dashboard.

"Idiot, you'll kill us all!" Dick shouted, grappling with Tom for the gun.

Harry lunged over the seats and grabbed for the gun, too.

Tom pulled the trigger.

The hammer clicked impotently on a dud cartridge. Harry fell back, cursing his brothers. Laughing now, too, Tom turned the gun to point it at his own head and pulled the trigger again.

The drum fell out of the gun, which spontaneously disassembled itself in his big, stubby-fingered hand.

Tom took the wheel and pulled back. They skimmed the flossy tassels of a cornfield, sending a terrorized farmer leaping from the seat of his tractor.

All three of them were laughing as they flew over the Illinois state line, heading for Chicago.

October 13th, 1931 | New York City

It was, all of it, the reporters' fault.

She never as a rule stopped to talk to them, for she was irked at every newspaper calling her by a different moniker and dismissing her as a lightweight. She had grown more confident in her second skin and wanted to try out the new pitch-shifter Ms. Benoit had rigged in her helmet. The doomful rumble it imparted to her natural voice would finally put paid to persistent rumors that the Silver Sentry was anything less than a red-blooded, all-American male.

Her psychoanalyst had repeatedly told her she should search for and take notice of moments when she was proud of herself, and though he knew nothing of her secret vocation, his advice rang true. She could forgive herself if she felt the need to take a bow now and again, couldn't she?

The day's batch of obligatory evildoers hijacked an armored car at a cash pickup in Hell's Kitchen. Two of them swapped uniforms with the guards and collected the deposits on the route. The cashier at the third place they hit was suspicious enough to call the police. A flying

135

squad shadowed the armored car, and two prowl cars staked out the remaining targets when they showed up at Cartier Jewelers on Upper Fifth Avenue and crashed through the display windows. Gunface Greer's gang leapt out to round up the handful of well-heeled patrons and sift all the diamonds out of the dunes of shattered glass.

The cops had the whole block cordoned off, a flying squad circling overhead, when Matilda alighted on top of an animated Bulova billboard across the street. She'd heard the whole saga on police band frequencies. While she waited and watched *The Spirit of St. Louis* repeatedly barnstorm through the wristband of a gigantic Lone Eagle wristwatch, she noticed the unsold summer fashions in the neighboring Georgette d'Paris boutique's display windows were being taken down, a rare symptom of sense, as the dresses made flapper frocks look like Puritan widow's weeds.

When the armored car backed out into the street like a mammoth, steel-plated pillbug, panicked orders to stand down roared in her ears. They'd covered it in hostages—nine men and women gagged, blindfolded, and chained to the running boards and back doors. The armored car sped north on 5th, pulverizing the gauntlet of police cars and rolling unimpeded over tire caltrops to veer down a ramp to the lower street level, leaving the flying squad hovering impotently in place. In the rooftop bubble turret, Succotash Jackson haphazardly sprayed the twin magneto-cannons in all directions, cackling and having a fine time.

Matilda leapt into the air and ignited her afterburners. They sputtered. She fell, a scream trapped in her throat. Close enough to touch the street before they caught and sent her hurtling north, nearly scraping the underbelly of an El train suspended over 34th.

With the throttle open wide, it was just like flying up a chimney. Overcorrecting with the merest twitch of a leg, she caromed off the hood of a taxicab and eased back on the throttle. Threading the crooked needle between overpasses and pedestrian walkways, she nearly smashed headlong into the side of a bus. With a clipped curse, she barrel-rolled and cut her thrusters. She landed on the roof of a paddy wagon, following half a block behind the armored car.

Since the upper levels, walkways, and flyovers had been added to Fifth ten years ago, the street-level businesses that couldn't make the leap up were literally buried alive. She flew through stagnant pools of yellow streetlamps, but the rest of the avenue was darker than a moonless night. Half the once-tony shopfronts were caged or bricked up to keep out squatters or had given way to flophouses, nickelodeons, penny arcades, clip joints, blind pigs, and automats. The armored car sped up, dodging or ramming through the slower traffic of trucks relegated to the lower streets.

Matilda knew if they weren't stopped, the armored car would be in an alley in Harlem with the hostages unharmed unless Gunface was feeling especially twitchy. And no one else could stop them.

Jackson sighted her from the bubble turret and opened fire. Matilda dodged a barrage that hit a moving van, which fishtailed and flipped on its side, leaving an improvised yard sale of damaged restaurant fixtures.

Nothing but a direct hit with an armor-piercing shell would punch through his reinforced plasteel bubble. She took careful aim with the Peacekeeper, telescoping sights extending from her goggles, and shot out the mount for the magneto-cannons. The hot artillery piece dropped in Jackson's lap. He threw up his hands to shove the guns away. The gimbaled turret mount gave way completely, and the gangster dropped out of sight.

Jackson was wanted in three states for armed robberies, car thefts, kidnaping, murder and a jailbreak in Georgia that burned down the work farm. Gunface would be inside with the take, and the third man, probably Virgil Bloodbath Bailey, was behind the wheel.

The armored car veered into oncoming traffic as it approached 59th Street. The cross-traffic was a rushing river of steel, rubber, and glass. They were headed for Brooklyn. She noticed that four of the hostages, all on the driver's side, were wearing breezy shifts in the unmistakable Georgette d'Paris style. As the car whipped into a hard turn to jump the line for the bridge, Matilda switched the ammunition in the Peacekeeper to white phosphorus rounds and shot out the right front tire.

Radiant sparks, smoke, and molten rubber gushed out the wheel well, engulfing the bodies shackled to the streamlined flank of the armored car, which heeled over on its left side and skidded sideways across two lanes of 59th Street. The traffic warden overlooking the intersection in his cherry-picker threw a lever switching the right-of-way, but two speeding flivvers still glanced off the flanks of the streamlined hulk before it came to rest.

The flying squad descended on the scene just as Gunface climbed out of the wreck with a sack of cash under each arm, snapping off gauss rounds from the double-barrel contraption famously strapped to his head. Circling directly overhead, Matilda popped a flare in his face and blinded him. The police ran in and tackled him, disarmed and wrestled him into a paddy wagon.

Succotash Jackson was taken to Bellevue's prison ward, along with two of the hostages, who'd suffered minor injuries in the crash. Several of them asked for autographs, but she politely declined.

The little snub-nosed guy from the *Times* shouted, "Silver Shrike! How did you know the hostages on the side of the armored car were mannequins? Or *did* you?"

"Silver *Sentry*." Matilda tapped her goggles. "They weren't warm," she boomed in a voice that gave even her the shivers. The reporters chuckled, and a photographer snapped off a few more pics of her posing in front of the 17th Precinct. Meanwhile, somewhere inside, the cops worked over Greer and Bailey and painstakingly sorted the diamonds out of the bags of shattered glass.

"This is the third time in two years Gunface has been pinched," someone in the press gang shouted. "Given how likely he is to escape again, are you sorry you didn't punch his ticket for good?"

The question got her dander up, but it was what she stayed for. "I'm honored to have the opportunity to support our courageous police force, but I am not, and would never willingly be, an executioner."

Fedoras bowed, they scribbled or checked their portable dictaphones. She took a bow as flashbulbs popped. "Well said," someone blurted, but the rest of the crowd went away grumbling.

If she'd cut the interview short, she would never have known. But just as the press dispersed like rabbits from a magician's hat, she saw two men come out of the motor pool entrance with hats over their faces and slip into the frenzied foot traffic on East 51st.

There was no room to fire up her rocket, so she had to shove her way through the crowd to catch up to the gaunt man in the pinstripe overcoat and the shorter fireplug in a worsted wool carcoat, with a porkpie hat snugged down to his cauliflower ears.

Pedestrians jumped out of her way as she pursued them, cheering or cursing as she pushed past. The noise surely must have reached them, but they didn't break into a run. Was she making a mistake?

"Gunface, Bloodbath. You're out early."

The shorter man turned on her with his hands in his pockets. Matilda braced herself and charged her gauntlet, the crowd backing up to make a circle around her and her enemies. "You got the wrong guys, buddy," he said.

She pointed a finger in his face, letting him hear the whir of the magnets spinning up in her forearm. His forehead and jawline were pink and freckled, while his facial features remained cadaverously white. "When you hid out in Florida, you should've taken the gun off." Seizing Greer by the lapel, she aimed at Bailey, who just shook his head like she ought to know better. "Don't know how you slipped out, but let's just go back inside."

Someone laid a hand on *her* shoulder. She jumped and nearly turned her guns on an aging cop in uniform. "There a problem here, gentlemen?"

"Just the revolving door in your jail," she shot back. "I assisted in the arrest of these men in the commission of a violent robbery. Maybe you heard about it on the radio..."

"That'll be enough of your tone," the sergeant said in his lilting brogue, one hand on a revolver that hadn't been fired in anger since before Matilda was born, if ever. "These men were arraigned, and bail has been posted. If you think there's been some miscarriage of justice...if that's what you're saying...perhaps you'll just take off that fancy mask of yours and come in to swear out a complaint."

"You got your picture in the paper, buddy," Greer sneered. "Everybody got what they wanted."

Matilda searched for the reporters. Dogging her heels one moment, but vanished when she had something they needed to see. She picked out a couple of them smoking and comparing notes on the steps of the precinct house. They didn't need to see it. They already knew. Everybody knew, apparently, but her.

"Now clear out, all of you, before I think of a reason." The sergeant turned on his heel. Greer and Bailey were already gone.

"Boy, you sure knocked him for a deck of tombstones," someone said in her ear. The unexpected voice, the familiarity of it, the mawkish vulgarity and the maddeningly knowing tone, strained her nerves to the breaking point.

"Murderer!" She drew down with her gauntlet, the ominous hum of the heavy magneto-cannon like a dynamo, spinning around, searching for the ventriloquist.

People reading newspapers bumped into her. Someone took her picture—no sign of him anywhere.

She looked up...

And saw him staring down at her from the Georgian roof of the precinct house, the cold, pale gold spirals of his eyes…

Matilda had prepared for this meeting since the last one. She had searched the city, tuned and refined all her gadgets. And she'd done her homework.

According to the old dime novels, Lionel Fanning was a wastrel playboy adventurer who tried his hand at smuggling and piracy in the South China Seas in the 1890s and found it easier and more rewarding than running his father's textile mills. When he was challenged by a monk in a golden mask on the deck of a junk he'd just commandeered, Fanning murdered him and set fire to it to escape a British patrol boat, only to discover the junk had been filled with women and children bound for the flesh-pits and sweatshops of Hong Kong.

On the riverbank, he found himself kneeling at the feet of the deceased monk, who offered him the golden mask. Rashly accepting the treasure, he found instead it was a curse that now fell upon his head.

The mask was the prison of a demon, conferring upon its wearer the ability to vanish in darkness, to travel without moving to a mystical monastery outside space and time. With his Evil Eye, he could also beguile men's minds to change his appearance and to strike terror into and wrest repentance from even the blackest human heart.

Condemned to wander the world trying to do good with the power of ultimate evil while frolicking manfully in his ageless secret identity, the Golden Ghost was once a household word since his first appearance in *Exotic Menace Magazine* in 1902. However, they changed his name from the more troublesome White Devil. He had appeared in fifty-one novel-length adventures and a syndicated newspaper strip when tragedy struck. The Lower East Side offices of Ziggurat Publications burned to the ground in 1912, taking the lives of the publisher, editor, and both authors who worked under the house byline Dirk Drummond. The crime was never solved, but witnesses saw a man in a black cape and golden mask leap from the window of the burning building.

The White Devil's true story was even murkier. From his first appearance in 1906 after the great San Francisco quake, the mysterious vigilante surfaced to clean up a town and then vanish for months or years before turning up somewhere else with very different methods and ethics. By any calculation, the real Lionel Lanning should be pushing seventy by now. She had concluded upon digesting every clipping she could uncover that there had been at least three White Devils, and perhaps this was the fourth. This one merited not a mention in the papers, had gone unnoticed in Bethlehem, and was not suspected of cutting the throats of every member of the board of Bethlehem Steel.

Matilda knew better, and she demanded an accounting.

She tried to, but even after she'd blasted off the sidewalk to alight on the parapet of the precinct house, she found herself still looking into his eyes. She knew he could confuse and paralyze his foes, but if he'd done it to her, maybe it backfired, for while her mind had wandered, *he* looked like the one who'd been hypnotized.

"I charge you with murder," she said.

She expected the White Devil to draw a weapon or try to flee. She was tensed to spring, but he meekly bowed to her. "Silver Sentry, I must humbly protest my innocence. I killed no one…in Pennsylvania."

"I hardly expect you to admit it."

"Do you expect me to prove it? If someone framed me, they're not working half as hard as you."

"You carry a sword. You were at the mill. You threw in with the strikers."

"I threw in with the *workers*." He tossed his head to stare at her, and she had to remind herself she was looking at a mask. "And you threw in against them…"

She felt trapped by those eyes but refused to look away. "I stepped in when their act of sabotage nearly killed hundreds on both sides of the picket line."

"Maybe you could have done more to stop it if you'd taken your mask off."

"You think you know all about me," she started. "You don't have to use your parlor tricks to pry open my head. Just ask."

"But I do, Miss Lynch." At her sharp intake of breath, he spun on his heel, so his cape belled out around him. She took in his broad shoulders, slim hips, and taut physique for just a moment before the cape enveloped him, almost like a jealous companion. It took all his operatic frippery to hide how much he enjoyed this. "You're the hood ornament on a runaway car. You could have all the power you'd ever need to make a real change, but you'd rather shoot your cap guns in the air and call yourself a superhero."

"You have me at a disadvantage, sir," she replied as cooly as she could. Not even the speech modifier in her helmet could contain the querulous vibrato in her voice.

"Would you like to know who I am? Would that set you straight about me?"

"Why should I believe anything you tell me?"

"What if I showed you what you've really been fighting and who the real enemy is?"

"I know who the enemy is. I'm only inches away from running down the Ochlocrat and his scheming army of fifth columnists."

If his earlier charm caught her off guard, now he poleaxed her by bursting into helpless, guffawing laughter. "Oh, I do apologize, but they're…oh, no…"

"What do you know?"

"I know they're no 'scheming army of fifth columnists; working to overthrow the fat cats," he said, "because that's *my* racket."

He threw something at the tarred roof between them, and a cloud of smoke enveloped him. When it cleared, he was gone.

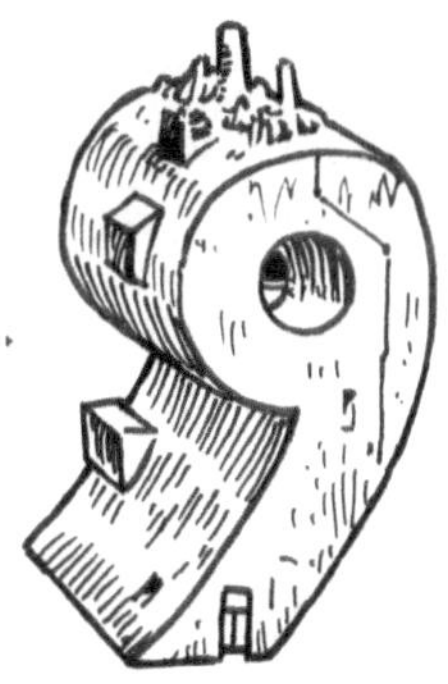

October 13th, 1931 | New York City

S pider McGowan stepped off the roof and plummeted nine stories to land as gracefully as his namesake on the roof of a southbound elevated train, one of the old ones still servicing the Lower East Side. He did not question how his cape spread out around him to arrest his descent just enough, so he didn't shatter both legs, any more than he questioned why sometimes, he seemed to be listening to himself talk, bemused and a little sickened by the windbaggery of his own voice. Too often, he felt like he was just running to keep up with the mask.

Even so, he nearly hit a flagpole and narrowly avoided crashing into a pedestrian bridge. He was badly out of tune, his mind wandering, his conviction shaken. He'd used the Eye of Fate on her, and it somehow bounced back on him. Never had he unleashed the Eye on anyone so disciplined as to resist it, let alone turn it back on him. He pushed the confusion away, throwing himself harder at the tangled cityscape until he left all doubts behind and beneath him.

The night sky was an electrified, sulfurous soup, visibility cut down to a few blocks. He looked back, half-expecting to see her hailing the flying squad down on him. He was pleasantly surprised to find her hovering overhead, a big Roman candle pointing out his position to anyone who cared to follow him, but a risk worth taking—he hoped.

Passing through the upper airship terminal of Grand Central, Spider jumped onto an eastbound train pulling away from the platform just as the southbound ground to a halt. Throwing a glance over his shoulder to see if she still tailed him, he ditched the train as it turned north on East River Drive, near Bellevue Hospital and the Knickerbocker Aero-Freight terminal.

Dropping from the underbelly of a tram just before it entered the Bellevue terminal, Spider landed on a ventilation grate in the right place to make it pivot and drop him down a shaft to the subway tunnels. If she couldn't figure it out, she would be useless to him in what came next.

He waited in the tunnel until he heard her come bumbling along. She pointed her gauntlet at him as if she'd run him to ground, rather than the opposite. He raised his hands but then jumped to tackle her and knock her out of the way of the Canarsie Line train.

They rolled in the clinkers and cigarette butts until the train had passed. "Don't mention it," he said, squirming out of her grasp to stand and offer her a hand up.

Even when she realized his intentions, the Silver Sentry seemed to think this was a fight. Maybe she'd take this as a surrender. "Right this way, ma'am," he said, stepping into a blind arch and triggering the opening of a secret entrance to his lair.

Beyond, a low gallery lined with arches faced with iron-barred gates. Most of the cells they passed were occupied, the prisoners cursing or howling indignantly as they passed. Raising her voice above the bedlam, she demanded to know why they were locked up.

"They're criminals," he answered. "This is the answer to the question you posed up there. You can't count on them going to jail, and you can't expect them to turn out any better if they do. I haven't killed nearly as many as the papers make out. I got tired of catching the same fish over and over, so I have my own jail."

That wasn't the complete truth, and she might've known. The lair had belonged to a previous White Devil—the ninth of nineteen, as near as he could tell. That one had been blessed or plagued by visions whenever he locked eyes with seemingly innocent people of the crimes they would one day commit. Perhaps the power was intended as a gift, or perhaps a further curse, an experiment, or a sadistic cosmic prank. Most likely, he was just nuts.

Whatever its motives, this far-sighted incarnation of the old Devil locked up those he didn't summarily execute until he could judge whether his interference had changed their terrible fates. When Spider looked at the list of names carved into the wall at the end of the gallery, he couldn't help but wonder if any of them were guilty or if the world was a better place with them out of it. His predecessor must have had his doubts; else, why would he throw himself, mask and all, into the East River? Regardless, within a month, someone else had found the mask and taken up the curse.

She walked up and down the cells, inspecting the prisoners like she was picking out a puppy at the pound. "You keep them down here for how long? How do you know they won't go back to a life of crime? Do you rehabilitate them at all, or just turn the old Evil Eye on them?"

"I'm trying to do it the old-fashioned way. The Eye of Fate forces them to confront their guilt, but it can't remake them." He didn't tell her what it cost to put the Eye on them. This lot, he'd tried to reform without recourse to his powers, but some had been in the cells for six months and still flung their meals back at the trusty who brought them.

"It's not enough for them to give up crime, though, is it? They must join this fifth column of yours. You recruit from the lowest of the low. To what purpose?"

"If you turn them loose, they'll find the only purpose they know. I take their old lives and give them a new one, fighting the unjust system that steered them wrong in the first place."

"What if they don't want it?"

It took him longer than it should to answer. "I give them more of a choice than they gave their victims." He hated to think of how many he'd killed or crippled because the crook had no remorse or simply because the Eye of Fate took too much out of him to be worth a particular human life. He'd had to be an executioner far more than he would admit, and many more, if the truth be told, he'd sent to a fate arguably worse than death.

Unlocking the heavy blast door in the blind wall, he led her into a smaller chamber like a wardroom for a police station. Half a dozen men and women bustled about in a workshop, ran a switchboard, observed the stock ticker and teletype machines, sorted packets of news clippings, or worked in a laboratory sealed off behind bullet-proof glass.

"What is all this?" she demanded. How she pulled off fooling the world there was a man in that can, he'd never know. Even in that suit of streamlined armor, her posture was that of a princess sitting on an overgrown pea.

"We're tied into the main telephone exchange in every borough. We can eavesdrop on any conversation in the city. It allows us to stop some crimes before they're committed."

Before she could lecture him on how unethical spying on criminals was, he led her into a smaller room bathed in a piercing blue-white light. She blanched as she saw freckle-faced Jasper Zwick and a headless man dressed in the height of 18th-century French fashion sitting at a big control console beneath the source of the eerie glow, a wall of strange little windows.

"The new cables are pulling in a lot more detail, Spider," Zwick said. "Come and see!" The headless man turned to favor them with an airy wave.

"That's Doc Guillotine," Spider told her, but that much she already knew. A science-vigilante wanted for capital murder in New Jersey, he used some kind of radio beam weapon to lop the heads off criminals. He wore a funny kind of cowl that used thousands of tiny mirrors to deflect light to create the unsettling illusion that he wasn't just the inventor of the decapitating beam but its first customer. Since Spider used the Eye on him, and he was a useful asset but still crazy as a bedbug. Spider was relieved the Circuit Rider wasn't here, as he was even harder to explain.

"I didn't mean…him. I meant *this*." She pointed most pointedly at the screens.

Jasper put his engineer boots up on a table piled with wiretap transcripts and dismantled or unfinished gadgets. "Ain't, you heard of television?"

She barely nodded, but even with all that armor on, he could tell she was spellbound. Once you get used to the piercing light, you can see tiny people moving around or talking in the windows, and with the headset around Jasper's neck, you can hear everything they say. "It's the coming thing if the radio people ever get off its neck. Meantime, it comes in useful for keeping an eye on people doing things they oughtn't."

She moved closer, leaning over Jasper's shoulder. "These are electrically transmitted images?"

"Sharp mind like yours," the kid said, "you ought to fight crime, maybe."

She leaned even closer, adjusting the filters on her helmet's goggles. "That's the mayor's office. How many cameras do you have?"

"Not as many as we need," he shot back.

"With all this, it seems like you could use it on real criminals."

Zwick sighed disgustedly. Spider asked, "Who clipped Arnold Rothstein? "Who nabbed Judge Crater? Who gunned down Legs Diamond in the Catskills last Christmas? Nobody knows, and nobody cares. Venal crooks prey on weaker men's vices until another takes their place. I'm after bigger fish. Men whose evil deeds get them invited to the White House."

"Who's the orphan?" she asked. Jasper twisted in his seat and opened his mouth wide enough to fit both feet.

Spider stepped between them. "You want to adopt him?"

"I'd like to knock his teeth out his ears if you must know."

Jasper grinned. Doc Guillotine found something to do in another part of the room.

"Remember the robot riot at Bethlehem Steel?"

She nodded.

"This kid made it happen."

"Did you have to stir his brains up with your voodoo or just double his allowance?"

"Aw dry up," Zwick said. "If you want to see a terrorist, look in the mirror."

Her shoulders hitched up in a dismayed shrug. "What a lovely addition to your little human zoo."

"I could use one more," Spider said.

He ushered her into a cloakroom, shut the door, and offered her coffee or tea.

Taking the hint, she looked long and hard at him, waiting for him to remove his own mask. When he didn't, she almost left, but he went ahead and poured a cup of black tea and set it before her. What did she have to lose?

She disconnected various hoses and, after a searching glance to ensure they were alone, removed her helmet. Brushing a stray curl off her shiny forehead, she came close enough that he could smell her sweat. Matilda Lynch, he discovered, was infinitely more fetching than she looked on closed-circuit television. "You guessed, and you guessed right. But it's only fair—"

"I don't know from fair," he said. He started to turn away, but something in her eyes made him believe—or want to believe—that he could trust her. "My mask doesn't come off."

"Oh honestly," she scoffed, reaching for it, but his hands caught hers and pushed them away less gently than he intended. "You could hurt me a lot more with what you know than I could hurt you…"

"I'm not fooling," he said. "When I was given this mask, I was nearly dead, and I can't take it off until I'm ready to finish the job. It's the only way I know of that I can die. This…*is* my face."

Her eyes widened, the bow of her lips parted to let out a sigh, but she bit back whatever she was about to say. A shield that obscured more than her helmet ever could was raised between them. "What's your real name, then?"

He meant to say the name on the tip of his tongue, but in the moment, it eluded him, and the mask spoke for him. "I am the White Devil."

She rolled her eyes. "Drop the Big Bad Wolf act. If you know who I am, you know I come from a long line of men who kill what they eat, and I haven't come that far."

"It doesn't take long for money to rot whatever it touches. If I can trust you—"

She took the paper cup of tea and sipped it, surprise cracking and letting some daylight out of her face, then tossed it back. "If you can trust *me*? Why should I trust *you*?"

"I'm not asking you to. You've seen what I do and how I do it. I'm offering you a chance to do something real with all those toys of yours. Or would your father take them away if he disapproved of your stepping out on your own?"

"Leave my father out of this. He has no idea what I'm up to…"

"And that's why you do it, isn't it? To wash some of the blood off all that money."

Her expression soured. She wasn't going to be baited again. "My father inherited the business, as I will someday. He's just a business-man. If he's guilty of anything, it's thinking he's one of the wise old elephants that holds up the world."

"Maybe he was when it was still flat. Your pop's gotten so used to stepping over blood that you don't know you're swimming in it. Big men like him have been sitting on little men with big ideas, stifling change and making a fortune off the world his kind broke—"

"Keeping the world safe, you mean. You never saw what the scientists did to Europe—"

"But I see what they do *here* every day. The ones hooked up with the big companies are making it smaller and more expensive every day, inventing little miracles nobody needs and almost nobody can afford. And the little guys out in the street have turned to crime. That much you can't ignore, how every gang has an egghead, every new crook has a science-pirate angle. But I'm not talking about that kind of change."

"Revolution, then?"

"Is it revolution to make a country honor the promises it was founded on?"

She crushed the paper cup like it was made of steel and tossed it in the wastebasket. "You're going to put it all right, are you? You're more dangerous than any villain I've put away and even more cracked if you believe that stuff."

"What stuff? The Constitution?"

"Don't play dumb. You come on like a wise old bird yourself, but you think like a villain."

"Anyone who wants to fix what's broken is a villain. Anyone who risks his neck to keep it like it is, they call a hero. I'm neither, just a realist."

"Go ahead then and tell me what's real. I promise I won't laugh." She practically quivered, and he was sure the wrong word now would lose her for good.

"History pretends everything changes when one great man with a vision changes everything, from Jesus to Edison, because it keeps everyone running, keeps the peasants thinking they're one great idea away from easy street." He resisted the urge to use the Eye, but it hadn't worked before. "But one man *can* change the world," he said. "One man as a tool of the world, remaking itself."

It was as if a cloud passed to obscure the light behind her eyes. "You know what happens to tools. They get used up, broken, thrown away."

He nodded, taken aback by her sudden cynicism. "But if one incident can change a person—one bolt of lightning, one fateful meeting, one World War—"

She flinched. "Like a match can change rubbish into a bonfire." Impatiently, she stripped a glove off her prosthetic hand and made a fist with it. "You said you could help me find what I'm looking for…"

"Every hound thinks it's a hero for running down the fox, Miss Lynch. Do you know how they get the greyhounds to race at the dog track?"

"I've never been," she shook her head, sullied by the mere implication.

"They have a little mechanical rabbit that runs on the inside rail. Drives them crazy. You should see it sometime."

"You promised me answers. Give them to me."

"Or else?"

"Don't make me beat it out of you."

"Don't threaten me with a good time." He handed her a slip of paper, crisply folded and pungent with whatever Jasper used for ink.

"What is this?"

"Your rabbit, Miss Lynch."

She took it mistrustfully as if it might be poisonous. "These are the mob who killed the board of Bethlehem Steel?"

"No. The board cut their own throats."

"How is that possible?"

"It's not all that tough if you know hypnosis."

"It's just a parlor trick. You can't make people harm themselves—"

"*I* can, and I must guess this bird is better at it than I am. You may not have noticed the phonograph in the corner of the boardroom, beside the open window. I chanced to go out that window and found a thing or two you missed."

Turning to a workbench, he held up a shard of a phonograph record in a clear glassine envelope. A flat dagger of glossy anthracite bore only a corner of the label at the wider end. "Chopin's funeral march," he said. Reaching across the bench to a bulky wiretap recorder, he played back the snippet of the wire spool on which they'd recorded the disk fragment. Through the crackling fireside ambiance, less than a bar of the ponderous death trudge played. Fiddling with the bank of equalization sliders on the recorder, he rewound and played it again. Now, the moribund melody and the distortion were muted, and a low, droning voice could be heard saying, "Cut the string."

She looked at the recorder for a long while, head tilted. "Is that all you found?"

He showed her a photograph of a dead woman, stocky, poorly dressed, lying prone on the gravel of Bethlehem Steel's administrative building rooftop. A police photographer's initials were etched into the corner of the photo. "A cleaning woman. She set the record playing, then threw herself out the window. Her thumbprint is on the disk."

"And this record made them commit suicide?"

At times like this, with people like these, Spider wanted sorely to remind her how they were dressed, what they did every day, and ask them how they could judge what was possible or even likely. "Is it so hard to believe? Our killer uses people as puppets. The recording could have triggered a posthypnotic suggestion in each man's mind. No way to know what they thought they were doing. That's how you kill a man with hypnosis. Get him up on a ledge and make him think it's a beautiful day for a stroll." Spider shut off the recording. "There have been three more that I know of and another half dozen that stink of our killer. But nobody else is keeping track because they look like suicides. Moguls doing away with themselves doesn't even rate the front page anymore, and one killed by his own servants… It's not the kind of news they see fit to print, lest it give others the right idea."

Her face went white. "But if he's still out there, why aren't you doing more to stop it? Maybe so long as he's knocking off the rich, he's not a priority." Spider figured she must be wondering if the list this killer was working included her father.

"I don't know who he is or what game he's playing, but I mean to end it. I need your help."

"Even if you don't believe what he's doing is wrong?" Her eyebrow arched, lips pursed, so it took him longer than it should to see how angry she was. "Not everybody thinks someone deserves to die just because they did well."

He was losing patience with her, but she had to be coddled a bit. A tropical fish couldn't be made to respect fire. "Rich men are getting richer off this crisis while the rest of this country's dying on its feet. Nobody's putting on a mask to fight them, but I can't think of any other legitimate reason to do it."

"What, the Depression? All it is, is a crisis of confidence. If people would just pull together and—"

Times like this, he almost forgot he had no human face. He had to shake his head at her blithe naivete. "It's the worst crack-up this country's faced since the Civil War…and maybe the start of the next one."

"That's exactly what I fear most. This killer hypnotist sounds like the work of the Levelers."

At last! "Your Levelers are anything but on the level, but that's where you'll find them. You should just see for yourself…"

"That wasn't what I meant." She pocketed the slip of paper as she moved a bit closer but held her helmet between them so he wouldn't get the wrong idea.

For a long, heavy moment, she only stared. He almost felt she could see his face through the golden mask. "Well…I suppose I should…" She trailed off. He didn't say anything. She donned her helmet and left without another word.

"So that's the one you been following?" Zwick said. "I don't trust her." The kid stood in the door with his arms crossed, a well-thumbed issue of *The Golden Ghost (Three! Complete! Novels!)* tucked almost out of sight. Jasper knew by now how the pulps annoyed him, so he was ragging him with an angle in mind.

"I don't either," Spider said, "but she can help us despite herself. Maybe the whole nine yards if she keeps her eyes open."

She probably wouldn't, though. She clearly thought he was cracked, but she was angry enough to go through with it. As he had to rely more on the loyalty of criminals he'd captured and brainwashed, so trusting a debutante who played vigilante wasn't such a long shot bet.

He'd failed to paralyze her with the Evil Eye. No one with any scintilla of real guilt could resist it. He'd seen inside her darkest memories, touched the painful sharp edges that made her what she was, and found nothing with which to trap her. *Instead, she trapped you,* he thought.

She'd endured the tyranny of her father and watched it crush her mother into howling insanity and death in a luxurious asylum. She'd witnessed horrors in war and suffered the death of her sister, the only one in her family she could trust, and then the loss of her arm and leg. All these things could and should have left her a scarred, bitter gargoyle, but instead, she took the hateful machines of her father's company and used them to protect people. She had confronted Gun-face when he skipped on the indictment, and when she followed his tip on the Levelers, her broken naivete would be tinder he could use to build a fire…but his feelings got in the way. He had to look at how his hackles had risen when Zwick said he didn't trust her to realize the truth. He'd been alone behind this mask too long and saw something in the first person to stand up to him that almost surely wasn't there. How stupid can you be?

He was quick enough to catch the glint in her eye when she'd shown him her face and expected to see his. But it was the look of a child at play, the anticipation of a card turned in a game. Even if she could see his true face, she'd never look twice at a mulatto Irishman—*quadroon*, the ugly southern distinction surfaced unbidden in his mind—and if she could see into his mind and memories, so much the worse. But he'd seen hers, and saw them still, whenever he closed his eyes.

He pulled off his gloves and looked down at the bronze skin of his hands as they knotted into fists.

He'd already told her too much of the truth, but hardly all of it.

Of all the things the old pulps got wrong that strummed his nerves, the worst was the Golden Ghost's secret identity. Whenever he liked, the eternally youthful Lionel Lanning could unmask and return to his playboy life. But Spider McGowan had no identity at all to speak of behind the mask.

He couldn't remove it, but he could have used the mask's power to cloud her mind, so she saw him without it, as he'd done when he collared Jasper on the train. But it took so much out of him to do it. He seemed to burn a little more of a reserve of fuel that was in short supply; he was only just beginning to recognize what it cost.

Zwick started to leave, but Spider called him back. "Did Junebug get the files from the Tombs?"

Zwick nodded and went to fetch them. Spider flipped through them, studying each in turn until Zwick left.

Whenever he took in new agents, he had a contact inside the central records division of the NYPD pull their files so the fingerprints and Bertillon statistics could be fudged. He'd asked for several so nobody, not even his closest associates, would suspect why he wanted any particular one.

When he got to the file for MCGOWAN, THOMAS, he took a deep breath and closed his eyes. The trick of clouding men's minds so they saw your face instead of the ghastly mask was easy. All you had to do was picture a face and project it into their heads, and that's what they saw. But it was a lot harder when you couldn't remember what that face looked like.

He opened his eyes and the file at the same time.

A champion is someone who gets up when he can't.

—Jack Dempsey

November 11, 1931 | San Francisco, California

I t was after the 27th round of the fight that Gouger O'Grady's trainer, Spiro Kazepis, decided the opponent his man was fighting had to be something other than human, so it was not only jake to even the odds, but damn near mandatory.

"He won't go down," the boxer growled. "I threw the works at him, but he keeps bouncing…"

"Ya ain't got nothin' on him in the last fourteen rounds but your blood," Spiro spat back. O'Grady couldn't box legit since he knocked an opponent's eye out and cold-cocked a referee back east. The ring was a waist-high rampart of sandbags lit by strings of firefly lamps to hold back the roaring mob, but beyond it, the satiny silver fog hid all but the most penetrating lights of Alameda, Oakland, and the new suspension bridge they were putting up across the Bay.

As boxing was technically illegal in the state of California, the match took place on a flatbed barge anchored in the middle of San Francisco Bay, on the Alameda side of the county line, because the sheriff there was more of a sportsman. The fix was most definitely not in—the local mobs actually *liked* clean fights—but from the opening bell, this bout had stunk from the tail up.

O'Grady had a cannon for a right hook but no speed to speak of, yet he'd danced around the southpaw, kneading the other fighter's face like a mound of bread dough. Sometimes, the southpaw brought the left up to block it, sometimes not, but it made no difference.

This freak of a southpaw…

He was hairless, so far as Spiro could tell, and a mute. His head looked like a bubble his neck blew, the features on it sculpted in putty or scribbled on the surface by one of those loony-bin psychos who made all the art these days. Built like a rubber tank, he lumbered in circles like he couldn't find Gouger, soaking up enough punishment to knock over a brickyard, throwing blows or blocking only when his trainer, some loudmouth ham & egger from Sacramento, told him to, like a goddam robot. His punches fell with all the force of water balloons. His name sounded Greek but didn't make a lick of sense. His age was impossible to determine, but he sure as hell was no kid. What kind of a name was Amoeba?

While the cut man stitched up the bleeder in Gouger's eyebrow, Spiro reached under his stool, took out a tiny carbide battery, and plugged it into the wires secreted in a circuit throughout Gouger's right glove. While Gouger would be insulated by the rubber lining, but any solid shot to the head while he was pushing the plunger would deliver a good stiff shock, enough to send him to the rusty iron deck and scramble his brains long past the referee's ten-count.

The bell clanged. Kid Amoeba came off his stool and slithered around the ring like oleo on a skillet.

"Put him down already," Spiro snapped as he shoved Gouger at his opponent. Kid Amoeba circled, deflecting Gouger's first tentative attempts to get the stinger into position. The loudmouth trainer kept barking, "Block," and the Kid kept shading his eyes, seeming not to realize he was in the ragged end of a boxing match.

Spiro grabbed his runner and hissed in his good ear. The boy nodded and burrowed into the crowd. Perhaps ten seconds later, a big man grabbed the Kid's trainer, forcing a beer mug into his hand. The trainer pushed the man away, but he was distracted long enough for Gouger to get a solid haymaker into the side of Kid Amoeba's head. It was beautifully executed, devastatingly timed, and all Spiro Kazepis could think was, *there goes another eye.*

The moment the juiced glove contacted the challenger's shapeless jaw, Gouger was flung back into the sandbag barricade like a bull had hit him. The southpaw challenger exploded into a hundred, a thousand ropy tentacles like the roots of a tree, and each feathery frond furry with a thousand horripilated tendrils, and all of them shot through for just a moment with lightning so bright that the image of the boxer's silhouetted skeleton would be burned on Spiro's retinas for a week.

The lightning chased itself in circles inside Kid Amoeba, arcing from its outstretched tentacles when they ripped down the lanterns strung up overhead.

Everything went black.

In the sudden darkness, a few in the mob sparked lighters, flashlights, or kerosene lamps.

"Where's the ref?" Spiro shouted. "Call the fight!"

The whole barge rocked underfoot, spectators shouting and shoving as all sides clamored for a disqualification. The referee was nowhere to be found, nor was Kid Amoeba, but in his place, a smoking mound about the mass of a big man lay splayed like a jellyfish across the ring. Gouger staggered across the deck, opening and closing his mouth and clenching his jaws like his head had been cut off and sewed back on wrong, but when he saw the mess underfoot, he kicked it and raised his gloves in triumph. "That is right, I am the winner!" He posed and punched air with sparks dribbling from the juiced glove.

Spiro started to climb over the sandbags to collect his champion when the gigantic wad of gum at Gouger's feet rose quicker than the lightning that felled it, congealed into an arm of Goliath, grabbed the champ by his neck, and swung him like the jawbone of an ass to fell half a dozen of the hoods, swells, and yeggs in the front row.

The crowd surged over the barricades. Men punched, kicked, stabbed, head-butted, burned, and shot it, hell-bent on destroying it because it violated their instinctual sense of what life is and must never be. It fought tirelessly, seizing men by their feet and flinging them head over heels into the Bay. By the time the mob parted and became a stampede for the rowboats, the blob reached the barge's edge, whereupon it slithered out of sight and into dubious local legend.

It made itself small and dense to sink into the chill, briny deep, away from the silver streaks of stray bullets and the lethal screws of a flotilla of rum-runner boats picking up the most well-heeled of the spectators from the spoiled boxing match and the sluggish, heavier engines of the Redwood City Sheriff's harbor patrol, which took a less pragmatic view of illegal sporting matches than their neighbors on the east side of the Bay.

All of which was, of course, incomprehensible to and unnoticed by the squirming nodule of battered protoplasm that sank to the murky bottom and lay mostly inanimate until even the local crabs and bottom-feeding fish had learned to avoid it.

Perhaps it should remain here. No matter what it tried, the dominant life in this alien place inevitably discovered it and reacted with hostility before it could adapt to their strange ways and accrete sufficient mass to destroy or devour them all.

Still, if it lacked the cognitive faculties to reason what it was doing wrong, it also lacked the ability to accept defeat and give up.

When it had engulfed enough marine life to repair the damage from the fight, it made itself into an eyeless worm to creep among the junked Gold Rush boats and lobster traps in a northeasterly heading.

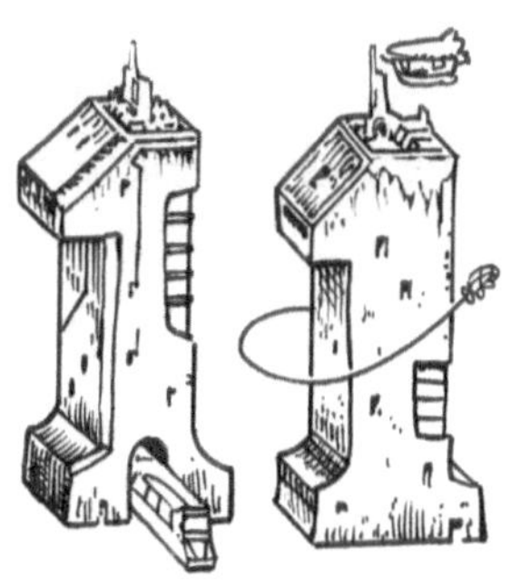

From Time Magazine, week of January 9, 1932:

AROUND THE WORLD IN EIGHTY MINUTES
by Damon Runyon

The world gets reinvented every week if you hearken unto the prophets of Madison Avenue, but how long has it been since an invention really changed anything? We still live in essentially the same houses and drive the same automobiles of our steam-driven childhoods. That shambolic national inertia, with complacency for a mother, economy for a father, and the big conglomerates playing the part of smothering governess, has stuck us with bigger, faster, more streamlined versions of the same old hardware. With the collapse of Black October and the ensuing stagnation, that ennui began to stink of the kind of doom that has condemned greater empires than ours to the dustbin of history.

But today (at 3:30 PM Eastern Standard Time), a hand-selected cadre of correspondents and photographers were invited to the stupefying new headquarters of the Chalice Company in New York City to bear witness to a revolution that will truly knock the world on its ear, and perhaps even wake America out of its collective malaise.

Looming over the Manhattan skyline like an embassy of sunken Atlantis, the mysterious Chalice Tower has been a lightning rod of speculation since its hasty erection next to Battery Park only a year ago. If one were attempting to hide something, the newest world's tallest skyscraper that upstaged the spanking-new Empire State Building even after the addition of its laughably ill-conceived mooring mast "hat," would seem to be a strategic blunder of the worst kind. But the true nature of its business was the most unlikely kind of secret in New York—the kind people keep.

This thing makes the Empire State look like a hat rack and Grand Central like a footstool. It makes the sky look small. And yet not even the late, eccentric Spanish architect Antoni Gaudi, who designed the submarine skyscraper as the Hotel Attraction back in 1905, could have begun to imagine to what purpose his outré masterpiece would be put.

Sylvester Chalice, the president and sole proprietor of his eponymous company, took the stage without benefit of introduction shortly after refreshments were served in the palatial "rotunda" of his tower, which makes the trading floor of the New York Stock Exchange look like a broom closet. An anonymous wag from a local paper loudly decried the meanness of the fare just before the rangy, dashingly dapper young man at the podium silently commanded our attention.

Mr. Chalice wore a charcoal pinchback double-breasted suit and a white linen shirt with an attached collar, heliotrope socks, and black patent leather shoes. He carried himself more like another Pecora than another Tesla. Lightning sprang from his fingertips as he made his airtight case for the future he wants to sell us. He nearly made us see it, too. Less is known about the man than the company, but schoolchildren will undoubtedly compose rudimentary paeans to him alongside Edison, Ford, and the Wright Brothers.

"For as long as humanity has set itself apart from the animals, it has dreamed of moving about the Earth and among the heavens as gods. Yet for all our inventions, we succeed only in imitating the animals—our cars and trains crawl upon the earth, our ships and submersibles sail the seas like fish, and our dirigibles and aircraft swoop through the skies as birds.

"Laudable, but where the journey is not a pleasurable end, such time is wasted. To finally master his domain, man must not travel at all but simply arrive. At last, the wish to be anywhere can be fulfilled instantly, and any destination is within reach…"

Or at least as near as the nearest door. When Mr. Chalice had finished his sermon, he cut the ribbon and invited us to follow him around the world.

We chuckled amongst ourselves at what we thought was a cute conceit, the prelude to a floorshow. What fools these mortals be…

Following him through a revolving door into a shadowy cavern that stretched over a hundred stories above us and had the atmosphere of a colossal beehive with restaurants, shops, and (one assumes), someday, a new home for the Yankees.

Ranks of galleries overhead gave the sense of a weird museum, but the exhibits were row upon row of revolving doors––or, as he calls them, "teleportals." In the center of the ballroom floor, Chalice asked for a volunteer and unsurprisingly called upon the lout who'd criticized the spread where he'd like to go.

"Champagne and dancing girls," came the answer. Chalice looked about as surprised as the farmer when the cow said *Moo*. Leading the junketeers up an escalator to the third-floor gallery, he ushered us to yet another revolving door. As we pushed through, the distinguished portly gentleman with whom I found myself enclosed in the revolving door asked me if I heard accordions…

We emerged into a lively, bustling upper-crust hotel lobby and noted that the clocks all said it was half past midnight. Many were struck by the sleight of hand involved in tucking a whole hotel behind one little door, while others noted the strange tongues in which passersby spoke, and one of our number, playing the Doubting Thomas among a flock of skeptics, rushed to the outer doors of the hotel lobby. I recall his awestruck face as vividly as I recall the sight that unmanned him, for the moon hung high over the icy streets of a city that was not our own. Beyond the modestly scaled gingerbread skyline stood the supreme apparition of the Eiffel Tower.

Paris!

A near-sighted gentleman who brought a portable dictaphone and clearly writes for *Popular Mechanics* was beside himself with commingled ecstasy and rage. Chalice had no right, the reporter insisted, to disintegrate and teleport us without our knowledge. Taking his case on the merits, he had grounds for a hearing. If we'd been disassembled at a molecular level and bounced off a mirror in space to Paris, he'd been all kinds of slick about it. Everyone loves a magic trick until they know the trick, but we couldn't finesse it. As near as we could tell, Gaudi's big beehive with all the revolving doors was the key; somehow everywhere and nowhere at once, but right next door to wherever you want to be.

Declining to answer our howled demands, our coy kidnapper led us to the Ambassador Hotel's grand ballroom, where a jazz orchestra led by Paul Whiteman provided dizzying accompaniment to a scorching dance by the notorious Bronze Venus herself, Josephine Baker. Under crystal chandeliers, Aubusson tapestries, and more marble columns than the Acropolis, the inestimable Mr. Chalice toasted the American spirit of innovation with the first crystal flute from a veritable Everest of champagne.

Before we could so much as establish a base camp on that mighty mountain or try wiring our editors half a hemisphere away, Mr. Chalice apologized for his poor hospitality, allowing that we must be hungry.

Another revolving door took us to our next destination.

Those of us who hadn't rashly checked their overcoats at the Ambassador removed them as the next revolving door disgorged us into a broad plaza fitted with an outdoor restaurant and wine garden.

Those of us who'd enjoyed a worldly education abroad clicked our tongues, all the more bedazzled than those who never crossed the Hudson River.

Between the Arch of Constantine and the imposing sprawl of the Colosseum and under the watchful panopticon eye of Rome's looming new Futurist Citta Nuova monstrosities, we dined on spaghetti and a Neapolitan treat known as *pizza* (which, for the record, is still better at Lombardi's on Spring Street). We enjoyed the liberty of unadulterated *frapatto, Etna Rosso, and Amarone del Valpolicella*. Mussolini may wantonly trample the four freedoms in hobnailed jackboots, but he makes the wine run on time.

Our whirlwind tour left little room for reflection, but even the least imaginative mind must reel at the implications of such a thing as Chalice has invented. If television and broadcast power were too hot for Americans to handle, what to make of this? Of course, the possibilities for commercial exploitation are legion, and the old cry of the American mercantilist echoes through Mr. Chalice's extraordinary gallery. *Oil for the lamps of China! An Arrow shirt on the back of every heathen!*

But it must be said that for every boon such a magical invention might bring, there is a lurking chimera. What will all of this mean for borders, treaties, tariffs, to say nothing of immigrants? Lady Liberty has tucked in her skirts and hung out the No Vacancy sign, but what will the nativists say when the teeming hordes of uninvited foreigners tumble to the new reality that America is just a revolving teleportal away?

Oh, brave new world and all that, unless you're a pilot, navigator, steward, engineer, brakeman, conductor, fireman, porter, truck driver, hotelier, bellhop, or travel agent…

Chalice spared no time for Cassandras: another revolving door beckoned. We pocketed the trinkets and souvenirs pressed upon us by hordes of street vendors and followed our guide to…

Cairo!

The pyramids gleamed dully beneath the full moon. Under the bemused gaze of the Sphinx, Bedouin nomads raced Arabian stallions. They engaged in a barbaric variety of polo or juggled gleaming scimitars by torchlight to warn us against straying too close to the belly dancers. Alas, the tenets of Islam are dryer than the desert sands, but we were fortified with strong Turkish coffee and cigarettes before we went through the next revolving door, stationed in the mouth of a humble tent.

The climate changed again, and the sweat on our backs turned to frost as we left the frenzied Egyptian scene for a frigid vista of serene majesty that finally put paid to the last nay-saying junketeer who'd been insisting that it was all done with mirrors and a cyclorama.

In a garden of delicate stunted trees, sculpted sands, goldfish ponds, and stately pagodas, we watched the rosy fingers of dawn caress the snowy crown of Mount Fuji. While tea was served, geishas danced, played, and recited scenes from the Tale Of Genji.

Perhaps it was the fatigue every man feels when bombarded with all the wonders, miracles, and libations the world has to offer, or perhaps it was the quiet oriental beauty all about us. Still, a somber silence reigned over this singularly shaken party. As the sun ascended over Mount Fuji, it was somehow not only possible but already accepted that we had emerged into another world from the dreary one we'd left behind only two hours before, by our wildly incorrect watches. We were now in Sylvester Chalice's world, and it might be quite a place for anyone he sees fit to allow into it.

We accepted the summons to file through the next revolving door, almost like children being roused from dreams to trudge through winter snow to school and emerged into the shadowy gallery of Chalice's New York pavilion chastened and a bit afraid of our convivial host. If the revolving door back to the rotunda had instead taken us to the icy wastes of Antarctica, or to Mars or the Age of Dinosaurs, we would have been no more nor less stunned than we were to find ourselves once again on the sidewalks of New York, just as the pale winter sun was setting over New Jersey…

I cannot read the minds of my comrades and competitors as we went our separate ways by subway or pneumatic car, in automobiles, autogyros, or commuter dirigibles. Still, they must, as did I, consider how shockingly antique is all that was new, shiny, and bright was only this morning.

In an era deafened by the celebration of every so-called breakthrough in speed and comfort, Mr. Chalice has shattered the very foundation of the journey and crushed an infinity of destinations into our trembling hands. Though the unspoken thesis of tonight's wondrous demonstration was that Happy Days Are Here Again, is it so difficult to conceive of a Tomorrow when a privileged few will literally have the world at their doorstep, able to tune in a private tele-portal to anywhere in the world—and beyond?—without recourse to rubbing elbows with the great unwashed who once drove our trains, flew our planes, and steered our ships? Oh, brave new world indeed…but a better one? And for whom?

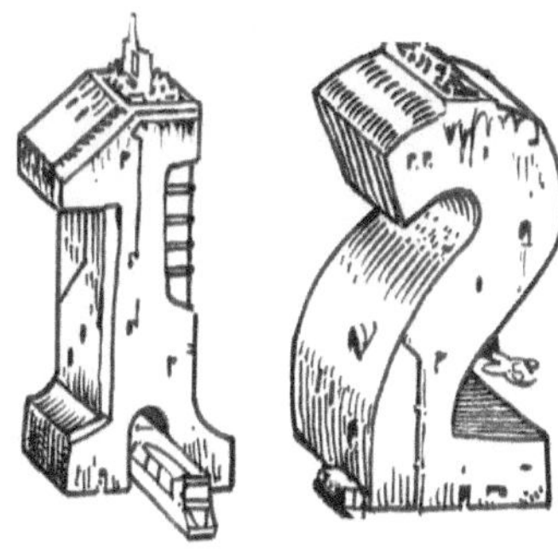

I can hire one-half of the working class to kill the other half.

—Jay Gould

March 10, 1932 | New York, San Francisco, New York

T he news, for a change, was good. All the men and women in both lines that wrapped around the perimeter of Battery Park were talking about the baby.

The ones waiting to enter Chalice Pavilion, many in tennis whites or golfing knickers, and carping jauntily that they thought they'd be in Palm Beach by now.

The other ones waiting in line for coffee and a donut from the Hearst newspaper truck: ragged, hollow-eyed men with no coats, many with old editions of the *Journal* wadded in their shiny trousers for insulation. After a harrowing month and seven ransom letters, the Lindbergh baby had been delivered safely home. Matilda bought a *Times* and read it as she waited outside the rotunda of Chalice Pavilion.

As of yet, all the tickets were by invitation only, in hopes that Manhattan's smartest, fleetingly famous cake-eaters would spread the good word. The market for second-hand tickets had become so hot that Matilda was reminded of the gilded notice she'd received—or rather Father had, but he had no intention of being "beamed across the aether like so much Morse code." She was reminded of the White Devil's tip.

She'd followed up on it straight away but thought he must be having fun with her when she researched the address on the slip of paper. Only when every other avenue proved a dead end, and the Devil himself had seemingly vanished, did she return to it, and then she thought of the ticket.

Dressed in a caracal fur coat with a cloche hat, riding boots, and leather aviator's gloves, she felt the chill only as a delicious novelty, not the ravenous beast at the back of every man waiting across the street. Her line moved briskly as liveried ushers verified each invitation at the doors with a strange kind of fountain pen that spat out blue light. An usher asked her destination, stamped her ticket, and told her to proceed through the main door to the pavilion and enter through Teleportal #7. She was not asked to present proof of her identity, for which purpose she'd switched wallets with Elvira Seaton. While Matilda was traveling incognito, the actress would attend a luncheon sponsored by the Mothers of Free Nations and then fly to the family estate on Long Island. She kept her head down as a brace of newspaper photographers blasted the crowds with flashbulb lightning.

The lobby was a bustling grotto, with all the commingled urgency and pomp of Grand Central Station and a gala at the Metropolitan. Porters shouted as they shepherded trolleys laden with steamer trunks and canvas sacks of shopping to and from the armada of cabs, vans, and gyrocopters out in the turnaround.

Matilda pressed a hand to her brow and wished she'd brought earplugs. The unusual design was something to see, at least. Matilda had no stomach for the busy, ruthlessly rigid art deco style currently in fashion and found the streamlined design craze reduced everything to dynamic expressions of phallic brutality. With its organic forms and strange materials, Gaudi's tower hearkened back to Art Nouveau while positing a weird new future, all green steel, tinted glass, malachite, and terrazzo marble.

The walls were some kind of not-quite translucent glass that must be stronger than concrete, for she saw no steel girders or other supports, just the light of gemlike lamps suspended in the walls shining dimly through the wall silhouetting the veins of electrical fixtures and the bowels of plumbing in the walls. She saw no seams between wall and floor as if the entire skyscraper had been breathed into existence by a colossal glassblower at the Lalique studios. Anything that wasn't made of glass—the railings, escalators, and revolving doors—was trimmed in two shades of gleaming green metal that evoked the shell casing and glittering underbelly of a Japanese beetle. It felt a bit like being inside a transparent termite mound or a gigantic pitcher plant, slowly dissolving in its saturated, syrupy light.

She breezed through a turnstile, a passport kiosk, and baggage inspection that were shuttered pending international travel approval. There were no uniformed police or security, but she noticed a few aggressively nondescript men in dark suits watching the passersby with hooded eyes and figured they must be Bureau of Investigation. Small wonder, as the Chalice business model promised no end of headaches for interstate commerce and law enforcement. Finally, the line filed into the pavilion through a maze of velvet ropes and stanchions and a great revolving door.

She showed her ticket to another usher, who helpfully barked and pointed out Door #7 across the ground floor. She fell in with the new line streaming into the teleportal, eyeing the reverse flow feeding out of it. They laughed, carrying light winter coats on their arms, hats, and shoulders dappled with raindrops. Outside, freezing winds off the Hudson would turn the rain to icy needles, but maybe they wouldn't go outside. Maybe they'd wander over to Door #23 (Miami, Florida), Door #44 (Houston, Texas), or Door #77 (Havana, Cuba), which she noted was lumped in between #76 (Honolulu/Sandwich Islands) and #78 (Hartford, Connecticut).

As children, Matilda and her sister believed you had to hold your breath when you went through a tunnel. A silly ritual to liven long car and train trips, but she found herself holding her breath as she went through the door. Emerging into a much smaller replica of the room she'd just left, she started to turn around to see if there hadn't been a mistake, but an usher took her arm, shouting, "This is San Francisco! Keep moving, please. Welcome to California…"

She kept moving, but she wasn't the only one craning her neck and staring around, waiting for some clap of thunder or shower of fairy dust. The pavilion here was only thirteen stories, and the escalators to the upper floors were roped off. Workmen toiled at installing revolving doors under signs that read Sausalito, San Jose, Stanford University, Oakland, and Berkeley. She wondered if they were still building that ugly bridge.

The crowd carried her out another revolving door into an arcade of boutiques and souvenir stands. Many of her fellow travelers stopped to collect pennants and other gewgaws that said San Francisco on them, before returning to New York. Door-hopping scavenger hunts were the new craze for the young, bored and rich.

She passed under a gauntlet of appraising male gazes and brought a defensive hand up over her face, a hand with which she could've blown them all away. She'd been warned about how brazenly the men undressed you with their eyes in Paris or Rome, but she found the artless scrutiny of overgrown American sheiks far harder to bear.

With an appraising eye that confused the worst attributes of an Arab slave auctioneer and a lost little boy looking for Mommy, they seduced you in their minds, whisking you off your feet and squandering your charms. With a glance at your hand, they proposed elopement and a whiskey honeymoon; with a compulsive assessment of breasts and loins, they plunged babies into you, ripped them out and found them disappointing; with a gander at your rump, they bought you a pre-fab Gladstone house and bemoaned how you decorated it, how you waited in the cloying, tearose-stinking parlor for him to come home from an innocent night out, and scowled at your legs and all the lies you told the judge at your divorce, just as they suffered you to walk on by, vaguely incensed at you for having led them on.

Maybe it was a lousy metaphor. Maybe any metaphor for love was lousy, if it made you mistake the poison for a drug.

Outside, she blinked at silver sunlight stabbing through ragged rain clouds. San Francisco's Chalice Pavilion lay across the Embarcadero from the ferry terminal. A squad of uniformed cops tweeted whistles at the dumbfounded pedestrians stumbling out of the revolving doors. In a week or so, this miraculous deliverance would be just another staple of the modern age, and none would think to ask how it was accomplished, any more than they asked how their cars carried them or electric lights lit their nights.

It was astounding, inspiring, and troubling, but she reminded herself she was here on business. Flagging down an aerocab, she folded her coat under one arm and resisted letting the pilot assist her with her satchel. She climbed onto the wing and slipped into the open passenger cabin. She gave the destination to the man, who whistled as he fired up the engines.

The cabbie asked, "So you came through the Chalice whatsit, ma'am?"

"As a matter of fact, yes," she answered. "I imagine you're getting a lot of traffic from there…"

"For as long as it takes 'em to finish that regional hub, maybe. But I won't see much custom if the swells can skip to their suburbs without leaving the building. Might have to trade in the wings for a bag of apples."

"I'm sorry to hear that," she said. "Change is always hard. But it won't mean the end of cabs, will it?"

"Not for folks who can't afford cabs," he said.

Before she could find a less hurtful line of conversation, the aero-cab dusted off, and the roar of the rotors spared her. She watched the Chalice pavilion recede to an odd little funereal urn on the mantel of San Francisco's teeming waterfront. They buzzed North Beach and Fisherman's Wharf, then skimmed the steely gray waters of the Bay churning with ferries, freighters, tuna boats, and the guano-streaked outpost of Alcatraz. All of this will be obsolete soon. The world just got smaller. Half of it is dead, and doesn't know it yet. And the new world, just being born? How many will fit in there?

She was letting her mind wander when she needed most to focus. To face this down was like staring into the sun. She had no idea what she was about to find, but even if the White Devil could be trust-ed, she was walking into the lair of the nefarious anarchist plot that had driven her to take up masked vigilantism. Her knees clasped the satchel, and she wondered if she weren't making a mistake not suiting up now and going in with all guns blazing.

The aerocab alighted on a landing pad awkwardly grafted onto a sprawling Georgian mansion amid a redwood forest on the shoulder of Mount Tamalpais. She couldn't see a sign, but places like Larkspur Cloisters didn't need to advertise.

Much like McLean Hospital, where her mother lived and died, Larkspur Cloisters was the kind of elegant private asylum where the quality families secreted their mad black sheep. "Sunny" Jim Rolfe, San Francisco's former mayor and, as of last month, Governor of California, was wont to dry out here after a particularly bad bender. If the Levelers were using it as a front, the trap could be sprung at any moment, but she still harbored doubts. Who did she trust less, the Ochlocrat or the White Devil? At least she knew her enemy's real name and had seen his face…

She paid the cabbie and asked him to keep the meter running. A weedy young doctor in a white linen suit with a starched collar and string tie greeted her on the landing pad. He looked askance at her, waiting until the noisy aerocab had powered down before asking, "Miss Seaton, good morning! Forgive me, but… you're a…Lynch… is that right?"

Matilda maintained her poker face, but her mind was in a tailspin. She'd been identified before she opened her mouth! Her mechanical hand twitched, and she realized by the wisps of smoke and odor of scorched fabric that she'd reflexively triggered the defenses concealed within it.

"I apologize," the doctor said. "I've overstepped myself. Dr. Throckmorton Crisp, at your service. We were told to expect a visitor, but…" She let an orderly take her coat, hat and satchel. Underneath, she wore a black suit of raw silk that looked quite smart and severe while being positively rife with concealed pockets.

"As per my telegram, I would like very much to interview these gentlemen." She handed him a slip of Majestic stationery. She didn't ask how the doctor she'd never met recognized her. Had the White Devil lured her all the way out west, only to ambush her? Had he given away her identity to her archenemies?

If this was an ambush, the short glass of sour milk between her and the trapdoor couldn't be in on the gag. Dr. Crisp smiled emptily at her for a long moment and said, "Well, that's… But of course." He pinched the fork of tension between his eyes, then polished his pince-nez on the lapel of his white coat. "I was about to inform you that it would be impossible, but seeing as you're…" Returning the spectacles to the bridge of his nose, the doctor waved his hands as if they'd fallen asleep. "That is to say, I'm sure something can be arranged. Of course, I thought…but never mind!"

He turned to lead her into the asylum, then slapped his forehead and said, "Oh, I nearly forgot…for your own safety, we ask that you wear this." He held out a peculiar metallic badge with VISITOR embossed on it above a tiny window through which two dials with numbers on them could be seen. While she looked blankly at him, he pinned it to the collar of her dress. The numbers clicked as they spun, then stopped at 43. His mouth quirked in a frown. He flicked the badge until it jumped to 53. "Not quite where it ought, but it'll serve… Are you, by any chance, wearing some form of magnet? They do play hob with the calibration."

"What is this?" she asked.

The doctor lifted his own lapel to reveal a badge that said STAFF, its dials set at 88. "A little invention of my own, actually… I call it a Sani-Meter. It passively monitors brain activity to determine a numeric estimate of the subject's mental state. We've had trouble with visitors who ought to be patients and vice versa, so this helps keep us informed."

Matilda looked searchingly at Crisp as her Sani-Meter clicked, dropping to 51. The doctor flicked it again, shrugged, and said, "Right this way…"

Matilda followed Crisp through glass doors that retracted into the wall, into a dazzling corridor of chrome, glass, and white tile, magnifying the gray day from rows of skylights. It made McLean look like some backward snakepit, and Matilda was reminded of the spas at Saratoga Springs as well-scrubbed inmates rolled past her in caneback wheelchairs by smiling orderlies.

"Dr. Crisp, I must confess, I'm a bit at sea here. These…patients… You keep them under these conditions?"

"Not like this, no. Our premium guests are sequestered in their own private ward. I have every confidence your family will find that we've done well by our charges."

"My…family…?"

Crisp leaned in close, wrestling with a devil on his shoulder before deigning to lay a hand on her artificial arm. "These are the most difficult cases to contain, never mind cure, but miracles almost happen every day, don't they?"

As if that explained everything, Crisp continued down the corridor to a nurse's station, a two-story panopticon tower overlooking four branching wings of cells. It looked like many other private asylums, except that the rooms were of plate glass and soundproof, if the naked fat man pacing his cell while blowing forcefully into a tuba was any indication.

Crisp signed some forms the nurse provided and led her down a hall past a spacious swimming pool, a salon, and a dayroom where a platoon of senescent oldsters performed an interpretive dance to Saint-Saens' "Aquarium" movement of Carnival of The Animals. They seemed happier as fish than anyone could ever be as a human.

Crisp stood by as an orderly unlocked a door like a bank vault at the end of the ward. She followed him down a flight of stairs into a deepening murk.

At the foot of the stairs, an orderly built like a circus roustabout escorted them down a corridor that passed a boiler room, an incinerator, and what appeared to be a museum of torture devices. At last, he stopped before a hatch like something from a submarine, turning to Matilda with his nervous hands clasped behind his back. "As you see, we've complied with every direction. I hope you'll relay that message to, erm, Mr. Lynch..."

Matilda smiled reassuringly though her head was swimming. As ever, Matilda found her steel in her father's gold. "He would be very disappointed to discover these...patients...were able to exploit contact with the outside world to...perpetrate criminal acts against society."

Crisp nodded, but he looked more than a bit nauseated, and his eyebrows tried to escape his forehead. "I...don't believe I follow... We were told—"

At her back, she heard the feeding slot in another armored door click open, and a husky voice whispered, "You here to see me, sister?" She stepped away from hot breath on the back of her neck.

Crisp reached past her and shut the slot with an acidic glance at the orderly. "I do apologize. We call none incurable, but..."

"I quite understand, Doctor. Open the door, please. I won't need protection."

"I trust you won't… The collars should serve as an effective deterrent, but if you require assistance, simply press the panic button on the back of your Sani-Meter." He smiled encouragingly until he said the word *panic*.

Twisting her wrist to ensure the batteries in her arm were properly seated, Matilda stepped through the hatch into the lair of the supreme council of the International Order of Levelers.

Two shadowy figures sat at an elevated table at the far end of a smoky cell papered with maps, manifestos, defaced photographs, and newspaper articles, all prolifically connected by lengths of particolored twine. An almost adorably tiny man in a strange sort of military uniform and a pointy crimson hood with a black capital A above the eyeholes stood and bowed deeply. "Signorigna War-Profiteer! So delighted you could at last answer our summons!"

Behind her, the door slammed shut, and a dreadful clank resounded as the bolt was thrown. "Summons?"

A split-second too late, she sensed someone behind her. Something clicked like a padlock about her throat, and she felt the merest tickle of electricity emanate from her strange new necklace. When her hand activated, the tickle became a lightning strike that sent her staggering to grab the back of the nearest chair. Her left arm hung from her shoulder like a ball and chain. She couldn't scratch her nose with it, let alone defend herself.

"Merely a taste of the local hospitality," the Ochlocrat replied. "They make us wear them to condition our behavior, but I am thinking perhaps you need it more than we. So many delusions, *Signorina*." The Ochlocrat took his seat. "You have flagrantly ignored our many attempts to coordinate our activities. Personal ads were taken out in the *Call*, the *Daily Worker*. Don't pretend you didn't see them!"

This wasn't going as she'd planned, to say the least. She had envisaged confronting her archenemies in costume, kicking their teeth in and dragging them to justice, or slyly interviewing them in the guise of a dilettante philanthropist to entrap them. She hadn't, in any of the scenarios she considered, imagined confronting the ringleaders of the cabal as a patron. "Baldassare Mucci, did your cabal sabotage the automata at Bethlehem Steel?"

The Ochlocrat laughed operatically at the mention of his real name. "You know we did, *cara mia*. But who else have you been seeing? Who was it that upstages us in so vulgar a fashion?"

"What do you mean?"

"The murders, the beheadings… It offends the sense of honor. This is not how it is done. Ask the Arsonist if you do not believe."

The man who'd collared her slouched towards his chair in an asbestos chainmail suit, his featureless mask wreathed in beetling blue flames from pilot lights in his collar. The hospital staff had confiscated his wrist flamethrowers, but she well recognized the Arsonist, a.k.a. Heiko Vikkunin, mastermind of the *Los Angeles Times* bombing and a hundred other heinous crimes. "I like women," he snapped, crossed his arms, and nodded vehemently as if settling an argument in his head.

"Ignore him," muttered the Ochlocrat. "He is quite insane."

On the Ochlocrat's other hand sat the notorious minister of propaganda, Dr. Pangloss, a cloaked apparition in a tricorne hat and a Venetian plague doctor's mask, the proboscis of which terminated in an outsized hypodermic syringe that dispensed a mind-enslaving narcotic, among other poisons. According to the White Devil, Pangloss was, in truth, a Dutch dope-peddler, pimp, and pornographer named Udo Clijsters, and had masterminded a terror campaign on exhibitions of *Wings* in which mustard gas was released into theaters, killing nearly 200 and wounding thousands more. "Opium is the religion of the muses," he said.

"You must admit, you haven't been keeping your end up," the Ochlocrat said. "In three years of hide-and-seek, your pathetic Silver Sentry has never once come close to exposing us. Give us a worthy adversary, at least. We should be on the top of the Most Wanted List, but nobody seems to know we hold their lives in our hands! One is measured by the stature of one's enemies. If I didn't know better, I'd suspect he was soft on us out of some perverse inversion of feminine timidity."

"Perhaps it's out of pity," Matilda said. She'd run the Ochlocrat down no less than twice, only to find that one was an automaton and the other a hostage bound and gagged in a replica of the anarchist mastermind's costume. It was only blind luck that she'd discovered the truth before she blew his head off. She didn't tell them that in all the years of red herrings and cold trails, she never thought to look at Father's financial records. "It wouldn't do for him to run you to ground in a posh insane asylum, would it? Perhaps if we were better apprised of your next nefarious scheme, we could make a better showing. Something at least worthy of the front page…"

"The end is packed into the beginning!" Pangloss roared. "The apple is in the bud, the worm in the blossom!"

Pumping a fist in the air like a mathematician calculating the final digit of Pi or an engineer who's just cracked perpetual motion, the Arsonist shouted, "I *like* women!"

"We are the makers of bloody revolution," the Ochlocrat ranted, leaping to his feet. "We kill kings! We behead nations!" Matilda had seen Mucci's mug shots and vital statistics. He was balding with bellicose eyebrows, no chin to speak of, and a preposterous mustache. Either he was wearing lifts or standing on an orange crate. "Trifle with us at your peril. Even as you foolishly give us succor, we plot your undoing!"

"This is the best of all possible worlds," growled Doctor Pangloss.

"I like *women*!" raged the Arsonist.

Her right hand searched various pockets, touching a derringer, tear gas, and throwing knives. Was she speechless, or was there simply nothing worth saying?

"Furthermore, we think that the iconoclastic currency of anarchism has expired. One never hears of deportations and Emma Goldman. It's all Stalin and the Comintern. Ergo! We must contemplate a new face for our campaign. You are not the only patron seeking our services, you know. Of late, our thoughts are much upon Russia. For myself, I am considering adopting the Crimson Curse as an operational nom de guerre and the rebranding of our whole enterprise." He unfurled a sleek new coat of arms. "Behold! The fearsome standard of the Total State Machine!"

Matilda had heard enough. Her left arm was sluggish, but she made it grasp the collar and snap it in half before they could shock her again. She flung it onto the table. "You've given us much to consider, gentlemen. Thank you for your time…" She bowed respectfully and banged on the door behind her.

"You have not been released! You must relay our demands to our patron and deliver our manifesto to the President—"

"I LIKE WOMEN!"

Matilda stepped through the door and came nose to nose with Dr. Crisp, who felt simply awful about the shock collar.

"Those men are using this asylum as a headquarters from which to launch a terror campaign against our government! They escape justice while giving orders that lead to strikes, chaos, murders—"

"As I told you," Crisp said with the earnest expression of one who would rather be anywhere else, "we followed your instructions to the letter."

She noticed his eyes pinned to her breast and took offense for a moment but then realized he was watching her Sani-Meter with a dismayed frown. Looking down as she tried to remove the badge without tearing a hole in her collar, she saw the number had dropped to 39.

She scribbled a terse note on a notepad and forced it into his hands. "We're changing the instructions."

Back in San Francisco, she checked into the Palace Hotel's presidential suite and sank into a hot bubble bath with a bottle of blind pig gin obtained from a trig bellhop.

She'd told herself that whatever else happened today, she would spend the rest of it getting drunk in the bath. She would sleep, then awaken at dusk to seek out a magnificent steak and a fine spaghetti dinner in North Beach, and then find a speakeasy she'd heard about where all the walls were waterfalls, and an automated jazz band so hot, no human dancefloor could keep up with it. She would play the only part that came harder than a flying armored crimefighting man: a woman at home in her own skin, enjoying her wealth, youth, and the limbs she still had left.

But it was no good. She could go to Chinatown and smoke opium or browbeat the ushers at the Chalice Pavilion to send her to the most scandalous gambling den in Hong Kong, but not for a moment would she forget what she'd learned or what it meant.

She soaked long enough for the steam to dissipate before springing back out of the tub, removing her half-sanforized clothes from the dry-cleaning caddy in the vestibule and striding to the elevators.

Damn him!

She checked out of the suite where Warren Harding died. After surveying the deadlock of taxis and cable cars out front, she walked eight blocks down Market to Chalice Pavilion in a driving rain just as all the streetlights ignited, making a jeweled mosaic of the streaming streets.

She waved her return invitation at the ushers and breezed through a much shorter line. She filed through the revolving door into the grand central pavilion, then out Door #1 for New York without sparing a thought for what had this morning seemed something of a miracle.

On the elevated train, she chanced to see the front page of the *American* in another commuter's hand, with a spectacular photo of a commuter dirigible engulfed in flames beneath a gruesome four-column banner headline: **TERROR BOMB EXPLODES OVER EAST RIVER; 17 AERO-FERRY PASSENGERS INCINERATED MID-AIR.** Between this Grand Guignol blow-off of a headline and the ensuing article were several portraits, presumably of the victims.

One of them was her.

At her stop, she double-timed down the stairs and bought a copy of each evening edition from the newsstand. She stormed the lobby of the Majestic and tilted her head so her hat hid her face as she passed the concierge, and used the express elevator by herself.

Just before she reached the penthouse, she pushed the Emergency Stop button and skimmed each front page as she sat on the operator's stool and had a good cry. They must have misidentified Elvira by her baggage and signature on the manifest. There was so little left that they couldn't get dental records or fingerprints.

When she'd read all there was, she was ready to confront Father. Funny how she always said *Father*, never *my father*, as if Romulus Lynch were the model, the only one, and the rest of humankind came out of eggs. Funny, the things you think about when you're dead.

She let herself in by the service door at the back of their kitchen. She found Father sitting in the library with a brandy snifter in one hand and an old family album in the other. The lenticular portrait of Father, Mother, Minerva, and Matilda on safari in South Africa in 1909, posing with a white rhino Father had just shot, danced on his trembling knee, glistening where his tears had fallen on it. She remembered the look in his eyes that day, staring into the molten red sun as if weighing whether to pluck it and wear it in his buttonhole.

He dropped them both when he saw her. Springing out of his overstuffed Moroccan leather chair, he crossed the room to clutch her by the arms in a fury of disbelieving relief. "My heart, my dove, I can't believe it's true. Say it's so, say you're no ghost, tell me…tell me…"

She returned his embrace, dropping the newspapers on the floor. "It wasn't me, Father." She let him cry into her shoulder for another minute, counting every tick of the ormolu clock before she told him, "It was all a mistake. They identified an actress who sometimes doubles for me at public functions. I've just been to San Francisco."

"What? Oh, you've patronized that upstart thug's teleportation palace, have you? Damned fool contraption. And why would you need to hire some woman to play you? You scarcely leave your rooms…" He ambled over to the sideboard for a fresh snifter, already recovered from his brief seizure of emotion. "So, did you get your father anything nice from San Francisco?"

"I went to Larkspur Cloisters, Father."

He dropped another snifter on the floor. The broken glass crunched underfoot as he approached her. "Why, girl? Whatever possessed you…?"

"You must have wondered when you heard the news if one of your little publicity stunts hadn't accidentally hit home."

He took her elbows in his hard, cold hands and shook her. "What do you know? Did you see…?" His oily eyes searched hers and found an answer to a question he dared not ask.

"Who are they, Father?"

"The Levelers? They are who they say they are…anarchists and madmen."

"But who finances their rhetoric? Who pays for these attacks, Father?"

"You already know, don't you? I taught you that, yes? Never ask what you don't already know. Yes, we pay for it. We arrange for their manifestos and sundry other nonsense to reach the papers; for all they know, the money comes from the Kremlin."

"Stop. They know, Father."

"What? But you asked—"

"Stop and tell yourself all of that again before you explain it to me. Explain to yourself how you paid for literal madmen to attack us, to kill workers and sow terror…to make me do this…!"

"My dear, the answer is so simple. I did it for you."

She stared into his glittering eyes until she couldn't bear it anymore. The worst part was, so far as he was concerned, it was probably true. Father's generation believed the bigger the lie you tried to live inside, the more grandly you hoodwinked the object of your affection, the more she was supposed to be won over. Years of frothy, stupid Fitzgerald stories had almost convinced her it was true, as well.

"Murders, Father. Bombs planted, factories burned, women and children abducted and held to ransom. Lies and propaganda spread, inspiring who knows how many more crimes. Don't lay it at my feet."

"But what would you have me do? Do you remember when you went out hunting Easter Eggs at the old family place and how irate you were when you didn't find any? Inconsolable. You cried until you wet yourself, then you fainted…"

Irritated at the digression, she nodded impatiently. "I was four." There was no point arguing.

"Well, it's just the same when you put on that fool suit of armor and take to the skies."

She raked tears out of her eyes and fixed him with an even colder stare. "You…know…?"

"Do you really believe I'm so oblivious, my dear?"

Suddenly, she was swimming upstream on a rushing river of long-bottled anxiety. "I was going to tell you…"

"I wasn't going to make you. I knew you'd probably quit the moment I gave my blessing, the same as your… Anyway, I've been proud as hell, naturally, of the way you've fought for us…"

"I fought them because I thought they were a threat to us, to the American way of life. If I'd known they were just some actors you hired…"

"Their rhetoric is quite sincere. They desire to overthrow the government and replace it with a new state of nature. They wish us harm. They work for our downfall. I just put them where they can be contained."

"They work for *you*, Father. The fear they foment is just a campaign to sell guns. Isn't it?" When he said nothing, she screamed, "Answer me, Father! I'm coming apart. I'm made of lies!"

"Yes, nobody could have predicted that you would react as you did, but consider the lilies of the field, Matilda. You are something more than you were. What you do…you help to preserve order, you inspire millions…"

"Don't change the subject, Father. Why…?"

"Why? I should've thought that much was obvious. We won the War to End All Wars and we don't make plowshares. The economy is whistling past the graveyard, and the strikes and marches are getting more violent, but some of the smart set can see what's coming if something drastic isn't done. Extremists on both sides have their own agendas. They're playing weak sister now, but if they worm their way into Washington, they'll have us all singing the Internationale. There are mutterings, but they're too timid even to act out their fantasies of class war. If they have their way, we'll never fight another war again."

"Would that really be so horrible?"

"It would be Hell on Earth! War is the natural state, my child. It's the only time any nation can be governed. Without war, men make everything else into war. Look at the state of us, limping away from another crash with no plan to guide us, relying on the whim of every drunken immigrant who can pull a lever to decide what, if anything, gets done. Ours is a necessary evil, and the world likes to forget it.

We needed a bottled enemy, Matilda. The government has been most accommodating with orders and oversight…and our products will be more necessary than ever, soon."

Her indrawn breath tasted like cold steel. "What's going to happen, Father?"

"You'll learn soon enough when all of this is yours. I won't be here forever, and when you're in my place, it'll take everything you have to hold onto it." Brushing back the wild silver wings of hair flaring from his temples, he turned to a stack of portfolios on the chifferobe. "I was going to save these for the right time, but I believe it's come now." Opening a folio with a nervous flourish, he held up a commercial artist's rendering of a new logo for Lynch Munitions.

She thought she'd fallen as far as she could. She'd thought there was no nerve within her left unplucked.

"Speechless, eh?" Father chuckled. "I was rather proud of them, myself…"

She couldn't bring herself to touch the picture of the old familiar logo, now superimposed over a stylized image of the Silver Sentry brandishing a flag and a gauss rifle.

"You've made me…a hood ornament."

"I made you what you already are. A walking, talking, flying, fighting advertisement for our product."

"I told them to stop it, Father. I told them that if the Levelers ever threaten the public again, I'll take the whole arrangement to the authorities. And then they tried to murder me…"

"You what?!"

"You heard me."

"Well, I'll straighten them out."

"Let's straighten it *all* out. I won't have you using my likeness. I won't go along with your insane scheme. And I won't…ever…run this company as it is."

His face flushed a deep maroon. His breath whistled out of his nostrils, almost steam. "You ungrateful termagant! You've never known real danger. If something were chasing you, how far would you get without the fancy leg I bought you?"

She'd been incensed—mortified—but only now, the raw rage that drove her to don the Silver Sentry armor flooded her brain with burning blood. The urge to strike him almost overwhelmed her. "If something were chasing me, I wouldn't run."

Did a flare of remorse fill his rheumy, tearful eyes? If so, it was the last gasp of a dying fire. "You can't mean this. You've had a busy day, but you… Oh, my dear, let's forget all this, I'm just so glad you're alive—"

"That makes one of us," she replied. "I'm sick to death of it, Father. A woman was killed because they thought she was me. I won't let you make us worse than the villains we fought in the last war."

"Then be dead," he said, "and damned." Throwing the portfolio in the fireplace, he turned his back on her to watch it burn. "I've been summoned to identify the corpse, and I will. I'll swear to it in court."

"Father, this is insanity…" She reeled, but she could feel a cold resolve stiffening her spine.

Under his breath, he said, "I can't lose my country."

"Of course, not. Countries are hard to come by. Have it your way, then." Wiping her face clean of ugly emotion, she offered him a chrome-dipped smile. "Yes, that'll be fine. It's the best idea you've come up with since you had Mother committed."

He moaned, searching for something else he wouldn't regret destroying with his bare hands. He looked lost. "Just go, won't you? Have pity on an old man. I lost a daughter today…"

She stormed out of the penthouse with a half-packed carpet bag under one arm and the satchel under the other. She took the express elevator to the hangar and ordered the valet to bring around her

Mercedes aeroroadster. Evidently, he hadn't read the paper. She threw her bags in the back and climbed behind the steering yoke, fired the ignition and was hurled out into the dark above Central Park.

She saw none of it. Steering by feel, blinking through streaming tears, she felt she had to talk to someone, but she couldn't return to the White Devil, not like this.

She turned on the wireless and strapped on the headset, and she requested the operator put her through to a mid-Manhattan commercial number.

No doubt, she was making a mistake. It was *her* mistake.

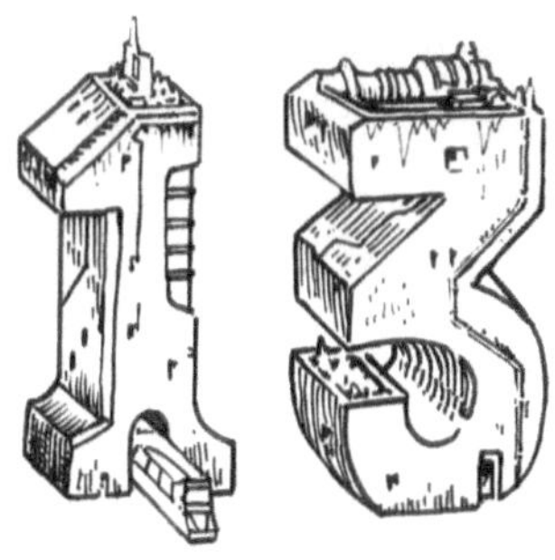

The reason for evil in the world is that people are not able to tell their stories.

— Carl Jung

March 10, 1932 | New York City

I n an improvised concert hall far beneath the sidewalks of Manhattan, eighty-seven men and women lifted their instruments at a twitch of the Conductor's baton. They commenced their rendition of the Viennese version of the overture of *Tannhäuser.*

The string section was weak in spite of his best efforts. It was difficult to find the right kind of fingers among the degenerate pool of mongrel masses of America. But the potential variety was so vast, the lines for bread and soup like an open-air slave bazaar, yours for the taking. What they lacked in innate gifts, they more than compensated with a vulgar vigor that he could not correlate with bloodlines and was forced to acknowledge as uniquely American.

If you knew where to look, there were even some with talent and training. Professional musicians drank in the bathtub speakeasies around the Musicians' Union Local 802 on West 48th or played for pennies in the park. But it was far more satisfying to find utterly raw materials, to sculpt beetle-browed subhuman laborers to coax achingly delicate music out of any instrument you placed in their waiting hands. Moreover, while musicians stuck together and gossiped incessantly, these milling legions of superfluous, hungry men and women were never missed when they failed to come home.

And for all their self-conscious egomania, he had never found a people so easy to dominate. A moment of casual conversation to reveal the essential self, a flash of eye contact, and the blankest of slates was yours to command.

He'd spent far too much time cultivating his orchestra to look for the right instrument to fill every chair. It was the only risk he took, but a large one. The quality of phonograph recordings here was abysmal, and he could not lose himself in any of the so-called orchestras in this barbarous zoo. He was possessed by murderous fury when anyone else conducted the band.

Another coded telegram this morning. Out of the mundane gibberish, as ever, the same commands: PROCEED. ESCALATE. And his next target.

In the two years since the crash, he had already eliminated over a dozen. In between, he had assiduously cultivated a cover identity that had blossomed into a life all its own while perfecting his therapeutic discipline.

How reverently he remembered the demonstration in medical school, the surgeon cutting into and performing an appendectomy upon a man sedated only by a master mesmerist. The man conversed in a sleepy voice, quite unfazed by the blood, the strange hands, and the knives violating his body. The young student had been so fascinated by the utter control, the calm command of the organism, that he immediately abandoned medical school to pursue the vivisection of the mind.

Studying psychotherapy under Jung and hypnotism under Caligari, reviewing the texts of Cagliostro and Mesmer, he took a doctorate at age twenty-five. However, his natural aptitude got ahead of his still-green character, and he ran afoul of the law for various abuses. The Kaiser's government saw enough value in him to give him a provisional army commission as a new kind of platoon commander. Soon, mostly by surviving all his superior officers, he held a Colonel's rank and ran a battalion. However, in the field, he preferred to wield a company that was closest in size and function to a philharmonic orchestra. When he controlled each and every infantryman, he could wield them like a sword. It was something almost indecently joyous to stride across a battlefield like that, all but invincible, looking out of a hundred pairs of eyes and smiting with two hundred hands.

When Wetzler came here, he was driven to form an orchestra in 1903, and he was foolish enough to invite Strauss to conduct a festival program of his work. The lumpen peasants humiliated him—fifteen rehearsals before the master could stomach the sound of them, and even so, they made a dog's breakfast of his *Symphonia Domestica* and broke down in the middle of *Don Quixote*. Not long after, Wetzler dissolved the orchestra and went home to Frankfurt. Much as the Conductor would have to do…but when?

Like the creation of musicians from mongrel trash, his greater mission could not be rushed. It required the selection and grooming of so many pieces, none of whom would ever realize until it was too late that they were part of an orchestra, or what the sheet music would compel them to play.

A blue light bulb set into his podium blinked. Someone was calling his direct emergency line rather than the answering service. His office was in the Modern Dentrifice Building on West 54th, between the Orthotex Private Detection Agency and the Mothers of Free Nations, twenty floors above his private concert hall.

He dropped his baton, and the orchestra fell silent. A tympanist erupted in a hacking cough, forcing the Conductor to gesture for two ushers to drag him out of the room.

He took up the telephone and said, "Hallo?"

"Doctor, I apologize but didn't know where else to turn…"

"I apologize. Who is this, please?" he asked, but he knew quite well. Only this morning had he taken rather drastic steps, sacrificing two of his favorite brass players, to bring about the crisis that had driven his patient to call him.

"It's Matilda Lynch, Doctor. I hope I'm not disturbing you. I'm at a sort of a rooftop speakeasy called the Hole in the Sky, and I'm afraid I'm a bit tight…"

"Not a bit of it, my dear. Only if something is bothering you am I disturbed, but if you would feel more comfortable, I can meet you at my office immediately…"

"Oh, I hope it would be no trouble…"

"No trouble, Miss Lynch. As it happens, I am merely listening to music… Anything I could do to help you would bring meaning to a meaningless evening."

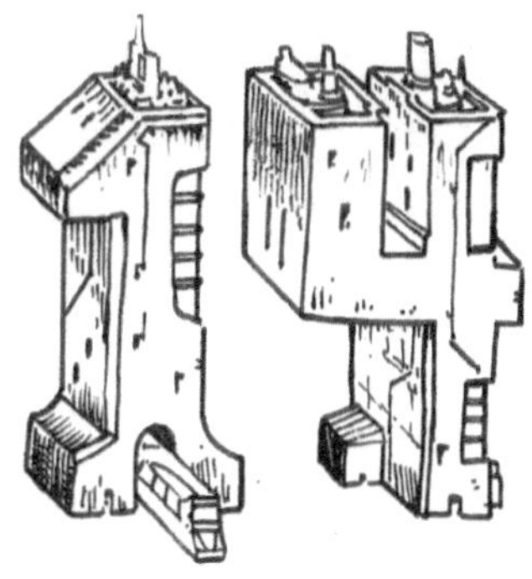

I've known what it is to be hungry, but I always went right to a restaurant.

—Ring Lardner

April 20th, 1932 | Rockwell City, Iowa

The Stutz Bearcat they stole in Fort Dodge threw a rod on the muddy road out of Pomeroy, and they'd been walking all night, each carrying a gun in either hand and a sack of cash slung over either shoulder. They'd hit nine banks in seven towns in the last four days and came up empty in all but two. Sleeping in abandoned farmhouses and listening to the car radio all night, they wondered where all the cops were. They hadn't had a square meal in two days, and they were just about ready to form a triangle and blow each other's brains out when they smelled the barbecue.

A full moon shone feebly down out of a sackcloth sky deprived of stars. Dick and Harry argued about whether they had strayed into Hell or the hollow center of the Earth. Tom swore at their stupidity. "It's the goddamn smoke, you idiots," and there was no disputing the powerful aroma of it. They all wiped sweat from their brows and drool from their chins as they turned off the highway to wade through the corn.

Halfway across the field, the smoke wafted through the stalks, and they could hear the squealing of a thousand pigs, so loud and urgent, it started to sound like amplified human speech. At the edge of the cornfield, they stopped under a stand of oaks.

An open pit the size of an Olympic swimming pool had been dug in the back forty between two cornfields. The pit was filled to the brim with pigs. Two tractors and a stake truck with a trailer were parked at the far end, and a pair of International Harvester Farmhands stalked around the edges, spraying the unfortunate pigs with flamethrowers. The bulky green diesel-powered suits made strutting ten-foot ogres of the hayseeds who operated them. Extra arms at their sides could do the work of forklifts or steam shovels. He whistled. Such a gadget could let one lucky rube put twenty on the breadline. If this was how they coped with surplus hogs, what'd they do with surplus people?

Only when they'd gotten a smoky eyeful of this maddening scene did they realize they were not alone. A couple dozen men stood under the trees watching the bonfire, licking their lips and staring in appalled awe. Most of them wore the dungarees-and-checked-shirt uniform of the local peasantry, but some were hobos in a motley potpourri of rags and castoffs. All looked like they hadn't eaten in days, and the squealing of the burning pigs only stoked the rumbling of their stomachs.

Tom sidled over to the nearest rube. "What're they, sick?"

The man shook his head, holding a sweat-cured straw hat like he was fixing to take a bite out of it. "Can't feed two-dollar hogs on forty-seven cent corn," he said.

Apparently, they couldn't afford to shoot two-dollar hogs with eighteen-cent shotgun shells, either. The pigs stampeded from end to end of the pit, trampling each other to escape the crisscrossing streams of flame.

"You a farmer?"

"Used to be," the hungry man spat. "Old bastard Squires bought up all the farms that went under, so I was lucky to work land that been in my family four generations as a hand. *Then* he got all them fancy machines on credit, so they cut us loose. *Then* they had a bumper crop after three years of drought, and now there's too much food to store in them grange bunkers, so they're just burning what they can't unload at a profit."

"They can't sell 'em, so they're just burning 'em up?" Dick cried.

"That's what the man said, ya lummox," Tom snapped.

"Reckon they'll plow it under before it's all too burnt," said a cadaverous old man in an ancient officer's greatcoat, dripping with grand epaulets and gold braid. "We'll have our share, boys. Ain't no worse than what we faced in Cuba when they left us to starve at Matanzas. A man learns patience in war, and this is just a new kind of war…"

"That just doesn't seem fair…" Harry muttered.

"You want fair?" Tom shouted. "They got all kinds of fair over in Russia, you go see what a handful of fair from Joe Stalin looks like. This here's America! We don't wait for it to be given to us. We take it!" Tom cocked his Thompson and dropped the sacks of cash at the farmer's feet.

Most of the men just stared at him with hungry, despairing eyes, but more than a few shouted, "Yeah!" They lifted shovels, pitchforks, and branches and came stomping out of the trees in a loose skirmish line.

Tom had to spray half a drum of bullets into the pig pit to get the Farmhands' attention. Most bank robbers and gangsters preferred the Lynch gun because of its silent efficiency. Still, the Haywire Gang's unique difficulties with complex machines, especially those with magnetic fields, made the old trench sweepers a necessary evil. Sometimes, too, the noise came in handy.

The two rubes in the Farmhands cut off their flamethrowers. A third rube came out from behind the tractor with a shotgun.

"Ain't nothing here for you," the armed rube shouted—a robust, ruddy man who'd never missed a meal.

Tom watched the pigs rush around trying to get out and saw how, if they worked in concert, they could make a ramp out of their bodies and climb out, but they just struggled in vain, and some of them were even gnawing on the charred flesh of their dead. When that wasn't enough to turn his stomach, he wondered if even burning human flesh would smell wrong now, if there was any motive stronger than hunger.

If there was, he held it in his hands.

"We just want a fair share of what you folks're throwing away," Tom called out. Circling one side of the pit while Dick came around the other at the head of a hungry mob, they approached the foreman by his tractor, and the engine developed an arrhythmia. The foreman pointed the shotgun but didn't put much heart into it when he saw the identical bookends of Tom and Dick with their submachine guns.

"Hell, take what you want, it's no skin off my ass," the foreman grumbled. A Farmhand came stomping up behind Dick, whirring and clanking but stealthy as an Apache brave amid all the porcine commotion. Just as it spread its claws to squash Dick like a bug, the Farmhand tripped on its own flamethrower hose and toppled into the pig pit.

Thrashing and honking, the overturned machine became the ramp the pigs had been pining for. Before the other Farmhand could move to stop them, they came scrambling up it and ran squealing into the night, many of them trailing flames from their bristly hides. The pigs fanned out into the cornfield, leaving smoke and blooming patches of fire amid the dry, combustible stalks.

"You blamed fool, look what you done did!" the foreman roared as he ran off toward the Squires farm compound. The still-upright Farmhand tried to run the hungry men off with his flamethrower, slinging wild gouts of aerosolized kerosene in their path. The rubes circled him and threw their backs into shoving the staggering man-machine into the pit.

"Everybody grab a pig!" Tom shouted, and the hungry men cheered. Lowering themselves into the pit, they formed a bucket brigade and passed several dozen blackened carcasses into the trailer of the stake truck. When the truck was full, one of the men told Tom about the hobo jungle where they'd been living, near a railroad spur on the edge of the next town. Between fifty and a hundred tramps and not a few families lived there and would be mighty glad of the feast.

"Can't call this a feast," Tom said. Lighting a cigarette off a burning pig and tipping his hat to a bloodied, beshitted farmhand as he clambered out of the pit and fled into the burning cornfield, he asked where to find the nearest decent general store.

The odd caravan of trucks and tractors rolled into Rockwell City on County Blacktop D20 just before midnight. When he saw them coming, a lone deputy took to his heels, leaving the Woolworths and the A&P unprotected. Piling out of the trailer and climbing down off the tractors, they smashed the big display window and rushed into the darkened emporium. The triplets, who had whipped them up in a fury of righteous rage stood back and watched from the sidewalk.

"This sure beats robbing banks," Harry said. "Beats it cold. Women love a hero of the people."

"You've been reading too many smooshes," said Dick.

Harry took a swing at Dick. He missed, but every streetlight on the little main drag blew out in a shower of sparks. Tom shouted at them to cut it out, and a fire hydrant burst and gushed into the street.

He heard a hand-crank siren wailing somewhere on the far side of the little town and whistled for the mob to beat feet. They came stumbling out of both stores laden with flour, sugar, coffee, potatoes, corn, canned goods, and various sundries. Several came out of the Woolworths in new coats and hats, with cigars and nylon stockings spilling out their pockets. Tom ordered them to mount up and got behind the wheel of the truck. Dick and Harry each drove a tractor to keep them as far apart as possible.

They found the hobo jungle just beyond a ridge overlooking the town rail yard, where the company had pushed a small mountain of decommissioned boxcars off the tracks. The new unmanned trains redlined in and out of the yard too fast to catch, and the automated railroad bulls fired rubber bullets at anything that moved within their domain. Sometimes, a freight train was sidelined or stopped for water on the curve, which the hobos had tapped for showers and sewage.

The result was a kind of junkyard high rise of haphazardly stacked apartments. A ragged, beaten-down crowd stood round a few barrel-fires when they came in, but the smell of barbecue and the triumphant cheers of the men clinging to the tractors hit them before they pulled into the jungle and a small army piled out to unload the trailer.

The pigs were triaged by the ladies of the camp. Moonbeam Sue chopped up and doled out those already cooked through, and spitted the still-pink ones to roast over an open flame. Queen Nell deputized posses to whip up side dishes. Jugs of shine and roll-ups of fragrant muggle were passed around, and a guitar, accordion, and a pocket Theremin were pressed into service. Someone called for a bugwalk number, and the combo assayed a pretty shimmy rendering of "The Wrong Side of The Room." A few of the more inebriated or liberated parties paired off to dance or just spin in circles until they got dizzy.

Just as the feast was ready, two big hobos buttonholed Tom and led him away to the carcass of an old coal-fired locomotive. An ancient tramp slouched in the engineer's seat like a throne and offered him a nip from a platinum flask. "Name's Doc How, Emperor of the North. Been riding rails since they were invented, and never gave the bastards a penny. We're mighty grateful for the spread, boy, but you must know you'll bring us heat."

A slat-ribbed tramp with ringworm sores all over him whispered in Doc How's ear. Tom heard him well enough to make out *that Haywire Gang, wanted men, and a big reward.*

"Sa'matter, Ringworm? Free food gotcha down?" Doc How yawned in Ringworm's face. "Not to worry," he told Tom. "We ain't rats. We abide by the Code Duello. The Calhoun County sheriff holds no sway here. We're just over the line…and a thing or two I know about the Sheriff of Dumont County makes him my slave."

"Aw, you ain't up to date," Ringworm flared.

Someone brought Doc How a pie tin piled with pork chops, an ear of corn, whipped potatoes and gravy, and a buttered biscuit. "Eat your pheasant, drink your wine," Doc How said by way of grace. Your days are numbered, bourgeois swine."

The conversation fell off as the Emperor sampled the fare. Makeshift plates were passed around only after he gave a thumbs-up. Ringworm's piping voice was a grave violation of hobo protocol. "These yeggs are on the Most Wanted list, Doc. G-men made a deal with that nabob what telephone-zaps folks wherever they wanna go almost before they leave. They can come through any proper door and get the drop on you. I heard—"

"It's called teleportation, Worm." Doc How sucked butter off his fingers. "And I need to know what you heard like my asshole needs taste buds. These boys tried to teach you bums a lesson tonight. Maybe you shut up and soak it in."

"But Doc—"

Tom noticed Ringworm's eyes riveted on the fire. Moonbeam Sue swanning around Dick and Harry, dancing languidly with both, each with a grasping hand on an amply curved hip. They looked ready to come to blows over her, which suited Sue fine, but the roasting pigs spat grease, the fires flared up, and the Theremin moaned painfully every time one of them looked daggers at the other.

"Let 'em go," How said. "She'll keep them both happy. She's a social welfare statistician. She's making one of every kind of male as part of a great experiment. You don't want her too, do you?"

Tom shook his head. He took a big drink of something in a jar without smelling it and passed it on empty, grimacing as his insides turned to fire.

"But not because you don't want her. You must do what they won't, want what they don't, to try to be special, not part of a set. Just as you ain't touched a crumb of this sumptuous repast you delivered. You ain't eating, 'cos something's eating you. Am I lying?"

Tom started to nod, then shook his head angrily. The old tramp was trying to get him all mixed up. "Me and my brothers…"

"You're not brothers, little brother Haywire. Anyone with eyes can see that. You're the same man three times, trying to fit in one pair of shoes. It's a big world, but the money power's trying to make it small. I wouldn't hazard a guess how you ended up like this, but if you can't make it right, you'll end up making a bigger mess than that Chalice fellow who's killing the trains."

"I reckon we'll get out of your hair with the next freight," Tom said.

"I didn't say that," Doc How said. "You got instincts, kid, but you don't know what to do with them. You listen to Daddy Long-Legs?"

Tom shrugged. "Folks are looking for answers…"

"He's a tool, but the bad feelings he's stirring up are real, so they let him rake the muck, so long as it serves their purposes. Kinda like you, son. You're playing their game. Stealing money that won't be good to wipe your ass with, come the revolution. Giving folks false hope, and that's why they play along. Slap your pictures up in every post office so folks will sing songs about you, then happily give you up and watch you fry. Keep the lambs in line for the slaughter while they're cheering for the Judas goat."

Tom thought about this, but it was hard to sit still for. The accusations got under his skin like bedbugs, and he couldn't find the words to scratch them.

"I don't approve of robbing and killing," Doc How went on, "but nobody seems to want to let us live, so far be it from me to tell anyone else how to try. I heard you boys never shot nobody down cold, but a lot of folks are dead, because of that witchy thing you do…I guess the eggheads would call it an entropy field, but folks around here would call it a jinx. Reckon, you got off on the wrong foot with the law because of that jinx. Maybe, if you were to give folks *real* hope, or at least more of what you gave us tonight…maybe you could turn that jinx around. If for no other reason than that, it sure would put a firecracker up the ass of whoever done you wrong."

Tom still couldn't find words. Smoke got up under his eyelids, and a single tear ran down his cheek. He wiped it onto the sleeve of his shirt.

"They stopped running passenger cars through here anyway," grumbled Doc How, "and less freight every day. Reckon all that rolling stock's going through those damned teleportals now. Soon, them trains will go the way of the buffalo, and we'll have to steal horses and become Injuns."

Tom looked around for Dick and Harry, but they and Moonbeam Sue were gone. He hit a fat, sloppily rolled joint until the hobo jamboree sounded like blue Harlem jazz. "I reckon maybe we could stay a while," he said.

Doc How smiled wearily and puffed on a fifty-cent cigar. "Well, son, I don't recall saying that, either…"

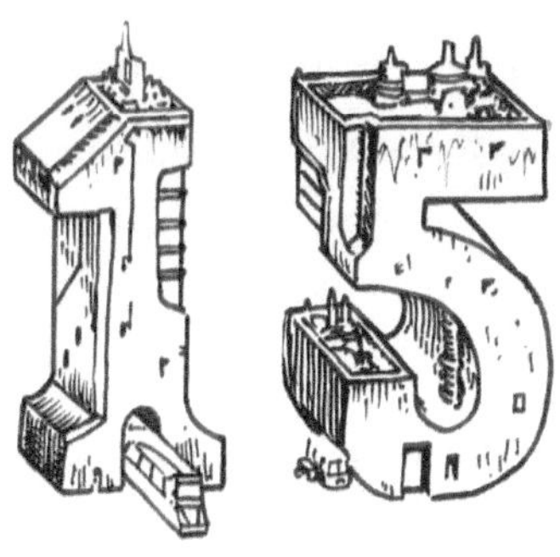

If you see ten troubles coming down the road, you can be sure that nine will run into the ditch before they reach you.

—Pres. Calvin Coolidge

May 2, 1932 | Cicero & Utopia, Illinois

To **Old Man Hussy, there was no more captivating example of** the eternal struggle betwixt man and his all-powerful nemesis, the World, than a fat man eating.

You could keep your boxers, your wrestlers, your dancing and cycling marathons and ipecac races. Man's eternal enemy was not another man, Woman, or even the World, if you wanted to put a fine point on it. Man's worst enemy was himself, and he used the World as a cudgel to beat himself to death, if possible, with an audience.

"You take a big, chubby boy," Hussy said, "one of those ham-assed apple-stealers with a nose pigged good and permanent from peering into sweetshop windows. He knows in his blubber-buried bones that his appetite will be the death of him, but he feeds it like a furnace because it's the only thing that puts out the gnawing fear that he has no other purpose.

"Every man is a big fat pig if you can see his appetites and the way he wears them. Everyone loves a fat man because he takes in the world at its sweetest and shows how even that turns to ugly, damning weight in the end, but he still can't help himself, so why should you?"

And that's why Hussy's Automat always had a chair on a platform in the front window, and any fat man of stature could sit in the chair and eat for free, so long as he did so in a colorful way that invited passersby to stop and stare, point and laugh, and then come in for a meal.

On holidays, the fat man would wear a costume, and on Saturdays, he was served by children dressed up as piglets and calves and chickens, the fat man in a gold-chased toga and laurel leaves in his role as Emperor Nero or Saturn, devourer of the gods. Hussy was no friend to men, but he was ever an astute and tireless student of the human spirit.

This new fellow had been a sensation all week, ever since Hussy was jawing with the cook about new gimmicks, and the cook suggested he find a fellow who looked like Herbert Hoover.

Hussy liked the President enough to take umbrage at the notion, but the cook convinced him it was the best kind of promotion, one that would equally motivate those who loved and hated him. For the hungry Republican, the robust leader dining carelessly on a never-ending banquet promised good times around the corner. And the malcontents could take it as a slur on a haughty president more likely to send aid to hungry hogs than starving voters.

Hussy was still chuckling at this idea and almost feeling remorse that as soon as he could afford it, he would fully automate the kitchen, and then he'd have no one to talk to, when he saw this fat fellow rubbing his belly and mooning over the window display. He nearly choked to death on a mouthful of rhubarb cobbler.

Speak of the Devil, he thought as he found himself looking into the slitted eyes of the man he'd voted for in the last election.

Never one to balk at grabbing fortune by the forelock, Hussy immediately put the Hoover lookalike to work. He wasn't nearly as fat as the sideshow oddities that usually filled the chair, but he was truly an eating machine. Hussy would have worried that he was eating more than he could possibly earn out if the bulk of the meals he consumed weren't cut with Avicel, a wonder additive of indigestible cellulose derived from sawdust, and Ambrosia, that new meat substitute everyone was talking about.

In its fight to adapt and go unnoticed among humans, Kid Amoeba had learned much from observing men but far more from the radio. Its favorite program was *Cassius the Tyrant-Biter*. Everyone who wasn't secretly an agent of sinister foreign powers loved that brave dog, but imitating him had only brought it grief. Far more useful, though most of the comedy went over its head, was *The Jungle Bunch*, sponsored by Mentone Brain Tonic, which followed the misadventures of a temporarily penniless Wall Street wizard, J. Hammond Egger, and his harsh education at the hands of his shrewd but clownish hobo cronies, Porky Pine and Woodchuck Woods.

There was something obvious yet unfathomable about how the financier, clearly a scion of humanity's ruling caste, was constantly humiliated by two of the most unfit specimens of the species, yet never bettered himself. From repeated listenings, the Kid had come to conclude that the lesson imparted, whether they knew it or not, was that even an elite specimen was helpless when taken out of its suited environment. Perhaps the only true measure of fitness was adaptability. Thus, it had concluded that it was far more fit to survive in this world than any of the sick, sad creatures who inhabited it. But it had traveled far and wide without finding anything like a home, let alone any creature like itself.

And so, the thing that still thought of itself as Kid Amoeba had decided to reproduce.

Of all the alien customs it still struggled to understand, it had been most difficult to learn all the rules that governed feeding and reproduction. Children were paraded around with little or no fear of predators, yet how the species hatched them was a zealously guarded secret. Its own instincts told it that before it could multiply, it must grow, and to grow, it must eat, but fulfilling even the simplest of its needs in this strange new world was a baffling ordeal.

Its native instincts told it to eat whatever was too small to eat you, but this had led to one conflict after another. While it had been easy at first because wherever it went, wild dogs seemed to follow, after hearing Cassius heroically save a diplomat's son from Bolshevik kidnappers, it felt a kind of sickness whenever it ate a dog or cat, as if the meat had somehow spoiled. From the Jungle Bunch, it learned that this novel form of poisoning was called guilt. It had resolved to avoid it and rededicated itself to living as the dominant species lived.

In the three years since it came here, it had roamed the nation, mostly on foot, performing odd jobs until something inevitably went wrong, then running away, changing its shape, and starting over. It had mastered most human behaviors except speech. Somehow, it could not use its voice without alerting all within earshot that it was not like other men.

By trial and error, it had perfected its camouflage, studying the rootless men walking, hitching, and riding the rails. They were innocuous enough not to attract the authorities but large enough not to present a target to predators.

Whenever it saw a line, it joined and waited and sometimes earned a sandwich, a cup of coffee, or maybe half a doughnut. Often enough, it was picked out of the line to do some odd job or other, usually lifting something that may or may not belong to its employer, and delivering it somewhere else. But no matter how it tried, something always went wrong, so it had become adept at running and hiding.

Since then, it had kept a low profile. However, where it once struggled to keep its membrane constricted into a fair replica of the human form, it became so accustomed to the strain that it had difficulty relaxing into its native shapelessness. It had grown so accustomed to wearing the articulated human skeleton it stole from a doctor's office that it never took it out anymore. This was profoundly disturbing to the Kid, for while it had no memory of its existence before it walked among humans, it felt at some molecular level the wrenching loss of its true essence and a fear almost as fundamental as that of being eaten and digested at the prospect of truly becoming one of them, and forgetting it was ever anything else.

Kid Amoeba soon realized that it could never hope to survive alone. The impulse to multiply arose soon after and became an obsession. Split into multiple daughter forms, it could establish enough of a presence to rediscover its true form and purpose, or at least stake out a habitat without having to hide. Maybe even take over…

To that end, the engagement at Hussy's Automatic Cafeteria was a happy accident. Each day, eating itself into a stupor in the display window, growing more obese until its belly sagged halfway to the floor. When its shift ended with the supper rush, it staggered to the hobo university on Bughouse Square if a cot could be found or sprawled torpidly in an alley when one couldn't, dreaming of the many stories embedded in all the myriad proteins it had consumed. Every night, as it pretended to sleep, it compiled and stored the day's haul in preparation for its imminent fission. Most of it was vegetal dross, an industrial by-product with no nutritional value, but some secret ingredient in it inspired disturbingly vivid dreams of home.

But just as its plan had begun to lurch towards fruition, fate dangled before it another irresistible distraction. It was tucking into a punchbowl of rancid chili spaghetti and a cold stack of stale hotcakes when something cut through the miasma of deep-fried sawdust to tickle its olfactory receptors like a horsehair in its nostrils. It found its attention irresistibly drawn to a pair of diners who'd just been seated in the middle of the cafeteria as they surveyed with dubious expressions the items they'd ordered for lunch.

Hussy's Automatic Cafeteria was open twenty-four hours a day, but the chairs were wired, so they administered increasingly painful electrical shocks if you sat too long without ordering anything. Customers came and went in waves and seldom attracted its interest more than the food on its plate.

Everything on the menu smelled basically the same, so it wasn't what they were eating but something they'd brought in. Both wore dark green coveralls with *Chalice Co.* embroidered on the back and a grail logo on the right shoulder. Once they'd finished ridiculing the food and the coffee that spurted out of a spigot on their table, they resumed an argument about something called the stock market.

"I'm telling you, Moe. This picture radio gimmick RCA is working on is the wave of the future. It's gonna change everything."

"In a pig's eye, it will. RCA stock has topped out. Everybody's got a radio, and if you think they're gonna let 'em drop that television jazz on the market in this economy, you should save your money for a bridge I wanna sell you."

"For crying out loud, don't start with that 'they' baloney again. If there was some nabob in the patent office deciding what can get invented and what can't, we'd still be on a breadline, pal."

"Listen, teleportation is gonna get this country moving again. Folks can live in Rapid City and commute to work in Hollywood. Something like television would have the exact opposite effect. Make the world come to them while they just sit on their couches. Fill people's heads up with a bunch of fantasy hokum until they don't know what's real and what ain't. Something like that would be worse than opium."

"Well, not everybody can afford to teleport. Maybe the rest of the world will need a pill or two of electric smoke."

"Save your money, Joe. The boss is gonna come around and take us public, and when he does, we're gonna be on the ground floor."

"Aw, you're nuts. *If* he sold shares, and I don't see why he would, we're in the basement. The swells will make out like Xmas on preferred stock, while the rest of us…" By way of emphasis, he elbowed the wreckage of a chicken pot pie onto the floor.

Understanding nothing of the talk and noting nothing remarkable about their appearances, the Kid was so driven to distraction by them that it stared at them with eyes extruded like a snail's, nostrils gaping avidly to drink in their mysterious odor as it absently shoveled rubbery pancakes into its ear.

"You'll see," Moe said as he scraped the last gelid glob of New England clam chowder from a paper cup and rinsed out his mouth with tepid coffee. Looking around before he continued, Moe leaned across the table and spoke in a voice even his friend barely made out. "The boss has us break a lot of eggs to get his show on the road. When it all changes, we're not just gonna be a company. There won't *be* any other companies. There won't *be* any market. A lot of people are gonna be mad about the new order, and he's gonna need protecting. Who do you think is gonna have to circle the wagons? You and me, and I'm betting we'll get more than a bonus for our trouble."

"He'd be the first rich guy to remember who put him up on top. I ain't waiting to get offered a piggyback ride."

"You're all wet. Sylvester was a little guy who had a big idea. He remembers what it was like." Moe wiped his mouth on his napkin and tossed it on his tray, and both men headed for the door.

Almost without willing it, Kid Amoeba stood up also, its pendulous belly upending the table and sending the special plates with the great seal of the president of the United States crashing to the floor of the display window. Its face was inflamed, eyes swollen almost shut, and cheeks and scalp sizzling with volcanic acne.

It realized with some discomfort that it was powerless to resist the aroma that engulfed those men, drawing it after them. It felt as it did whenever some new stimulus triggered a flicker of memory from within the cloud of its earlier life before it had been forced to become like the things of this world.

Kid Amoeba stepped off the display stage and immediately bumped into Old Man Hussy. "What's eating you? Lunch rush is coming up. All the panhandlers will come in with what they got off the working traffic. Get back up there, push the meatloaf, and try to enjoy yourself. You looked like you were eating your own dead mother up there."

It stood motionless except for its right ear, which was still a mouth, noisily sucking in the last straggling spaghetti noodles.

Old Man Hussy blinked and adjusted his glasses on his nose. "What in hell's gone wrong with your face, Kid? You allergic to something?"

Kid Amoeba looked more like a walrus or an elephant seal than the President of the United States. Toothless mouths and gulping nostrils opened all over its face in a threat display until every pore on its puffy red face screamed, "NO!"

It shoved Old Man Hussy. The boss shoved back, and Hussy was a prison guard and a strikebreaker in his strenuous youth, so he knew a thing or two about shoving. It fell back into its chair, rocking back to bang its head against the picture window. Outside, the men got into a green panel van with the logo painted on the side and accelerated into the flow of traffic.

Old Man Hussy was an immovable object. So, it leapt through the window of the automat. An apple seller and a couple of street urchins dove for cover amid the torrent of shattered glass. Flexing its membrane to constrict all the yawning vacuoles on its face, it bounded down the sidewalk after the retreating van.

It was a sweltering early summer afternoon, the sun pounding down from directly overhead and off a dazzling array of reflective surfaces. Traffic on Roosevelt Road was heavy enough that it could barely keep the van in sight while navigating the churning river of pedestrians. A crowd gathered in front of a radio display next door, listening to the news. A shopkeeper berated Kid Amoeba as it thundered past, arms pumping, big, cracked leather brogans slapping the asphalt, breath gasping out of every hole in its face, and hundreds more distributed over its stocky, heaving body.

One of its shoes split open like a banana peel when it leapt off the curb, narrowly dodging a taxi. Kicking off the ruined shoe without stopping, it never took its eyes off the van. It passed under an el track, bounced off the bumper of an omnibus, and turned sideways to slip between a baby carriage and a beat cop who shouted and shook his nightstick as it barreled by.

The next block was even more crowded. A drugstore, a cigar shop, a movie palace, and then it crossed in front of the facade of the Hawthorne Hotel just as a group of swarthy men in fedoras and bright phototropic suits sauntered out onto the sidewalk. They walked with their hands inside their coats, their hooded eyes intent on the traffic. As they moved, their jeweled suits shifted from gold to magenta to aquamarine, every angle a completely different color. Before Kid Amoeba could alter its course, it blundered into their midst, knocking them down like ninepins and clotheslining a somber man with a face the color of brick in a conservative wool pinstripe suit despite the heat.

Kid Amoeba didn't follow the news and would never have recognized the name Al Capone. Even if he had, he might be unaware that the Hawthorne was the de facto headquarters of Capone's mob. Most Chicagoans knew Scarface had been convicted of tax evasion the previous October and was already serving an eleven-year sentence at Atlanta's federal penitentiary. His favored lieutenant, Frank Nitto, better known thanks to a hectoring press as Frank Nitti, had himself only returned from a federal sentence six weeks before, and had called today's summit meeting to plot the future of the mob without its figurehead. Just emerging from their old stomping grounds after a heated exchange over the ongoing feud with the North Side Gang, Nitto and his minions were on guard for another ambush like the one that had left the Hawthorne riddled with thousands of bullets in '26, and determined to avoid the kind of street warfare theatrics that made Capone so infamous.

It knew none of these things and would have done nothing differently if it had. The aroma that drew it onward could not be ignored, and it was growing fainter as the van pulled away, heading west towards the edge of town, where traffic was thinner. It kept running as the gangsters fell on their capo and drew handguns, searching for the next attack before setting their hooded eyes on the retreating fat man who bore more than a passing resemblance to Herbert Hoover or maybe W.C. Fields. When they piled into a car and gave chase, their quarry was two blocks away and still picking up steam. When a line out front of a soup kitchen blocked the sidewalk completely, it jumped off the curb and ran into the street.

Accelerating to keep up with the traffic, it burned through its recently consumed meals like a blast furnace. Its shiny old suit coat burst at the seams, and the seat gave out of its pants, but it kept running, shedding the tattered rags and running in grimy underclothes. Sweat, or something like it, bubbled out of its gasping pores.

Hot on its trail, a wailing siren split the stultifying summer air. A police motorcycle with a sidecar accelerated alongside it, the rider standing up in the sidecar, shouting at it, "Get out of the road, ya moron!"

On either side of the street, the buildings grew shorter and farther apart, until after a traffic light, the street became a road with fallow fields of weeds on either side.

The cop in the sidecar rapped Kid Amoeba on the head with his nightstick. The blow rippled through its fluid form without achieving the desired effect, so the cop tried again. Kid Amoeba snatched the nightstick out of the cop's hand, nearly pulling him headfirst out of the sidecar. The motorcycle veered away, then swerved back to knock it off its feet. Moving quickly for a body its size, the Kid jammed the nightstick into the spokes of the motorcycle's front wheel.

The motorcycle turned a disastrous forward somersault, flinging both cops clear as it smashed end over end down the road.

Kid Amoeba ran on, eyes fixed on the sliver of green, now almost a mile ahead on the highway. An eastbound delivery van bopped its horn as it passed, swerving as the running fat man threaded the needle between it and a farmer's pickup truck. It didn't notice the glossy black Packard bristling with Lynch rifles and shotguns until it was literally nipping at the Kid's heels.

After being tackled in front of their old headquarters, the Nitto-Capone mob had abandoned all caution to teach the fat man a lesson. When they saw how he dealt with the cops, they had half a mind to offer him a job.

A man in a dazzling phototropic suit, emerald in shadow, orange where the sunlight splashed off it, leaned out the window and brandished a gun at him. "Hey, fat boy, slow down! Boss wants to talk at ya!"

Kid Amoeba poured on the speed, surging ahead of the Packard, which skipped over the center line and nearly collided with a Greyhound bus.

It didn't notice gunfire, but it spasmed violently as a salvo of bullets stitched its back. Tumbling through its torso, the gauss rounds shattered several of its second-hand ribs but emerged out of its chest with little velocity lost. It stumbled, legs flailing at the tarmac, but its straining membrane threatened to burst, its lumbering bulk to fall beneath the wheels of the pursuing car.

If it was forever confused by every new experience, it never knew what past mistakes might prove vital. In Sacramento, pressed to compete in something called an "ipecac race," the Kid had run in a crowd of competitors from the City Cemetery to the capitol building, stopping at each corner to drink from one of a batch of milk bottles, one or more of which was spiked with the potent emetic. It left the other contestants violently heaving their guts out at every intersection and reached the finish line alone. The police moved in to break up the unruly event. Kid Amoeba had violently disgorged eight gallons of milk on them and had to flee without collecting its prize, ten dollars and a year's supply of Dr. Benoit's Gastro-Blast Tonic.

Now, the unpleasant memory provided a way to defend itself.

Without breaking stride, Kid Amoeba vomited at the Packard. The jet of disgorged chyme sizzled where it hit the doors, blistering paint off the car's armored flanks. The gunman retreated behind bulletproof glass, frantically swatting at smoking gouts of caustic ooze on his sleeves.

The Packard swerved again to run the Kid over when it expended the balance of its last meal into the passenger-side wheel well. The tire exploded and flew off the wheel in smoldering scraps. The armored sedan slewed sideways on the highway. Its once-turgid belly flapping emptily between its legs, Kid Amoeba lurched and left the ground, barely clearing the hood of the tumbling Packard like an airborne hot-water bottle.

It rolled and bounced along the shoulder of the road before bellyflopping in the ditch. Two gangsters clambered out of the Packard, which lay on its side across the center line. They sprayed bullets in the direction of the ditch while the others jumped out in front of the next oncoming truck, trying to hijack a ride.

Scuttling away in the weed-choked ditch, Kid Amoeba crawled back onto the shoulder when the coast was clear and doggedly followed the scent trail of the long-gone panel van. When it came to a fork in the road and a sign that proclaimed, WELCOME TO UTOPIA, POP. 316, it left the highway to hop a barbed wire fence and follow a rutted dirt track in the grass. The trail led it over a hill and through a pasture dotted with dairy cows until it reached a building that even the Kid recognized was not a farm.

The featureless, four-story rhombus of glass block and Vitrolite was all dynamic curves and no visible doors or windows. The heat haze rising off the ground added to the illusion that the stationary building was a dynamo racing across the plains.

A crackling electrified fence topped by razor wire surrounded the rhombus, and the Kid was too exhausted to spring over it or burrow under it, too cowed by memories of past brushes with lightning. Panting in the shade of a tree and watching the sun pour through the wilted leaves, it waited until another van came and then crawled under it on all fours to pass through the gate.

The van circled the glass rhombus twice before the blank black wall retracted to allow access to a loading dock. Clinging to the truck's undercarriage, Kid Amoeba waited until the engine had subsided and cooled before crawling out. Now, the elusive scent that had driven it into a frenzy was a suffocating miasma persistently blooming up under the pall of vinegar and bleach.

Though it teased out the cilia on its membrane to catch any vibrations in the air that might denote a threat, it froze when it found itself hugging the oil-stained concrete between two pairs of hip-high rubber boots.

"Well, well," said one of the men in those boots, "if it isn't the Forgotten Man!"

Kid Amoeba looked up, striving to remake its face into a sheepish human expression, but it couldn't get the features right. Its eyes chased each other across a Cubist confusion of mumbling mouths, twitching nostrils, and cauliflower ears.

"Are you seeing what I'm seeing, Moe?"

"It ain't a pink elephant this time, Joe…"

The Kid knew it was cornered. Before it could abandon its disguise, forked cattle prods jabbed into its neck. Lightning shot through its cytoplasm. Its membrane convulsed and lost any semblance of a bipedal shape. Exploding in an ecstasy of tentacles, it grabbed both pairs of legs and slammed them into each other like cymbals. Breaking every bone in their bodies, it flung them away, and then tried to climb into the cab of the van. It didn't know how to drive, but it had hitched enough rides to try. A mob of men in canvas and rubber suits and gas masks swarmed the Kid, jabbing it with cattle prods until it was a quivering puddle. Unable to will even the most primitive limbs and organs into being, it contorted and expelled its skeleton, then contracted into a gelatinous smear on the pavement.

"Remarkable!" exclaimed a mutton-chopped man in a long white coat. "Complex somatic mimesis! This is our most momentous discovery yet!"

"Keep with it," one of the workers in gas masks shouted back, "after you eggheads figure out how it got loose!"

"It couldn't possibly be one of ours, you simpleton! Though I suppose one of the technical staff could have left the gate open…"

They kept arguing, but though the Kid was too exhausted to try to escape, it finally grasped what it had sensed, which made it so important to come here.

At last, it realized the source of the smell pouring off these men, or rather, off the rubber suits they wore.

It was the smell of itself, its own kind, and the world from which it came.

No man can swim unless he enters deep water.

—Helena Petrovna Blavatsky

May 16, 1932 | Mara Dzong, Tibet

S pider emerged from the shadows of a blind arch to stand in the courtyard. Roaring wind rattled frozen prayer flags, clawed at his cape, and glazed his golden mask with a patina of frost.

Every time he returned here, it was the same storm. If he scraped away the snow at his feet, he might see the freshly frozen blood that poured from his guts the first time he set foot in this place.

The naked monks meditating in the icy deluge paid him no notice as he crossed the courtyard and entered the *gompa*. The monastery clung to the sheer wall of a twisted chasm nearly two miles deep, the walls of which almost met in a jagged seam high above its steep, slate-scaled rooves. The white pillar of a frozen waterfall loomed over the parapets, forever thrumming with the howl of the eternal storm.

For a lost monastery somewhere in the Himalayas, it was most striking that almost none of the monks were Oriental. Ever since Marco Polo, European explorers and fortune-seekers sought in droves the legendary place called *Shambala* or *Beyul Pemako*, a sacred hidden land where no man ever died. All but the strongest and most resolute perished in the maze of icy gorges, bottomless crevasses, and impassable, savage-haunted jungle far below, but more than hostile terrain sheltered this place from the outside world. If they were simply too evil to win their way to the fabled paradise, they might find themselves here instead, and gain a sort of immortality few would prefer to a swift death.

At first, Spider thought they shunned him because he never had to brave that hellish gauntlet to win his way to this place. To return, he had only to conceal himself in perfect darkness and whisper its name. Later, he thought they were jealous because only he could leave. How stupid he'd been…and did he know any more, even now?

This fortress was one of seven consecrated by Padmasambhava in the 7th century A.D. as isolated refuges for devout Buddhists, but *Mara Dzong* was more of a prison colony. For centuries, it had existed outside of time; for centuries more, its denizens would be both blessed and condemned to meditate upon the world's suffering, to atone for the pain they had caused.

Spider stepped into the atrium and sealed the great door against the wind, inclining his head not to bow but to avert his gaze from the brilliant mural on the curtain wall shielding the great hall. The depiction of the wheel of Life, with its six realms of enlightenment and suffering, was clutched in the talons of a fiery-eyed demon whose face was the model for his mask.

He shook the snow from his cape, swept past the mural, and entered the great hall. He searched for a familiar face among the impassive, frostbitten acolytes eating or studying beside the fire pit. Neither of the two who had ever condescended to talk to him was among them, nor were any of the men he'd sentenced to live out eternity in this place.

He hadn't been completely honest with Matilda Lynch, of course. Let her think he killed all those he couldn't redeem, but many of the shaven-headed penitents sentenced to live out eternity in this place were brought here by his hands.

None acknowledged the malign effigy in their midst, but an acolyte ran from the hall while the others looked away. Spider stood beside the charcoal fire, still but for the wisps of steam emitted by his dripping cape, watching with a wistful air as the others sipped hot buttered tea and ate honeyed rolls. He felt neither hunger nor thirst, but whenever he saw someone eating, his mind went back to his last solid meal, on the night he busted out of jail—cube steak, freeze-dried potatoes, boiled peas, and a stingy slice of pound cake, with coffee that burned the roof of his mouth so he could taste almost none of it, anyway. His tongue went to the spot now, probing it to bring back the memory.

The acolyte returned and gestured down the corridor. Spider followed him out of the great hall, down corridors lined with golden Buddhas, fierce gods, demons, and *bodhisattvas*, up the terraces of a cloistered garden courtyard where it was forever spring, with riotously flowering rhododendrons, poppies and sundry herbs and spices bursting out of cracked stone pots and fruit trees bowed to the ground with dates, apples, and figs; through the winding stacks of a labyrinthine library with scrolls, folios and leatherbound books piled unto the sagging ceiling; up winding staircases, ramps and finally, a ladder to the cell of the master, inside the uppermost stupa of the monastery.

For all its vaunted isolation in space and time, this place was nonetheless world-famous, even if nobody believed it existed, though the dime novel writers, as always, made a hash of it. In the short-lived *Golden Ghost* radio serial, a British actor with a swank accent played Master Fan. The real Fan Li was once a half-caste tong hatchet-son of Shanghai who ran the lion's share of heroin into San Francisco, but he repented of his evil ways and sought salvation here. Though he had come here only half a century ago by the outside world's reckoning, he had always been here and presumably always would.

The wizened, hairless lama remained seated on the bare floor with his back to the door. "Have you brought us more of your foreign devils?"

"Not this time. My need is great, Master. A dire threat imperils millions—"

"You have come to use the Ear," Fan Li scoffed. "So, you still seek to do good with evil, eh? Go, then. You need not ask. Only the damned are truly free."

Spider started to leave, then said, "I didn't see Ugly John…"

Fan Li stiffened but did not turn to face Spider when he said, "John is in solitude, meditating upon his destructive appetites."

"You found his still again?"

Fan Li didn't deign to offer a reply.

"Only the damned are free, my ass," Spider said as he closed the curtain.

The lama's voice cut through the curtain. "You scoff at our lessons but fall into the same trap that has claimed so many before you."

Spider ripped the curtain back. "I've done everything I could. I've turned bad men into agents for good. I am at war with darkness, but I lose a little more of who I am every time I use it. How am I save anyone if I don't know myself?"

"How can you not? The Eye of Fear and the Eye of Fate pour the illusions of this world into men's minds to bend them to your will, but are you not lost in illusion yourself? Why do you fear the face of the demon whose likeness you wear? Why do you fear even mirrors? You know the answer.

"Only when you have cast off all worldly attachments, all illusions and selfish fantasies of free will, will you open the demon's third eye and gain the power to truly serve the highest good, which is harmony between light and darkness."

Scalding words poured into his mouth, but Spider backed out of the lama's cell without speaking to them. The only thing about Master Fan Li that the dime novels and the radio show got right was that he always got the last word.

In the four years he had worn the mask of the White Devil, Spider McGowan had raised a small army and turned it loose on New York

City. He had gone from thieving and riding the rails without care to waging a clandestine war against the wealthy and powerful, but he still knew almost nothing about where it came from, who gave it to him, or how he could free himself from it.

When he first came to Mara Dzong, the monks treated his wounds and let him recover, but they deigned to answer none of his questions. Fan Li told him to return to the world and sort it out for himself. When Spider couldn't even make the mask do that, he was forced to abase himself to take on the most odious chores of the monastery as Ugly John's apprentice. The hunchback, at least, was only too willing to tell him how damned he truly was.

The monks who turned their faces away from him were all exiles or fugitives. They came from every corner of the earth to atone for crimes and vices that should have been punished with their deaths. A frozen hell for those who still desired the world, it was a harsh sanctuary for those seeking absolution for the unforgivable. In all the world, there was no human being lower than them except those who, in their death, took on the curse of the mask of the White Devil.

It was said that a demon set upon *Padmasambhava* in this deadly gorge. It offered him powers to destroy evil, but the enlightened one saw the trap in the demon's promise and defeated it, capturing its essence in the golden mask, just as it imprisoned any mortal condemned to wear it.

To those damned souls, the demon freely gave its powers—to shrug off fatal wounds, to cloud men's minds and stop their hearts with their darkest fears and smother them in guilt if they could be made to feel it, and so offer them a chance at redemption. But every use of those powers wiped away more of his memories and claimed a bit more of his soul, until only the demon was left.

None who wore the mask had lived long enough to be free of it. Most of them simply went insane. With it, the wearer need not eat or sleep and was all but impossible to kill, but few could bear it more than a few years and willingly passed it on and died in the hope of oblivion if not eternal peace.

Ugly John told him the demon could be stymied and power served by acts of goodness, and so many of Spider's predecessors had tried to become crusaders against evil as they saw it, but the hunchback liked his jokes.

Spider had read more than a couple dime novels in his misspent youth. In the stories, the Golden Ghost rescued Christian missionaries from Singapore slave traders, saved hapless botanists from Kalimantan cannibals, and crossed swords with China Sea pirates and Japanese samurai. Unlike the White Devil, the Golden Ghost's alter ego never changed, and he never diminished for use of his powers.

Once the shock and disbelief gave way to resignation, he thought he would do this sentence standing on his head. Spider truly believed none of the previous White Devils knew what evil really was or how to fight it. But the monks knew that good and evil were two sides of a counterfeit coin minted by desire, which was the antithesis of the enlightenment they sought. To prove this, they gave the evilest man seeking to make good the power of the mask and let him strive and fail.

Spider had begun as he meant to carry on, thwarting and exposing the crimes of industrialists as a vengeful apparition. But his crusade had been run into a ditch by two agents who might otherwise have been his allies—Daddy Long-Legs and the Conductor. One held millions spellbound with his seductive promise of a populist revolution, while the other killed Spider's enemies faster than he could ruin them.

He had listening posts eavesdropping on an ever-growing list of targets, moles inside the police and federal agencies, newspapers, and radio networks, as well as informants and operatives in the underworld of five major cities. But every lead on Daddy Long-Legs or his musical mesmerist had run into a brick wall, only confirming what he already knew.

Neither of them was affiliated with domestic radicals, so they must be either agents of foreign powers or catspaws of the wealthy, like the Levelers. Various cabals of industrialists had backed fringe political groups like the Liberty League and the Technocrats, and many more were guilty of fifth-column schemes like Lynch's. Of those he suspected were backing the terror campaign, three prime suspects had already fallen prey to the faceless, music-loving assassin.

He regretted not throwing what he'd learned about the Levelers and their warlike patron into the Bureau of Investigation's lap as soon as he discovered the truth. He'd kept it to himself for Matilda's sake, hoping to liberate her from the delusions she labored under, but the discovery had all but broken her. He hoped she would pick up the pieces and return as more than a pawn. He hoped she would—but how much did she care what *he* hoped for?

He had come here to use the Whisper Dish with no other leads.

Of course, they had a poetic mumbo-jumbo name for everything around here. They called it the Ear of the World among themselves, and even among the monks, its existence and purpose were a secret.

When he was a kid, the nuns sometimes took Spider and the other orphans to Coney Island. While the others played and fought on the playground, Spider was fascinated by a pair of metallic saucers standing at either end of the park. When someone spoke into the opposing dish, you could lean in and listen to the ghostly voice magically transported across the playground of howling children. No less magical for Sister Eugenie's explanation that it was a simple trick of acoustics. It was one of those little moments that might have led a luckier little boy to a career as an engineer or an architect or something better than a thief.

The monastery had a Whisper Dish too, and it *was* magic.

Spider sat and crossed his legs in a low, empty chamber chiseled out of the living rock. The cell's only feature was a golden disk like a concave gong mounted on the ceiling of a niche in the back wall above a narrow, bottomless pit. The heavy stone door hushed shut behind him, muting any outside sound. The disk was like an eardrum; the bottomless shaft branched and penetrated, so it was said, the whole interior of the earth, and was privy to all its secrets. If you whispered a name into it and listened patiently in perfect stillness, you might hear their voice subtly conducted through air, water, stone, and the global web of magnetic force with the intimacy of a lover's whisper to your waiting ear.

Ugly John used to lock him in this cell as punishment and let Spider discover for himself what it could do. Spider would sit beneath the Whisper Dish for hours on end and eavesdrop on people he knew, famous crooks, important political figures, and even fanciful names he made up, just to see if anyone answered.

In the case of the mesmerist, he had more urgency and less hope, so he tried it first. He'd failed to trace the phonograph fragment to a record pressing plant, as it was individually recorded on a commonly available transcription cutter. A small orchestra produced the music in a resonant concert hall. His network had gathered the names of missing men and women on the Bowery and found a pattern. Many were musicians, and a string of recent burglaries in Brooklyn and the Bronx had involved music shops. No money was taken, only instruments. The thread connecting them was tenuous, but his suspect had put together one hell of a band, if the record was anything to go by.

He whispered the names of the missing ones into the ear one by one. Waiting an interminable minute after each, he reached the end of the list without hearing anything but muttered conversations among other bums asking after, mourning, or lambasting the missing.

He tried another—the name on everyone's lips.

If the previous trail went cold for lack of whispers, now the noise amplified itself until the sibilant din forced him to cover his ears. It was as if every human tongue joined in a chorus to sing a tortured paean to Daddy Long-Legs.

He had never heard such interference. He'd come to think of the Ear as the center of a web enfolding the globe and learned to attune himself to the subtlest twitches of its strands. But the longer he listened, the more the web vibrated with an intangible, invading force. Spider felt the spastic convulsions of a multitude of ensnared prey. Earth's subtle energies were taxed to their limit as if some unseen alien presence was using the web itself for its own unknowable purposes.

Science would say it was sunspot activity. Fan Li would say the world was out of balance but would soon correct itself. He was about to give up when he noticed something else. A sound so faint he had to stick his head into the concavity of the disk to make it out.

Whoever and wherever he was, Daddy Long-Legs blasted the entire United States with a million-watt signal for a few hours every day. His signal was as erratic as his schedule, but his rhetoric consistently harpooned the government as a tool of the ruling class. The Federal Radio Commission had been hunting him for over a year and was no closer to finding his transmitter, or his true identity, than Spider was.

For an uncounted span of hours, he forced himself to lean into the roaring of worship and curses…but nowhere on Earth could he find the voice of the man they were talking about.

Maybe he wasn't on Earth…but that was ridiculous…wasn't it?

He sat with his head inclined against the rim of the Ear, frozen lest some tiny gesture set him back hours in recovering his sensitivity. Whenever the voices subsided, his body drifted into something deeper than sleep, only to jolt to full alertness whenever a new voice emanated from the dish. His hand absently scratched names, dates, and places on a grubby notepad, but otherwise, he remained motionless, for he knew not how long.

He'd told himself he wouldn't, but his other inquiries had gotten him nowhere, so he pressed his hand against the Ear to still its susurrant din, emptied his mind, and whispered one final name.

"Matilda Lynch."

Almost immediately, she heard Matilda's voice. "Yes, I hear you." A dreamy murmur on the edge of sleep. It seemed as if she spoke to him, like on a telephone, but she was with someone else.

In the background, a record played Beethoven's 7th, second movement, but it skipped, endlessly repeating the same bar.

Another voice replied, hushed but charged with a piercing intensity. "Your progress has been remarkable. Your armor is a chrysalis from which you will soon emerge. Autochthonous in your rebirth, self-created. Do you feel fear or guilt over the cost of your transformation?"

"No, Doctor. I'm ready to be reborn."

Spider shuddered. She was under hypnosis with a psychoanalyst. This man knew her secret identity, her innermost fears, and was using them…but to what purpose?

"You should be proud of what you've accomplished. You have erased your false persona. Dead to the public eye, you are free to kill your last connection to the failed world. Free you will be. Free to soar. But there is one more string attached to your old life that must be cut away. Have you taken the steps we discussed?"

"I've already done it. It's only a matter of time…"

Spider was jolted out of his reverie by something the psychoanalyst said that echoed another muted, commanding message—

Cut the string

Mind racing, Spider methodically massaged blood into pincushion limbs. He noticed the candle at his knee had melted into a cold puddle on the floor. He had to warn her, to stop her…

A keen wail like an untuned radio startled him so badly that he nearly tumbled into the bottomless pit.

When it resolved into a voice, it was like a trumpet blast in his ear; for all its clarity, the voice might have been in the room with him.

The voice of Daddy Long-Legs.

"Hello, you. I hear you've been asking about little me. It's an astounding age we live in, isn't it? New inventions, but so many are only rediscovering ancient knowledge. Nothing new under the sun, as the man said. You think you're something new, though, don't you? A champion of the little man, waging a private war to bring about a better world, not so? Perhaps it would surprise you to learn that I also see myself thusly, and recognize in you a misguided ally.

"We should like to know you better, to demonstrate how our ambitions are not so different, but you will soon be entertaining visitors, as we cannot afford to let you meddle in our great work. Please understand that what we do is not in anger but regret…"

The voice seemed to trail off but then came back, though muffled, as if to itself. "No, I don't think there's any point in telling him. I suppose he would have put it together on his own, given time, but there's never enough time…" The Ear resonated with the last echoing words, trailing off into maddening silence. He forced himself to stand and shook the circulation into his hands and feet, the sensation somehow no more unpleasant than the last time he'd been shot. By the time he reached the door, his steps were steady, and his hearing so trained from listening so intently for so long that he might otherwise not have noticed the heavy booted footsteps in the corridor until he'd blundered into them.

He stood between two men in leather-sheathed armor, gas masks, and aviator helmets, carrying oddly sawed-off hunting rifles with bell-shaped barrels.

"Get him!" one barked helpfully. Spider dropped on all fours and kicked one man's knee. The blow should have shattered it, but padded shin guards saved him. Lunging at the other man, Spider drew his sword to skewer him at the junction of groin and thigh.

The man he'd kicked pointed his rifle in Spider's ear. Spider heard the click of the trigger and some kind of crackling hum. He laughed at what must be a misfire. Withdrawing his sword from the dying man, he stalked the other, who doggedly kept pulling the trigger and shaking his gun.

Just as he drove his sword through the chink between gas-mask and breastplate, he began to feel something. His insides were boiling. He swayed on his feet and staggered to lean against a column. His ears throbbed with an oceanic roar. His gloved hand went to his chest, and the front of his shirt crumbled and fell away like autumn leaves. The floor and the ceiling traded places with every step he took. Maybe it wasn't a misfire after all…

Kneeling over the men he'd killed, he stumbled and fell on his elbows. Through the roaring in his ears, he could barely make out the crackle of a voice coming from a dead man's gas mask, which was connected by corrugated tubes to steel oxygen tanks on the man's back. "Sully, check in…Sully?"

The guns were some kind of radio rifle with a blunderbuss barrel lined with reflective crystals, and a big uranium battery where an ammo drum ought to be. A Colt long-barrel .45 hung from each man's belt, along with manacles, a shock baton, and a canteen.

Wireless headsets, radiation guns, bottled air—these yeggs came prepared for anything, but he wouldn't bet on them against the monks. Still, if these two had found their way to the innermost sanctum, something must be horribly wrong.

Staggering from column to doorpost, Spider retraced his path back to the great hall. On the stairs leading to the garden courtyard, he found heaps of smoking corpses. All were monks, so badly burned as to be unidentifiable. He turned one over by its arm, which popped out of its socket like a charred drumstick.

Brittle ash and smoking meat were all that remained of the monk's face.

More bodies choked the outer corridors, piled where they died charging the invaders without landing a blow. Some still smoldered, bluish flames lazily licking at fabric and hair. Spider abandoned hope of finding anyone alive.

For 1300 years, this place had stood aloof from the world, and these bastards had wiped them out in minutes. Spider bit his cheek, fighting waves of vertigo and nausea. His stomach was empty, but if he vomited, he might choke on it—a fitting end for the White Devil. Of course, one of the mercenaries would find the mask and take it, and the cycle would begin anew. For all he knew, the monastery would be restored when the mask changed hands, and all would be as it was.

Spider unsheathed his sword at a sound coming from the direction of the great hall—a piercing scream that transcended almost beyond his range of hearing. That scream had no language, identity, or even humanity, yet he thought he recognized its source.

Drawing his cape over the glaring white of his tuxedo, Spider skulked to the threshold of the great hall.

Five men in padded leather armor stood in a circle around the charcoal fire, their faces bare and gleaming with sweat, their eyes intent on the writhing body staked down over the guttering flames.

"Getting tired of your act, old man," one of them rasped. Playing his shock baton over the soles of his victim's feet, he leaned in close and growled, "Where is he?"

The body arched and let out that blood-curdling cry again, but the convulsive breaths that followed were no plea for mercy but haggard, ragged laughter. "Have you looked up my bum?"

Ugly John.

Spider closed his eyes, clenched his fists, and made a wish. Every lamp and lantern in the great hall dimmed and guttered, then died. Only the lurid red glow of the charcoal fire illuminated the room, sending wild shadows writhing across the walls and roof beams.

"What gives, Slim?"

"Don't go to water, you mutts. He's here somewhere…"

The White Devil became one with the shadows, swimming through the darkest corners of the great hall until he had a clear view of the leader. Two of the men hoisted microwave rifles and nervously swept the room. The other three drew their pistols, kicking over tables for cover.

He couldn't hope to cut down all five before they raked him again with those damned invisible beams. Thinking of the awful damage they wrought on the monks, he had reason, yet again, to be both grateful for and repulsed by the protection the mask gave him. He'd been shot, stabbed, burned, and endured pain far beyond the domain of death, but never had he seriously contemplated removing the mask and ending it once and for all. Even so, his guts still churned with the cooking they'd been served, his legs trembling under his weight. Giving up would be a mortal sin to the nuns who raised him, but in the rigged game that hardened him, it was worse. Giving up was worse than never having existed at all.

"You gentlemen have come to the wrong house," he said. His voice boomed and whispered, echoing and seeming to come down on the wind and from right behind them. "The man who sent you here will suffer for it, but sadly, not as much as you."

Their rifles scanned the hall in every direction. The White Devil threw a chair into a corner. One of them jumped and licked off a wild shot. Slim, the leader, cuffed him upside his head. "Spread out, idiots," he hissed.

Scuttling across the floor, the White Devil popped up among them and drove his sword through Slim's throat. Throwing his cape wide open so the flash of white dazzled them, he kicked Slim's upright corpse into the charcoal fire and retreated into the shadows.

One of them screamed as he blasted everything that moved, setting two of his comrades ablaze. Backing up, he tripped over a table and fell flat on his back. The invisible beam from his rifle raked the ceiling, sending flaming banners, timbers, and tapestries raining down on the other survivor. Another tossed his rifle aside and opened up with his revolver. The White Devil danced and dodged the crazed gunshots until the mercenary's gun clicked on an empty cylinder. Before he could draw his bayonet, he was enfolded in the cape.

"Do you know where you go when you die?"

Shivering with mortal terror, the man could only shake his head.

"I don't know where other men go," the White Devil said, "but you will burn forever…inside *me*."

Gently as a mother tucking in an infant, he slid the sword between the man's ribs to transfix his galloping heart. His dying gasp of "God damn you" was an almost tangible wisp of mist that wafted between them, only to be drawn up into the flared nostrils of the White Devil's golden mask.

Spider let the body fall, hideously quickened by the dead man's stolen vitality.

"My lad, I know ye've a lot on your nasty little mind," said Ugly John, "but if you could speed a poor old man on his way without making a meal of his soul, he'd be much obliged."

Spider's hand had already hefted the sword before he recalled himself. He looked around at the dead men still merrily blazing on the floor. Sheathing his blade, he knelt beside Ugly John and untied the leather thongs binding him over the fire pit.

The stocky monk threw an arm around his neck and let himself be laid down on his side. Smoke and a sickeningly savory stench wafted from his back. "Give us a taste of the rare old mountain dew, and we won't need your blade."

Following the monk's directions, he located a hollowed-out statuette filled with his peculiar brand of moonshine. Ugly John took the cup but wouldn't drink until Spider joined him.

"To your health," Spider said.

Ugly John laughed and then coughed and moaned. "To our deliverance," he amended and drained the cup, coughing again but aglow with his customary cheer, even as he was dying.

A washed-up Shakespearian actor renowned for his Falstaff played Ugly John on the radio, but he turned out to be a traitor, and the Golden Ghost had to throw him into an icy crevasse. Spider had a good mind to tell Ugly John about it. He'd probably laugh himself to death.

"I have a line on the man responsible," Spider said. "Rest easy. He'll pay for what he did."

"And when he has, will *your* debt be repaid? Lad, it matters not. There's no balance sheet, no redemption. There's only blood..."

"Easy for you to say. You don't know what it's like out there now, how the rats run the farm. You want to go? You should see the mess they've made..."

"The rats always ran the show, lad. It was ever thus..."

Spider looked down and realized he was alone. Ugly John lay curled on the floor around the question mark of his spine, the empty cup rolling in a circle just beyond his outstretched fingers.

Spider laid a tattered banner over the monk's body. He sat in a chair and crossed his arms. Perhaps if he closed his eyes, everything would return to its eternal status quo. The monks would be eating and drinking and studiously ignoring him. As soon as he realized what he was waiting for, he stormed out of the hall into the courtyard and the roaring wind.

Stepping over a tangle of charred corpses, Spider searched the walls until he found a rectangular formation of chalk marks on a buttress between two columns. This was where they came in and thought they were leaving. Steeling himself, he stretched out a hand to touch the wall, smiling grimly as his gloved fingers passed through the semblance of solidity into another unseen space.

The ones who did this expected their hired killers to return at any moment. They would not be expecting him.

He stepped through the doorway and into fire.

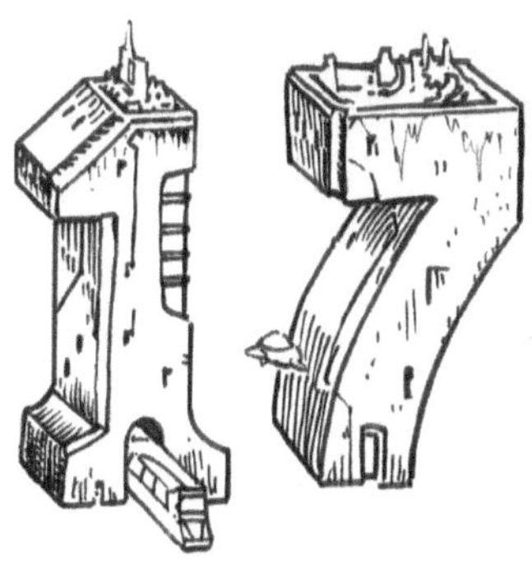

If you want to know what God thinks of money, just look at the people he gave it to.
—Dorothy Parker

May 16, 1932 | New York, New York

Two years ago, a corporate attorney named Gerard spent his convalescence from a surgical procedure at Cornelius Vanderbilt's Newport estate in a thought experiment. He composed a list of the fifty-nine rulers of America, the powers that bought and sold thrones and laws.

Even after it was amended to sixty-four, Sylvester Chalice had not made the list, so it was with sour satisfaction that he watched eight of Gerard's top names file into his conference room. Oris and Mantis Van Swearingen, railroad barons; Alfred Sloane, General Motors; David Sarnoff, chairman of RCA; Robert Whitney, representing J.P. Morgan & Company; Pierre DuPont, of E.I. DuPont de Nemours; Walter C. Teagle, Standard Oil; Linus Hedison, Vulcan Robotics.

A good crop. Only three who were invited declined to attend after receiving his letter, and Chalice wasn't surprised about Ford, Hearst, or Lynch. They were right to see it as a declaration of war.

Anticipating the enmity of the guests who had chosen to attend, Chalice played the upstart huckster to the hilt in a shiny aluminum brocade double-breasted suit with a green velvet vest and no tie at all. The looks of commingled disdain and bemusement were sweeter than the tarted-up Ambrosia dishes set out for the luncheon. After he followed the last of his guests through the teleportal, he pulled it shut behind him.

The walls were covered in pale green, patterned leather, tastefully lit by buttery-tinted lamps. Three long mahogany tables set for a three-course lunch stood in a horseshoe formation, with a podium at the open end. After the meal had been served, Sylvester Chalice took his place at this podium, emptying a tall tumbler of ice water down his throat before he commenced his address.

"Gentlemen, what would you say is the principal cause of the nation's current troubles? Mr. Whitney, I would like to hear your conclusions, in particular."

Robert "Icicle" Whitney talked like a cheap man's telegram, as if words cost more than air. "Conglomeration of market forces. Can't be helped. Like the weather. Shouldn't knock it. Natural cycles healthy, purge dead wood. Renew the soil. Indians knew it."

"Oh yes, the Indians. Do you know any Indians, Mr. Whitney?"

"Why, no…why?"

"I would recommend you find one posthaste and learn what else they know, because today, you—all of you—are standing right where the Indians were, on the day the *Mayflower* arrived. Now… this country sleepwalked into the industrial age with no central planning, unaware that it was a world power. The only initiative they took was to stifle innovation, but they needn't have bothered. You moguls did a fine job of it yourselves. The government clamped down and yoked business to the plow of war in Europe, but as soon as the Armistice was signed, they dropped the reins, letting the oxen steer the plow. Your monomania for driving up productivity and keeping wages down was slow-motion suicide. When nobody could afford to buy all those superfluous goods, you'd cut your own throats. Small wonder we're in this ditch, and all the laissez-faire in the world won't get us out. What's needed is robust central planning from *within* the business sector."

"Here, here," cut in Linus Hedison, de facto head of the Technocracy Party, seeming to dip a paintbrush in a can of pure superciliousness before applying it to the room. A late addition who barely cracked Gerard's top twenty, but Chalice included Hedison to goad the others. It seemed to be working. The nabobs applauded Vulcan for replacing tens of thousands of unskilled laborers with his products. However, his cockeyed proposals to put every obsolete worker on permanent relief stuck in their craws. Hedison was famously rumored to be assaying a run as a third-party candidate for President.

"I very much doubt he's advocating anything as idiotic as business handing control of the economy over to engineers, any more than laborers," said David Sarnoff. "But the gentleman is always free to prove me wrong."

Chalice looked at the wall, coughed into his fist, and let them fume. This was going better than he'd hoped. "Gentlemen, whatever the cause, it is inevitable that when this depression ends, and the new list of the men who rule America is drawn, few, if any, of you will be on it."

This provoked exactly the hoped-for outburst. He had to shout to reclaim the room, which caused a brief coughing fit. "Beg your pardon…must be that virus that's going around. Consider the source of your fortunes. The wealthiest of you monopolize raw resources—steel, oil, timber, electricity, land itself. Below those worthies are the brokers of transportation, information and entertainment." He nodded to Mr. Sloan, who'd only accepted his invitation when he learned Ford had rebuked his, and winked at the twin railroad barons. "All of your models have benefitted too long from the retardation of progress, and the only growth has been in the field of distracting the masses from that fact.

"Consider Mr. Whitney's boss, J.P. Morgan, Jr., reduced to a dotard on the witness stand, unable to explain the Chinese puzzle-box of holding companies concealing his wealth, or why he couldn't stop slopping his prize hog shareholders with dividends even as his bank teetered on the brink. Sam Insull's utility empire collapsed with the banks, and now he's fled to France while the rest of you have been reduced to eating out of cans for fear of poisoning.

"I know that some among your number have conspired to use radical uniformed thugs and phony fifth columnists to settle your labor problems while a slightly more ambitious clique has started a fascistic gentlemen's club soliciting volunteers to join a military coup against the next president, whoever it is. Their only defense in court would be that no judge or jury would ever believe men of such means and influence could be so stupid. I'm sorry, but there's no other word for it. Whoever takes power this November, you'll be lucky to escape jail or, if some voices on the air are to be believed, lined up before a wall.

"The people are demanding a new way, and revolution is in the air. While you've dithered, a rabble-rouser is urging millions to burn down your plantations, and some boogeyman you *haven't* fabricated out of thin air claimed two more of your number in the last month. No matter how many high walls and bodyguards you hide behind, he can get to you as easily as he got to the entire board of Bethlehem Steel."

The earlier furor of the room had given way to a morbid silence.

"Gentlemen, I did not invite you here to be insulted or terrorized. I am here to broker a treaty between yourselves and the vanguard of the new, as the only one who can save you."

"And by what right do you claim to speak for the *new*, Mr. Chalice?" Mantis Van Swearingen, seated alongside his sphinx of a twin brother Oris, controlled 30,000 miles of railroad track and all its rolling stock. "We salute progress, yes, but not parlor tricks."

Chalice smiled indulgently and poured another tumbler of ice water. "I beg your pardon, sir?"

Mantis went on, "Innovation is one thing, but this 'invention' of yours, it's an aberration. Even if it does work, such reckless leaps into the unknown seldom come without casualties. The cost, when it comes due, we have every confidence, will be as high as the leap forward it pretends to. We'll still be here when your little game has played out."

Chalice was hardly surprised. The sudden shortage of credit hit the railroads and utilities hardest. He'd noted that Mantis took the opportunity to buttonhole Whitney and a couple others before the meeting, no doubt for a loan.

"I'm glad you asked. I, with my little parlor trick, hold all the resources I need to bury each of you, who get all your eggs from only one chicken. My portfolio is more diversified than you can imagine and mortgaged to the hilt on a bright new future.

"Those of you in the business of transportation must see the threat most clearly. Expanding my teleportal network is making railroads and airlines obsolete, and cars and planes returned to their status as playboys' toys. You lot who dream of saving the gold standard should know that if I so chose, I could bring to market a single ingot of pure 14-karat gold equal in mass to the Matterhorn, thus destabilizing your entire economy. But why would I bother, when I also have a diamond the size of the Ritz? A formula for artificial oil. A method for harvesting asteroids to make steel for cities in the sky. Ambrosia, the meat substitute on every working-class table in these lean times, is also one of mine; it's just something I stumbled upon during my travels—even an organic alternative to your clumsy automatons, Linus.

"You gentlemen underestimate me at your peril. I'm not just a man with one patent for a magic trick. I'm another Marco Polo with the key to open the road to the stars."

Pierre DuPont made a grand gesture of tossing his napkin on his plate. "I've endured as much as any man could," he said. "Perhaps I am a bit slow. Comes with age and experience. But as I've listened to you strut, preen, belittle, and boast, I've yet to hear anything like a plan. Because men like you seldom know how to draw one." Slipping on his bowler hat, he took up his coat and rose from the table. "I bid you all good day."

Chalice let him get to the door. Let him open it and turn back from the blank wall that had once admitted them to this chamber. "I think you'll find getting home a bit more complicated than getting here." Turning a dial at his podium, Chalice crossed his arms and let his audience watch as the shutters retracted, revealing the utterly unearthly landscape outside.

"Good God," Whitney said, "we're not on Earth."

"At last, the sparkling intellect that conquered the markets reveals itself," Chalice said. "What you're seeing is the actual hub of our operations, though our best guess is it's on the far side of the Milky Way. Suffice to say, it's a long walk home. For want of a better name, I call it Circe, after the Greek goddess of transformation and initiation."

"So, this is a kidnapping?" asked Mr. Sarnoff, who had at least some inkling of the business of force from his humble beginnings as a newspaper boy.

"Merely a demonstration. This meeting ends when I've said my piece, and you've said yours.

"Now, to the plan. Mr. Hoover is doomed but has no intention of dropping out. The Bonus March is at his door, and he's sure to send them packing, which will be the final nail. The Democratic convention will choose Roosevelt because he's an affable cipher. Unless a miracle intervenes, he will win. He won't preside over a revolution, but he'll exact concessions for labor that will cut into your respective yacht funds. He might even steal some of Mr. Hedison's fantasies and impose relief taxes.

"The only viable option is to run another candidate to galvanize and unite the nation. A candidate who simply can't lose."

Sarnoff was blotchy and apoplectic. "Forgive me if I'm missing another magic trick, but your plan sounds like ours in short pants."

"Forgive me, but you hope to overthrow the government with a military coup. I've got a man in my back pocket. A man who commands more admiration and awe than anyone in or out of Washington…"

"Good Lord," Sloane said, "don't give us Huey Long…"

"No, sir. I give you Charles Lindbergh."

"That's rich," said DuPont. "We tried him. He's got no stomach for politics."

"Yes, we've discussed it. He's had a change of heart. After his son was returned to him, he came to see how society at large must be delivered from the kind of desperation and lawlessness which led to that hideous crime. He'll run, and if he runs, he'll win, and his experience will lend credence to a law-and-order platform that gives business a free hand." All the bitter pills he'd fed them were as molasses compared to this last item. "But as you say, Lindbergh isn't interested in politics so he won't be top of the ticket."

"And who will?" Sloan shot back.

Chalice humbly bowed his head. "I will."

They laughed. Laughed! He let them.

"Even a third-party candidate with some credibility can only spoil the Democrats' chances," put in Walter Teagle of Standard Oil, "and we're right back in the mud with Hoover."

"I won't be a spoiler. If you throw in with me, you'll see I only offer what it says on my business card. I'll get you there almost before you leave."

"And how do you propose to make any of these soap-bubble promises stick?" Sarnoff demanded.

"You, of all people, should appreciate how I mean to do so. Mass communication is what unifies a polyglot nation, is it not? Father

Coughlin in his little chapel, the Kingfish fulminating from his bully pulpit in Louisiana. I have such an arrow in my quiver, and I daresay he could be your best friend or worst enemy."

"You're saying you pull Daddy Long-Legs' strings?" Sarnoff stood up. "That's supposed to make us fold our tents and follow you?"

Chalice indulged in the most elaborate of shrugs. "Now… I do not flatter myself that my little presentation has either seduced or cowed you into sharing the fruits of my ambitions…"

Chalice returned to the podium and pushed a button beside it. Linus Hedison was rushing towards him but he froze, gasping and covering his ears, then fell at Chalice's feet like one of his own robots. "So allow me to introduce," Chalice said to the paralyzed assembly, "my not-so-silent partner."

Nobody moved except DuPont, who drooled a bit.

"What happened?" Chalice demanded. "You told me they would listen—"

And they did, came the voice of Daddy Long-Legs. His partner extended a tapered, chitinous forelimb and slid it up Hedison's left nostril, deep into his skull. *Rest assured, if your message doesn't get through to them, mine will.*

"But they laughed…"

They'll laugh out the other side of their faces soon.

"I don't like this," he said. "If you knew they'd buck us, why tell them at all?"

They can't stop us. They're much more useful to us like this… Scared, sick—

Chalice was wracked by another coughing fit. It got so bad he started hiccupping. "I'm not worried about them. I worry about you."

You shouldn't—

"You're stirring up your audience. Bringing too much heat before we're ready—"

Daddy Long-Legs moved to the next millionaire. *I'm setting them up for you to knock them down. When the dust clears, everyone else will be gone, and they'll be yours...*

"I don't know," Chalice mumbled. "I don't know if I want them anymore."

Don't be a fool. We've come so far...

"Exactly. We've come too far to trip ourselves up. You don't know them. You're not one of us. You don't know how we..."

Relax, Daddy Long-Legs hissed as it impaled another of the nation's most successful brains. *I understand how you Earthlings work. Trust me...you're not that hard to figure out.*

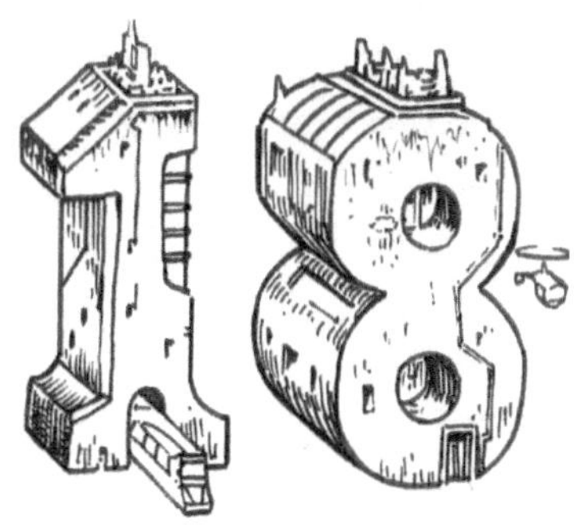

And someday, I believe that everyone will have wings and be able to soar from the housetops. But there must be a lot more experimenting, before that can happen.

—Clem Sohn, parachutist, inventor

June 3rd, 1932 | New York City

L ooking out the window of the elevated tram as it raced alongside Central Park, she loved how the icy light from the new streetlamps illuminated every scaly leaf on the trees without dispelling one whit of the mystery of what they truly were, letting them be dragons and airborne krakens in the greater dark.

All other things being equal, there was very little in life that wasn't lifted out of mundanity and imbued with a sickly, ironic sweetness simply by being dead.

If the last moments of life are suddenly endowed with a sharpening of the senses, a wild, wholehearted passion for the moment, how much sweeter was every stolen strawberry, every sip of water, with the aftertaste of mortality?

It seemed fitting that this gift came from her father, who had spoiled her rotten all her life without ever making her feel loved. That it forced her to shift for herself had brought no small amount of pain, but it only allowed her to define, for the first time, what she was and what she wasn't, and love herself a little for it.

She never intended to play along with his puerile stunt for more than a day or two, but three months later, here she was. Thrown for a loop after the argument, she'd used the identity ready at hand and gone to ground at Elvira Seaton's flat at 44th & 6th, just off Times Square and across from the Hippodrome. Drawing on funds she'd squirreled away in a safe deposit box at a nearby bank, she bobbed her hair, dyed it Titian red, and set about creating a new life, or at least escaping her old one.

She ate in automats, cafeterias, and chop suey houses; she toured the Natural History Museum daily for two weeks, until she'd studied every exhibit. She haunted libraries and bookshops and sat up all night with all the books she'd never found the time to read. She went to the theater and the movies, devouring plays, musical revues, and double features with a gourmand's indiscriminate but bottomless appetite. She spent hours every day and some nights walking the streets, observing and learning not to be observed, relishing the anonymity that the city provided as the first and finest of its gifts.

Every so often, she suspected that she was being tailed by discreet detectives, no doubt in her father's service. Other times, she caught a panhandler or a man in a soup line studying her with more than mere envy or lust, and she thought of the White Devil's extravagant claims of universal surveillance. Any day now, she expected one of the detectives, or perhaps her father's favorite attorney, an oily-voiced little man who walked like he'd just had his other six legs lopped off, to present her with a bank deposit book and a blind contract promising never to disclose her true identity, in return for a generous stipend.

She had gone a month before she confronted, in the midst of guiltily cleaning out the clutter of Elvira Seaton's possessions to make room for her own, the satchel containing the Silver Sentry armor in the back of her closet. She'd buried it the first day and willfully forgot it as part of a life from which she now felt amputated. She felt no burning desire to put it on anymore, no sense of purpose in what she now acknowledged was little more than a dangerous hobby.

This hit home the first time she saw a billboard for Lynch Munitions' new line of "silent personal firearms." In stark contrast to Father's logo so peevishly thrown in her face, the graphic showed the Silver Sentry brandishing a compact short-barreled rifle and an automatic pistol against a shadowy horde of torch-wielding peasants. The implication was all too clear—Father saw the next martial windfall in a war at home, and even in death, she was to be its mascot.

Putting aside any notion of donning the costume and going hunting then became a moot point, as any pride or pleasure she'd taken in it was poisoned. But she would not let herself be burdened with internal debates about what was, and should never have been. Such pastimes were for the living.

So it was with some trepidation that she answered the anonymous summons to Harlem before dawn. The message stuck under her door had addressed her as "Matilda," which sent a procession of geese over her grave. Only her father and, she supposed, the White Devil could know her true identity.

But the locale for the rendezvous spoke volumes, and so she went.

She took no notice of the wary glances she received from the other passengers on the IRT elevated tram as it floated north up Third Avenue. The exhausted porters, shoeshine boys, and washerwomen, the doormen in their operatic livery returning home from the night shift in brighter neighborhoods, looked mistrustfully at the soberly dressed white woman in their midst.

She had chosen her outfit carefully. The smart, sporty gabardine skirt and wrap covered a bespoke Tiffany chainmail tunic that was supposed to clench into plate to deflect knives and even small-caliber bullets, and she carried a Winchester gyro-derringer in one riding boot. No doubt, she looked more formidable than she felt. Still, at this ungodly hour, with sunrise a bloody rumor peering over the eastern horizon, a white woman riding alone into Harlem was a baited trap only the most desperate hoodlum would try. But on the streets would be another matter entirely...

Out the windows, the view became murky as the lesser lights of Jefferson Park failed to compete with the flickering fluoro-lamps in the tram, and she found herself facing her reflection. The grand march of vertical development fell off drastically after 98th Street, the towering, setback-crazed ziggurats surrendering to crowded tenements, boarding houses, and shuttered storefronts. Matilda's heart went out to the people for whom this was New York, but she'd come to understand that the march of the monoliths would never uplift them, only sweep them further away from the heart and light of the city that needed them to live.

She disembarked at 125th, following a handful of sleepy home-ward-bound commuters and fighting the stream of equally bleary-eyed workers crowding up the stairs to go to work. Her left hand covered her purse, but nobody tried her.

At the bottom of the stairs, she had only to raise her hand when she spotted the burgundy Packard she'd been told to expect. Opening the door for herself (another delicious little liberty she'd only learned to appreciate as a ghost), she climbed in, and the car pulled away when she still had one foot on the running board. She fell into the plush cushions and pulled the door shut behind her.

"You're recovering nicely," said Aurora Benoit, "for a dead girl."

Aurora looked older and almost regal in a long velvet-trimmed overcoat with a pillbox hat perched like a boat on the stormy sea of her hair.

"Oh, Aurora, I'm ever so happy to see you..." Matilda smiled and threw out her hands, so overwhelmed with gratitude for a familiar face that she visibly flinched at the somewhat scornful tone, the smoldering anger in her old secretary's wide, dark eyes.

She knew every rich person took their servants' obsequies at face value. *But Aurora was different. She was my friend…* "I'm so sorry, Aurora. I should have written you, but I was adrift. Please try to understand…"

"I understand perfectly, Miss Lynch—"

"Aurora, you're not my secretary anymore. Please, call me Matilda."

"And if *you* please," Aurora said, giving her back her hands like an inappropriate gift, "you may call me Ms. Benoit."

Matilda recoiled as if slapped, searching for the right words, but it occurred to her after a painful stuttering spell that what was wanted here was not words, but listening. She kept her eyes low, watching the procession of storefront churches, blind pigs, and brownstone apartments on Lenox Avenue.

Aurora let her stew for another couple blocks. "We suspected the truth, but we kept mum. Your daddy fired us all on the day of your funeral and had the house dick search us when we left the Majestic. It was cruel…"

"Well, you know he's a beastly man—"

"I'm not talking about his cruelty, but *yours*. We stuck our necks out for you, and you forgot all about us. I always knew you were one for drama, but you left us behind without so much as a fare-thee-well. You could've waved your hand and ruined that rotten old bastard, had him committed like he did your Ma…"

Matilda raised a hand to the driver to order the car to stop, but the reflex passed. "I didn't mean to, but I suppose you know what I *did* mean, and I apologize for that, too. I was thinking only of myself, as you say. I'm trying to…I *am*…correcting a lifetime of unexamined mistakes. When I received your note, I was hopeful that…perhaps…"

"We're grateful to you, Miss Matilda. Knowing you did it for yourself and your sister's memory makes no difference. But that isn't possible right now. We do what we think we have to, and maybe do right if we live long enough to make up for it."

They rode in silence for a block. Matilda could've said *I'm sorry* a hundred times more, but there seemed little point.

"We were working on something a long time before it all cracked up, and my sisters don't approve, but I felt we owed you this much…"

"You don't owe me a thing, Ms. Benoit…"

"Maybe not, but it'd ease my mind, just the same." The sedan turned east off Lenox at 142nd Street and parked in front of a five-story tenement beside the 369th Infantry Regiment Armory. Beyond the ornate little fortress, the Harlem River rolled towards the Triborough Bridge and its rechristening as the East River.

The driver came around and opened the door for Matilda and Aurora Benoit to alight on the sidewalk. An armed Negro guard escorted them up the steps to the portico and opened the front door. The lobby looked more like the reception room for an embassy than a crowded tenement, with unfamiliar flags and a massive portrait of Marcus Garvey, who founded the Universal Negro Improvement Association and forcefully urged all American Negroes to go back to Africa.

Less a zealot to Matilda's mind than the biggest charlatan to hit Harlem until Father Divine came along, Garvey was deported to his native Jamaica after a prison sentence for shady stock dealings. She felt chagrin at the realization that Aurora could harbor such radical beliefs. But then again, she chided herself, she'd never asked Aurora what she believed, nor even where or how she lived when she wasn't devising new toys for her mistress's distraction. Another unworthy thought surfaced in her unquiet mind. *What if this is a kidnapping?* Ridiculous—Ms. Benoit knew that nobody would pay her ransom.

Aurora swept through the lobby and up four flights of stairs in the run-down but scrupulously clean building. Matilda sensed people sleeping behind every door she passed. She heard a child crying, someone coughing, and a hushed argument. She followed Aurora to a fire door that led to the roof.

"What you see here, nobody is to know, is that clear?"

"Dead men tell no tales," Matilda said. "Whatever it is, show me."

With a final warning glance, Aurora used a key to unlock the fire door. Outside, the clammy night pressed in, condensation suspended in the air. She saw what looked at first like a pigeon cote, a relic from the homing pigeon craze. But behind the chicken-wire fencing stood an improvised machine shop with lathes, drill presses, a die-cutter, welding torches, tool chests, and a drafting table. She recognized more than a few pieces from the mad scientist's lair they'd built together in the Majestic.

Aurora strolled to the eastern edge of the roof with her hands in her pockets. Matilda followed her, waiting for her to speak. For a long minute, they stood looking over the roof of the armory at the river and the wharves, warehouses, railroad yards, and Yankee Stadium on the opposite shore.

If this was some kind of trap, this would be the place to spring it. Turning to her erstwhile friend, Matilda said, "I hope we can still be friends, Ms. Benoit. I always felt…"

Matilda's colorless appeal died in her throat when she noticed someone else standing in the shadows behind Aurora. A hard, implacable silhouette seemed to command her submission without lifting a finger. Matilda's hand went for her holster just as Aurora flicked a fountain pen flash to life and splashed the cold blue-white beam on the face of their interloper.

"Good Lord!" Matilda drew the derringer out of its holster and stepped back, looking for cover.

"I made this one for you."

She shook herself and let out a giddy giggle. She hadn't realized how nervous she still was. "Ms. Benoit—Aurora—I think you should know; I left all that behind with my…family. I haven't so much as—"

"I know, Miss Matilda. Go on and look it over, in any case."

Shamefacedly putting away the tiny pistol, Matilda stepped closer to the shadowy figure, still apprehensive, though she knew it was only a suit of armor on a shop mannequin.

It was somewhat lighter than the old armor. The prosthetic left arm was a veritable Swiss Army knife with a modified magneto-cannon, a flamethrower, smoke grenades, and even a chainsaw. Overall, it looked more like a coherent costume and less like a jumble of components. Walking around it, she noticed the biggest difference. "The rocket looks different… *Is* that a rocket?"

Aurora only shook her head, but Matilda could see the mad engineer was holding herself back, waiting for her to figure it out for herself. It took a minute longer for her to catch on.

"It's so much lighter. What does it use for fuel?" Noticing the lack of tanks and hoses, she gasped, finally getting it. "Why it's a big magneto-impeller, isn't it?"

Aurora nodded, straining to keep from smiling.

Remarkable! She remembered a time or two that Aurora had mused upon using the gauss impellers that powered every Lynch firearm and the launchers at the Majestic's flight deck as a means of propulsion. "But I don't see how it could fly…at least not safely…"

"When did that ever stop you? It works alright, but that's why we needed you."

"How's that?"

"Nobody else crazy enough to strap it on."

"Well, don't look at me. I hung up my spurs."

Aurora just looked at her and crossed her arms. "We cracked the global positive repulsion factor."

"The mendacity! Your mother would wash your mouth out with soap if she heard you lie like that!"

Aurora cracked a smile.

In spite of her resolve, Matilda let herself be shoehorned into the contraption. Aurora went over the control stick, which plugged into her left hand. The studs just behind her knuckles activated the thrust, while a bubble underneath her left thumb adjusted pitch, yaw, and acceleration. "It's calibrated to directly repel Earth's gravity, in effect pushing you away from it. We lost a couple unmanned prototypes over New Jersey, so—"

Whatever Aurora's next words were, Matilda was several hundred feet away by the time she said them.

Her helmeted head whiplashed back and bounced off the impeller. All the blood in her body pooled in her foot and fist. Unlike the violent skyward yank of the rocket, the impeller silently and smoothly hurled her into space. She came to rest hovering steadily at about 2,000 feet on the altimeter. She felt strangely safe, as if she rested on the invisible but quite tangible ball of force that separated the like-charged poles of two magnets. The skyline to the south glistened and stretched up to clasp the moon while the blinking patchwork of Harlem, Brooklyn, and the Bronx lay a half mile beneath her feet. Rolling the accelerator caused her to slide forward like on a greased glass plane. By thumbing backward, she climbed, and by pushing it forward, she deactivated the thrust and went into a barrel-rolling dive.

Once she got the hang of it, she lost herself in maneuvers that would've been impossible with the old internal combustion rocket. Dropping out of the sky, whistling like a buzz bomb, she skimmed the roof close enough to see the whites of Aurora's eyes, reversed course, and dragged back on the bubble to arrest her motion, hovering directly above her friend.

"Come fly with me," she said.

Aurora's eyes went wider. "Not on your life." She turned away. Matilda swooped down and carried her off into the sky.

Locking her arms under Aurora's, she felt the other woman's body tense against her own, felt it vibrate with the terrified, exultant scream that she gave to the wind as they ascended until even the distant pinnacles of midtown were misty footlights, and hovered in place. "I can't believe you wouldn't build one of these for yourself," she said.

"I like my feet on the ground," Aurora said. They'd only flown together once, which terrified the younger woman, but she'd laughed harder than Matilda had ever heard anyone laugh. But then something else almost happened, and they never spoke of it, or flew together again.

"How long does it stay charged?"

"Thirty minutes at full exertion, but you're pushing it right now…"

"Can it recharge off alternating current?"

"If you want to cause a blackout…"

Matilda felt Aurora relax in her arms and squirm to face her. She went into a corkscrewing power dive until the tenements rose up on all sides, and the street became a narrow slot that could surely never contain them.

They buzzed the river over Aurora's objection that the water would play hell with their stability. Matilda veered north and circled over the enormous punchbowl of Yankee Stadium. When Aurora's gay whoop turned to a warning, she dropped into the bowl. She flew around the infield like a horsefly buzzing a manure pile, gathering speed and turning in ever-tighter arcs before popping back out and circling over all of Harlem, from Sugar Hill to the fringes of Spanish and Italian territory. When Aurora shouted, "That's enough!" Matilda brought her back.

Dropping out of her embrace, Aurora stumbled and fell on a broken heel. Matilda landed clumsily and bent to help her up, nearly hugging the other woman when she caught her breath enough to say, "That was something else."

"Something else? Why, it's everything! Aurora, with this invention, you could start your own company and revolutionize flying cars. Hell, flying cities! You could… What's wrong?"

"A white man could," Aurora said. "Maybe even a white woman, but we'd be lucky to have our work stolen and our names ruined if we kicked up a fuss."

"Oh, that's not true," she said, already feeling like a liar. "Why, it's hard for Negroes to overcome discrimination, but with your talent and vision…"

"Why must *we* overcome it? My father couldn't wait to get to France, but he couldn't care less about the Boche. He thought we'd have a chance to prove our worth. He died, and he still wasn't any more than an animal to white folks. If you hadn't lost that arm and that leg over there, would you have pestered your father to put us through school? You had to be broken in the same meat grinder to recognize that we were human beings, too. What would it take to break a country?

"We've been talking about what it would mean for Africa… Why should we build flying cities for folks who hate us when we can build a home in a country where we don't have to prove we're human?"

Matilda shook her head as if to dislodge a bee in her ear. She'd never imagined such fierce enmity burned in her friend's heart. "You belong here, dear. The letter of the law promises you equality. It'll come. Inventions like this, contributions to progress, that's what'll win you a place."

"Maybe we don't *want* a place at your table," Aurora said in the cold, brassy voice with which she'd dressed Matilda down in the car. "Anyhow, it's a ways off from being what it ought to be, but I always thought if anyone could do good with it, it'd be Miss Matilda. Maybe you don't feel like flying anymore," she allowed a wry half-smile and tipped Matilda a wink, "because you lost your reason. When you find a better reason, you can still do what you do."

Matilda felt too warlike to shuck off the armor and take a cab, so she flew home. As the first fingers of dawn broke over the ocean, she zigged and zagged among the towers with fluidity and control she'd never known before. She played tag with a flying squad radio car, leading it a merry chase from Battery Park back to Central Park, and ditched it by hiding under the leafy canopy of the oaks along the Ramble. She was trying to wear herself out, but she found she didn't want to go home, and it was some time and many more reckless stunts before she admitted to herself where she wanted to go.

A fleet of Knickerbocker Air Freight blimps bobbed on the spokes of the East River Skyport. She dodged under them and dropped into the shaft on the Skyport's buttress and into the lair of the White Devil.

A steel mesh barrier had been installed across the tunnel. It spat sparks when she touched it, and another dropped into place behind her. "Anyone home? I'm canvassing for the Universal Negro Improvement Association…"

"He's not here," said an amplified voice from the bottom of a dry well. "Dangle." Taking hold of the steel grill with her prosthetic hand, she ripped a hole in the barrier and stepped through it.

She heard whispered pleas at the end of the tunnel and the gallery of cells. "Hey buddy, they're starving us to death in here. Be a pal…"

She went to the reinforced door and pounded on it. "Open up, or I'll introduce you to my good friend, Walter Winchell."

A bolt retracted in the door that swung open with a portentous groan. Matilda entered the room, almost hoping for an ambush.

"Is that a new suit?" Jasper Zwick slouched in a sprung swivel chair in a stained undershirt and pajama pants, illuminated by the wall of television screens. She loathed the cold, ghostly light, the tawdry electronic spying. Zwick's eyes roved over them as his hands absently made notes on a clipboard with a mechanical pencil. The console upon which he rested his feet was buried in empty food cartons, crumpled napkins, and paper silverware.

"If you could tear yourself away from peeping on our city's leading citizens long enough to tell me where to find him, I'd gladly depart."

"If you must know, I'm trying to keep them alive. Any of them could be next on the hypnotist's hit parade." Leaning forward, he punched a button on a console and picked up a telephone operator's headset. "Dispatch, get eyes on #129. The housekeeper looks like a sleepwalker."

"Copy, Control…"

"So, he left you in charge. How long ago?"

Jasper got up so fast that the swivel chair scooted backward across the grooved concrete floor. "Listen, Tin Man, I don't recall the Devil deputizing you before he left. He went where no one could follow and didn't say when he'd be back. And you know what he said to do if he didn't come back at all?"

The last breath of wind just about knocked out of her sails. She only shook her head, feeling suddenly ridiculous.

"No, you don't. Because you're not one of us." He crossed his arms as if to keep from taking a poke at her, this lost little boy.

She almost started to explain herself to the pimply little commissar before she recalled herself. "Then tell your friends to stop following me."

"We didn't put a tail on you, sister. If we did, you'd never see it."

"I won't try to justify myself to you. You're worried about him. I am, as well, but it's not a competition. I only want to help, but if you're so sure of yourself, I'll just leave you to it." She reached out to touch his arm. Maybe she forgot she was in a suit of armor that could fly and electrocute people by snapping her fingers. Maybe he was even jumpier than he looked.

Jasper threw up his hands as if whisking her away, whipping his head around and ripping the headset's patch cord out of the switchboard. He opened his mouth to say something, but then he thought better of it and went to get his chair. She wasn't there when he turned around.

On her way out of the White Devil's lair, she wondered why she'd come here at all. She wanted to do something. She'd cocooned in Elvira Seaton's life long enough to know she wasn't going to heal without taking some sort of drastic action. Her father had amputated her from her life, and she had to be forceful in reclaiming what could be salvaged, what she still loved. She had been reminded that she still loved doing this and wanted to do something good with it. But why did she think that deranged gargoyle and his Wobbly orphan sidekick would have any answers?

Goosing the throttle bubble, she felt the impeller spin up and had just enough time to brace herself before it flicked her up the shaft and into the rosy dawn.

"Doctor, I haven't been completely honest with you…"

"You should know by now that my discretion is unassailable. So much of what our sessions draw out is for your discovery, your benefit, not mine. To omit vital details is to lie to yourself, dear Matilda. Are you in the habit of lying to yourself?"

"Why no—that is, I'm trying to come clean, but it's hard to see what's a part of me and what's just pasteboard and spangles… I've always felt this stirring to fight for what's right. I know you'll read into that any number of things, but I've gone to great lengths to pursue what I thought was a noble and laudable goal. To protect innocents, to strike at evil, and yes, to redeem the tainted, blood-drenched family name, even if only in my own heart. And then I met someone who showed me that what I was doing was all an empty charade… a 'fox hunt,' he called it."

It had taken her a long time to warm to Dr. Frauenwahl, and their sessions were still a sort of conversational sparring. She scored by how far off the mark his rare observations fell, and how often her confessions left him frowning in owlish silence. But after the crack-up with Father, he'd been the only willing ear she could trust, and sometimes it seemed when he removed his spectacles and favored her with his cautious smile that he already knew everything about her and was only waiting for her to find it for herself.

Now she'd trusted him with her most vital secret and could only wait for judgment.

He crossed and recrossed his legs before bringing one hand decisively down like he was cutting a bolt of fabric with shears. "You feel as if you owe some debt and have found an arena that vitalizes you as you haven't felt since before the war. A means of escape that doesn't infantilize, but completes you. A mask that allows you to confront the world as a powerful, complete individual. A hero, even."

"Yes, that's it, but…" She turned to stare at him.

Without breaking their gaze, Dr. Frauenwahl pivoted in his chair and dropped the stylus on the phonograph on his desk. A lilting, sinuous melody played on a flute seemed to darken the room, to paint the walls with the stray beams of golden sunlight through the leafy canopy of a sylvan glade.

She couldn't take her eyes away from his hands, which seemed to direct the seductive flow of the music.

"Tell me," he said, "everything…"

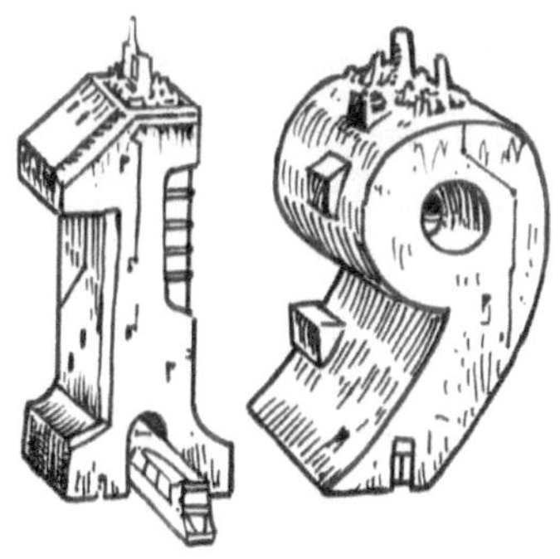

We have had the alternative of humanizing the industrial city or dehumanizing the population. So far, we have dehumanized the population.

—Lewis Mumford

June 24th, 1932 | Utopia, Illinois

If you were to have told young Sherman Peeler that someday he would be a scientist working to uncover the secrets of life on other worlds, he would have scoffed, and you would have been tarred and feathered and run out of town, because that's how they dealt with fortune tellers, where he came from. If you would have told him as he set forth on his career as an assistant professor of biology at the University of Chicago that he would be among the first humans to meet an alien visitor, he would have swooned before you could add that he would come to despise it and fervently wish he'd never left his benighted hometown at all.

When he was recruited to work for the Chalice Company, Peeler was whisked away from his Evanston bachelor flat by a truculent pair who might've been G-men. He half-expected to find himself tossed into a rocket and hurled up to a Bernal habitat in a hollow asteroid or a secret laboratory on the dark side of the moon, whereon he'd help to crack the secrets of the first emissaries from Mars…

If this was a pipe dream for a novice assistant professor with not so much as a published article to his name, they did nothing to disabuse him until they arrived at the Utopia Research Laboratory, barely an hour out of town. The murderously streamlined structure had been built by the Austin Company not more than a year before and was more stiffly guarded than Fort Knox.

Inside, he'd received his first demonstration of a teleportal, and his wildest dreams were insufficiently wild to address the possibilities. His lab was modestly equipped, but he was told that he had only to ask for any resources he needed for a project. There would be new frontiers crossed with every day, a fistful of discoveries every shift. He would be a legend ten times over unless he tried to leave the building before his term of service was ended—two years, with an option to renew at the company's discretion—and if he did, he would be shot dead.

Faced with such stakes, no red-blooded man of science could fail to rise to the occasion.

Indeed, it rained discoveries in the ensuing weeks and months. Still, they remained concealed from the world, and little time could be spared for experimentation or documentation because he had to serve as a coroner for every bit of dead or partially incinerated flora and fauna the reconnaissance parties brought back—if they returned.

The uncultured, scientifically illiterate goons who composed these parties were mercenaries, ex-Marines toughened by endless campaigns in the banana republics down south, who delighted in scraping their boots off into petri dishes and throwing them at him.

Haphazardly collected specimens piled up in his lab faster than he could categorize them, let alone ascertain, as per the company's mandate, any immediate commercial value. Whenever he did manage to study a potential breakthrough, he returned the next shift to someone telling him his experiment had escaped or reproduced so alarmingly in the night that it had to be destroyed. Finally, he was charged with feeding liquefied pastes made out of his specimens to rabbits to see if the new species could be added to the company's biggest cash cow, Ambrosia Meat Substitute.

To his dismay, his colleagues were a mistrustful clique who jealously guarded their own work and sniped at or outright sabotaged each other at every opportunity. The director of research was a Dr. Leopold Lasky, a brazen exemplar of the new Haeckelian school, who delighted in pitting them against each other and siccing them viciously on lesser lights like Peeler. Every meal in the cafeteria and every morning meeting was like a game of liar's poker, and Peeler came away feeling like everyone else could see his poor hand.

He was well and truly at his wit's end when they brought him the thing that he believed would enshrine his name alongside Darwin, Wallace, Cuvier, and his personal idol, Lamarck. And to think, the discovery of the ages had skulked into their labs by way of the loading dock!

Peeler had dissected more than a few of the blobs, and the macroscopic single-celled organism was remarkable, but nothing could be done with them. The creatures consumed almost any organic matter and reproduced by fission at an alarming rate, suggesting a far more competitive native habitat. They adapted to any threat with an alacrity that would've made Lamarck stand up and cheer.

And this specimen showed not only startling resilience but also the rudiments of actual cogitation. It had learned to camouflage itself in the semblance of a human form, to walk among humanity unnoticed, and to observe and even predict phenomena. Once burned by a booby-trapped feeding tube, it avoided the trap and, when denied any other food, contrived a way to open it without getting burned.

Surely, this was a sign of intelligence on par with the wily octopus, but his colleagues were unimpressed. Someone must have taken note, however, because the deluge of maddeningly damaged and unidentifiable specimens stopped, and his superiors unexpectedly agreed to grant him extra working space and materials to build a maze.

His star pupil handily navigated its every configuration. It could manipulate keys to open locks, alter its shape to slip through a barrier, disarm simple traps, and use lessons learned to overcome more complex ones. It had even assumed a rude approximation of Peeler's form to try to convince a janitor to let it out of its cage. By Sherman's most skeptical estimation, the thing showed at least the mental capacity of a human child of grammar school age. Surely, they wouldn't procure a child for him as a control group, but he still pondered how best to word such a request.

Even his archenemy Lasky had taken an interest. Peeler got in the habit of locking up his lab after finding evidence that someone besides the janitors had been rifling through his research.

Now, it sat in its cell, probing at the feeding slot, barely keeping up the wilted outline of a bipedal form. Far less convincing than it must have been with the captive skeleton inside it when captured. Its talent for mimicry had presented a bit of a puzzle, for while it demonstrated intelligence, it also promised any number of hazards. Prof. Peeler could not help but consider the ramifications of their finding this thing out in the world, where it may have imitated countless humans and wreaked untold havoc on the environment. If it had reproduced outside like its kind had in the lab—he shuddered to think of it.

Security was increased fourfold, and Sherman was ordered to avoid association with his colleagues. More explicit orders were delivered only this morning in an express communique that he was specifically ordered to destroy after reading, with the courier ordered to stand by and watch as he did so. Today, he was to test the organism's capacity for chemical transfer of acquired memories by feeding samples of human tissue to the blob to observe its reactions—specifically, if it could learn from what it was fed. Subsequently, he was to harvest cytoplasm from the thing for injection into other blobs and run them through the maze.

This experiment presents a host of challenges, both procedural and ethical, he wrote in his journal. *Chief among them, the question of acquiring sufficient cytoplasmic samples from the donor subject without destroying the integrity of its membrane. Assuming that is not a desirable outcome,* he added, before erasing it. He'd found it best to write everything he had to write around here in pencil.

While a fearsome predator in extremis, the paradoxical blob was actually quite fragile. Its membrane could sustain damage from scalpels, firearms, and blowtorches without lasting harm, but electricity and extreme heat could damage or even destroy it. Experiments on other blobs had shown that their elasticity did have finite limits, beyond which the creature burst and disgorged the myriad organelles and bizarre structures suspended within its cytoplasm.

To proceed as ordered posed an enormous risk, to say nothing of the question of where the "human tissue" was coming from. He knew less, rather than more, every time he faced this thing, and in spite of everything, he had to admit he'd become rather fond of it.

Peeler was sterilizing a set of trocars, which embalmers use to drain blood from corpses, when Dr. Lasky and his lay assistant, Mr. Kercheval, blustered in. The latter pushed a large, hooded cage on squeaky wheels into the lab.

"What is the meaning of this?" Peeler demanded.

Kercheval began connecting a hatch in the side of the cage to the negative-pressure airlock of the blob's bullet-proof plastic cell.

"You can't do this! I am conducting a vital experiment—"

"So are we, bud," Kercheval grated.

"But mine requires strict dietary controls to preserve the integrity of my results."

"What're you, its mother?" Lasky demanded. "It eats everything you put in there, doesn't it?"

"I am attempting to ascertain the extent of the chemical transmission of experienced memories in this species—"

"That's a big idea, Peeler," Lasky said. "Did it hurt coming out?"

"I don't take your meaning, but I deeply resent your impudent tone. I'll register a complaint with Dr. Carr…"

"Like fun, you will." Rolling up his sleeves, Kercheval expansively prepared to administer a beating. At the last possible instant, Lasky stepped in. "What my assistant is trying to say is that our very different projects have intersected in their value to scientific inquiry. We see vast potential in your ongoing experiments to shed light on our own hitherto irresolvable conundrum."

"What?"

Lasky threw up his hands as if ready to thrash Peeler himself. "We want to feed this mug to your pet and see what shakes loose. Cripes, I thought you said you understood science."

Kercheval ripped the hood off the cage. Peeler blanched at the sight of the thing behind the fine steel mesh.

Just to have somewhere to retreat, he picked up the clipboard and fanned through Lasky's slapdash records on the test subject.

Near as he could tell, the subject was recovered from a reconnaissance mission a month before, with orders from the top to "experiment unto destruction" on the subject. Nowhere in the sheaf of grimy carbon-copy invoices, transfer forms, and experiment digests did it stipulate that the subject in question was a human being.

"Experiment" seemed to be a euphemism for "interrogate under torture," and the results, judging by the flurry of transfer forms, seemed to satisfy no one. When the hot potato ended up in Lasky's lap, the focus of the experiments shifted to separating the subject from the golden mask on his face. Surgical intervention, fire, hydrochloric acid, and good old-fashioned elbow grease had been applied, with no results that satisfied the home office. One had to read between the lines to gather that two of his colleagues and no fewer than seven orderlies had suffered grievous bodily harm while trying to remove the mask—many, apparently, by their own hands.

So that's what became of Schweinfurter and Fugate, Peeler mused. He put down the reports and polished his spectacles, and then it dawned on him, quite unscientifically, that he recognized the thing in the cage.

Lasky and Kercheval probably were too busy as children bullying their peers to waste much time reading, but Peeler still guiltily requested an armload of the pulps from the newsstand in Cicero whenever he was allowed such luxuries. Even clad in charred rags, blackened and flayed to a gruesome stick figure that by rights shouldn't be intact, let alone alive, he'd recognize that demonic, bug-eyed skull visage anywhere.

But that was, of course, ridiculous, wasn't it? The Golden Ghost was a fictitious character. Though newspapers had extolled the antics of countless crooks and amateur vigilantes who dressed up as the Golden Ghost on occasion, it had no basis in fact, which was precisely why Sherman Peeler found it so compelling.

"Gentlemen, this is most irregular, but in light of your pressing urgency, I believe we can combine our projects. I will, of course, be cited in your reports and share credit for any discoveries this encounter might yield?"

"Oh, you'll get all the credit," Lasky said, crowding Peeler out of the way to withdraw the divider between the two cages. "We just want whatever comes out when it's done with him."

Kercheval stood by the door. The burned man didn't move, but the blob flushed a vivid pink and seemed to palpitate with curious undulations of its membrane. Did its pigmentation change as some sort of agonistic display, or was its chemical composition changing in preparation for predation? The shapeless mass contracted into a rigid pillar and extended two forelimbs and a rude semblance of a head. "Do you see that?" Peeler shouted. "Predatory mimesis! That's what sets this remarkable specimen apart—"

Lasky lit a five-cent cigar off a bunsen burner and took out a roll of bills. "Wanna bet?"

"Surely you can't be serious!" Peeler sputtered. "This is a travesty of the scientific method! I implore you…" He reached for the airlock controls, but Lasky planted the flat of his palm in Peeler's face and shoved him away.

Kercheval dug in his pockets. "I'll cover you. Your boy's been through the wringer. Ten says he doesn't even wake up."

"Twenty says the dinge rips the jellyfish a new vacuole." Lasky blew smoke into the cage. "Hey Peeler, hold our money."

Kercheval prodded the caged subject in the back with a shock stick. "G'wan, get in there, ya lazy skell."

A seizure threw the masked man halfway into the airlock. He did not move further, even when the blob throbbed across its cell and stretched a cautious pseudopod into the airlock, just as it did with any unfamiliar meal.

Peeler could have fainted from relief that this wasn't going to be some kind of gladiator arena when the burned man threw out an arm at the last split-second. The charred stick bundle of its hand trapped the blob's bulging appendage against the wall. For its part, the blob was like animated chewing gum or a deformed balloon twisted into a vaguely humanoid form by a sadistic circus clown. Peeler somehow felt beguiled by its seeming harmlessness every time he fed it, and he could hardly suppress a giddy giggle such as he let out the first time he saw a python eat a rat.

All at once, it swarmed over the masked man's arm and torso, engulfing the entire body from outstretched hand to twitching toes. The thick, pulsating membrane obscured all but the bare outline of the man.

"Would ya lookit that," Kercheval said. "Easiest twenty bucks I ever made."

"My boy ain't done yet," Lasky snapped. "C'mon, ya bum." He banged the cage, but his heart clearly wasn't in the wager anymore.

"Won't be long now," Peeler said, peering over the other men's shoulders at the prone form. Bubbles burst on its surface, first a few, then a stream.

Kercheval put an arm on Lasky. "Where's my money, ya welsher?"

"See the bank," Lasky said, pointing at Peeler. "I gave it to him."

"You did no such thing," Peeler cried, "and this has gone far enough! See here, it's out of its containment." The torpid blob seemed to be occupied with its meal, but Peeler knew it could escape through the fine steel mesh like water through a basket at any moment.

"G'wan," Kercheval growled, "crap out the gizmo and go back in your cage." He jolted it with the shock-stick. The blob jerked its human meal erect, its membrane standing on end like gooseflesh, flinging it-self against one wall of the cage, then the other. It slammed into the mesh, and its tendrils stretched through it, reaching for Peeler's face.

He blundered backward until he hit a solid wall, his eyes fixed on the ghastly mask he saw gleaming through the bubbling pro-toplasm. The membrane seemed to peel back from the snarling fangs, the goggling eyes to swim up out of the slime until they filled his whole vision, until he tumbled into the infinite black-ness between them…

You were always a doormat. They walked on you before you knew what you were, so that's all you've ever been. You never hurt anyone, forever bent over backward to help your fellow man, but they always knocked you down and took everything you had. You thought it would be different here, but there's always a bully where there's a weakling. You might have achieved great things here, but you'll be fed to a giant amoeba by a bully who'll take credit for your discoveries. His name, his face, will be in the journals and textbooks and the facades of lavishly endowed university research facilities. Not yours…

He thought he'd already been eaten by the blob, devoured and di-gested when he came to lying on the floor with a scalpel in his hand, wet and red up to the shoulder…

He turned over and found the shattered, empty cage, the bodies of Lasky and Kercheval, islands in a lake of blood. He struggled to his feet and went to pull the alarm by the door, but then he looked with a more objective eye at the scalpel, the blood all over himself and the two dead men.

Good Lord, had *he* done this? He dropped the scalpel, wiping his hands on his lab coat, then stumbling to the sink. He didn't remember anything after it engulfed him… No, he remembered a nightmare where he'd finally stood up to them… He remembered—Oh dear.

Maybe he should clean up a little first. Even in this place, such things could stain a researcher's reputation.

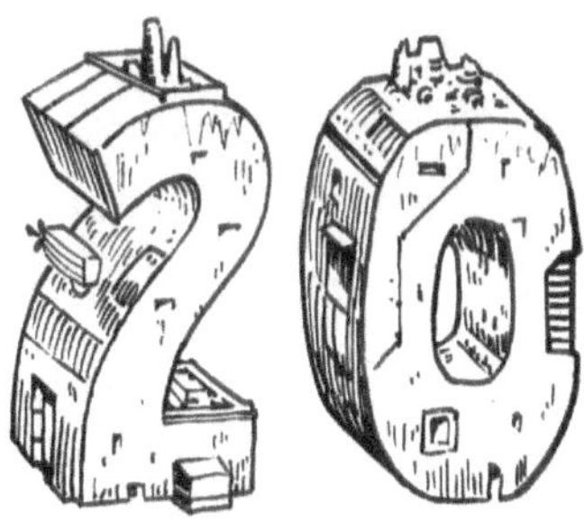

While I do not like to say so, I would be less than candid if I did not say that in such circumstances, I would steal before I would starve.

—Daniel Willard, President, B&O Railroad

Kankakee, Illinois | June 28th, 1932

"**M**ighty hot," the leader of the Haywire Gang said to the man behind the counter of the Kankakee Grange storehouse, not by way of making conversation but of ending it.

Not that the supervisor of the Grange Food Vault took his meaning. Swatting away flies with a tattered copy of *Policeman's Gazette*, he replied, "Mighty hot indeed, but it's not much of a man who lets a little heat keep him from his business."

Whereupon the gangster leveled a Colt Commander at the supervisor and said, "Mister, heat *is* my business."

The man behind the counter, a truculent marshmallow named Abner Bove, raised his hands, but he seemed somewhat unimpressed. "Mister, we ain't got but petty cash on hand—"

"We know what you got, and we're taking it all. Open up them loading doors, or I'll open one in your face."

Two useless local coots who'd been passing the day with Abner tilted down the brims of their straw hats and made for the door. When they saw what was waiting outside, they didn't need to be told to sit on the floor with their hands on their heads.

Reaching across the counter to grab Bove by his collar, Tom steered the clerk into the sweltering recesses of the Grange storehouse. Here, the combined agricultural output of four counties was purchased at ruinous current market value from farms teetering on the edge of the auction block and hoarded. At the same time, the association's lobbyists dickered with politicians over Canadian scotch. While whole towns starved, the food that wasn't destroyed in bonfires was piled to the rafters here, awaiting a chance to enrich the bankers back east. Or at least, it should have been…

"Where's the damn food?" Tom shook Bove and shoved him across the barren concrete floor. "We clocked loaded trucks coming in all week, and nothing going out." Only a few palettes of flour and corn sat in the far corner of the storehouse, and the refrigerator and freezers stood empty.

"I was tryin' to tell you, Mister. We got one of them new-fangled teleportals to stow our stock, so crooks and rabble-rousers can't come forcing a hand-out. On a trial basis, the man said. First in the state, if you care to know…"

Tom's head whipped around, jaw clenched like his teeth were trying to escape his mouth. "Where is it?"

Dick stomped inside with a Thompson at port arms and a ten-gallon Stetson askew on his head. "What's the damn holdup on this holdup?" He saw what was left to be stolen and charged Abner with both guns pointed. "Name the ants that spoiled our picnic."

Abner took Dick's threat a bit more seriously and became a signpost. His left hand pointed quiveringly at the gleaming machine in the back beside the refrigerators. It might have been a furnace or even a crematorium, with a heavy roll-down gate over a wide, low door that faintly hummed like distant cicadas.

"Am I invisible?" Dick shouted. "Don't you see this typewriter, pappy?"

"I'm sorry, young feller… But like I was tellin' your brother…"

"He ain't my brother…" Tom growled.

His beady eyes bouncing from one face to its clone, Bove bit his lip and opted not to dig any deeper.

Tom hoisted the gate up so it banged in its frame. The space inside it was a solid darkness. It wasn't so much the absence of light, but the sunbeams streaming through the high windows bent away from it, or his eyes simply couldn't fill in the blanks or perceive its color. It made his teeth itch and his bones vibrate; it tickled his eyes every time he looked away and then stared back at it. It seemed to grow towards his outstretched hand in scribbles of black stardust that shimmered a negative rainbow as they melted. His fingers pleasantly tingled, vibrating with the machine's hum in perfect syncopation with his galloping heartbeat. Before he knew what he was doing, he'd ducked down, closed his eyes, and stepped into the dark—

"Hey!" Dick kicked the machine. The cosmic blackness dissolved into mundane shadows. Tom hit his head on the machine's low ceiling and came back out swinging the gun. "What in hell'd you do that for? Turn it back on!"

Dick shouted, "Idiot! What were you trying to do, get yourself killed?" He stood between Tom and the knife-switch on the machine's control panel, his crooked smile like a half-discarded mask.

Tom advanced on Abner Bove with his pistol outstretched until it was almost between his teeth. "Turn it back on!"

The farmer's stolid absence of fear would be a source of wonderment in less trying times, as if he didn't believe he could be killed or that guns shot bullets. "Once it's shut off, it has to be recalibrated, or some such, by the home office. I told you; I got nothing but them bags of flour and some lard that's gone rancid, which you're more than welcome to…"

Tom stood staring at the machine like an infant watching a rattlesnake climb into his crib. Dick had to drag him out by his arm.

In the few short weeks since awakening to their new purpose, the Haywire Gang had broken up a dozen-odd farm auctions, raided grange stockpiles and general stores in nine counties, and acquired a small army of hungry hobos and dispossessed farm boys. When they stole money—when they could find any—they'd been vilified in the press for their greed and wanton violence. But when they stole food, they were limelighted as the figureheads of America's desperation, as the face of a peasant revolt, perhaps even a new revolution.

The crowd that came swarming out of the shanties of the Kankakee Hooverville when the trucks rolled in honking were whole families, rootless working men, women, and children among the runaway boys and wizened brothers of the road. They'd come to the squatter village hoping to catch a freight for anywhere else, knowing only what they'd heard about riding the rails from the *Jungle Bunch* radio show, but the new unmanned freights pounded out of the yard at over sixty miles per hour. Stranded here, they tended a little garden with loose seeds stolen from neighboring farms, but they had nowhere to go and no way to get there.

The bucket brigades lined up at the trucks groaned as the weevil-infested bags of livestock-grade oats were passed down the line, but the canned goods taken from every general store on the county road eased their disappointment a bit. The kitchen crew went to work on a cauldron of slumgullion, a catch-all hobo stew liberally seasoned to conceal the spoliation of its ingredients.

"Leeches," Dick grumbled. "Sucking us like a tit."

Harry was beside himself at Moonbeam Sue's having hitched a ride out of camp while they were raiding, but turned to prowling the crowd, making sure everyone knew where the grub came from and bracing every runaway who was fair of face enough to be a girl in disguise. Tom stormed off while they were still unloading the food.

Someone had an old crystal set, and the sugary sawtooth voice of Daddy Long-Legs smothered the whole jungle. "Them old doughboys are laying siege to the Capitol to get their bonus, but what are you doing to get *yours*? You who think they're just shiftless bums looking for a handout, you're dead men reaching up out the ground to salute the rich ones who buried you. Every one of you hearing this voice should hit the rails and march on the Capitol, too. Get back what they took from you. When will you stand up to get the bonus you earned in the war they declared on *you*, the war you're still losing every day?"

Dick sauntered over to the far corner of the Hooverville, trying to look like he wasn't searching for his twin. He sat down on a half-crushed oil barrel and lit a cigarette. "What's eating you, anyway? You got your way. Everybody's getting fat off our hard work…"

"All I got is nothing," Tom snarled. "One life, split three ways. None of us can be satisfied."

"Tommy," Dick said, wheedling with his jaw clenched like two fists, "listen to your big brother."

"We ain't brothers," Tom shot back, "and you ain't so big."

"Nonetheless, I'm bigger than you." Dick crowded him with his ballooning bulk, languid smoke leaking from his nostrils. "What's eating you, anyway?"

"What we are is eating me. I don't rightly know, but when I looked into that machine, all my atoms got goosebumps, and I felt like I'd been there before. Like we was born there… And I been thinking, maybe we're all just carbon-copies of some fella who went through one of those doors and came out split into three. Don't any of us belong on this earth, and those doors are the only way back to where we belong. Maybe we should…maybe if we all went through it, we'd go back together…"

"Nuts!" Dick took off his cowboy hat and swatted his duplicate. High above, a bird fell dead out of the sky. "You wanna go through one of those doors so bad? What's stopping you?"

Blood flushed Tom's face and seemed to coagulate in new bruises on his cheeks. "What're you afraid of?"

"I ain't afraid of catching lead, but tell you what…I'm scared stiff of that dark light. But you know what scares me worse? Every bit of this world is lined up against us, and we're all we've got, but we don't got any enemy gunning for us who hates us half as much as you do."

Tom took off his hat, pinching the crease in it and punching the inside to make room for his swollen head. "I just want to know, or I want it to be over. I can't take no more not knowing."

Dick ripped Tom's hat from his hands and shoved him away, flinging the hat into the high weeds. "Go on, then! Get yourself dead. We don't need you!"

Tom clenched his fists and jaw, seething, tears glistening in his slitted eyes, but he turned and walked away.

Harry came running and tackled Tom, knocking him flat on his face and falling hard on him, crushing out his breath. "Traitor! I'll kill you—"

Dick jumped into the thrashing tangle of identical men. All over the Hooverville, jury-rigged electric lamps brightened, then exploded in showers of sparks. The radio drowned Daddy Long-Leg's voice in a hailstorm of static until every word was thunder out of the speakers. Men and women grabbed their children and ran for cover, ducking into tumbledown shacks and canvas lean-tos. "It's them damned Haywire boys again—"

Tom kicked and bit and butted heads with Dick, only for Harry to knee him in the groin and rip out a fistful of Tom's hair. The trio went rolling down a weedy embankment towards the railroad track. Tom came out on top and busted Harry in the jaw. He grabbed a big rock and lifted it high above his head with both hands. Harry squinted at him and said, "Do it, you yellow he-bitch."

Tom glared down at the hateful faces that were his own face. Snarling, he flung the rock aside and staggered over to a track inspector's one-man velocipede that some enterprising hobo had set up on the short spur beneath the water tank.

Kicking the switch, he sent the velocipede rolling down the track, jumped on it, and began pumping the pedals. Once primed, a little battery engaged, and the velocipede scooted away at the speed of a motorcycle.

Dick and Harry ran along the tracks after Tom, calling him every nasty name they could think of and hurling loose rocks, but their aggression only seemed to speed the velocipede faster. They didn't hear what was coming up behind them until the tracks throbbed with its imminence.

Dick looked over his shoulder and saw the Super Chief Special pounding towards them. Coming out of the bend beneath the Hooverville, it had braked to just under eighty miles per hour, but no human engineer was at the switch. A horn brayed as the locomotive's blazing cyclops eye detected motion on the tracks. Dick hurled himself at Harry and threw both their bodies out of the way. They rolled in the high grass just as the speeding train bore down on the velocipede. Steam and diesel exhaust washed over and blinded them, but Dick saw the locomotive effortlessly smash the velocipede to matchsticks as it highballed north, bound for Chicago.

Time and again, Tom Haywire was confirmed in his one conviction that the world was out to get them. Machines broke down; clothing ripped, and sharp things licked their rusty chops in eagerness to cut them and give them lockjaw. But almost as often, the crazy-making magic that fouled their every play seemed to turn tail and grant them an equally unlikely deliverance. The other two thought this was some kind of superpower, but Tom believed it was some kind of jinx and the world was toying with them like a cat, letting them slip free only to savor the delicious surge of hope in the doomed mouse.

Tom had a split-second to leap into the air before the Super Chief overtook the velocipede. Straddling the seat, he couldn't dive sideways, so he jumped straight up, clawing and kicking at thin air when the locomotive smashed into him. He took the impact on his left shoulder. The bone fractured just below the joint. Tom slid like a squashed bug off a windshield, his right hand and both feet scrabbling for any purchase. The wind whipped over the streamlined engine, trying to pry him off and fling him under the screaming steel wheels. Tom's foot caught on the prow of the cowcatcher. He flung out both arms, nearly fainting from the pain of the bones grinding together, but he clung to the speeding train like a baby to its mother's breast.

The Super Chief barreled into Chicago less than a half hour later. Tom's muscles finally gave out and dropped him as it braked coming into the yard. He barely had the strength to roll off the cowcatcher and throw himself clear of the rumbling juggernaut.

He lay prone in soot and gravel. By painful degrees, he realized men had gathered around him, and was trying to get up and challenge them to a fight when they picked him up and carried him to the far corner of the yard.

"Big brass balls, this kid's got," one of them said. "Bigger'n his brains, anyhow…"

"Mind his wing, Sarge. It's got too many elbows." The man who said this carried one of Tom's legs with a hook instead of a hand.

Tom kicked one of them in the belly and tried to pull free. They let him fall on his broken arm. He bit back a scream, curling up in the cinders like a smashed spider. He didn't kick when they carried him the rest of the way to a signalman's shack. There were dozens of them standing around smoking. A few wore garrison caps or doughboy helmets. They all looked and smelled like gentlemen of the road, but something else about them put him on his guard, or as high an alert as he could muster with his head ringing and his arm singing. They laid him out on the warped floorboards. One of the men gave him a shot of brass polish by way of anesthetic, while two more set the broken arm and did it up in a sling. Another shot of poison, and he was weepingly refreshed.

"You yeggs are alright," Tom mumbled through gritted teeth.

"Aw, shit," said the lantern-jawed fellow the others called Sarge. "Trouble with this country. Everybody wants to be a hero, pull a man out of a flash flood or a burning building, but nobody gave a tin shit how he ended up there. Fewer would need rescuing if more folks looked out for their neighbors."

"We ain't yeggs, and we ain't hobos, neither" spat a skinny, stoop-shouldered man with a whole pouch of chaw in his cheek. "We're with the Bonus Expeditionary Force, bound for Washington."

"The what, now?"

"We served in the Great War, kid. 40th Infantry Division, out of San Diego. We were promised a cash bonus of a dollar a day served, and more for those who went over there. Men are coming from every corner of the land any way they can for that bonus. And we mean to get it or bust!"

"It's bust then," said a sour-faced man who looked like he'd just shaved his head with lard and a Bowie knife. "We ain't getting a step closer than we are now unless the railroad folds and lets us ride."

The circle of vets parted for an older, distinguished gentleman with a politician's head of thick silver hair and a mannequin's stiff bearing. "Who's this man?"

"Some bo who came in on the cowcatcher of the Super Chief, Cap'n," said the Sarge. "Don't know his way around a train, but he sure got sand."

"Well, he can't help us unless he knows how to stump those damned bulls." The officer, for Tom figured he'd have to be, wore some sort of electrified metal exoskeleton that held his head upright and whirred faintly every time he moved. Looking down his nose at Tom because he couldn't incline his head, the

Captain started to turn away and leave the shack when the bum with the broken arm spoke up.

"If you fellas want to get to Washington, you're going the wrong way."

"Listen to the kid," the sourpuss said. "He's got this whole hobo thing on a string."

Tom wasn't sure if that was a dig or not, but he let it dangle. "There's a way you could get there before moonrise. Makes a magic carpet look like a tortoise."

"Aw, he's talking about them fancy tele-whatever doors," said Sarge.

"G-men and Pinkerton goons all around them places," added another, "because of gangsters…and probably because of us, too."

"Stick with me," Tom said with his most winning smile. "I'll get you to DC before that chinless wonder can say, 'Bust' again."

"Young fellow," said the Captain, "if you're sure you can get us there, we've got no choice but to trust you."

Remembering something a smarter man once told him, Tom said, "Don't trust nobody, hunkie, and nothin' but your own nose."

They marched out of the rail yard in formation. There were just under a hundred of them, a few with wives and children and even babies in tow. Brown clouds of manure dust from the stockyards rolled over them as they mounted the overpass at 35th Street and continued north along the canal. Tom stayed at the front with the Captain but was running to keep up with what he'd set in motion. All of them were ten to twenty years older, and none of them heavier. They marched at a pace none could sustain, but damned if any would let the company down.

It took almost an hour to reach downtown, the strongest among them carrying those who wilted in the brutal summer heat. Standing across Adams from the new Union Station on Canal Street, the Chalice Instant Travel Pavilion was an architectural retort to the fusty Beaux-arts train depot.

Looking like a grand art deco movie palace blown out of green glass, Chalice's place had lines going out the door and around the block, a convoy of trucks unloading at its rear freight entrance, a fleet of cabs and cars clogging the grand swoop of a turnaround. The people in line were all well-dressed and jocular as they chatted while the porters ferried their baggage out of sight. All jaws dropped and fell silent as the parade of scarecrows in rags and barrack caps hobbled past.

"Make way for the Bonus Army," Tom shouted, and they made way. Whatever had infected these grim, ravenous men, they didn't want to catch it. The line parted at the front door, and they got three steps into the foyer—the marble so cool, Tom could feel a chill through the soles of his shoes—before a line of security goons hemmed them in.

A frosty-faced concierge with the haughty air of a floorwalker at Marshall Field headed them off, bird-dogging the Captain and inviting him to join the line outside if they'd already purchased tickets, but they were booked through the following weekend.

"We're in a hurry," Tom cut in, "and seeing as your boss is such a great patriot, we thought you'd let us go on through to DC in honor of the service these men have rendered to their country, so just point the way to the right door, and we'll be out of your hair lickety-split."

The concierge let his gaze be soiled by the long line of road-weary, rail-dirty tramps spilling out onto the avenue, and the color drained from his face. "I suppose something could be arranged if you gentlemen can pay the fare..." When nobody leapt to ask, he smiled mincingly. "It's thirty dollars a head." Satisfied, he turned on his heel and started to walk away.

"To walk through a door?" the Captain brayed in an operatic voice that winnowed any reporters out of the teeming crowd. "Mister, I spent two weeks on a tramp steamer to France, and nobody charged me a thin dime. We're going to Washington to get what we're owed. Why don't you call your boss, and we'll be right here waiting for his answer."

Blinking at the flashbulbs popping off all around them, the concierge screwed a monocle into his left eye and stormed off through the hurtling foot traffic. Security guards, porters and clerks in Chalice livery dogged him all the way to the front counter, where he picked up a phone and reported on the invasion.

A squad of ushers corralled the Bonus Marchers with velvet ropes and iron stanchions. Jostled by security, elbowed to drop his last two bits into the Captain's Stetson, Tom stood flabbergasted by the sight of a Roustabout, bulkier cousin to the Farmhands they toppled in Iowa, lurch into the lobby and stand in front of the tall double doors to the pavilion, stopping the foot traffic cold.

Uproar made its way down the line. Tom heard folks with more money in their pockets than he'd ever taken from a bank wondering why someone didn't call the police. *Who do they think they are, anyway? If they get their way now, you can see how their appetite for handouts will never be sated...*

Tom tugged at his hair, turning on his heels. He wondered if he was the only one in the line carrying a gun. He saw no metal detectors, but some folks were sent to a room where a couple ushers went through their baggage. The security goons looked like second-hand Pinkertons, with gauss guns, shock batons, and manacles on their belts. In an alcove beside the door at the back of the lobby, a man in an unseasonably heavy overcoat and snap-brim hat stood watching, talking into a telephone. A G-man, no doubt.

Maybe it was a mistake leaving Dick and Harry, but he was drawn to it. He had to know, and more, he liked these guys and their cause, and he wanted to help them. Some part of him that had always dreamed of adventure, of doing big things, told him this was where he belonged.

The concierge came back, looking as if he'd just bungled the ransom call for a kidnapping. "We'll deliver you to your destination in just a moment...sirs," he said, turning the last word to a slur, then dismissed the Roustabout. The line resumed flowing through the revolving door and into the pavilion. The people who came out of it—tanned, laughing, swaddled in exotic clothes, and swimming in shopping bags—looked wonderingly back as they exited the lobby or searched themselves for baggage claim tickets. The door hummed as it turned, but the people stopped coming out.

About a minute later, one man came striding out in a flashy suit, almost like some kind of fine chainmail. Scanning the lobby, he made a show of being startled by the sight of the Bonus Army as if he'd been looking for them all day.

"Gentlemen, I do apologize! Had I known, I would have arranged for your travel, perhaps even a brass band and refreshments. I know the roads have not been kind. The old ways of transportation are archaic wastes of time and resources for those who can afford them and barbaric for those who cannot. Sylvester Chalice, at your service." Playing to the scribblers in the crowd, he offered his hand to the Captain, who shook it until the gears of his automated brace whined.

"I like a man who handles his own affairs, sir. Captain Miles Wendell Danforth, at your service." They gabbed for a minute, and the reporters crowded in for another shot of Chalice shaking the Captain's hand. The Captain's hat came back with almost fourteen dollars in it.

Chalice told the Captain to keep the money for lunch in Washington, D.C., then pushed several others aside to approach Tom, of all people. "Do I know you, young man? I seem to recognize you…"

Tom looked away but could feel the tall, unnaturally handsome man studying him. "I'm from, uh, San Diego, sir, so unless you served in the trenches, I don't know when we might've met…"

"Seem a bit green for a doughboy," Chalice said. His hand trapped Tom's and gave it a good squeeze. A minute electrical shock passed from palm to sweaty palm. "What's your name?"

"Tom, uh… Danforth."

"Your father is a hero, son. If nothing else, I hope this pilgrimage helps you recognize that." He finally gave Tom back his hand and told the concierge to send them through.

The Bonus Marchers gave a cheer and followed the humbled concierge through the big departure door. Tom's heart knocked on his sternum. He felt both exhilaration and dread as the tangible darkness beneath the arch refused to part for his eyes until he walked into it…

He closed his eyes and stepped through.

Someone trod on his heel and he stumbled, looking around and rubbing his eyes. The Chicago pavilion they'd entered was maybe four stories tall, but the ceiling of this room was so high that clouds of smoke obscured it. Galleries climbed the concave walls of the corbel-vaulted cavern, reached by open cage brass elevators and escalating stairs. The floor of the vast space was an arcade of restaurants, shops, and amusements. Tom was so stunned by all he saw that he almost forgot why he'd come. He'd passed through the gate and come to no harm, and if he didn't learn anything from it, maybe that was just as well. Maybe abandoning his twins set him free of the bad luck that stalked them all. Wherever he was going, at least he no longer needed to worry about them.

"I beg your pardon, sir…" Someone tapped his shoulder and he turned, not even reaching for his pistol, when a sap came down on his head.

A pair of brass knuckles slugged him in the gut and folded him like a laundry sack over a man's shoulder. He gasped and tried not to vomit as he was manhandled through the crowd. "Fainted man, make way!" the man carrying him called out. The noise of the crowd was cut off by a slammed door.

He was carried down a long corridor with shielded, flickering incandescent lamps. After they'd made a few turns and gone through another door, Tom threw his good arm around his assailant's neck and kneed him in the gut.

The man staggered but twisted and smashed Tom into the wall. Tom fell flat on his ass and wheezed for breath. The man kicked him in the face. Tom let him kick him again, taking it on the ear so he wouldn't black out. The blinding pain galvanized him. He flopped over and let the man think he'd knocked him out, but then Tom let him have two in the groin.

The man dropped to his knees, reaching out for Tom. Backing away, not wanting to waste his last three shots, Tom went for the door by which they'd come in, but it had a crazy crank on it that refused to turn and had a red light blinking above it. Casing the room, he took in a bunch of deep-sea divers' suits and helmets hanging on pegs along one wall and metal tanks like artillery shells piled up against another. *What kind of crazy grift is this?* he asked himself, but he couldn't figure it out. He turned the crank on the opposite door, the one that looked like it went outside.

It did…

But not to *his* outside, nor anywhere men belonged.

The air was hotter than hell and almost as thick as water. His vision blurred, and his lungs burned. Maybe he should've grabbed one of those helmets, but it was too late now. He moved slowly, looking up—

Gigantic jellyfish swam through the sky. The sun was not his sun, unless his sun turned red and was being eaten by its shadow. Its light was the ruddy glow of a burning city, the stars shimmering and winking as if they were all hurtling towards this utterly alien but maddeningly familiar planet—

The earth quivered beneath his feet like gelatin. Translucent, it allowed light to penetrate deep within to buried strata of honest rock, to things that might have been manmade, and to eerie, crepuscular lights pulsing deep down below.

He turned around and jumped for the door just as it slammed shut. It had a big crank on it, but he was too weak to make it turn.

The deep-sea divers who came bounding up to surround him had no trouble carrying him away. He tried to fight, tried to trigger one of those storms of unlikely luck that had always saved his skin. But he was all alone and nothing special, now.

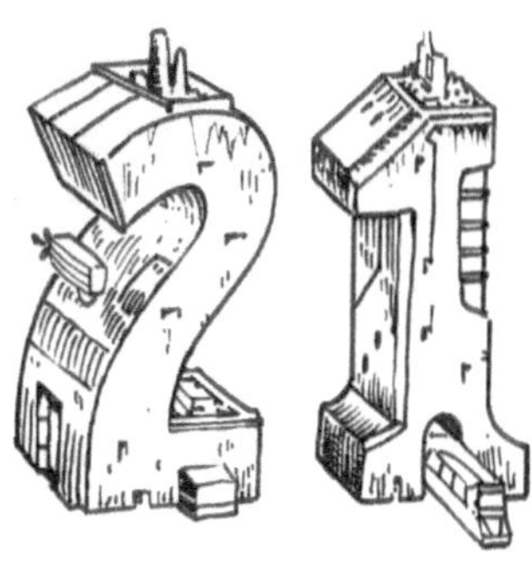

Why, it's the best education in the world for these boys, that traveling around! They get more experience in a few weeks than they would in years at school.

—Henry Ford

July 1st, 1932 | Chicago, Illinois

There were things you had to learn your first time riding the rails, if you wanted to live to try it a second time. You always catch out on the leading edge of a boxcar to ride the blinds, as jumping the caboose-end will likely end in a double amputation. You never ride the jakes or the catwalk without cinching your belt to something, lest the wind and cold sweep you away in your sleep. You never climb into a reefer compartment without propping the lid, or you'll get trapped and freeze, starve, or crushed under a load of ice. And you never, ever sleep in a boxcar with unsecured freight.

Spider had learned these lessons at a frightful cost in friends and fellow travelers lost in moments of lapsed judgment or plain bad luck. He learned to revere the seasoned hobos who shared wisdom for the price of a smoke or a half a stolen chicken. Now, he was forced to pass these lessons on to his new partner, who had neither ears nor eyes nor, so far as he could tell, anything like a brain.

He remembered little or nothing after he blundered out of the portal and into the laboratory, but they were waiting to burn him.

After the fire, there were worse tortures and questions he couldn't answer, and then a voice roaring in his head that he thought must be the voice of the mask, telling him to cooperate or be eaten. The thing that enveloped him did try to eat him, but it must have found him indigestible and resorted to using him as a crutch. The slime coating his ruined body was a rude substitute for all that had been burned away, wielding his charcoal limbs to make their escape and pummel anyone who got in their way. The thing used every weapon they came across, and when necessary, it pointed the mask at them, crushing them with visions of their own guilt and leaving them more badly damaged than those they simply stabbed or shot.

Somehow, they got outside and made it as far as a ditch beside a branch railroad line. They lay in a muddy culvert under a trestle bridge for two days and nights, listening to the sounds of trains passing overhead and men searching. Rank water and a gruel of algae and insects filtered through the membrane covering him sped his recovery. Sometimes, the thing slipped away, presumably to hunt. Agonizingly, his body began to heal the worst of its damage, slowly at first but then showing an eagerness that he had to resist for fear of what else it would cost him.

I was Lionel Fanning, wastrel and soldier of fortune, but now... No...

He pushed these delirious thoughts away, but for the life of him, he couldn't remember his name.

I am the White Devil, the Golden Ghost. I am Hell's judgment on the evil of men—

When he wracked his brains trying to figure out who he was and where he came from, all he could remember was who put him *here*.

Daddy Long-Legs.

This oily cipher, this grinning *salesman*, had caught him eavesdropping, called him out, and brought the fireworks to the monastery. When he tried to repay them, he'd walked into a trap, and now, he was a dead thing in a ditch, with only a faceless monster for company. How did he know? How did he find me?

Chalice.

People said his wondrous instant travel network was nothing short of magic. Maybe they were right. He seemed more like an insurance salesman than a scientist, so perhaps his new invention was no invention at all, but really something very old. If so, he was the most dangerous man the White Devil had ever crossed and perhaps the one casting all the shadows he was chasing.

He wasn't chasing anything now but sweet oblivion.

The mask wanted him healed and would even regenerate his trademark white tuxedo and blacker-than-black cape but at the cost of his every last memory. When he resisted, it punished him with such visions as he used to demolish the will of his enemies. He re-lived all the shameful moments of his life that he could still recall until he wanted only to cease and be nothing.

He rode in a boxcar on the Empire Builder, a cocky teenage runaway who laughed up his sleeve at the three greenhorn Boy Scouts who rode with their legs dangling out the open door. He could have told them the dangers. When the train crossed a narrow bridge over a canal, all three smiling, carefree boys were hooked by their feet and ripped off the train so fast that not one of them so much as screamed. He told himself they deserved what they got for being stupid, but then, what did he deserve now?

Another boxcar on the Great Northern out of Detroit on a frigid, icy night with a couple dozen riders, all of them white, who went deadly silent when a Black boy no older than himself climbed aboard and tried to lose himself in the shadows and warmth of huddled bodies.

He heard the boy cry out as something was done to him in the dark, but nobody stopped it. Nobody said a word. For all he knew, everyone but he was participating in whatever they were doing to him. He kept his hands in his pockets and his mouth shut. Hour upon hour, it went on, but he only thanked his own good luck that he could pass for white in the dark.

When the boy finally broke free and ran, naked and howling for the open door, when he leapt out into the white blur of the night, the empty young man he was then only felt grateful that, at last, it was quiet.

He robbed, he stole, he beat on those who wouldn't give it up and laughed at their stupidity. With the mask, he struck viciously at those he saw as evil but let his own petty villainy fester. He wallowed in the scum of his every cowardly, evil deed, but never was he allowed to remember who he had been and if he could ever have been better. If this was who he was, why remember it at all?

Who are you to rub my face in the world's shit? I didn't ask to become this and don't deserve it. I was no devil, and I'm not even white. I was just as the world made me and barely bad enough to get by. I remember that much, and I won't let you take it away—

He resisted but did not do the only thing that would set him free. Once, he lifted his hand to touch it and feel where the edge of it met his skin, but he did not try to remove the mask. He knew where he needed to go, but he could not stir from the muck until his inhuman partner came for him.

Even when no other memories plagued him, the lama's stinging words came back to haunt him. *Only when you have cast off all worldly attachments... will you open the demon's third eye... harmony between light and darkness...*

Someone jostled him, and he reflexively cursed Ugly John. The sight that met his gummy, half-opened eyes was uglier still.

The blob prodded him impatiently and disgorged a bundle of farmer's clothing out of a pocket in its liquid flesh and then nudged him until he clumsily forced his limbs into baggy, damp denim overalls, a frayed flannel shirt, and a broad-brimmed straw hat. The bridge rumbled with the passage of a slow train. The thing throbbed with urgency and then enveloped him.

Again, he endured the queasy sensation of being a puppet. They staggered drunkenly from the ditch, and then they were running alongside the train. They lunged for the rungs of a ladder up the aft end of a boxcar, deaf to his warnings that this rookie move would cut them in two the wrong way. They caught the ladder and were dragged over the cinders, then climbed into the boxcar and collapsed in a quivering heap behind stacks of wooden crates, so taxed by the effort that they slept as deeply as a hibernating bear.

Their rest was rudely interrupted hours later by the shriek of brakes and a rumbling of shifting crates. The cargo skidded across the floor to smash him into a wall. Before he was completely awake, his silent partner jackknifed his ruined body out of the path of the crates.

They were rolling into the Indianapolis rail yard. Some 500 men crowded the incoming train short of the gate. Loudly chanting slogans and tossing rocks at the vastly outnumbered yard bulls, they swarmed the train. The engineer and the fireman powered down the diesel dynamos, and then they tried to decouple the locomotive, but they were chased off. The bulls cordoned off the locomotive and were swinging clubs at the vets who tried to commandeer the train for themselves.

He'd never seen anything like it and wanted to help them, but he was overruled. Together, the strange duo climbed out of the boxcar, pushing past the legions of veterans, hobos, and rootless rabble-rousers climbing in. The White Devil clouded their minds, pushing the last human face he saw at them in place of his golden mask. No one took much notice anyway. He staggered out of the mob and took cover among the shunted freight cars. He heard bulls cursing the Bonus Army, the Reds, the railroad, and each other for having to enforce the unenforceable.

They kept looking for a quiet place to hide until they could hop a ride east. A warehouse bursting with goods offered little shelter. Automaton workers furiously moved palettes of freight from the loading docks to the boxcars. At the far end, another loading dock, and beyond that, a big open lot with towers, elevators, and trailing ropes anchoring a looming fleet of Knickerbocker Air Freight blimps.

"No," he managed to speak his first word in weeks, but it did no good. His mind lost focus: he was just struggling to keep up with the unrelenting coating of slime forcing him onward. He felt their disguise dissolve, and he heard men shouting. No wonder. He must look like a scarecrow slathered in strawberry jam, something that shouldn't be walking like a man.

The merciless thing pushed him across the loading dock against his feeble resistance. He heard shouting and then a shot. Something tugged at his arm. He saw a hole in the rubbery protoplasm close over the passage of a bullet.

They leapt into a cargo net with a palette of assorted produce just as it was hoisted skyward. While their pursuers searched and shouted below, the gaping underbelly of a Knickerbocker blimp swallowed them up. Pulling boxes over themselves, they lay silent until the palette was dropped into a refrigerator and the crane descended for the next load.

They lay among the produce for a long time, the White Devil watching the faint fumes of his breath in the chill, so welcome after the sweltering summer heat. Perhaps, at last, he could rest…

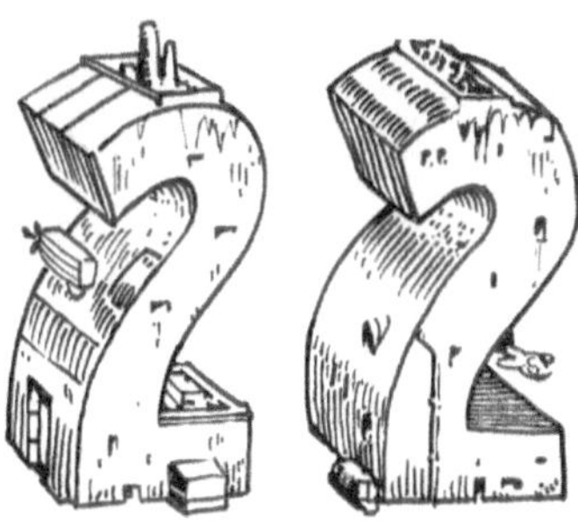

Backward, turn backward, O Time, in your flight; Make me a monkey again, just for tonight.

—Rev. Z. Colin O'Farrell

July 4, 1932 | Waterloo, Ohio

In spite of all it had suffered and all it had learned, the thing that some called Kid Amoeba was still struggling to cooperate.

Like the herd animals they raised for food, humans, it knew from hard experience, banded together when threatened, only to turn on each other when one saw a selfish advantage, for each two-legged sheep imagined itself a wolf in disguise.

It had no choice, at first, but to throw in with the masked creature. Since it had been captured, Kid Amoeba knew only testing and torment and had regressed to its basest instincts. When the not-quite-human thing was thrown into its cage, it tried to eat it. Everything alive was its enemy and its prey. Everything but this one…

Its flesh was poison, the touch and taste of it utterly repellent. That it was barely alive yet unable to die, and inspired fear in its captors, only piqued the Kid's simple curiosity, which in turn sparked a plan. Even if it could not be eaten, perhaps it was still useful.

Using the poison thing as it had used the stolen skeleton, it had broken free and fought its way out of the monstrous place. The masked creature proved more useful than a skeleton, its terrible gaze freezing the armed men and the torturers in white coats or compelling them to kill each other while it fled.

Outside, at last, it tried to communicate with its host, but the masked monster was deaf to even the simplest and most urgent chemical messages. After their escape, the moribund thing could barely put one foot in front of the other on its own and collapsed in the nearest ditch.

But somehow, together, they'd made it this far. Soaring high above boundless fields of tame vegetation with no enemies in sight, Kid Amoeba still trembled with a most alien sensation— dread. As soon as the gigantic sky-blob had begun to swim on the wind, Kid Amoeba detached itself from its host and forced its way out of the cold container where they'd been entombed. Inspecting the steel deck and bulkheads, the polarized windows, it had to conclude that this was some kind of parasitic habitat or vehicle implanted in the sky-blob's flesh. Perhaps the entire thing was a construction of dead, inedible matter, and it had again been fooled. Alone out of all the things of this world, the sky-blob had reminded it of home.

Not for the first time, Kid Amoeba combed its tangled scribbles of vestigial memory from the time before, but nothing offered a path out of its current troubles. It had been forced to adapt beyond its limits and change into another creature entirely, but was it any more successful? An endless cycle of hiding, capture, and escape was the sum of its life so far, and where was it going?

The prospect of a future was just as troubling as the murky reflection of a past. It took less effort now to constrict its membrane into a human form, but it could never hope to walk among them undiscovered or navigate the baffling transactions that made up their world. It had searched for a place where it could exist and reproduce undisturbed, but when it considered the perils of past and present, now it wanted only to find a way home.

Home—

When it had found no immediate threats in the cargo compartment, it returned to the cold container to find its host stirring, shivering with cold and weakness, but driven as if by an engine like those that pushed them through the sky. The mask of pale gold snarled ferociously, its eyes forever spiraling in a disquieting way that made Kid Amoeba's own rudimentary eyespots pop like soap bubbles. Strangest of all, he was now clothed not in the homespun garments that Kid Amoeba had procured for it but a long black cloak that shrouded its emaciated form.

This thing had become a man again, and Kid Amoeba knew that sooner or later, he would betray it, as humans always did.

"You have earned the gratitude of the White Devil. It isn't worth much," he said. "I don't suppose you can talk, but you can hear... can you think?"

The words bounced off the Kid's membrane, but the White Devil's tone, posture, and odor told it much. All it had learned about reading the subtle changes in human faces was useless here. The gleaming visage was inert metal fused with his true face, so it had to look elsewhere. He reeked like something dead and yet had regenerated his muscles, and his myriad of burns and surgical incisions had scabbed over with new skin. With hands out and open, the masked creature showed that he accepted it and was trying to communicate not as host to parasite, but as a partner.

"I don't know where you come from, but I've got some idea how you got here. You came through an open door from somewhere else, didn't you? The one who opens those doors is the one who puts us both in the meat grinder back there. The bad men in the white coats. You savvy?"

Kid Amoeba blew a bubble to signify that the masked creature's tone was agreeable. Dimly, it grasped that he was talking about the ones who'd hurt them both and tried to pit them against each other.

It made the noise it had heard human children make at each other to signify aggression and disgust.

"That's right, raspberry… Maybe you're wise, after all. If we stick together, we can help each other out…" The masked creature stretched out a gentle hand in that gesture that humans employed to trade germs and search each other for weapons. Kid Amoeba drew itself up to the height of a human adult and assumed as human of a shape as it could manage and reached out its own forelimb to shake—

An ear-splitting Ka-DOOM set the whole gondola swaying violently. The concussion smashed in all the windows. Kid Amoeba and the creature were flung head over heels across the cargo hold.

The gondola remained canted nose-down, every loose bit of cargo and even the hulking refrigerators tumbling across the deck to smash into the forward bulkhead. The masked creature caught Kid Amoeba in his arms, dodging and leaping towards the aft end. They were falling to earth, faster and faster. The nose of the great balloon streamed smoke and flames. The horizon tilted obliquely as the fire consumed the beautiful floating blob that held them aloft.

The masked creature leapt into a container anchored to the aft wall and slammed the lid just before the gondola smashed to earth.

They were brutally jolted and then dragged across the ground for some distance. Jerked to a stop, the heat and flames descended on them with the collapsing, flaming skin of the sky-blob, but they'd been spared the worst of the impact. The White Devil kicked open the container and climbed out. "That was no accident," he said. "We were shot down."

Kid Amoeba oozed out of the container. Fire raged overhead, but the creature threw his cloak over it and spirited them both out into a flattened cornfield. Half a dozen men in gray coveralls came scrambling out of the wrecked gondola's forward compartments and ran off into the corn.

Out of the green maze of stalks came another bunch of men. Carrying rifles and axe handles, pickaxes, and torches, they circled the gondola and dared each other to brave the fire to loot the balloon.

The masked creature retreated back into the smoke at the sight of their numbers and obvious hostility. One at the front of the mob, who seemed to be the leader, held a long metallic tube on his shoulder—the weapon that had shot them down, judging by how the others slapped him on the back and cheered. Kid Amoeba enlarged and multiplied its eyes to see the man more clearly, then leapt out of the masked creature's arms.

Bounding and bouncing across the field, it flung itself at the man with the bazooka, knocking him down and looming over him in the most perfect imitation it could manage of the man's likeness.

Of all the faces to find! Before it could recover from this shock, another man who was an exact twin of the first jabbed it with a rifle barrel and kicked it away. Once, all men and women looked the same to the Kid, but slowly, painfully, it had refined the senses necessary to tell the differences in appearance and temperament that could mean life or death. Only dimly did it recall its first, fiery trial in this strange, hostile world, but how vividly did it recall the face of the one who saved it from the fire.

Now, the same familiar face stood over it like a wish come true one too many times, frozen and undecided whether or not to blast it with their guns.

"You figure this is the same critter we dreamt up?" the one with the bazooka asked his twin.

"Looks a fair bit like it," said the twin, "but I ain't dreamed about it since Tom lit out."

The leader elbowed him halfway off his feet. "Never say that name."

"It's some kinda monster from outer space!" screamed someone behind them who didn't look familiar or friendly at all. He aimed a shotgun at Kid Amoeba, and the others raised their weapons.

The man with the bazooka knocked it aside with an offhanded slap. "Nobody touch it. Dinner's burning on the stove, ya hayseeds."

The crowd broke up and ran to the ruined gondola. Kid Amoeba turned to look for the masked creature, to tell him as best it could that this man who was two men would not harm them, but he had vanished into the endless sea of corn.

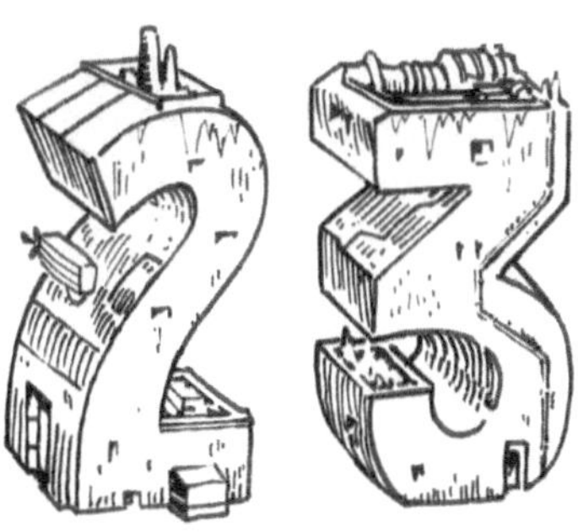

July 8th, 1932 | Hell's Kitchen, New York

"**T**hat's all we know, boss," said Jasper Zwick. **Not for the first** time, he ran his fingers through his unruly hair, chewing his lips. Only minutes before, he'd almost turned a cartwheel when his mentor stormed into headquarters after weeks without a word. "I know it ain't much, but if we had more to go on…"

"Don't beat yourself up, kid." The White Devil pushed away the pile of maps, diagrams, typed and handwritten reports, stood up from his chair, and planted his knuckles on the desk, staring at the papers so intently, they almost smoked.

He was exhausted and wobbly, but shut down Zwick's concern to demand any new dope on Matilda Lynch and the hypnotist. Something big was cooking, and they were ten steps behind. Jasper had made a few breaks while the White Devil was away, but they were still flying blind.

"The dame skipped town in June," Zwick told him. "Right after she dropped in here, looking for you…"

"What'd she want?"

Zwick shrugged. "Show off a new frock." Traveling under the alias Elvira Seaton, she'd taken a train to Washington, DC, and paid for a night at a modest hotel, then disappeared.

"Let her dangle," Zwick said. "We got heat on your hypnotist." Every operative under their thumb had followed the leads without uncovering anything new. Even the phonograph shard had proved a dead end. The record was cut with a Presto portable transcription cutter, so it could have been made anywhere, and no records turned up at the other murders. But as with every aspect of this goat-rope of a case, there were shadows that suggested invisible hands at work all around them.

They'd found a tantalizing pattern of thefts and a sharp uptick in demand for instruments and sheet music from pawn shops and union halls all over Manhattan until about a year ago, suggesting the unknown party had assembled his orchestra. Another tasty lead had almost gone unnoticed under a pile of dead bodies. A report from the Central Morgue detailed several dozen of the dead men routinely collected off the streets of Lower Manhattan every morning also had bloody, tattered fingertips as if they'd been ruined in some kind of repetitive work. The police declined to follow up on it, and the bodies were consigned to unmarked mass graves in Potter's Field.

But there was a name, or at least a word, on the blue lips of some who were not quite dead when shoveled off the pavement. Der Kapellmeister—the Conductor.

"Ring a bell?" Zwick smiled when the White Devil shook his head. "I read once about this kraut Field Marshal who hypnotized his men into sleepwalking suicide troops, but I didn't connect it until we got the name. He used music, boss. I think it's the same guy. We're this close—"

He didn't tell Zwick he already knew who the Conductor was.

This bird was unlike any stripe of criminal the White Devil had ever come across. He could keep a secret and had no loose-lipped associates. He took what he wanted with authority, and he possessed an ability more powerful than the Eye of Fate. His agents were sleepwalkers, and those he didn't simply use up emerged without memory of what they'd done or for whom.

And Matilda Lynch was one of them.

All those weeks in captivity, he'd never put it together, but now, it was unmistakable. No wonder she'd shrugged off the Eye. She was already enthralled by a master mesmerist who had masterfully bound her deepest animus to his own agenda.

He targeted only the richest, but it was old money—oil, railroads, mining, banking. If he was a spy for some foreign power, the Devil's operatives could've intercepted his orders. If it was some long-buried Wobbly faction, they would never shut up about it. They would claim each blow against the ruling class as a clarion call to the masses to rise up and lynch the rest of them with their broken chains. The new money power and the moguls pressing to open the market to their automatons, ray guns, and teleportation devices were not on his list. None of the swells who attended Sylvester Chalice's luncheon had been clipped, but two who'd declined had since gone into seclusion. Hearst was in hiding at San Simeon behind a private army, and Henry Ford holed up at his Dearborn fiefdom, and was served only by automata of his own design.

The third to decline was the subject of a confidential report from a mole within the New York PD. Romulus Lynch, president and chairman of Lynch Munitions Company, was found dead in his penthouse apartment at the Majestic. Though the apparent cause of death was a fatal heart attack, police were seeking to question his housekeeper, Mabel Hildebrandt. The White Devil wondered if the Silver Sentry would come out of retirement to avenge his death.

It was too late to warn her. The chilling conversation he'd eavesdropped upon came back to haunt him.

Dead to the public eye, you are free to kill your last connection to the failed world. Free you will be. Free to soar...

Perhaps he was wrong. It could all be a coincidence. If she was an unwitting tool in her father's demise, she would be destroyed if she learned the truth. She must be protected if she could be saved at all. Such thoughts were attachments that could only confuse him and deflect him from his aim, which was total justice—evil to destroy evil.

Whoever the Conductor was, the Devil had more reason than ever to suspect he was Chalice's stick. But he'd gladly trade all the suspicions piled up in front of him for just one solid fact.

"I want to see Lynch's autopsy—"

"It's a cinch the Conductor did it."

"As much as he did any of them." If he was right about Matilda's analyst, she herself could be the greatest threat, wherever she was. If she was in the Conductor's power, she might be closing in on his next target...but who was it? Zwick's shoulders settled, and he licked his lips, eyes shifty like he was about to throw down a winning poker hand after bluffing his freckled ass off. "Just this morning, Moose spotted this track rat climb up onto the IRT platform at Penn Station... Looked like death spread on toast, and he was hiding something under his overcoat..."

Zwick let the silence ripen until the White Devil snapped, "What, already?"

Zwick's crooked mouth straightened out painfully into something like a smile. "A French horn."

"Do tell. What did he have to say for himself?"

Zwick combed his hair with his fingers and held them up in front of his face. "Not a word. We tried to get soup into him, but he wouldn't eat. Just sat there like a wind-up toy, running down..."

"Where is he now?"

Zwick took a ring of keys and led him to the gallery of holding cells. Even before the heavy door opened, the White Devil could hear the fractured tune skirling out of his toothless mouth.

The track rat had sallow skin like used tissue paper. Gnarled hands were held up before him, the fingers of the left fluttering as if working the valves of a horn. The White Devil was no music lover, but he recognized it well enough, and it answered every question he could have asked.

It was "Hail To The Chief."

A Salvation Army band slowly murdered "Onward Christian Soldiers" on the corner of Tenth Avenue and 34th. The White Devil flipped a quarter into their collection kettle as he passed, crossing 34th amid a stream of bleary-eyed men and women going to or from soul-killing jobs. The sun's dying rays touched the roofs of the tenements and smokestacks high overhead, the leaden heat stored up from the sweltering day seeping back out of the half-molten asphalt. Everything west of 10th had been swept away by bulldozers and wrecking balls to make way for a new tunnel to Jersey.

Once, Hell's Kitchen was the most dangerous place in the nation, ruled by gangs like the Gophers, Gorillas, and Hudson Dusters, who ransacked and robbed the trains out of the Thirtieth Street rail yard with impunity until the cops broke them, twenty years back. Likewise, the burlesque houses, opium dens, and brothels of the Tenderloin, which once painted the streets scarlet from Fifth to Seventh Avenues and 25th to 42nd Streets, had been snuffed out, overtaken by the more respectable garment and fur trades, but the greater obscenity of the tenements continued unabated.

The waterfront warehouses, factories, stockyards, and docks had pushed the unskilled immigrant labor that worked in them into denser slums to the north and Lower East Side. Still, many of them had fallen silent as the flow of finance dried up or diverted to other venues, and more were boarded up but churned out products day and night with automaton labor. Hell's Kitchen today was like a notorious convict paroled from prison, a shadow of itself looking for honest work with a blackjack in its boot.

He combed the streets for hours, lurking outside pawnshops and soup kitchens in the layered disguise of a vagrant, listening and watching for glimmers of a trail that dissolved like a handful of fog. A girl skipping rope in a tower block courtyard whistling a snatch of a Strauss waltz, a busker in a tattered swallowtail tuxedo playing "The Thieving Magpie" out front of the Old Grand Opera House, a drunk playing the French can-can on the steps of the 8th Avenue subway line on a harmonica, which the White Devil had once heard was part of a symphony called *Orpheus In The Underworld*.

All of them were like player pianos, eyes fixed on the sheet music inscribed on their brains as if by the recording device the Conductor used to press his murder music.

For over a year, the White Devil had beaten his head on a brick wall, and now, he couldn't turn a corner without having bait dragged under his nose. He was being led into what could only be a trap, but powerless to turn back. What was his life balanced against this? It was all he had. There was something else, some half-forgotten pipe dream that once blunted his resolve, but now his mind was clear.

By the time he returned from Chicago, he didn't even care that he and the mask were one.

Taking the stairs two at a time, he hopped the turnstile and followed two flights down to the platform. He pressed his back against a wall to let commuters shuffle by onto a northbound train, watching the few stragglers left on the platform. When the train rumble had died away, he could just make out a fragile, plaintive sound coming up the tunnel to the south. The faint, mournful call of a horn led him off the platform and down the track, spatted shoes straddling the electrified third rail. It seemed to repeat the same mournful phrase over and over, one he knew all too well.

Chopin's Funeral March.

A hundred yards or so down the track, he found the source of the sound—a loudspeaker mounted on a tunnel wall that had conspicuously been rebuilt. Its cord disappeared into a crack in the newer brickwork. At the first vigorous kick, the bricks collapsed, the mortar little better than wet sand. Climbing through, he found himself in a stairwell descending into a wide, lightless cavern.

Even with the dark-adapted eyes of the mask, he saw no one, but he heard snores, furtive scraping, and grunts all around him.

Hundreds of homeless New Yorkers moved underground in the first hard winter after the Crash, and many never came back up. There was a world down here beneath even the various subways, freight rail, and private pneumatic tubes that honeycombed the island.

This godforsaken cave was lined on both sides with boarded-up shops, and the tunnel bisecting the long promenade was a cylindrical tube, so he concluded this must be the old Arcade Line. It was to be New York's first underground railroad, back in the runaway steam boom after the Civil War. Every savant with a degree and a rich backer sent digging leviathans to chew the substrata to Swiss cheese before the city imposed a moratorium on private subway lines and set up the IRT. The Arcade Line got a lot further than the others before funds ran out, and the spoilsport developers bricked up what they'd carved out of the bedrock rather than share it. Like Gramercy Park, it was to be a privately held, self-contained subterranean city, with pneumatic tunnels connecting the island's posh high-rises, shops, theaters, and other diversions, so one need never sully their fair patrician skin with the harmful rays of the sun ever again.

The greedy developers' dream had come true after a fashion.

He searched the rubble-strewn floor for the speaker cable, but he needn't have bothered. When he listened, he could hear the source of the music. Following the melody into the grotto of an aborted concert hall to rival the Orpheum, he found a lone, dead cellist propped up on a folding chair on the bandstand. The music led him through a fire door, he barely flinched when it slammed and locked behind him.

Down the stairs he crept, drawing a pistol and his short, curved sword. The dirge washed over him like a fever of rotted flowers. The stench of ancient sewage wafted up from the depths. His shoes plashed in shallow, scummy water. This chamber was part of the city's oldest sewer system, an octagonal drainage hub. The inflow pipes were all plugged with pig iron caps, the floor of rusted iron grating beneath which black water eddied and gurgled into still lower depths. Even as the music limped on, it took a moment to realize that the room was full of people.

Perhaps half a hundred men and women sat in chairs around a makeshift stage. A man stood motionless at a podium, arms outstretched with a baton pointing imperiously over their heads. The White Devil stalked through the ranks of chairs, noticing many slumped with their instruments across their breasts where they had died. The rest labored on, dehydrated and starved, fingers bloody sticks. Their various clothing marked them as hoboes, debutantes, hoodlums, cops, priests, prostitutes, bohemians, stockbrokers, and stevedores. However, all had the exact same blank, impassive stare a yoked ox gives the rutted field ahead as it pulls the plow.

Leveling his pistol at the base of the Conductor's skull, he commanded, "Turn around."

The Conductor remained frozen at the center of his circle of misery. The erect curve of his back seemed to defy, if not demand, the fatal stroke. The White Devil hated to do it only because doing so might not break the spell that held his victims, and if he was here, then whatever he'd set out to do was already in motion.

The White Devil came close enough to know the truth but fired the weapon anyway, so profound was his fury.

A mannequin's head burst into sawdust. The orchestra played on, but louder, with missed notes and off-key seizures spreading out in ripples through the headless death march.

Searching the room for an exit, he noticed the cage of a service elevator against the far wall, but there were no buttons to summon the car. The cage was sealed by some kind of magnetic lock and could not be forced open. By pressing his face between the bars and staring up the shaft, he could just make out a pale scrap of dingy artificial light against a wall, perhaps twenty stories up. Indeed, it must lead to whatever public front the Conductor used when he wasn't playing with his toys.

Casting about again, he returned to the podium and stood where the mannequin had been placed. A man so used to controlling everything in his life would have more than one means of escape at his fingertips. He ran his gloved hands over the podium and its lamp. Brushing aside the curled sheaves of moist sheet music, he saw a row of recessed brass buttons on top of the podium. He pushed one, and there was a growl of stone on stone, a sudden downpour.

The ceiling caved in.

The White Devil flung himself from the podium and dove into the orchestra pit just inches ahead of a slab of granite six feet thick, which crushed the stage and the whole woodwind section. A torrent of rubble and wastewater sluiced down from the gaping hole in the ceiling. Before the White Devil could find his footing, he was knee-deep in black water, and it was rising faster and faster.

The orchestra finally awakened, but not to their senses. They climbed over each other to get at him, clutching at his cape, tugging his sleeves, and throwing arms around his neck and legs, so he had to drag a dozen of them up the stairs to the locked fire door.

He broke off the doorknob with the butt of his blade, but the door refused to budge. He fired into the lock, but the bullet ricocheted and glanced off the fangs of his mask, knocking him back into the arms of the orchestra. They pulled him back down the stairs. His gun was ripped from his hand by fleshless fingers, his sword arm pinned, and he sank with them into the rising flood.

His feet couldn't find the floor. They piled on him and dragged him underwater and rolled him until he couldn't find the surface. His breath gushed out in silver bubbles. He crept hand over hand among the drowned, but more came thrashing in and clung to him, holding him down. His lips clamped shut on his last stale breath…but he stopped fighting as another awful truth of the mask revealed itself.

Who needs to breathe?

Only the living—

The White Devil went limp and let himself sink under their weight, let them bear him down to the bottom, let them all die. When the last galvanic twitch had subsided, he kicked off the floor and pushed through the thicket of outstretched hands until his fingers knotted around the bars of the elevator cage. He crawled round it to the door, which now slid easily back. The elevator was disabled. He climbed the wrought-iron cage of the shaft, corpses clinging to his cape. He emerged from the water and gasped in stale air like an infant's first breath, but it didn't revive him any more than being held under for so long had killed him. Something inside him had drowned and died, but he climbed on, a machine more relentless and emptier than the puppets who failed to stop him.

Climbing the shaft, floor after floor, with no doors until the 12th and top floor of this building. He pried open the safety cage and the doors, then a sliding barrier of blond wood that turned out to be the backside of a bookcase. He stepped out of the shaft and into a well-appointed office. A desk big enough to land a biplane on with a green-shaded lamp, a blotter, and a notebook held open with a fountain pen, as if the occupant had only just stepped away to consult with his receptionist. More bookshelves with leather-bound volumes on psychology and art and everything else smart men pursue to make life seem less empty lined the walls that weren't covered in oblique geometric art. A plush padded lounge upholstered in lush green velvet sprawled across the middle of the room. Just behind where patients rested their heads was the cone of a phonograph.

Rifling the desk, he found a stack of engraved business cards on buff paper like raw silk. *DR. GERHARD FRIEDRICH FRAUEN-WAHL, Clinical Psychotherapist.* The White Devil pawed the journal, sodden gloves turning the paper to dripping rags almost before he found what he was looking for.

A regular appointment with ML every Tuesday afternoon for the last six months. The last one was a month ago and was crossed out with a short, terse, precisely lettered remark: THERAPY COMPLETE.

When I marched off to war in 1917, I remember a Civil War veteran, over seventy years old, telling me, "Son, you are all heroes now, but someday, they will treat you like dogs."

—Benjamin Shepherd, Bonus Marcher

Washington, D.C. | July 26th, 1932

"**The vultures still flock to Gettysburg,**" cried the rabble-rouser, "so potent is the memory of the feasting their ancestors did on that bygone day of battle." He pointed his finger at the Capitol Dome. "What vultures will descend on yonder grand temple of dead democracy in the last days now upon us? Their numbers will black out the sun, and their feast will be upon your flesh—"

"Nuts to you!" Someone shouted. Someone else threw a rock. The speaker jumped off his soapbox and tried to lose himself in the angry crowd.

Matilda watched the veterans of the Bonus Expeditionary Force run the Socialist orator out of camp as she played checkers with Ralph, a grizzled old private in a sweaty union suit and his old breeches and puttees. A shabby little marching band struck up a forlorn rendition of "Over There." Her opponent flinched and dropped his piece on the board. "Your move, Miss Seaton."

"I'm sorry, where is my mind…?" With only a distracted glance at the battlefield, she moved one of her few surviving red pieces over the crease in the well-worn board. "I know the music's supposed to keep up our spirits, but..."

"I heard the other woman say you was at Nesle, Miss? April of '18? You couldn't have been..."

"Oh, but I was," she said, tapping her left arm against the edge of the camp table. The dull clang brought a sad smile to the veteran's whiskered face. It served better than any doctored identification, and no one asked after seeing her wounds who she was, where she came from, or why she used a dead woman's name.

"Then you heard it."

She wasn't sure what he meant, but his eyes were cold stones under icy water, and then she did know.

"To this day, I can't abide the sound of orchestra music. That cold-blooded puppeteer drove his men over us. They kept coming into our crossfire like we were throwing out candy. I remember his shadow blown up real big against the smoke from their eighteen-inch field guns. Those arms waving in time with the music, throwing the wave attacks at us like he was flinging little tin soldiers... Forgive me, Miss, for going on, but I never felt shut of that damned war without knowing we sent the Conductor to Hell..."

"Never mind all that, Ralph," Matilda said, but she couldn't take her own advice. She remembered the funereal music surging on the operating theater intercom and the blood-red sound of it outside when the line collapsed, and they had to flee. "I heard stories, but... why do you mention it now?"

"King me," said the veteran. Looking down, Matilda realized she'd been triple-jumped, and her last piece was boxed in between Ralph's other two kings.

"Just as well," she said. "Thank you for a very stimulating game, Ralph."

Adelaide Weiland came around over wiping her hands on her apron. "Elvira, could you mind the counter for a moment? I really should speak to the General about where our next cup of coffee is coming from."

Adelaide was an Alaskan oil man's widow and had been the directress of a Salvation Army canteen in France. She still wore her khaki uniform with skirt, gold epaulets, and the red emblem on her doughboy helmet. Scrounging furnishings and diversions from local attics and junkshops and soliciting donations for food, coffee, and cigarettes stood her in good stead running the BEF canteen. She'd managed to fill out the war surplus mess tent with three rows of picnic tables, mismatched chairs, and even an old upright piano.

Outside, Camp Marks sprawled over a couple dozen acres of the Anacostia Plain, just across the river from Washington. It was the greatest Hooverville in the nation, a city of over five thousand housed in dead cars, tarpaper shacks and castoff materials from the neighboring junkyard. There was a lending library, an official post office, a blacksmith, and a boxing ring. One veteran slept in a coffin to protest the cruelty of the "Tombstone Bonus." Not to be outdone, another just down the row had himself buried alive, and you could pay a nickel to look down into his coffin via the funnel through which he breathed.

As the summer wore on without the meager victory they'd come from every corner of America to claim, the shanty-town had become less like an army camp and more than a little bit of a human zoo or a circus sideshow.

The oddest thing about this experience was how odd it wasn't, or at least, how right it felt to her when so much had gone wrong.

At the last session with her psychoanalyst, Dr. Frauenwahl had told her she should seek a less perilous outlet for her need to serve a higher good. She had seen the newsreels about the Bonus Army converging on Washington and felt like she could do something real there. She packed a bag and bought a train ticket, presented herself at Camp Marks for whatever duty they saw fit to assign her.

They opened the hospitality station with reveille every morning and served 2,500 doughnuts, fifty pies, and two hundred gallons of black coffee, "a maximum of grace with a minimum of grease." Matilda served and circulated, helping men write letters home or playing canasta, cribbage, chess, or checkers.

It brought back the war for her as vividly as for the soldiers, she could tell, and reliving their youth's greatest adventure and time of terror was as overwhelming for them as it was for her. Her heart would've gone out to them in any case, and she believed she'd still be here even if not for Frauenwahl's urging. Still, even though she hadn't come for the Bonus and was never promised one in any case, she felt she was one of them, having made the same sacrifices, with her head now on the same chopping block.

The rabble-rousers were coming in greater numbers and shouting louder every day, but no one gave them a moment's notice, though morale in the camp was at rock bottom. For nearly two months, they'd marched and waited and watched as the House passed Wright Patman's Bonus Bill to the Senate. The papers that were on their side said their cause was just, and the rest could go to hell.

She had arrived in DC on the night the Senate voted. On June 17th, 700 men stood vigil on the Capitol lawn, and when the word passed that the bill had been defeated, many of them were ready to riot. Instead, they gathered to sing "God Bless America" and march in an orderly procession back to their camps. That they had neither turned violent nor abandoned the cause altogether was less through the will of the weedy little fellow in charge, Commander Walter Waters, a former sergeant and out-of-work cannery worker from Portland, than the goodwill of Police Chief Glassford, who'd bought the BEF provisions out of his own pocket and was now handing out train tickets at his own expense to anyone who wanted to go home.

Over a month after their last hope was gone, the overwhelming majority of the Bonus Marchers still clung to the camp, waiting for victory or whatever was coming.

She saw Adelaide trailing after Commander Waters, who'd taken to high cavalry boots and breeches and twitched a swagger stick as he harangued the scrum of reporters dogging his review of the camp. They wanted to know why he wasn't mobilizing the BEF to go home and what they hoped to accomplish by staying.

While she still wanted to believe their cause was just, the last issue of *B.E.F. News*, a grubby mimeographed pamphlet published here in Camp Marks, outlined Waters' plan to form a new organization that had little to do with the Bonus. Who the Khaki Shirts would fight and on whose behalf was left unspecified, but that they took more than their fashion sense from demagogues like Hitler and Mussolini was spelled out in rabid clarity.

Waters was losing his grip on this ragged band. Only two days before, they shouted down his impassioned plea to retreat to nearby Camp Bartlett and set up "permanent quarters," whatever that meant. The City Commissioners had refused to meet with him, and only this morning, the apologetic Police Chief told him to move or be moved. Today.

The BEF would probably fold in the face of armed force, but they weren't the only ones in town. Rumors abounded that the small army of Reds who'd been exiled from the BEF camps and set up their own tent jungle on Pennsylvania Avenue were stockpiling weapons and planned to make a shooting war of the evacuation.

"We just want what we came for," Waters shouted, but he was hoarse and melting like a snow cone in the broiling heat. Someone whispered in his ear and passed him a telegram. Reading it with white knuckles, he waved it in the air and shouted, "There you are! You're double-crossed! *I'm double-crossed!*" He bit his lips and strutted off double-time before Adelaide could get a word in his ear.

Adelaide hurried back into the tent and began picking up as if President Hoover had announced he'd come by to sample the doughnuts. "It's happening, dear. They're starting to roll up the camps in the city limits. They'll all be coming here. I hope you remember your nursing…"

"I don't understand," Matilda said, but she noticed the camp springing into high dudgeon all around her. Vets raced from place to place or just shouted at each other. Some were sure they were about to be overrun, and others just as sure they wouldn't dare, and still others defiantly waved sticks and stones and said let the bastards come.

Whatever the yellow presses said, the Bonus Expeditionary Force had no weapons or order of battle. Even the MP's detailed to preserve order were empowered only to mediate and in no way physically punish those who violated camp regs. Perhaps it was asking too much of an embittered army of old soldiers to see that their playacting at war was inviting a real one.

After helping Adelaide secure the canteen, Matilda visited the hospital tent, only to be told they were bracing for the worst and to stay within earshot. Standing outside the tent, she looked to the north and saw columns of smoke rising from somewhere near the center of the city.

Someone jostled her and pressed something into her hand. She unfolded a scrap of the same pulp paper used to print the BEF News, but her eyes fell upon a hastily scrawled note: YOUR FOX AIMS TO KILL PRESIDENT TONIGHT. WILL YOU HUNT OR HIDE?

There was something else on the note, but if she saw it, she didn't read it; if she read it, she didn't understand; if she understood, she didn't remember.

Balling up the paper in her fist, she fell in with the racing throng, running to her own billet and a footlocker under her cot.

Even Adelaide had fretted that she'd be safer and more comfortable at a nearby hotel, but Matilda had felt safe here and part of something good and right. All the same, she had brought the footlocker with her and kept it close, unwilling to admit but unable to deny that she would need it here and others would need her.

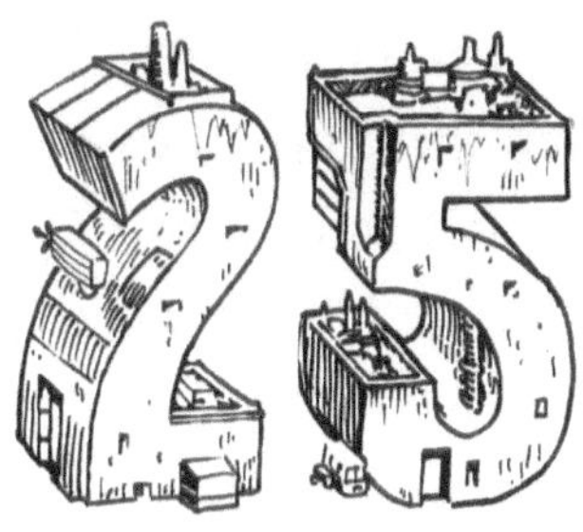

Hang together and stick it out till the gate bars of Hell freeze over; if you don't, you are no damn good… Remember, by God, you didn't win the war for a select class of a few financiers and high-binders.

—Gen. Smedley Darlington Butler

July 26th, 1932 | Washington, DC

On a sweltering July afternoon, with the Bonus Army milling angrily on the Mall and police out in force, the city simmered with uneasy anticipation. It had suffered the two-month occupation with generally good humor, but with no end in sight and local charity banks stripped to bare shelves, they looked anxiously for any change in the weather.

Congress had adjourned for the summer, having buried the question of the Bonus, but the camps had swelled across the capitol until nearly 100,000 marched in ragged bands, panhandled door-to-door, and waved signs at passing motorists. Perhaps half of them were the veterans stubbornly pressing on with no hope of redress, while the rest included Communists, labor agitators, and assorted nomadic refugees who'd come at the urging of radio demagogue Daddy Long-Legs, whom the powers that be saw as an existential threat not only to the safety of its citizens but to the fabric of democracy, itself. In strategy talks between Generals MacArthur and Mosely and Secretary of War Hurley, the possibility that the Army might impose martial law on its own if the President did not immediately put Plan White into effect was leveled more than once.

While official business had ground to a halt, the press was treated to a brief address from the north portico of the White House by Chairman of Chalice Electric & Transport Sylvester Chalice, before his informal luncheon with President Hoover. NBC carried the speech on its news program, which was syndicated via more than 200 stations nationwide, in what was seen by many as a subtle declaration of a third-party candidacy for the Presidency.

In response to a reporter who asked if he was sorry he let some Bonus Marchers use his teleportals to come to Washington, and if he'd be willing to let them use it to return home now they were beaten, he said, "I salute the brave servicemen who sacrificed so courageously for the cause of freedom, and I hereby pledge my resources to their safe and orderly return home, but I would hope that some more forward-thinking leadership in these parts come November might find a better solution than to spread the unaddressed grievances of these dispossessed sons of liberty across this still broken and beleaguered nation."

Chalice coyly declined to report what he and the President planned to discuss, but he forcefully declared his intent to address the next session of Congress about the onerous regulations impeding the growth of his company.

Someone else asked him how he slept at night knowing his whiz-bang Buck Rogers toy for rich folks was slated to put four million more out of work.

"I've had little choice but to maintain fares at higher rates than the average citizen can afford because of all the restrictions imposed to protect entrenched labor and capital interests, and in response to the gentleman from the *Post's* line of questioning, it's never been a company's responsibility to retard its own success for fear of putting obsolete industries out to pasture. You say four million will be put out of work if my network is allowed to expand to its full potential. But tens of millions are out of work now, and nobody's asking the old money powers how they sleep at night.

"I freely admit that what I've offered the world will make it smaller and that many of the changes will be painful ones, but I can only offer the reassurance that every new invention that snuffs out old markets has always in turn opened new frontiers, which Americans have always courageously conquered."

A reporter from the *Wall Street Journal* demanded to know if Chalice was promising, or threatening, to open America's borders to other nations.

"Gentlemen, I submit that we must reconsider not only the borders between nations… but between worlds."

Over an eruption of disbelief and outrage, Chalice added, "I know full well that each and every citizen of this great land harbors dreams and fears of where the future could lead us. But I only hope that every sensible person within the range of my voice will ask themselves today whether this great nation, or someone else, should lead the future.."

Mr. Hoover was not available for comment, but his office cheerfully disclosed that he would be entertaining German Chancellor Heinrich Bruning at a six-course state dinner with entertainment provided by celebrated Theremin virtuoso Rutherford Royce.

Camp Glassford was the name given to the largest BEF camp within the District limits in honor of the police chief who'd taken every pain to feed and support the Bonus Marchers while preserving order in his jurisdiction. The string of gutted, abandoned office buildings at 3rd & B Streets SW were slated to be demolished to make way for a new federal complex, so the first Bonus Marchers to arrive in town had squatted in the ruins. Hundreds lured by the siren song of Daddy Long-Legs vastly outnumbered the few legitimate veterans left there. Clusters of tents, lean-tos, and shanties filled the broken ground between the gutted buildings. Maybe a hundred cops poured out of a fleet of black Mariahs and paddy wagons to face off against several hundred angry, hungry squatters. Behind the cops, a bunch of trucks lined the street, and a pair of demolition cranes came creeping into the camp on great, gnashing tank treads.

It was the most excitement Harry Haywire had ever seen in about a week.

He sat with his feet up on a ledge where part of the third-story wall had collapsed, eating navy beans from a can and sipping bathtub gin before a panoramic view of the ranks of police forming up outside. "Hey Dick, come see… The bulls got themselves a wrecking ball."

From his bundle of horse blankets, Dick shied a tin can at the blob where it skulked in the shadows. The blob undulated to catch and throw it back, provoking a curse and a display of Dick's hold-out pistol.

Harry drew his own revolver and aimed it at his twin. "Mind you, don't mess with the Kid," he said. "He's worth two of you when it comes to foraging."

Dick sprang from his bedroll and paced the rubble-strewn floor in his sweaty undershirt and holey trousers, with his suspenders flopping around his knotted fists. "Blamed freak of nature is what it is! Just cuz you and me both dreamed it don't make it right. It ain't done nothing but eat more than its share and make a mockery of us, and it don't sit right with me, when it tries to act like a man."

"Hey Kid, how many fingers'm I holding up?" Harry held up three fingers from across the room. The blob blew wobbling bubbles that chased each other under its membrane before sprouting a pseudopod that held up three digits.

"See?" Harry said. "How dumb can it be, if it can count higher than you…"

The Kid drew itself up into a boneless pugilist's stance and took a few tentative pokes at Dick, who tried to pistol-whip it. The blob engulfed his arm. Dick screamed and yanked his empty hand free, wiping it disgustedly on his trousers. "Give it back, ya damned booger!" The blob slithered across the room like an ice skater, juggling the purloined pistol in its churning cytoplasm.

Harry chuckled as he dropped his own pistol into his side pocket. "Ain't nobody comes out the oven into this world cooked all the way through," he said. "If you throw in together, you take the bad with the good, and don't write your pals off when they come up short. You help each other get where you're going, even if it ain't the same place."

"Yeah? What about Tom?" Holding his marinated brains inside his skull with both hands, Dick poked through his blankets for a fresh bottle. "We ain't done so right by him…"

Trouble like thunderheads swept across Harry's face. "We're here, ain't we?"

Indeed, they had resolved to find their missing partner only after the peasant army they'd found themselves leading had decided the Haywires were too hot to follow. Unable to agree on anything else, with no clue how to find Tom, they'd robbed a newsstand in Kankakee, and there he was…

Dick spotted Tom's big dumb face on the front page of the newspaper, posing with a gang of Bonus Marchers who invaded the tele-pavilion in Chicago, bound for DC. Hijacking a delivery truck, they'd stormed from Ohio to Washington, DC, in a red-eyed crime spree, sure that all they had to do was follow the signs. But after a month bumming around the capitol, the trail had gone cold, and Dick wanted to give up. But he couldn't. It drove Dick half-mad, the itching need to find Tom, but he couldn't fight it any more than he could begin to guess what they'd do when they found him.

At the end of the line, they'd holed up with the Glassford squatters for no better reason than it looked like a storm was coming.

"Look," Harry said, oddly subdued. "They're dragging them out of the joint next door." Dick came over and watched the police carrying limp bodies, most of them black, out of the derelict Ford dealership. At first, they looked dead, but they were just resisting, if you wanted to call that resistance. "Strange, all these boys who had to fight a war expecting to get their fair share by just standing around, holding their breath."

Sometimes, Dick came across almost as sharp as Tom, but then he reminded you he was still Dick. Stomping back to his corner, he returned with a Lynch gun and a couple gasoline bombs they'd made from old wine bottles.

"Hold on, we ain't at the Alamo yet," Harry said.

The mob of vets and bums and onlookers had swelled to more than a thousand jeering, angry faces and upraised fists. A group bearing an American flag tried to force their way through the police lines, but the cops shoved them back. Someone ripped the flag out of their hands and a scuffle broke out, the milling dots of humanity surging to a boil.

From the windows of the neighboring ruins came a hailstorm of rocks, bricks, and garbage. The cops took cover behind their cars, but one of them caught a brick squarely on the crown of his skull and sat down hard on the trampled grass. The cops opened fire, sending the mob scurrying. Two men lay prone on the grass in the widening gap between the opposing forces, shot in the back. Chief Glassford his own self roared up on his motorcycle, shouting at the cops to hold their fire and wait for the Army.

"D'ya hear that?" Harry asked, a wild glint in his eye. "The cavalry's coming."

"Guess that makes us the Indians," Dick said. They opened fire.

The Lynch gun silently delivered a magnetic projectile the size of a man's pinky finger through the windshield and engine block of every police car. The rain of rocks and bricks intensified. Caught in a crossfire, the police dove under their crippled cars and fired in every direction. Harry was mindful not to shoot anyone because he obeyed the rules of any house where he was a guest, but he sent the police scampering off down the street with the laughing vets pelting their backs.

Dick suggested maybe they should retire to another locale to plot more deviltry when the intact wall at their backs suddenly collapsed into the room in an avalanche.

Both men fell in each other's arms and rolled away from the implosion. The wrecking ball swung through where they'd been only moments before, then swung back, taking out the remainder of the wall. The ceiling sagged halfway to the floor, blocking the stairs. Dick aimed and fired, but even the Lynch rounds only bounced off the crane's armored cab. Foolhardy to the end, he walked towards it just as the wrecking ball pivoted and came swooping back in to finish the floor. Harry came up alongside his twin and hit him as hard as he could in the face.

Something like lightning squirted out of the impact and scrambled every orderly imposition of molecules in the immediate area. The wrecking ball jerked short, reversing its doomful pendulum arc with a wrenching screech.

Harry and Dick rolled on the floor, grappling, slapping, and biting each other. The Kid squirmed between them and swallowed both men, propelling them down the staircase just as the roof gave way.

Outside, the crane swung round and round, completely beyond any human control. The operator leapt from the cab and ran for his life. Faster and faster, it spun, teetering on the edge of its treads. At last, it heeled over and collapsed when the wrecking ball snapped free and sailed off into the dazzlingly bright blue summer sky, passing high over some who watched in disbelief and many more who moved obliviously through their day, until it smashed through the dome of the Capitol Building, plummeting to the floor of the rotunda of the most hallowed heart of these United States like a cosmic judgment… or an omen.

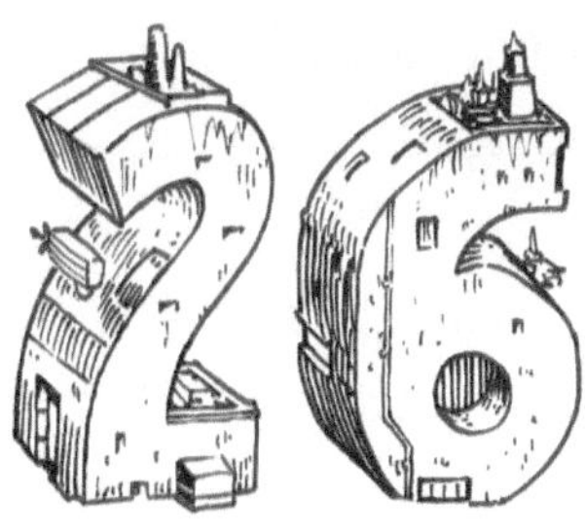

Thank God we still have a government that knows how to deal with a mob.

—Herbert Hoover

July 26th, 1932 | Washington, DC

The squatters were still clinging to the Glassford ruins three hours later when the Army began to rally on the Ellipse, just south of the White House. Army command and the police had received intelligence detailing a coordinated Communist plot to incite mass rioting and were briefed to expect a hostile armed march on the White House. The troops had trained for weeks in riot control and urban combat but had also been deluged with handbills: *Soldiers! Marines! You are Workers! No red-blooded American soldier will allow himself to be used to shoot down fellow workers—his wartime buddies—his father or brothers who are unemployed...*

At the spearpoint of four companies of cavalry and four more of infantry, a mounted machine gun squadron, and six "Red Rooster" Juggernaut tanks, General Douglas MacArthur gave a hand signal to his adjutant, Major Eisenhower, who detailed an orderly to rush to Fort Meyer to fetch the general's tunic, service stripes, sharpshooter medal and English-style whipcord breeches. When he'd returned an hour later, and the general was properly attired, he mounted a white stallion and gave the order at 16:15 to advance on the mob.

The infantry donned steel helmets, gas masks, and fixed bayonets on their gauss carbines. The mounted machine gun units rotated their barrel loads and gunned their diesel engines. The tanks lurched off their flatbed artillery trucks, gun turrets swiveling all over beetle-green carapaces like eager antennae, bayonet spurs flicking out from their reticulated stilt legs.

For eight blocks, they swept down the broad, willow-lined promenade of Pennsylvania Avenue in an orderly phalanx to thunderous applause from crowds on either sidewalk. Flags waved, spectators cheered and whistled, and a few brass bands playing competing Sousa marches made it feel like a second Fourth of July. But the cavalry surged ahead behind their eager leader and was charging at a full gallop with sabers drawn by the time they reached the Bonus Army. Even most of the vets thought this was some kind of martial parade, and saluted proudly as it rode them down.

The cavalry charge split into two wings at 4 1/2th Street, one herding spectators to the north and the other driving the vets south and out of town.

At the head of the line of vets defending the billets of Camp Glassford, Kid Amoeba stayed squashed down between Dick and Harry in a doughboy helmet and a tattered overcoat.

The charge didn't turn or stop.

"Don't you boys know a thing or two about horses?" Harry shouted. Linking arms with Dick and everyone within reach, they threw themselves to the ground. The nearest charging horses balked at the writhing bodies on the ground as they would a nest of rattlesnakes. One rider was thrown from the saddle, and several more crashed in a whinnying tangle rather than step on them.

The Bonus Army cheered raggedly, but the cavalry was already regrouping. Dick and Harry ran south through the billets of the Camp. Kid Amoeba contracted its cytoplasm until the pistol it'd taken from Dick jutted out through its membrane and clumsily shot at a tank as it tottered past.

A vet standing beside them lost an ear to a slashing cavalry saber. Another was trampled by a horse's thundering hooves. The cavalry drove the men back into the midst of the billets, and the infantry launched volley after volley of tear gas canisters at vets and spectators alike. Men, women, and children staggered blindly through the caustic fog, walking into rifle butts or stumbling into shanties the infantry had begun to put to the torch.

Something came barreling out of the sky, so low and so fast it was gone back into the clouds when its thunderclap rattled windows for several city blocks. Horses reared, flung their riders onto the grass, and stampeded from the field.

All eyes searched the sky for the unholy airborne terror. When it came again with a flash of blinding light, the few cavalry who'd kept their seats after the first barnstorming were flung or dragged by their stirrups.

It was a rousing show, but the camp was afire, the infantry wielding their weapons through the crowds, cavalry troopers riding down combatant and bystander alike, Juggernauts kicking and blasting shanties and tents and anything that moved, and few of those deafened by the sonic boom could hear the police ordering them out of the riot zone or coming after them with clubs.

This was not proper work for soldiers, Major George S. Patton told himself. This was a job for cowboys.

Once the civilians were culled from the milling herd, his men had made short work of pacifying the rabble who refused to flee Camp Glassford. Amid the flames and tear gas, Patton rode like a trail boss, rounding up strays, laying about him with the flat of his saber, the M1913, a blade of his own design. *Git along, lil doggies…*

He'd heard a lot of loose talk among his unit commanders, questioning the right or wrong of it, and though it disgusted him, he hated internal doubt more than he hated punishing his own. Some of these beggars served under him over there, for God's sake, but what did that mean when they turned on the noble cause that had been the only bright spot, if not the purpose, of their little lives? If they wanted to play-act like they were still in the Army while defying all protocols of command and heaping shame upon those forced to correct them? No, the betrayal was theirs, and the only indignity was that this shabby Wild West show had to unfold on the hallowed streets of the capitol and not in the confines of a proper military tribunal and a firing squad.

How quickly he'd come around from his own qualms about the order once he saw their signs, their slovenly hovels, and heard their childish demands. No plan survives conflict with the enemy, but no doubt can survive, either. Once his orders were cut, he was only another soldier, and there was only duty.

In less than an hour, Camp Glassford was a pyre, and a lieutenant rode up to let Patton know that Camp Meigs in the northeast quarter and the Reds' camp on the Mall had been routed with no resistance. Cowards and traitors all, they limped south towards Anacostia with their tails between their legs, and good riddance to them.

As the last rays of sunset failed in the west, the cavalry regrouped on Pennsylvania and Maryland Avenues on the steps of the Capitol. Patton found the General enjoying a flask of sherry in the saddle while his weak-kneed underling Eisenhower mopped his brow and cast about him like an understudy bucking to play King Lear. As the Major saw it, MacArthur was exactly the kind of perfumed prince whose political aspirations proved a greater impediment to victory than any enemy.

"Lovely night for a game of polo, eh, George?" the General sang out. Patton snapped off a gruff salute. Plan White called for the expulsion of all hostile and seditious elements from the city proper, but as soon as the smoke had begun to rise, dispatches had come vomiting out of the White House, urging restraint. Aging boys who'd never seen the elephant, dictating tactics through a telescope. "Women and children are to be afforded every courtesy," ran a typically idiotic dispatch, but the men hiding behind their skirts and short pants would be hunted down like the stray dogs that they were.

"All camps in city limits are ours, sir," Patton said. "Are we hanging up our spurs for the night?"

"I see no reason for that," the General sniffed. "Any meaningful resistance? We were told to expect teeth."

"That aerial bogey gave us a scare…what in hell was that, anyway?"

"Nothing to fret about. We've scrambled the air corps, and they'll shoot him down."

"Sir," Patton said in a dutiful tone, "just to be clear, our orders were to drive them out to Anacostia and stand down…"

The general leaned over to hand Patton the flask. Out of the bellows pocket of his greatcoat, he took a fistful of crumpled dispatches in one kid-gloved fist and flung them into the smoky, bitter wind. They both laughed.

Patton took a lusty swig—fruity stuff, not to his liking, but it scratched the itch—and waved it under Eisenhower's nose, knowing full well the milquetoast would refuse it. Handing the flask back to the General, Patton tipped his peaked cap and reined his horse around.

"See you at Anacostia," MacArthur said with a wink.

"Form up and double-time!" Patton roared. As the order went through the chaotic swarm of pawing, snorting beasts, and the slightly tamer animals carrying them on their backs, he watched his forces come together like a blazing sword materializing out of mist. He had only to grasp it and swing to cut away all the sickness out of the world.

Without further incident, the 600 troopers of the 3rd Cavalry drove the mob southeast down Pennsylvania, swatting and chopping at anyone who wasn't running for his life. Bricks flew from a parked truck, knocking a few men down and spooking the horses, but they were gassed and sent packing, the truck put to the torch. Patton himself laid the flat of his blade across the seat of one vet's pants as he retreated.

Meaningful resistance, my ass, he thought. The greater hazard, by far, was the spectators. Civilians staggered blindly in the path of the cavalry charge, carrying a baby, a child, and a three-legged dog. You had to choose between riding down some fool bystander or being thrown, which was no choice at all. Whatever doubts his men had entertained during training were well behind them. They shouted to each other, laughing and joking more than he liked, but he couldn't begrudge them a bit of levity. Not only the seditious backsliders, but all of the general populace needed an occasional reminder of what real order meant. Yes, sir, if a few more military parades ended like this, America would put all this depression nonsense aside and be a proper country again.

MacArthur had retired from the field to soothe his saddle sores and recite love poetry or something, and Patton had the mop. It was a charade of an operation until they reached the 11th Street Drawbridge, which was the only crossing over the Anacostia River to Camp Marks.

The Major called a halt to let the rats run for cover, and the infantry catch up. They knew when they were licked but didn't know what was still coming. He had tactical command of all forces, and if complications arose, the USS *Constitution* was anchored just downstream from the bridge with its forward artillery trained on the enemy's stronghold. If the President was still watching from the Oval Office, he was finally leaving the war to the generals.

"If we had guns," one of the Bonus traitors shouted, "we'd show you what for." Patton didn't doubt it, but he sent the loudmouth scurrying with his saber just the same. "This ain't over, Major," shouted an old man with the Croix de Guerre and the Distinguished Service Cross on the breast of his baggy doughboy tunic. A chill ran up Patton's back, for he recognized the Sergeant—indeed, he'd received that medal he wore for saving Patton's life. "The whole world will hear of this."

The night air was sultry, soft, and fragrant with the dogwood blossoms along the shore. Half a moon hung low and orange over the horizon. Four Juggernauts lined up on his flank, and a gunner on the nearest tank reported that the fifth had tumbled into a foxhole at the Red camp and was scratched unless the mechanics could right it. Their company commander had broken a leg in the tumble, so Patton told them to take direct orders from him in the action to come.

The drawbridge was blocked with a slipshod barricade of wrecked flivvers, sandbags, and miscellaneous debris. The refugees from the city camps straggled through the obstacle course, running for the guttering lights of Camp Marks on the far shore. One of his younger lieutenants was salty to cut them off and take the bridge, but his orders were to usher them out of the capitol, and he meant to do so.

"Let them run to their nest," Patton barked, "then we'll kick it over." The bitter human river fleeing the city had dwindled to a stream, then a trickle when he sent word to the General over the company's portable wireless that the enemy was all bottled up, when the ground opened up beneath them and spat fire into the sky.

It was as if Hell itself yawned, cleared its throat, and spoke.

A Juggernaut tipped over and fell into the midst of his mounted cohort. Horses reared and galloped, screaming, flinging riders like jackstraws. The other three tanks staggered away from the bulging mound in the ruptured macadam road. "Artillery!" someone shouted, but they were wrong. Patton was perhaps the first to recognize the enemy in the ambush, but between knowing and accepting, he found, lay a gulf into which the best-laid plans could plummet into defeat.

The massive mound broke apart, clods of soil rolling away from the spinning, gnashing drill of an old Regenwurm. The armored bulk of the Boche tank undulated up out of the tunnel like a terrible metal mockery of its tiny namesake. Stubby magnetic cannons bristled and flung a fusillade in every direction, firing over the cavalry's heads but chipping away at his Red Roosters like a scythe through a field of flowers. Two Juggernauts backpedaled too hastily and stumbled into each other. Their spurred legs tangled in a gigantic, comical cockfight, tipping them off the bridge with a colossal splash in the shallows of the Anacostia River.

Patton himself was hard-pressed to keep his seat. His horse wheeled and galloped for the cover of the trees. Cold horror clutched his palpitating heart, but he felt the weight of years drop away as the atavistic vision of the Great War burst forth in their midst.

Where did they ever get such a thing? Even as Patton's mind unraveled the insane surprise, he detailed his companies to new vantage points to engage it. Someone must have broken into the Smithsonian Institute, but it hardly mattered.

The lopsided charade had at last become a proper battle. All that remained to be done now was proper soldier's work.

Scattered small fire began to pepper them from the barricades at the far end of the drawbridge, which the opposition was working feverishly to raise. Ordering his infantry to take the bridge, Patton deployed the surviving Juggernaut to knock out the Regenwurm, which had slithered out of its burrow and humped down 11th Street in hopes of blockading the drawbridge. The Juggernaut harried the tank like a hungry rooster on a worm, rolling it into the river.

The lip of the bridge was a foot above the roadbed when the infantry leaped onto it. The first charge was repelled by a pair of Lynch guns in the wheelhouse. The infantry couldn't punch through its armor, and the drawbridge continued to ascend, blocking his advance.

Dismounting, Patton scanned every noncommissioned officer who raced past, looking for his confounded wireless operator. When at last he found him, he cuffed the man about the face, stripped the rig off the hapless corporal, and howled down the operator, demanding to speak with the commander of the *Constitution*. "We need that drawbridge, Navy. Can you or can you not put fire on that wheelhouse?"

The Navy, as usual, needed its food chewed for them. "We can't hit what we can't see," they complained. It took some doing, but he got word to his mobile artillery to drop signal flares on the roof of the little pillbox where those vets were furiously cranking up the drawbridge by hand. By and by, the message worked its tortuous way through the nervous system of the gray behemoth downriver. The big ten-inch guns of the battleship spoke up, and a moment later, the wheelhouse was a plume of dull fire. A few more salutes took the starch out of the enemy camp's other gun emplacements.

The infantry fell back to let the cavalry lead the way over the bridge, which was wide enough for two lanes of traffic and a streetcar track. At the head of the charge, Patton had burnt away the last cobwebs of doubt. His command had not seen casualties since the War, but the shock of it was nothing compared to the gnawing horror of having one's hands tied. Whatever these fools hoped to achieve with their ragged resistance, they had forfeited any claim to mercy.

Coming off the bridge at a dead gallop, Major Patton limbered his wrist and abandoned the flat of his saber for the leading edge as he charged into Camp Marks. Men and women ran pell-mell between tents, shacks, and shanties in complete disarray. The resistance at the bridge might've been another bunch altogether, for these folks acted as if they'd been waiting for the Army to rescue them. Women with babes in arms pleaded with soldiers for time to get their personal effects. Men shouted their serial numbers and battlefield citations like prisoners of war. The front-line infantry pounded the camp with tear gas and herded them back with bayonets. The second wave went from tent to shack, clearing out stragglers and tossing torches into every hovel. The Juggernaut stalked the camp, kicking over shanties and splashing jellied gasoline on the larger tents, the canteen, the lending library, the blacksmith, and the hospital. Scattered from camp with nowhere to go, the demoralized vets and camp followers ran for the far trees or waded in the river or took shelter in the neighboring garbage dump, only to find an ever-constricting ring of infantry herding them towards a fleet of deuce-and-a-half trucks. Plan White hadn't provided for the round-up of the routed army, and he was glad someone else had stepped up to remove them.

As he rode herd on the mopping-up, he saw something shimmy up the lanky leg of the Juggernaut like a blob of grease racing up a pole. The tank froze in place with one leg pawing at the air. In a trice, the gunner was flung screaming from the cockpit, then the driver tumbled and landed face-first on the turf. The tank jerked backward, legs pedaling like a new-hatched chick stumbling from its egg. Patton drew his sidearm and spent the whole magazine at the runaway tank. He heard more than one bullet ping impotently off its hull. All its guns went off at once. Patton's horse nosedived, throwing him headlong into a burning shanty.

A bleary climb to consciousness later, he found himself lying in a quilted coffin beneath a sign that proclaimed, SEE THE UNKNOWN SOLDIER—5 CENTS!

He climbed out of the coffin and waded through smoke and blazing canvas in time to see the runaway Juggernaut trip on its own spurs almost directly overhead. Patton had to dive out of its path and must have hit his head again, for he would swear later, if anyone had asked, that he saw an animated wad of pink slime climb out of the wreckage of his last tank and go galloping off into the night.

Major Patton shivered and prayed to the god of war as he reloaded his Colt revolver. He'd seen things to shake the soul in France, and he knew the measure of men. But if this was the shape of war to come, he wondered if he was not too old for it.

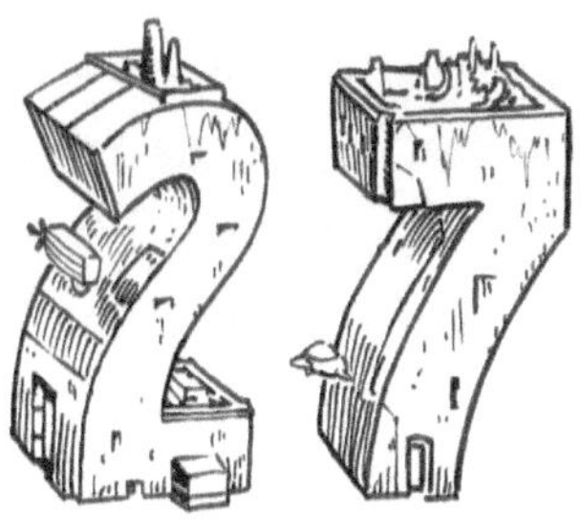

There are old pilots and there are bold pilots, but no old bold pilots.

—E. Hamilton Lee, U.S. Air Mail pilot.

July 26th, 1932 | Washington, DC

From the moment she'd received the White Devil's note, Matilda Lynch had felt a time bomb somewhere out there that she could only defuse by somehow disarming the ticking clock inside her head. Again and again, she had to stop and take stock of what her body was doing, what her brain was saying. She had opened the footlocker and begun to strap on the armor without thinking about how it would look for mild-mannered Elvira the doughnut girl to go into a tent and an armored vigilante to come blasting out of it. No one would notice amid all that was going on, but what was she doing?

Tonight, the note had warned. It could only have come from the White Devil, but how much could she trust him? She'd felt him spying on her but when she'd sought him out, he disappeared. Who was he to send her bumbling into the White House with some story about sleepwalking assassins?

Discretion had won out, sending her back to the canteen. Every able-bodied man had run towards the ominous pillars of smoke to the northwest, but the camp was still haunted by the shouts and crying of frantic women and children. Matilda assisted in the hospital tent and donated a pint of blood. Still half out of her mind with worry, she went outside and copped a cigarette from a stolid old hobo with a brace of French medals on his sunken chest. Casting about for anything to occupy her mind, she settled on the bullpen someone had labeled in carefully stenciled letters, THE NEWS OF THE WORLD.

A lofty title for the collage of scrounged newspapers posted where the men gathered to smoke and drink coffee. Her eyes took refuge in the bold sans serif headlines, the unvulgar absence of grubby photographs standing in for honest words.

The headline was like a spear through her chest.

Just below the fold of the *Journal's* front page: ARMS MAGNATE ROMULUS LYNCH SUSPECTED MURDERED; POLICE HUNT FOR MISSING SERVANT.

She sucked at the cigarette until her head swam and her meager breakfast threatened to repeat on her. She closed her eyes, breathing slow and deep, then opened them and forced herself to read the two columns.

There wasn't much to it. Romulus Lynch, 72, was found dead in his study on July 8; poison was found in the autopsy. The housekeeper sought for questioning apparently vanished immediately after the demise of Mr. Lynch, a widower survived by none but the owner and sole proprietor of a company with assets in excess of fifty million dollars.

How had she not known? She'd avoided the news even when someone tried to catch her up over checkers, but somehow, it didn't surprise her. Funny how seeing it spelled out in a headline could make everything else seem unreal. How could the declaration of a corrupt organ of some political machine set events into history as if they were inevitable when, in the noise, confusion, and shock of the world, everything almost didn't happen at all? If only she'd stayed…

But if she could have, she would have, and nothing would have changed. She was stunned to find herself feeling absolutely blank on the subject of Father. Her heart went out to Mabel Hildebrandt, for the author of the Bethlehem Steel massacre would be mercilessly thorough.

It was a tar pit, the grief and the guilt and the grief again until you buried yourself in it, and no ray of light could reach you. It would claim her unless she moved.

She returned to her tent and suited up before she could change her mind again. She ducked out the back of the tent before engaging the impeller. Nobody seemed to notice right away, but at first, "Look at that shiny man, Mommy!" she goosed the ignition stud on her gauntlet and was lofted into the sky.

The city was tearing itself apart, with troops and military vehicles converging on the Ellipse and a chorus of sirens converging from every corner of the capitol.

Where would she go? Who could she help? Surely, if the message was true, then no action was excessive. The President must be warned, but what kind of reception could she expect if she dropped out of the sky on the White House lawn and told them to arrest all the servants?

They'll listen to you, she thought. You're only a bottom-drawer science vigilante and known associate of a radical fifth columnist on the FBI's Most Wanted List. Maybe you'd fare better as the resurrected munitions heiress whose father was just murdered by his own housekeeper… Surely, they'll listen. Who wouldn't listen to a hysterical woman with a gun for an arm?

She buzzed Lafayette Square, where police maintained a cordon around the White House, and spotted a pair of men with binoculars on the roof. They would be Secret Service and the tip of an iceberg draping the grounds in unseen security. Hoover was the safest man on Earth, or he should be. But his assassin could be anyone, even one handpicked to protect him.

He had to be warned, but they would arrest and interrogate her and might still fail to stop the one sent to murder him. She dropped behind the Treasury Building and swooped in low enough to touch the wrought iron tines of the fence. Even before he became the scapegoat for every symptom of American misery, Mr. Hoover was known to be less approachable than past presidents who would occasionally walk the lawn and wave to sightseers or press the flesh at holiday gatherings like the Easter Egg Roll. Cleaving close to the lawn, she hovered beside the grand gable window of the Oval Office on the second floor.

Feeling like a foolish child spying on the adults, she peered around the frame at a stout man sitting with his back to her behind an enormous fiefdom of a desk. A taller, younger man with a certain dashing, exotic quality nervously paced and gesticulated as he spoke. The man looked familiar but didn't carry himself like an advisor. No, he was a salesman. Tonight, she reminded herself. There was a state dinner with the chancellor of Germany. She must have noticed it in the newspaper just before reading about—

She was losing her mind and would soon be Public Enemy #1 if she was spotted here. She took out a micro transmitter and affixed it to the top right pane of the window.

She remembered touring the White House once with Father, several years before. She remembered Harding's ruddy face, the burst capillaries in his nose and cheeks almost sizzling, and his erratic heartbeat thumping out of his soft, sweaty hand into hers.

She dropped below the Oval Office and zipped past four ground-floor windows with curtains drawn, then peeked into the State Dining Room. The long table was being set and dressed in massive floral arrangements by a team of uniformed servants. A small stage was furnished with microphones and instruments, including a concert Theremin and a baby grand piano.

Her mind fixed on the piano. She thought of the fatal phonograph at Bethlehem Steel, the mayhem incited by music. What if the President was his own assassin, post-hypnotically compelled to cut his own throat at the first strains of the National Anthem?

Before falling into another paralyzing reverie, she placed a second micro transmitter on the window. She took off at high speed, staying below the White House's roofline until she'd put the willow oaks between her and the Treasury Agents on the roof.

She should feel quite proud of herself for such a feat of stealth. She should feel—something…

She landed on the roof of the International Hotel and startled a little man in a formal swallowtail tuxedo. With his foppish tie and vest, he looked like an ambassador someone left out in the rain. Evincing no surprise whatsoever at her descent from the sky, the little man offered her a magnum of champagne and slurred, "To the new American Revolution."

She lifted her visor to look him in the eye and drink off the rest of the bottle. To his goggling, incredulous stare, she said, "To liberty," threw the bottle into the street, and sidled down the fire escape.

Her new batteries took several hours to charge, so she risked breaking into her hotel room for the spare. She was resolute in sharing the hardships of the Bonus Army, but she didn't have to stink while she did it. Only visiting the hotel room thrice a week to shower and use the laundry, she had kept the armor here until last week, when it began to seem as if something like this would happen.

Something like this—

She rooted under her bed and found all the unread *Washington Posts*. And then she realized who the man in the Oval Office must have been.

Checking again that the door was locked, she put on her helmet and tuned into the micro transmitter she'd left on Mr. Hoover's window.

"—Mr. President, I fully recognize that we don't see eye to eye on many issues of the day, but you must know that your political fortunes hang on the outcome of the fighting in the street today. I come to you as someone with no dog in this fight but someone who could win you a victory.

"These hungry ghosts of a bygone war are going to hang their chains around your neck and drag you down. Everyone knows it. A mule could whip you in November. But I can make all of it go away."

"If only that were so," the President stated, his voice like a flywheel engine pushing a mountain uphill. "I've heard your proposal. It is laudable, most public-spirited if it can be made to work, but I don't see why the federal government should be asked to underwrite it."

"You can, and you most likely will, one way or the other. I'm not offering safe transit back to their home states, where they'll continue to agitate and demand. You've got a cancer, sir, and dispersing them would only spread it. What I am offering is on the order of a final solution. All men willing to lay down their arms and walk away will be given safe conduct without cost to them… but they won't go home."

"I don't follow you. Where will they… where will you send them?"

"I am only asking for five dollars a head for each traveler. But to know where I send them would cost you much more than money."

"This is all… highly irregular. I hope you realize this is not how the nation's business is done. There are simply too many unknowns. Sir, I must consider this meeting, and our business, as closed."

"It isn't," Chalice said, and his voice drilled down to a cold stage whisper. "Listen, little man. You've got a choice between going down in history as the hapless hand on the tiller when the ship of state ran up on the rocks or the man who opened the door to a new frontier… I can't show it to you, I won't describe it, but I assure you, as a man who thought five years ago that he would die a shopkeeper, I secured this meeting with no advance notice, only this morning. Consider, sir. I offer you the key to an empire not of nations, but of worlds. And I won't offer it twice."

A long, leaden silence ensued, during which she thought she heard drops of sweat plashing on the blotter of the President's desk. At last, seething through flared nostrils, the president replied. "I believe I said good day, sir."

Without further word, Sylvester Chalice turned on his heel and vacated the Oval Office.

She took to the sky again as the sound of the cavalry charge rolled over Washington. She buzzed Pennsylvania Avenue at such speed that a sonic thunderclap unseated dozens of riders, and she used a flash bomb to blind the attackers. The charge stalled, but the Army fired wildly into the sky. She turned back over Union Station at the city's northeast border and circled for another pass when five fighter planes dropped out of the clouds and harried her away from the action.

 It was the sweet spot of a Southern summer evening when the heat breaks like a fever, and she was a sitting duck against the setting sun.

Matilda dropped out of a barrel roll with a plane's machine guns chattering on her tail. She led her pursuer down below the rooftops framing the Mall and through the curtains of smoke over the Red camp, then climbed until the pilot's brain must be mashed against the back of his skull and his gunfire chewed the tail off his wing commander's plane.

She performed an Immelmann to get clear as the monoplane on her tail nearly crashed into its four mates. The squadron scattered like drunken horseflies a few thousand feet over the Potomac. She took cover again in the smoke, then came in for a rough landing atop the castle keep of the Smithsonian.

They passed overhead, props growling like frustrated bloodhounds. She couldn't hope to keep tripping them up, but she couldn't seem to ditch them. She was faster and more maneuverable, but the quintet of P-26 Peashooters from the 8th Pursuit Squadron out of Langley, Virginia, had the luxury of wanting her dead. Watching the rudderless plane glide out of the dogfight, corkscrewing uncontrollably as it limped away for the nearest open field, she fretted that they wouldn't have to shoot her if they kept her in the air too long. Naturally, the batteries were draining faster than Aurora had said they would, and she hadn't even gotten off a shot. Every time she had to engage her magnetic deflectors, their bullets zinged off like fireflies in a wind tunnel, but her reserves took a hit, and she became as dumb as a June bug when she tried to maneuver, a vicious circle she could see swallowing her up if she didn't take charge.

Though the sound of men screaming gave her a special kind of headache, she tuned into their wireless channel. Their panicked, profane chatter burned her ears, calling for another squadron, which would only add to the confusion, and she'd been driven halfway across the city. For all she knew, she was already too late.

"Spread out, take the bastard's goddamn ass off…"

Matilda tilted her chin to activate the helmet in her transmitter. Unlike her old armor, this one didn't have a damper to give her a man's voice. "The only asses you boys seem to be able to take is each other's…"

"Who said that? Was that a broad?"

"Ma'am…whoever you are, sign off… this is a secure military channel—"

"I'll get off your channel when you washouts get out of my sky."

She cut off their outraged replies and switched to her micro transmitters at the White House.

She faintly heard music through waves of static before the roar of a rocket drowned out everything. The sound seemed to come from everywhere at once, cracking the sky in half. The sound was as terrifying as it was familiar.

She saw a lance of fiery witch-light arc across the horizon, the exhaust trail of a missile out of the north streaking over Washington to descend on the White House. Shaking her head in disbelief, she leapt onto the parapet and blasted off. With her new magnetic impellers, the only sound spectators on the Mall heard was the scream of a madwoman hurtling across the night sky.

Skimming over treetops, dodging searchlights and smoke, she roared down over the Ellipse and then the White House lawn. The transmission signal grew louder in her earpiece as she closed in on its source. More than a dozen Secret Service on the roof opened fire as soon as she came into sight. Divert power to shields… Her speed dropped off, but she still smashed through the window of the state reception room like a shell from a Howitzer.

Matilda stuck the landing atop the long banquet table, but her prosthetic leg locked up. She skidded the length of the table, sweeping aside fine bone china and Waterford crystal and linen napkins. Guests and servants and heads of state flung themselves to the floor. A pair of Secret Service agents lunged between her and the President of the United States, who looked stolidly up at the armored apparition that had burst in upon the gathering. The music shuddered to a halt, the Theremin quartet sitting frozen in their chairs.

The moment was hers to win or lose. Looking around the room, she wondered yet again if she wasn't losing her mind. She'd seen it and heard it, and there was no mistaking it or where it went. But where was it? *Who* was it?

"Mr. President, you're in grave danger. An assassin has hypnotized someone to murder you. It could be anyone…"

The bullet-headed bald man on Hoover's left, whose eyes might've been painted on his spectacles, flung his napkin onto his plate and moved to stand, his hand tucked into his coat as if to draw a weapon. Matilda's hand twitched, and the magneto-cannon in her left arm punched a soup can-sized hole in his chest. The bewhiskered diplomat beside him cried, "Gott in Himmel!" The chancellor of Germany fell back into his seat, and Matilda swept the room again.

The Secret Service agents opened fire. Bullets bounced off her helmet and breastplate. She powered up her deflectors, sweeping the room with her gauntlets. No one else moved, but she could hear the house stirring all around them. The President squinted up at her, clutching his chest. Her left arm completed the circuit of the room and pointed dead at Mr. Hoover. With a queer detachment, as if she were watching herself through one of Jasper Zwick's peeping television screens, she observed as her metal fingers depressed the trigger.

Something blasted her squarely in the back, sending her sprawling off the table. Her shot took the headrest off the President's chair. Rolling to come up on her knees, she tried to boost her deflectors, but the impeller only coughed and spat sparks from her back. Someone dropped in through the shattered window to land atop the banquet table. Matilda goggled at the new arrival…

The Silver Sentry, wearing her old rocket pack, blasted her off her feet.

She hit the wall and slid down it. Breathing in desperate gulps, but somehow, they didn't reach her lungs. She had holes in her. Her lap was filling with blood.

The Silver Sentry kept the gauntlets leveled on her chest. "You're safe now, Mr. President," boomed an amplified basso voice.

The President was very safe indeed. He looked at the hole in his chair, then patted out a smoking cowlick on the back of his head. He stood up from the chair, waving away the Secret Service, servants, and his wife to come stand over her. "I want to see his face," he said.

She did not know what was strangest of all the strange things that happened next. The President knelt beside her.

"Mr. President, if you will allow me," said someone who caused the President to recoil in disbelief.

The corpse of Chancellor Heinrich Bruning pushed the President aside, and his face turned to smoke. Beneath it, a fanged golden skull leered at her and whispered her name. His cloak fanned out to eclipse the room and drape her in shadow, and then she was falling into a darkness deeper than sleep.

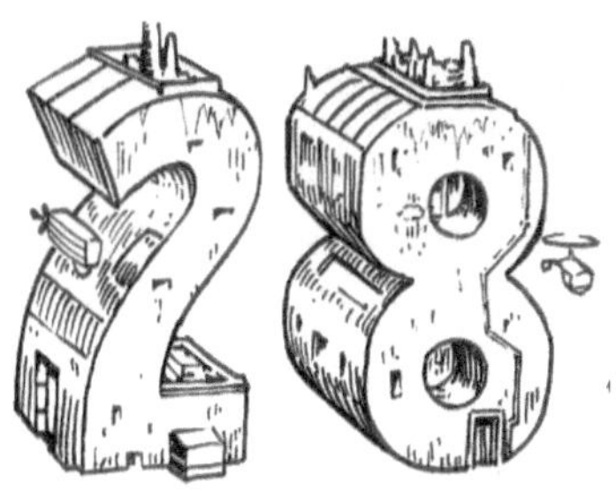

If the lightning strikes, it will find me a willing victim.

—Bernarr McFadden

July 27th, 1932 | Washington, DC

NEWS ON THE WING!

Chaos in Washington, DC! As General MacArthur finally moves to purge the Capitol of the disgruntled ragamuffin army, the Red agitators among them show their claws! It's a sequel to the Somme as Boche tanks tunnel under our brave Juggernaut artillery! But our boys' mettle isn't rusted, and the traitors are ushered out of town more politely than they deserved.

But what's this? A high-flying aspiring assassin foils our newest pursuit planes in a spectacular aerial battle over the Mall and invades the White House! But this dastardly attempt on the life of our President is foiled by the Silver Sentry! The cowardly killer escapes with the aid of a shadowy accomplice disguised as Germany's Chancellor Bruning, but he won't get far. A grateful Mister Hoover thanks freedom's champion, who says he won't rest until he's bagged the cabal of fifth columnists who murdered munitions magnate Romulus Lynch and sent their killers to behead our beleaguered head of state.

And whither the Bonus Army? For tens of thousands stuck without train fare home, Sylvester Chalice rides to the rescue! With no Bonus in sight, the young innovator promises them the next best thing. Those doughty doughboys who want to work will have honest jobs with fair pay on Mr. Chalice's new frontier. Wherever you are, don't work too hard, boys!

§ Providence, Rhode Island §

All his life, Sylvester Skolnic dreamed not of wealth, success, or fame, and certainly never of becoming an inventor, but merely of being a big man, in the most literal sense.

Without inheriting any of his father's business acumen or his mother's gentle tenacity, he'd gleaned from their genes a short, slight physique that silently cried out to be bullied. He was a small boy when his parents immigrated to the United States from Latvia and settled down in Providence in 1905. He was scarcely much larger when his father, driven by a ferocious excess of nationalist fervor, impulsively returned alone to fight for his homeland in 1914. Young Sylvester dropped out of high school to manage the family tobacco shop less as a solemn duty than as a refuge from the world. The other kids found Sylvester an irresistible target for beatings, and there was no Latvian enclave in which to hide, no gang obliged by blood to protect him. But behind the counter, Sylvester soon became an avid reader of the periodicals he sold. In them, he found not only a fantasy life to sustain him, but tantalizing glimpses of a secret path to repair all that heredity and nurture had broken.

In particular, he hewed to the health magazines of Bernarr MacFadden. He devoured each new issue of *Physical Culture*, and unlike any number of his winking, nodding clientele, he eagerly consumed them for the articles on physical fitness and embellishment, not for the grotty rotogravure prints of oiled, near-naked bodybuilders contained within. When MacFadden began leading a morning calisthenics regimen on WOR, he tuned in religiously.

But strive as he might, no isometric or circular breathing exercises served to augment his stunted, wiry musculature; no products ordered from its myriad of advertisements increased his thoracic circumference or general appearance of vigor. Hours spent skipping rope or tossing a medicine ball brought him no closer to being mistaken for one of the models pinned to the wall of the Skolnic household attic, which Sylvester had converted into a makeshift gymnasium. Even his mother got the wrong idea about his pursuits. "Why don't you just go downtown and pay one to lay you?" she said once, the last time she was allowed into the attic.

Sylvester continued striving and dreaming until one day when a new ad in *Physical Culture* caught his eye. Promising to reveal the "ancient Oriental secrets of physical perfection in a single pamphlet," the ad demanded a steep $2.75 for said revelations. For "nigh-instantaneous bolstering not only of muscle mass and bone density but even height and symmetry of facial features," $2.75 was a small price to pay.

Nine weeks later, the portentous pamphlet arrived, but the revelations promised within fell far short of miraculous. For one, the author seemed to have stitched together a slew of charts and unsourced passages from Asian and Hindoo texts on acupuncture, meditation, and mysticism, larded with a lot of hot air about the body's secret electricity reserves. The author, one Col. G.K. Livesey, concluded that a specific configuration of needles inserted into the chakras while meditating could induce the desired physical metamorphosis, but the needles must be of "purest silver forged by a true alchemist" and a lot of other banana oil intended to backfill the extraordinary claims beyond any mere mortal's reach.

Where another man might have tossed away the pamphlet in disgust and chastened himself against such frivolity, Sylvester forged single-mindedly ahead. In the years since he'd had leadership of the Skolnic household thrust upon him, Sylvester had developed a shrewd head for business, expanding the tobacco shop into a small chain throughout Rhode Island, and his scattershot but indefatigable efforts in the attic had given his compact body a spring-steel quality. But the Italian toughs who once hounded him from schoolyard to front stoop in childhood now came round to lean on him for protection and beat him within an inch of his life, and laughed at his futile efforts to defend his shop.

Picking up the pamphlet again, he scoured the surrounding towns until he found a village blacksmith at Lime Rock who was willing to make the proper needles. The beetle-browed brute scoffed at the strange charts and diagrams but took Sylvester's sack of silver coins and in a week, delivered the requested needles.

For weeks thereafter, Sylvester mortified himself in a litany of uncomfortable postures—standing on his head with legs akimbo, or supine and balanced on hands and feet in agonizing rigidity under the light of the full moon. Though acupuncture was billed as being painless, the needles were of such thickness and the placement close to sensitive nerve clusters that it seemed more an exotic form of self-torture than self-improvement. In any case, it didn't work.

The pamphlet's true magical qualities revealed themselves only as it leaked hitherto unnoticed caveats with every new perusal. To affect changes upon the skeleton, the needles must directly contact the bones; the body must be in such a geographical position as to conduct the earth's subtle electromagnetic energies; the subject must make his mind a supremely blank slate. The treatments must take the place of and provide all the benefits of sleep.

Only when he had begun to succumb to nervous exhaustion and brought the pamphlet to a professor of anthropology at Brown University and prevailed upon him with a generous cash offer did Sylvester learn that Col. G.K. Livesey, whatever Oriental wisdom he might've picked up while fighting to preserve the British Empire in China and India, wasn't worth a tinker's damn as a translator.

The needles required for his wholly fraudulent procedure were not to be made of silver but of "celestial ore," by which the professor supposed they meant metal from a meteorite. Such metals were indeed rare, but the university's astronomy departments had several on exhibit. But not even the right metal would induce the kind of farcical transformation promised by this hogwash, the professor felt constrained to warn him, for the text promised not "transformation" at all, but "transportation," though to where, not even the original text deigned to specify.

Not even the hapless anthropology professor thought to connect the chain of incidents when, a week later, a burglar broke into Lowell Hall and absconded with several prized meteorite specimens.

Sylvester coerced the blacksmith into smelting the meteorites and extracting half a pound of ferrous sidereal iron, which he, in turn, cast into a new set of needles. Never daring to ask what the client wanted with such instruments, he only hoped never to be bothered by him again.

Back home, Sylvester resumed his nightly treatments with obsessive vigor, leaving the tobacco shop to underlings who robbed him blind, sleeping in all day on bloodied sheets as the open wounds at all his chakras became grievously infected. His mother observed that he now argued in vicious whispers in the attic at all hours with some unknown, inaudible party.

Sylvester learned only that this alien entity who intruded upon his meditations wanted him to succeed in his efforts, but he was going about it wrong. In describing the place where he could channel the earth's energies into his body, he put Sylvester onto how to finally do it right.

When Sylvester asked the identity of the voice, it might've plucked an image out of the shopkeeper's mind, because Sylvester was deathly afraid of spiders.

Call me Daddy Long-Legs, it said.

"Where are you? What are you?"

I come from another world—a better world—a breath away from yours. One where you could be everything you are not… Jaunt here but once, and you will return home a giant.

On the night of the summer solstice in 1924, Sylvester took his needles to the top of College Hill, where, on a vacant lot across from a decrepit Victorian mansion, he found a low, large stone in the high weeds that Daddy Long-Legs told him was once sacred to people who were gone long before white men settled it. At midnight, he disrobed and impaled himself, one by one, with the terrible star-born needles, and there, he began to realize results far more complete than even Col. Livesey could've envisioned.

At last, Sylvester Skolnic was transported out of this world and into the next.

How vividly he recalled that threshold moment when he found himself in a new universe of undreamt potential, unexploited resources, untapped possibilities—and unable to breathe. Drowning with every futile gasp, he cried out for the disembodied voice that guided him to the other world. Only waiting for his cue, Daddy Long-Legs appeared in all his glory and attached himself to Sylvester's dying body, allowing him to breathe.

Their partnership, at first, was purely a pact of mutual survival. The ecology of the other world was not so different from where he came from, although symbiotic and parasitic relationships invisible on Earth were writ large here. Daddy Long-Legs was a wise and affable companion and a formidable predator by terrestrial standards, but on his home planet, he was little more than a virus. Of the months and years he spent on the planet he christened Circe, Sylvester remembered little and longed to remember even less. Daddy Long-Legs called it another Earth, but it was nothing like home. The changes wrought upon his body were, by and large, everything he could have hoped for, however, and by the time Daddy Long-Legs revealed the way back to his own world, he was ready to conquer it.

On the summer solstice of 1927, Sylvester stepped out of a hole in the darkness and looked once more upon the lights of Providence. His only thoughts were of returning to his old life, but Daddy Long-Legs coaxed where he could, and took the reins where he must, to drive Sylvester to change his name, and his destiny.

Together, they set out in search of other standing stones, ancient remnants of a forgotten network that connected the worlds. To render the star-born stones into a working prototype teleportal consumed the best part of the next year. To fabricate entangled teleportals on the other side, which would return the traveler to any designated point on Earth, took only a few months.

After he successfully demonstrated the prototype to a consortium of New England bankers at the end of 1928, he raised more than enough private investment capital to begin serious exploration and exploitation of the Otherside, and he'd paid it all back with generous dividends to hold onto sole proprietorship. Diamonds, gold, platinum, and elements for which they didn't even have names yet, funded his rise until he had to stop for fear of destabilizing the economy.

It was all so unreal, so easy, that Sylvester never stopped to ask why Daddy Long-Legs had never asked for anything in return.

The only real hitch had come when he found that other fellow nosing around his turf. The Kurtzberg operation was a big mess to just sweep under the carpet, but when something wants to happen badly enough, the way is made smooth, and all obstacles swept aside.

When the stock market crashed, they picked at the corpses of the Insull and Foshay electrical empires, scalping utility grids across the Midwest, Canada, Alaska, and Central America, merely to acquire the necessary camouflage until he was ready to reveal what he was really up to. At his research labs in Utopia, Illinois, and throughout the Otherside, small armies of nameless eggheads converted new discoveries into more potential inventions than he could ever bring to market. He could make Edison and Tesla look like shiftless pikers just by opening his hands and letting the magic spill out.

If the oil companies didn't play ball, he had a cheap and plentiful organic substitute that would make them all obsolete. If the railroads and automakers continued to give him grief, he'd expand the teleportal network and lower fares so nobody but the lowest of the low traveled any other way. But his biggest windfall had come from Ambrosia. The new tins came with an internal heating coil—just pull the tab, and it was steaming hot, ready to eat out of the can. The meat substitute was outselling pork and chicken and driving meat prices even lower, and he hadn't even had to bribe anyone. Nobody seemed to want to know what was in it.

He still felt troubled about the Lindbergh situation, however. When the aviator's son went missing, he saw an opportunity not only to win his loyalty but to right a wrong. Even Daddy Long-Legs told him what he proposed was dangerous, but as always, it numbed him to any instinctive fear of failure.

To do it was as simple as walking through a teleportal, then side-stepping into another variation of the room you left, as if that made any sense. He lost track of how many alternate earths he had to visit before he found one where the child hadn't been taken—and he took it.

In the weeks after the child was returned, he'd watched the newspapers with something approaching dread as the police ran in circles trying to find the kidnappers. There'd been a close call when the corpse of an infant was found on the side of a New Jersey highway a month later, and Chalice had to frame a patsy, but none of that mattered now. Charles and Anne had their baby back, and Charles was extremely grateful.

How would he feel, Sylvester wondered, if he knew that this child was not truly his and had been taken away from another Charles Lindbergh? The man was wooden and rather shallow but far from an idiot. Would he want to give the child back, knowing that some other Charles Lindbergh was devastated by its loss? Perhaps another Sylvester Chalice would restore another baby to that Lindbergh, and the endless rippling conga line of kidnappings and rescues would eventually resolve itself. It still rankled him to wonder if there ever had been a kidnapping or if every abduction was performed by another Sylvester Chalice, seeking to right each other's infinity of wrongs.

Now reunited against all odds with his family, Lindbergh had returned to work an invention he'd dreamt up when his wife's sister suffered from lasting heart defects after recovering from rheumatic fever. His perfusion pump would allow surgeons to remove organs from the patient and work on them outside the body, he insisted, but it was a pipe dream. Still, Chalice knew he could count on the aviator to lend his good name, if nothing else, to a third-party ticket in November.

And then there was Hoover…

After the extraordinarily costly stunt in Washington, Hoover folded and accepted his plan to clear out the Bonus Army but would not concede the nomination. It would've been easier to kill the sonofabitch. The Lynches put the fear in him, but nothing would make him see the world had moved beyond his power to influence it. Perhaps if he only introduced the pig-eyed reactionary to Circe in all its crepuscular glory, he would see how outmatched he was. If he could only get him alone, Daddy Long-Legs would show him…

I told you he wouldn't, said Daddy Long-Legs.

He fretted that he'd lost the Conductor, who tried to take the Chancellor and the President in one throw and was cheated of both. A very expensive hired hand, the German had his own agenda, and his wounded Prussian ego would make him as dire a threat as he'd been to Chalice's enemies. But even the worst he could do would only serve the grand design, in the end.

He'd wanted only to have a perfect body and be the envy of the whole world. What a fool he was. Now, the whole *world* would be his perfect body and the envy of the universe.

"It will be mine…yes?"

When it is complete, when it is perfect, I shall give it to you…

Sylvester believed it.

A young aide with nose-glasses and crooked teeth came into his office. "We're ready for you, Mr. Chalice."

Sylvester rose from his desk with a winning rictus fixed on his prematurely lined face. He swaggered towards the door to the recording studio when a bolt of pain shot through him. Two of his teeth cracked under the strain.

Almost forgot your speech, said Daddy Long-Legs.

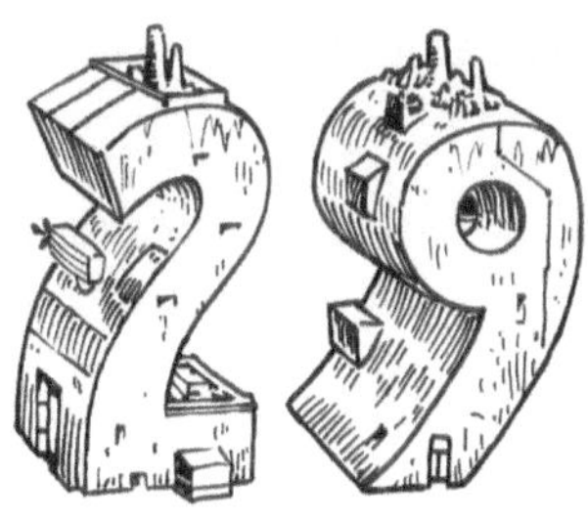

The great trouble today is that there are too many laws.

— House Speaker John Nance Garner

July 30th, 1932 | Virginia

The amphibious Duck-Truck raced over winding, dusty country roads all that seething summer night. The two men riding in it kept guns in their laps and watched the road before and behind and the sky above as if some silent pursuer might appear out of nowhere at any moment. Every bend or covered bridge could hide a roadblock. Every gas station attendant could be a spy.

When they stopped just outside Manassas and Spotsylvania, one went in and brandished a pistol and demanded any food they had handy while the other filled up, nervously studying the road. A heap of moth-eaten Army blankets lurched up out of the backseat to press against the flyblown window, whereupon the man pumping the gas hissed at it to stay down in a livid whisper.

Speeding through the dark, they'd made Richmond just before dawn. Model Y trucks blocked the road just outside the city limits. A vigilante mob with rifles, lanterns, and pitchforks crowded the road, forcing them to stop.

A jug-eared deputy sheriff looked them over with the dumb cunning of an absolute master of two square miles of the world, putting a boot on their running board and scratching his unshaven neck with the sight of his deer rifle. "Where y'all coming from?"

The twins looked at each other. One said, "Baltimore." The other said, "Delaware."

Looking back over his shoulder at his posse, who drew closer, the deputy smiled indulgently and asked, "Where y'all headed?"

"We gone to Florida," the driver said, affecting a Dixie accent as if the issue was already decided.

"Ya fool," the passenger shot back. "We ought go to Mexico." He hadn't the vaguest inkling what a Mexican accent sounded like, so he made up his own.

"Ain't seen any of them Bonus Army bums on the road, have ya? We heard they're all comin' out every which way from DC with their tails twixt their legs."

"Oh, we went clear round that rat's nest, I tell you what," said the driver, scratching the stubble on his head. "Could see the fire from a hundred miles away. I heard tell they's all gone ape-y ramblin' from town to town with Hoover's head on a stick, rapin' all the white men and hangin' all the women. You best not believe what you hear on the radio, cos they already been subverted by the Comintern. You heard it here first, brother."

They peeled out and sped through Richmond without further incident.

Too angry and confused to come up with a plan, they rode and watched while going south. When Harry spotted a brand-new emerald Essex Terraplane in the driveway of a banker's house in Chesterfield, he made Dick pull over. They bickered about stealing it until the lights were flickering on and off throughout the neighborhood, and Dick sped off.

Neither of them tried to talk about what they'd seen, what any of it meant, or where they were going next. Dick was annoyed that they'd not been recognized as the notorious Haywire Gang, but Harry was so wound up about ditching the Duck-Truck, he stopped complaining, and thus had nothing to say. He fidgeted with the radio, looking for music or news and shouting, "Nuts!" whenever he came across Daddy Long-Legs, who seemed to be everywhere up and down the dial today.

The memory of last night blazed brighter in his mind than the sun when it shone through the trees lining the highway. The old, dead-eyed soldiers scattered, whipped by their own government on the Anacostia plain, the gas-masked infantry loading them into trucks at bayonet-point that took them to the teleportals. Harry wanted to go with them, maybe they were going where Tom was, but Dick told him to forget Tom, and spat that they wouldn't get far with their new friend, anyway.

The men running the trucks weren't from the Army; they had padded leather armor and different guns, with Tesla coils and diodes and such. They gave Dick such a bad feeling, he ran away down to the river. They'd found the Duck-Truck parked on the bank, under a camouflaged fishing net. Someone in Camp Marks must've stashed it for a hasty escape. "The old Haywire luck strikes again!" Harry crowed. Dick ripped the netting off and jumped behind the wheel. Harry dove into the passenger seat, and the blob hopped in the back, which was full of old crates labeled as Army rations. After a brief shouting match over which wires to cross, Dick somehow got the engine started, and they drove into the river.

They heard someone yelling from shore and saw a gray shape chasing them down the bank. They didn't realize he was shooting at them until a salvo of silent projectiles punched holes in their canvas canopy. Harry figured out how to start the propeller, but Dick nixed it, holding his breath until the floating fortress of the *USS Constitution* had passed by on their starboard side. All hands-on deck, klaxons wailing, gauss cannons throbbing, the Navy never noticed the little olive drab boat floating by on the lazy current. Not until a bend in the river hid them from the battleship did he fire up the growling propeller, and soon, it was all behind them, but then a flotilla of Murphy boats came pounding upriver towards them, and they diverted back onto the Virginia shore, just north of Alexandria.

Fort Myer, Fairfax, Manassas, Bristow. Farm trucks and delivery vans, revival tents, roadhouses and filling stations, sharecroppers and cotton, tobacco, hemp and corn.

Neither said a word to the other until they were crossing into North Carolina at mid-afternoon. Harry got hungry enough to rummage in the crates in the back, but they were all full of antique dynamite, sweaty with nitro, and crumbling like old cheese. "Figures," Harry grumbled. "Hungry enough to eat my hand."

"I'm hungry enough to eat your face," Dick said, ensuring silence for another sixty miles. Staunton, Lexington, then Roanoke, and another roadblock, so they ducked off on a rutted country road, heading more or less east.

Stopping at a general store outside Mecklenburg, Dick came running out just ahead of a shotgun blast that ripped apart the screen door and snatched off his hat. They took off with the nozzle still screwed into the gas tank, ripping the hose off the pump. A spark from the hose bib dragging on the cracked macadam ignited the gusher of gas, leaving a lake of fire in their wake.

Dick stuffed a Moon Pie in his face, tossed a wrapped ham sandwich and a pack of Lucky Strikes over the seat for the blob.

"Where we going?" Harry finally demanded. "We gotta find Tom."

"We don't need him, and he surely don't need us."

"Damn it, where we going? What're we doing? Why're we even alive? You don't know, and I don't know, and we won't ever know because he's our head. I hate him too, but I hate *my* head even more…" Harry punched his head by way of emphasis.

"He left us…"

"No, he went looking for answers, and we stayed. He's looking for how we came to be three. He's lookin' to make us one…"

"I ain't no fraction of a man." Dick hunched over the wheel and picked up the pistol between his legs.

"That's it, ain't it? You don't want go back."

"Why should I? He plays the angles, and we take the pain. Why would I want to be just the ass end of a pantomime horse? It's less than nothing at all. Who made you the brains of this outfit, anyway? When did *you* ever get to call the shots?"

"Whenever *we* call the shots, it goes wrong," Harry shouted. "You damn near got killed for a handful of Moon Pies back there…and when'd you get him smoking?" The blob had five or six cigarettes smoldering in its trembling vacuoles. Noxious vapors emitted from simmering bubbles bursting like ripe acne all over its membrane.

Harry fell silent as they heard the wail of a siren, far behind them but growing louder all the time.

It was getting dark, and they were miles from any town, swerving back and forth across the oiled dirt road as they battled over the wheel.

A bullet starred the back window. Then, they started coming down like hailstones. The Kid tried to ooze into the front seat. Harry slapped an ammo drum into his Lynch gun and barked, "Hold 'em off, will ya, Kid?"

The blob fumbled out a handgun and snapped off a couple rounds, but the kick threw the barrel almost straight up, and it shot more holes in the roof than in their pursuers. "No, dummy!" Dick shouted, jabbing it with a stick of dynamite. "Light 'em up and pitch 'em!"

The Duck-Truck swerved onto the span of a quaint covered bridge, like a drive-thru barn. The Kid took the stick of dynamite in its pseudopod and touched the fuse with the ember on one of its cigarettes. The sputtering fuse startled the blob, so it tossed the dynamite out the back of the speeding jeep. They bounced again at the end of the bridge, flinging the open crate of dynamite into the air. The blob spasmed and spat out the rest of its cigarettes as a fusillade of bullets smashed through it. The rest of the dynamite spilled onto the road.

The strain of constricting itself to absorb the barrage that would surely have chewed its human friends' heads off left it sloshing exhausted around the truck bed like a dying jellyfish.

The posse ran hard on their heels in two open civilian cars and a black Mariah, fishtailing onto the bridge just as the fizzing fuse disappeared into the waxy butt end on the tumbling stick of dynamite.

The first explosion blew the shingled roof off the covered bridge, but it was only an appetizer. The rest of the crate lofted the sheriff's posse high into the sky and utterly pulverized the bridge.

A fiery wind washed over the careening Duck-Truck. Dick fought the wheel, shouting at Harry, cussing out the blob, when Harry screamed high and hard and slapped his own face.

The engine died and the brakes locked up. An eerie whistling drowned out whatever Dick said next. It grew louder and seemed to hang over their heads like a buzz bomb coming down. Dick turned to punch Harry in the mouth just as the black Mariah tumbled out of the sky to land on its roof in the road, just a few yards ahead of them.

The Duck-Truck slewed into the inverted grill of the police wagon. Dick and Harry jumped out and gazed up in wonder.

There was money blowing everywhere.

Dick ran around the back of the police truck. The back door hung wide open, and greenbacks floated out of it like a conventioneer's back pocket. Harry danced around, catching them in his fists as they fell out of the sky. Dick did the same until he saw Harry doing it and realized how idiotic they looked. "Gotdamn, get a sack, you big dope. Get the freak out here…" He climbed in the open door of the overturned paddy wagon and was standing ankle-deep in loose cash like a drift of dead leaves. It was dark in there and getting darker, faster, even, than the sun was setting. He knelt to stuff his pockets; they must have robbed the entire town. It didn't make any sense, but for once, luck was with them, so he wasn't kicking—

He tore the side pocket on his trousers and the lapel pocket on his shirt and was cursing the money he'd just been kissing when he realized he wasn't alone in the truck. "Move, Harry, you're blocking my light," he said.

It wasn't Harry.

A black silhouette blocked the doorway. Dick went for his other side pocket and pulled out a fistful of money where his gun ought to be. He threw it at the black form. Transfixed by glowing eyes that spun and flashed and pulled his brain apart like monkey bread, he fell almost willingly into perfect blackness.

Harry and the Kid had picked up most of the money off the road before Harry noticed Dick was gone. He peeked into the black Mariah, more than a little scared of the dark and the quiet and thinking maybe they ought to beat feet to Mexico. He'd always wanted to see a bullfight.

When the demon with the golden mask reached out of the black Mariah to seize him by the lapels, he had time only to say, "Tom, help me—" before he was tugged into the dark, and it was as if he'd never been.

Kid Amoeba abruptly ceased gamboling around, trying to engulf the last of the bills, when it saw the White Devil standing in the doorway of the upside-down Black Mariah, beckoning like he was selling tickets. It contorted, twisting itself out of habit to "look" for its human friends, but when it failed to see them anywhere, it bounced willingly into the doorway of the truck and out of this world.

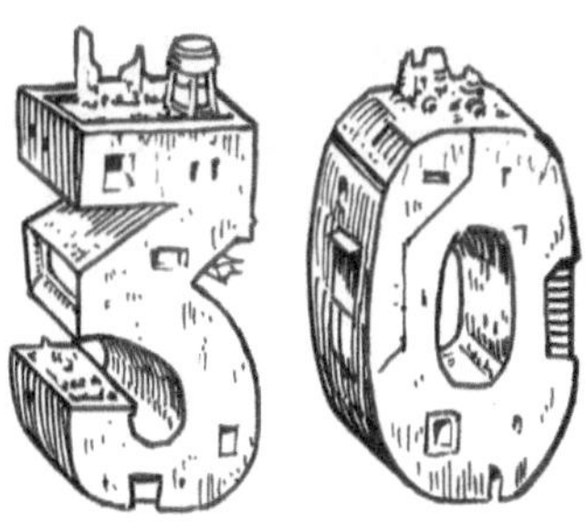

True love is not possessive or demanding; it is selfless and freeing.

—W. Somerset Maugham

August 1st, 1932 | Mara Dzong

She awoke, and her first thought was, I'm dead, this is death— Her eyes opened, and nothing she saw told her she was wrong.

Darkness thick as molasses, broken only by the dull orange glow of coals in a brazier. The light illuminated nothing but a wall of golden demonic faces leering down at her as if waiting to judge her. Startled when one of them seemed to blink, she sat up and threw off musty animal hide blankets and found she was still wearing her flight suit, but it had been unzipped to the waist, her prosthetic limbs disconnected, and the bandaged wound in her chest nearly blacked her out again when she tried to sit up.

She supposed she'd known all along where she'd end up, but it still upset her more than it should to find herself in such a cheaply operatic Hell, with exotic props and dancers with cucumbers in their tights, and cheapest of all, the philosophy. Didn't she deserve it?

Breathing through her teeth, she looked at the eager demons again and defiantly pushed out her lower lip. "Well, what did you expect?" she asked her infernal judges. "Wasn't I always a puppet? I only ever tried to do good..."

One of the golden demon faces stepped out of the parade to loom over her. "All of us puppets, trying to do good by evil means," it said. Its voice was like a sword on a whetstone.

She recognized it, yet how different he sounded now from that impudent, idealistic guttersnipe who'd confronted her at Bethlehem Steel. How drained of **humor**... of humanity. "You drugged me... brought me...wherever here is... Why?"

Did that implacable mask tarnish with something like a blush? "I had to...you were shot."

"Then why am I not in a proper hospital? Where am I, anyway?"

"Mara Dzong," he said, as if that explained anything. "I had no choice. As far as the world knows, Ms. Lynch, you're dead. And after what you did..."

"What did I do...?" She combed at a tangle of fragmented memories and recoiled from the kind of ghastly nonsense one dreamt under heavy anesthesia. She remembered, and her heart cracked wide open. Oh, what hadn't she done? The White House and the President and the poor little man she shot who turned into an apparition, but she was sure she must be dead because she was stopped by...herself. "Am I one of your prisoners, now? Are you reforming me?"

"No... I only hoped to free you from the prison in your mind."

"Why didn't you come to me? Why did you only send a note? Why did you send me... into that...?"

That stopped him in whatever game he was playing for almost a moment. "I sent no note... I went to the White House myself when I learned you were the assassin. I'm sorry. I should have...—"

"Wait, what is all this?" she demanded.

"Your psychotherapist, Dr. Frauenwahl, hypnotized you. Used you to try to kill the President and the chancellor of Germany."

Aghast, she shot back, "That's ridiculous! I'm no assassin..."

"But you were. And you still are." His head tilted maddeningly. "There's no shame in it. You saw what he could do in the War.

Frauenwahl's real name is Egon Schuiten, but you knew him…as the Conductor."

"You're out of your mind," she spat, but she knew with fatalistic certainty that it must be true, for it was exactly the most unbearable thing she'd ever heard.

"You set a trap for me but didn't try to warn me. Someone else beat me to the punch. Someone…" She clamped her hand over her mouth, shook her head, and pulled her hair. It came back to her, that trail of vapor across the sky, too quick to see what made it, the winged knight standing atop the banquet table and pointing her own weapons at her…

"The newspapers and the radio say it's the Silver Sentry. As a registered trademark of the Lynch Munitions Company, the Sentry foiled the assassin after he murdered your father and saved the President… from you."

"Go to hell." It beggared rational thought. Someone else was flying around in her armor. She wondered if Father, or whoever was in charge of the company now, had given the job to someone else. And the man who killed her sister had been toying with her mind for months. How could she have been such a fool? Perhaps she was an even bigger fool to believe this ghoulish revenant. Disgusted by its own train of thought, her mind jerked out of its morbid rut all at once. "What happened to the Bonus Army?"

"They were rounded up, and all went through Chalice's teleportals, and they haven't been heard from since."

"Well, I don't know what to think of that… Maybe they're better off."

"The Conductor kills for Chalice—or he did. I don't think he worked on you as long as he did, only to be upstaged. Let's stick to that. What do you remember?"

She started to tell him it was none of his damned business but found she couldn't force her mouth to make the words. Nor, she discovered, to her horror, did she need to.

So, this was the Evil Eye…

Those unbearable, bulging orbs began to glow and spin, pulling her out of her skull. She tried to block it, but she could see them with her eyes closed, see what they saw as they ripped it from her.

All those weeks hiding out as Elvira Seaton, the only time she'd felt truly grounded was in Dr. Frauenwahl's office, pouring out her thoughts and her life at the silent direction of his masterful fingers, those hooded, endlessly inviting eyes. He had played her like so many human instruments—

It was horrible, but as she looked into his eyes, she realized the Conductor was not the only one who'd meddled with her mind.

Her idle time in the flat off Times Square was like a net with more holes than substance. Her memories had been edited with a rusty butcher knife. When she searched them for proof of what he'd told her, she found only stumps as rudely abbreviated as her limbs.

"What did you do to me?"

"Only what I had to," he answered. "I erased what he put inside your head. If I didn't, you'd never know when he might jerk your strings again…"

Her hands clawed at her head as if she could pull out what he'd put into her. It was as monstrous as any crime for which he'd ever killed a man. Without ever laying a hand on her, he'd violated her mind, then stolen the memory.

"What else did you erase? And what did you put in? What magic word would you say to make me dance for you?"

His voice betrayed no anger, no emotion at all. "I would never," he sputtered, but somehow, she knew he was lying. "This is… trivia, Matilda. There is much to do…"

"You don't feel the least bit guilty about it, do you? You dirty little thing, hiding behind that devil's mask, trading your soul by the ounce, but you're less and lower than a devil, for they're only doing what they're made for. You were a man… once."

If he heard her at all, he gave no sign. Perhaps his head shook a little behind that infernal mask as if what she said disturbed that fragile, broken thing behind it. Maybe it sank a little into itself, as that last thread connecting him to who he once used to be was almost imperceptibly severed. Perhaps the mask had only shown her what he'd done, so she would do her part to rip that thread away, and give the mask what it wanted.

Matilda strapped on her arm and leg and changed into gray whipcord riding breeches, a fleece-lined sweater, and a fur-trimmed leather flight jacket, wondering vaguely how her clothes from her Manhattan flat came to be here.

She was looking for the exit when she came into the hall. A pair of identical twins in grimy shirtsleeves and dungarees warmed their hands at the fire pit while a restless mound of translucent pinkish ooze, like something out of her mother's daft picture books, stretched and contracted before the flames. Opposite them stood the White Devil. She looked around, expecting…an army? She approached the pit, her eyes drawn to the dancing flames until she realized what was burning in them.

A linen shroud crumbled away in ashes from a face gnawed down to the skull. She gasped in disgust, but there was no stench. The smoke was aromatic, like sage and herbs, rather than the stench of burning flesh.

When Matilda took her place at the fire, the White Devil raised his head. The glint and gleam of his mask was dazzling, yet another reason she couldn't bear to look at him.

"This is the last of the monks of this place," he said. "He was its leader for a hundred years. Mara Dzong has stood outside of time for so long, I hoped that by returning, I would find them alive again; so powerful is the spirit here. The man who murdered them claims to have invented something new to usher us into the future, but his power is very old. If he is not stopped by those few who realize it, the world shall return to a past so dark, no history will record it."

"Mister," snapped one of the twins, "you better start talking straight, or we gone pound it out of you." Holding up a fist, he slapped his twin with his other hand. The fire leapt up and Matilda saw crackling wisps of tiny lightning squeeze out between his fingers and the close-set, beady eyes of both men. "We got no reason to throw in with any of you without knowing what the job is…"

"And I'd like to know," Matilda put in, "who these men are, please…and this… thing…"

Much as the slack-jawed bank robber's bluster merited her attention, she shuddered and took a step back from the undulating blob as it came humping and slurping around the fire to blow bubbles on the toes of her boots. Biting back a scream so as not to let down her fragile front, she took a step back.

The other twin tipped his hat. "Pleased to meet you, ma'am. We're the Haywire Gang. This is Dick, and I'm Harry. Tom, he—"

"She don't care, dummy," Dick grumbled.

"And this here's the Kid." Patting the oleaginous blob like a dog, Harry said, "And who might you be, ma'am?"

"She's the one who tried to kill the President," Dick said.

"He's pretty harmless, ma'am unless you cross him," Harry said, leaning into the fire to light a cigarette. Patting out a smoldering spit curl, he observed, "Fella smells awful sweet for a burnt-up body… but I reckon we done paid our respects, so…can we go home now?"

Now, she looked at the blob with the light shining through it. She was less frightened and more fascinated. It was not just a pile of jelly as it first appeared, but filled with strange organs and structures that defied description yet somehow gave it life and, undeniably, intelligence. Watching as it rolled across the flagstone floor to coagulate between the White Devil's shoes, it tugged his cape with a forked tentacle.

"For once, he's right," Dick said. "Get to the point. What's in it for us?"

"They have your brother. You know you have only turned to crime because you hungered for a purpose, a great wrong you could prove your worth by righting. Here it is."

"You don't know us from Adam, Mister Magician," Harry snapped. Dick nodded, surprised as anyone to be in agreement with his twin. "Spell it out plain, plug-ugly."

"Sylvester Chalice's teleportals lead to another Earth, and he's racing to cut it up and sell it by the pound. Any obstacle to the growth of his company, he has erased—the Conductor assassinates the swells who stand in his way, and Daddy Long-Legs stirs up the working class to make them a tool for his political aspirations."

"You trying to say he's a Red?" Dick asked.

"No, he's a fascist, but without the politics. He's making speeches on the radio, promising to destroy the old money power and end the depression with free food for the poor and worldwide teleportation for the rich. He's calling it the New Tomorrow plan. Daddy Long-Legs is urging his listeners to write Chalice in for president in November."

"To do what?" Matilda cut in. "Forgive me for stating the obvious, but how is he different from any swell-headed nabob who thinks the sun shines out of his ass?" She surprised herself, but she rather enjoyed it.

"He's making good on his promises. Even if you don't care what happens to this country, the Conductor killed your father. He used you to try to kill the President… and he's just warming up."

"So all one can hope for is to be used by the right monster," she said. It was like a bad dream, but every time it came back, the memory pumped black sludge into her blood.

"Wait," Harry said, his hand raised like in school. "Where's this other Earth you keep talking about? Is it on the other side of the Sun or thereabouts?"

Staring fixedly into the flames, the White Devil shook his head. "Just as our world was always but one of countless millions in the universe, so are there as many more universes. Some say they are laid atop each other like pages in a great book, others that they are all here but vibrating at another frequency."

"Mister, you just talked your way out of a job," Dick said.

Matilda held her right hand up to the fire, working the heat into her cold, cramped flesh. "I don't follow this, either. The Conductor is still out there. There was a war in the streets of Washington between the Army and its own veterans. What is this nonsense about another Earth?"

White Devil pointed at the twins. "All of it leads back to Sylvester Chalice. These men are proof. An inventor named Kurtzberg dedicated his life to studying megaliths—sacred stones that served as ritual centers, observatories…and something else."

"Like Stonehenge?" Matilda asked, curious despite herself.

The White Devil nodded. "For those who knew how to use them, the stones could transport ancient shamans across continents, between worlds. There is evidence… Ancient Egyptian jewelry found in mounds in Illinois. Chinese jade in pyramids in the Yucatan."

"But how do any of these crackpot theories help us?" Matilda asked.

He touched the golden prison of his face. "It's no theory. This mask allows me to travel without moving between Mara Dzong and anywhere in the world. I know Chalice's doors operate on the same principle because he sent men to kill the monks who lived here, but he doesn't know how it works any better than I do."

"Where is this Kurtzberg now? And what the hell is that thing?"

"Dead, most likely. Killed by Chalice's goons when he tried to demonstrate his theory."

The White Devil inclined his head at the twins and the pile of goo purring at his feet.

"That thing is a native of Chalice's other Earth. These men were once a cub reporter named Millard Crabtree, who went through Kurtzberg's portal just as it was shut off. They came out at three far-flung locations across the country but were drawn to each other by the same energy field that disrupts everything they touch."

"He means us," Harry said, elbowing Dick in the ribs. "We're lucky."

"We're just two dopes who went through the wrong door," Dick retorted. "And the blob here ain't even housebroken. Mister, you seem like you got sand and a trick or two more than Houdini, so I don't see why the rest of us are even here. If you can't fix us, leave us out of it. Why us?"

"We must strike at Sylvester Chalice before he opens his teleportation service worldwide."

"So, we're just going to charge into the home office and shoot up the place? Just the five of us?"

"No. We go in the back door. Chalice has tried to seek out Earth's ancient stone circles to make more doors, but he hasn't found all of them. We will use one to travel to the other Earth. And there, we shall raise an army. And we'll shut the doors."

Matilda's hand went to her mouth. She recalled what he'd told her in her room. "No, you can't be thinking of using the Bonus Army! They're just a bunch of broken-down old soldiers… They should be rescued, not led into another battle!"

"So, you're saying Tom is over there, and if we go, we'll get him back?" Harry put in.

"He'll say anything to get you to stick your necks in his noose," Matilda said.

Watching as the lama's blazing ribcage collapsed into embers, Dick cracked his knuckles and scraped his face with his dirty, broken nails. "I can feel him itching in the back of my head. We both can. We'll go where it leads. If we end up in the same place, I guess you got us."

"You don't even know what's over there, but you're going to lead us to another planet to launch an insurrection and overthrow… a travel agency, basically? So, however, many of the thousands of people passing through it at any given time will turn out like these two, if they're lucky?"

"Hey now," Dick sneered, "I wouldn't trade with you, even if you had all your arms and legs."

"You couldn't handle it." She crossed her arms and stamped one boot-heel on the floor, activating the last-ditch armaments in her prosthetic leg. It wouldn't come to that, would it? "It's been a lovely outing. Thanks ever so much for all you've done, and I wish you every success." Taking a big step back, she found herself pausing, tensed for the White Devil to berate or just attack her, and wasn't there any way out of here besides going into the shadow of his cape? But he just stood and watched the fire with his arms crossed.

The wheeled suitcase with her armor was parked where she'd left it, behind a charred wooden pillar. Looking over her shoulder one last time at the odd gathering, she dragged it over the rough-hewn stones, cursing under her breath. She reached a massive double door behind which she could hear the whipping wind of a storm. Though she was scarcely dressed for it, she should get her bearings, as it would no doubt prove fruitless to ask for a telephone to summon a cab…

She put her head against the doors, barred by a log as thick as her thigh.

This must be what Mother felt like when she was committed. She would not end up like Mother—or worse, a part of this doomed sideshow. With her left arm, she flipped the heavy bar out of its clasps and let the wind throw the doors open.

He was standing there in the wind, the frost clinging to his mask.

"So, you are the only way out," she had to shout over the wind. "If you're here for anything else, you really can go back to whatever Hell you came from…"

"I won't stop you," he replied as he crowded her back inside and slammed the doors. "But you should know one thing before you go."

"I don't have the stomach to hear anymore. Haven't I been used enough? I want to go home and reclaim what's left of my life…"

"The Silver Sentry revealed her true identity to President Hoover…"

"*Her?*"

His eyes did not light up in the gloom of the antechamber. Indeed, they were as cold as the rest of the mask. "The new Silver Sentry is your sister…Minerva Lynch."

Her mind reeled. She stepped back as if he'd slapped her. It was preposterous, insane… so it must be true. She remembered the flicker of guilt on Dr. Crisp's face when she visited Larkspur Cloisters, the relief when she said she was there to see the Ochlocrat, the sour, rasping voice that had assailed her from the neighboring cell—*You here to see me, sister?*

Tears sprang hot from her eyes, but she wouldn't cry in front of this monster. "Oh, do stop! Shut your filthy mouth and bite your forked tongue off. What a monstrous lie, and you know, even if it's true…even if… Oh God, what happened to you? What happened to *us?*"

He only stood and stared beyond her into emptiness.

So weak, she almost threw her arms around him, but instead, she turned away and grabbed her case. "I want to go home now." She was starting to shake with sobs. "Now, please…"

Minerva alive? All these years, locked away somewhere? Someone had put her in Matilda's old armor and sent her to save the President. It was almost too monstrous, even in a world where doctors turned their patients into murder puppets, and veterans were trampled by their old commanding officers in the streets of the Capitol.

But who would do such a thing? Only a man who drove his wife mad and locked her away in an insane asylum; only a man who hired anarchists to throw bombs to drum up business; only a man who could use an innocent woman's death to disown his daughter.

"How did she do it…?" She pushed him back. "Never mind. I don't want to hear it from you."

"She's quite insane, and she's vowed to avenge your murder. You'll be framed as your own assassin if you go back to New York."

"Enough! It's over! I'm just talking to the mask now, aren't I? There's nobody behind it anymore. I watched as you killed him… You know, I might have been rather fond of him, if he didn't owe his life to you, if he could take you off and be an ordinary man again. And I hate myself a little bit for that, for being as shallow as any man who made himself scarce when he saw what I'm missing, but there it is, and thank you for that little lesson.

"So I'll just be going, and good luck saving the day from your windmill. I just have to ask, though I know the answer. How much do you hate yourself?"

"I don't know a hero who doesn't," he muttered, so low it might've been a trap to draw her closer.

"A hero," she spat. "How sad when you could've been a man. And I don't even know your real name, but I begin to suspect that you don't know it, either."

He tossed his head, suppressing a thousand angry arguments. "I…" The White Devil hung his head. "I…am…so…"

"SEND ME HOME!" she screamed.

He obliged and spread his cape until it was an alcove. She stretched out her left hand, closed her eyes, and walked forward, ready to blast him in half.

She stepped into his cape, and when he closed his arms, he held only himself.

August 2, 1932 | Washington, DC

Of all the hazards an agent of the Bureau of Investigation faced, nothing was more dangerous than briefing the Director when he was in a mood.

"Sir, we have ascertained some very disturbing likelihoods regarding the Daddy Long-Legs investigation…" This was a grievous sore spot, and the Assistant Director paused to see which way the wind blew. At first highly agitated over radical elements threatening the stability of the upcoming election, Hoover had lately chilled the pursuit of Daddy Long-Legs, even threatened agents who brought him routine reports on the rabble-rousing phantom.

"I've told you more than once not to bother me with trivialities. I want the Bonus Army assassin stalking our leaders of industry. I want the White Devil and the Haywire Gang."

He knew he was plunging into an abyss but couldn't avoid it. They had become Hoover's new *bete noire* and clogged the top of the Public Enemy list. "Sir, Daddy Long-Legs has told his listeners to write in

Sylvester Chalice on November 8th. We've worked with technicians at the Federal Trade Commission, comparing the timing and signal strength of his broadcasts, and we've eliminated all other possibilities…"

Hot black blood flushed the Director's face. "How many times must I tell you…?" Of late, the Director had goat glands on the brain and waxed paranoiac about the "border blaster" transmitters unscrupulous entrepreneurs had slapped together just over the southern border to skirt Radio Commission regulations and bathe the nation in salacious programming and miscegenated music. The infamous goat gland transplant mogul had pioneered what had become a chronic national scourge, but Daddy Long-Legs seemed to operate on a higher plane altogether.

"Sir, we believe the broadcasts originate on the Moon."

This stopped the Director in his tracks, if only for a moment. "That's preposterous… Isn't it?"

"As I said, all other possibilities have been assiduously debunked. We've intercepted a huge volume of telephonic chatter suggesting coordinated mass marches on Chalice's franchises across the country to coincide with his declared intent to open his teleportation network worldwide…"

Again, the pregnant pause. The implied threat to America's borders was another pet obsession of the Director, who rose to his present position on the deportation of seditionist and anarchist elements.

"We already have that situation well in hand. Mr. Chalice has personally assured me that he will work with our immigration protocols and won't seek political office…" The Director was almost talking in his sleep. "Isn't there anything out there that *does* merit our attention this fine morning?"

The Assistant Director shuffled the manila folders still piled in his lap, completed a series of calculations in his head, and stuffed them back into his valise. "Nothing that won't wait until tomorrow, sir…"

"Fair enough. Detail men from all coincident field offices to observe proceedings at relevant sites. Collate and prioritize all known and unknown threats. Our priorities are clear. Rescind all deviations."

The Assistant Director made a show of copying down this sphinx's riddle, excused himself, and vacated the Director's office.

"It's as if I'm talking to myself," the Director said.

They perceive you as weak, said the voice in his head that had come to be his closest—indeed, his only trustworthy advisor. *They bury you in minutiae, so you won't see their devious machinations…*

Of course, they did. The Ivy League set always looked down on the little man with the little degree and no friends in high places. They would love to send him chasing populist demagogues on the Moon while they plotted his downfall. "Perhaps I should issue a policy memo…"

Not strong enough. A surprise inspection of all field offices. Today. Show them you see them…

The Director was musing over this when he was seized by a wracking cough. Reaching across the blank expanse of his desk for a disposable handkerchief, he cleared his throat into it and hesitated before looking at what he'd expelled.

The discharge was marbled with dark threads and gobbets of hard foreign matter that almost reminded him of the tiny eggs his father had used to catch fish.

"I think… I think I'm getting worse…"

Ransacking his desk drawers, he found a hand mirror, but it took an act of will open his eyes and look at his face.

Tiny, vigorous things like mosquito larvae skittered around inside his eyes.

No sir, said the voice, which sounded like how he imagined his own voice sounded—not the high, unmasculine voice he cringed from every time he heard it in the newsreels.

It was the voice on the radio.

You're getting better…

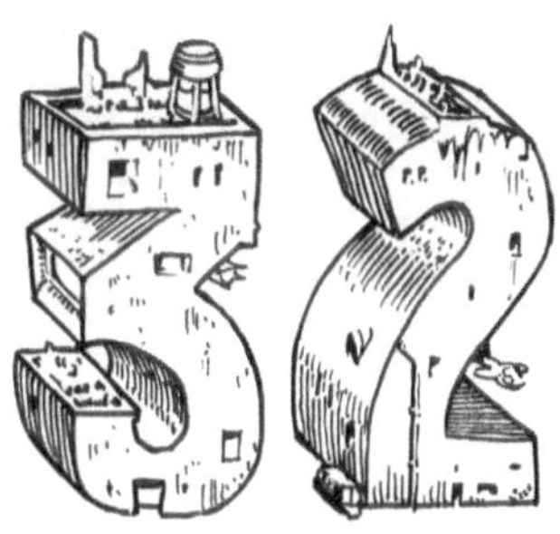

So in Scotland witches used to raise the wind by dipping a rag in water and beating it thrice on a stone, saying: "I knok this rag upone this stane, To raise the wind in the divellis name, It sall not lye till I please againe."

—James G. Frazer, The Golden Bough

August 1, 1932 | Woonsocket, Rhode Island

T he town below the hill was dead but didn't know it.

Even as the economy sputtered and failed, the hulking six-story mill at its center had run day and night because of Rhode Island's lax labor laws until this year, when cheaper labor down south silenced the last New England mills and condemned countless towns like this one to almost total unemployment. Only a corner of the old combing floor was still used by a radio assembly concern. Even at midnight, with the full moon and stars glittering in the cloud-raked sky, men walked the streets gibbering, searching in a drunken rage for work.

The high hill was once used to hang condemned criminals, and before that, the worn nubs of stone circling the peak like a giant's half-buried dentures were the site of rituals meant to keep the world turning by the first people to live here.

"Yep," Harry said, "this looks like the place…"

The White Devil didn't need to be told. He'd probed Harry's mind and retraced his childlike memories back to their wellspring in this place.

It was lucky they had not been uprooted and carted off, as were all the megaliths Professor Kurtzberg had identified in his research at 214 sites in North America to power Chalice's tele-portals. Maybe these ones were overlooked because not even Kurtzberg knew about them, or maybe they just didn't work.

Harry had come out through here. The White Devil knew it had to be so, but there was much he still didn't know, and it was too late to learn.

Back at the monastery, he'd tried and failed to learn more than he told them, and none of the knowledge he shared seemed to do them much good. "You're so smart," Dick had railed at him, "how'd we get this way?"

The White Devil had given this much thought, putting it together with the massacre at the monastery and his ordeal in Utopia. He had decided to wait for them to ask and to let the newspaper clipping he passed to them speak for itself.

According to the article, 22 were killed in an explosion and fire in Eureka, California, on September 29, 1929—their birthday. Some crackpot inventor invited a bunch of the press to see a teleportation demonstration, but his makeshift laboratory burned down, cause unknown. Among them were two *Examiner* reporters who were shown at the bottom in an office party snapshot—Busby Aaronson—balding, beady-eyed—and baby-faced, gormless Millard Crabtree. Harry and Dick stared for a long time at the picture. Harry started to say something and, for once, thought better of it.

"You went through the portal Kurtzberg opened," the White Devil said, "but something went wrong. Maybe they cut the juice, maybe somebody stopped them…and you came out as three men in three places…that we know about…"

"But which one of us is the *real* one? Which are the copies?" He'd worked himself up so badly that the White Devil had to find a skin of Ugly John's Himalayan applejack to calm him down. Even in a place with no electricity, the Haywires sweated entropy, and it played havoc with everything they touched.

"I don't think any of you are. You all have the same fingerprints and dental work and no memory before the day Crabtree died."

Dick looked at his feet as he talked. "We fought plenty, but we both always figured Tom was the original, because he was smarter, but he kept us running from one crazy scheme to another. If he had his way, we would've built a rocket to the moon or become cowboys or something. Was me and Harry wanted to rob banks, cos it was the only thing the hoodoo would let us be good at." Now he looked at the White Devil, and his face went slack, as so many did when they remembered they were talking to a violent amnesiac in a magic devil mask. "What are we, doc? How're we supposed to live one dead guy's life?"

"I don't think you could be put back together if you wanted to. What do you want to do, both of you?"

Looking over at Harry sleeping on a pile of pillows, Dick said, "We got to find Tom. No two ways about it."

"Do you still feel him? Is he close?"

"He is, and he isn't, if that makes sense." Now he closed his eyes, holding his breath, shrinking when he let it out. "He's not dead, but at the same time, he's nowhere at all. I bet he could explain it better… I guess he's the brains of the outfit, I'm the heart, and Harry is the muscle, guts, what-have-you."

"I disagree," the White Devil told him before leaving him to sleep if he could. "I think you are the head. If you follow me tomorrow, I will help restore your heart."

He'd regretted the hammy promise almost as soon as he made it, and he felt a twinge of guilt when he looked at them now, but he had already lost Matilda Lynch—in so many ways, he bitterly reminded himself. And yet, a strange instinct made him feel that she would be of greater use elsewhere, or the mask would never have let her leave.

Now, they stood looking at each other across the circle. That instinct had left him high and dry.

"So, Mandrake," Dick shouted through the modified gas mask strapped to his face, "whatta we do now?"

"Be quiet," the White Devil said. "Be still. Midnight is near. We need to focus our attention, open our senses, and take what's offered."

Harry and Dick closed their eyes. Dick had two gauss revolvers in a cross-draw shoulder rig. Harry had a Lynch rifle and some Army surplus grenades. Both wore gas masks to which Jasper had attached cans of compressed air, which would buy them at most ten minutes. He knew next to nothing about what they were stepping into, beyond that the air was unfit to breathe and that they had to go now.

He believed that Chalice somehow energized the teleportals to continuously activate them, but the ancients had used the alignment of the planets and ritual offerings. He hoped to accomplish the same end with the Haywire twins as an amplifier and the Kid as a focus. Their connections with the other side should help them to pick the lock.

Funny, the things you can believe when you can't sleep or remember your own name.

In stillness and silence, he opened himself up completely. He felt—did he feel it? Yes, the tingle of imminence. Once, he'd known it when the tumblers of a safe turned on their back for him, or a grift was about to drop coin in his open palm. It felt familiar, even if all he remembered was that he had much to repent.

"Take my hand," he said. Dick reluctantly edged closer and let his hand be trapped by the White Devil's glove. Harry wouldn't touch him, but then he realized why. The blob undulated in between them and stretched itself to match their height. Extending a pseudopod to each, it trembled and flushed as it took its place among them. Its tentacle in his hand was cool and pulsed with a false heartbeat.

The White Devil called up in himself the silent mantra that let him travel to the monastery. Picturing the energy flowing from the mask and out of his arms, he passed it on to Dick and the Kid. A startling sizzle and pop jolted the brothers. Both men grunted, and the Kid twisted on itself like a candle's flame in a high wind, but when the White Devil opened his eyes, they were still standing there.

"Maybe it wants a whatchamacallit… sacrifice," Harry said, giggling nervously. "Like a virgin."

"Go to hell," Dick snapped, tugging his gas mask down around his neck. "You're twice the virgin I am. I can't breathe in this damn mask, and I gotta smoke."

These stones once opened on a world next door, but we forgot the way of it. Chalice turned the ancient magic into another modern convenience, but the folks from the old times knew there had to be a sacrifice. What's Chalice sacrificing to open all those doors, and who's paying for it?

Dick lit up. In the fitful match-glow, the White Devil noticed the old woman watching them from the high weeds just the other side of the stones.

She was bent over a cane, and her lank hair spilled out from under a colorless knitted hat. She wore a shapeless black dress over a plump, crooked body.

How she snuck up on them, he couldn't figure, but she looked anything but surprised to find them there. The old woman tilted her head to take him in with her good eye, regarding him with both accusation and awe. "Have you come to open the Old Way, Black Master?"

"Go on, Devil," Dick said. "Zap her with the Evil Eye."

"Old Nell keeps the true high days and the old rites," she said, lowering her head but grinning even wider, "but the rest of them… They let the town die, let the work go away. But if you show them, they'll come around. See if they don't."

"How do we do it, ma'am?" Harry asked, like a child asking where babies come from. "What's the magic word?"

Old Nell cackled. Her hands tracing runes in the clammy night air. "Your familiar knows the way home. But you, black master…to open the way, you must sing, and you must dance."

The White Devil drew himself up and tried to present himself as whatever arcane bogey the witch suspected him to be. As if testing her, he demanded, "And do you know the words of this song?"

"Oh, we all know the song, master," she said. Her good eye twinkled mockingly. Lifting her head so the wattles of her neck stretched taut, she let out a long, low moan and twirled with a strange, stolen grace. She uttered a bloodcurdling howl that trailed away and echoed off the sky. Reeling around them, she commenced a gibbering, tortured caterwauling exactly like the broken drunks wandering the streets below. For a moment, he thought the old woman—the witch—must be just another lunatic, but he felt a subsonic refrain answering her voice, throbbing up through the ground and the soles of his shoes.

Dick and the Kid must have felt it too. Their hands caught his and pulled him in a circle counterclockwise. As her voice lifted in pitch and urgency from a growl to a wail, the Haywire twins joined in, and even the blob emitted a rasping thrum from yawning pores that opened up all over its membrane.

When he began to feel it racing through him, running away without him, the White Devil joined in. There were no words, but he knew the song all too well. At once, curse and prayer were the sound of all the pain of this world, all the torment and despair and wrong, and all the longing for an end or a new beginning. Once he added his voice to it, there was no stopping. It ripped its way out of him. The Haywire twins added their grief and rage and dislocation, their hunger for a home and a purpose in a world that utterly rejected them. The Kid added its alien variations on the same universal theme, bolstered the song and made it an invocation, a key to an invisible door.

Faster and faster, they paced the circle, the sympathetic vibration of the earth making it toss and heave like the ocean, flinging them into the air until they seemed to dance above the ground, to rise up on the wind of their own motion.

The world became a roaring blur. His throat felt as if it was tearing itself apart. He clung to the others' hands and screamed himself hoarse. The sound of the witch's lament grew fainter while the Kid's alien crooning filled his ears. He had to lift his voice still higher to be heard above it.

Suddenly, they were flung apart and tumbled into a dark compared to which the full moon night was high noon.

Old Nell coughed and stumbled, putting out a hand to catch herself on one of the stones, but then recoiled when it raised blisters on her palm.

Looking about her, the witch saw she was alone on the hill. Smiling to herself and muttering, "Fools," she took up her cane and began tottering down the winding path to her cottage on the edge of town.

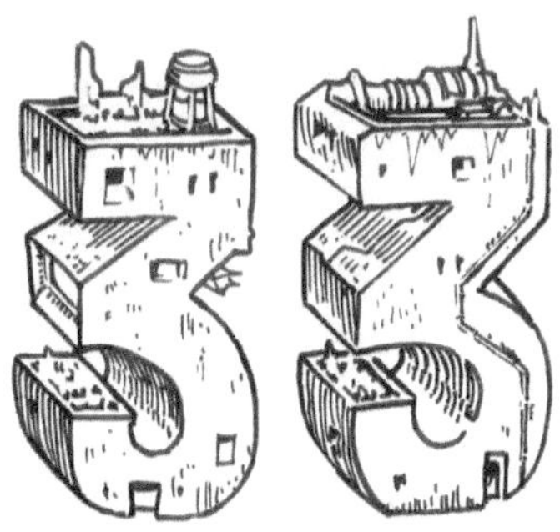

There are invisible rulers who control the destinies of millions. It is not generally realized to what extent the words and actions of our most influential public men are dictated by shrewd persons operating behind the scenes.

—Edward L. Bernays

August 2nd, 1932 | New York City

S he stepped out of perfect darkness into the mottled murk of an alley off Times Square. Lights and the noise of crowds echoed and reflected to where she stood, but she found herself flattened against a grimy brick wall, fighting panic.

She should feel relief that she was finally home after so much trouble. But none of it reassured her. Nothing felt safe. If the White Devil wasn't lying, she was now being hunted by her own sister—and why would he lie, when the truth hurt so much more?

Her hand shook on the grip of her rolling suitcase. She should throw it in the nearest garbage bin and run away. Burn her fingerprints off with acid and relocate to Hollywood, a fresh start for Elvira Seaton—

She'd run away from her father. She ran away from the debacle she caused in Washington. She ran away from the White Devil's quixotic scheme. She couldn't run away from herself.

Whatever happens, I will change what I can and change myself when I can't. I won't run from Minerva, and I won't let the Conductor get away with what he did.

As for the armor and its flying device, she would decide when she had finished whatever she did next.

That settled, Matilda stepped out of the alley. She was just around the corner from her apartment. She felt a bit peckish and turned toward the Automat (signs in the window proclaimed YES, WE HAVE AMBROSIA!), but the smell of it put her off. She got a red hot and a cup of cold coffee from a vendor on the corner and finished them, heading back to her flat. The parade of impassive faces that used to make her feel safely hidden now all seemed to study her as they passed, making her shoulders tense in anticipation of a hard hand falling on her. Dragging her suitcase, she moved as fast as the pedestrian current would allow, feeling buried alive in humanity.

If there was a trap, they would spring it now as she entered the lobby. The enormous old man snored on the couch. The cockeyed little man behind the counter told her there were no messages, but he picked up a telephone as soon as she went up the stairs.

She may as well recognize that she wasn't cut out for this and stop punishing herself for it. Despite all, it seemed as if she'd fallen yet again into the trap of doing something to prove that a woman could do it when she never stopped to ask if other women simply didn't know better. Only men would think the world needed their particular skills, their fabulous deformities, their obsessive will to punish, to save it from itself. There were only a handful of lady science vigilantes and none who were taken seriously by the press or public. She'd taken that as gospel when she hid her sex, but was it her sex that let the Conductor turn her into a weapon? Was it her sex that let her be manipulated by men from the moment she took on the role? If nothing else, she could still assure herself that she would have made no bigger of a mess of her life with a man's plumbing between her legs.

Letting herself in with the key, she stopped and studied all the other doors and listened for furtive sounds through the soda-cracker walls. Would the rest of her life be like this? Looking over her shoulder and always running, measuring her time in days stolen from her rightful fate?

No. Tomorrow, I will broker some kind of reckoning with Minerva. I will work within the law to bring the Conductor to justice, and then—I will live however I can.

The door groaned open, and she dragged the suitcase into the tiny flat. She turned on the chintzy floor lamp, and in the yellow light that barely reached the window, she saw the sloppily plastered, ear-wax-tinted walls. She heard the steady dripping of the faucet and reminded herself that she was safe at home.

She sniffed the air, wrinkled her nose, and noticed a small pot with African violets resting on the windowsill, drinking in the stuttering neon light from the Sensoria Nerve Tonic sign outside her window.

From the overstuffed chair in the corner, a voice said, "Fraulein Lynch, I owe you an apology—"

Dropping her suitcase, she twisted her wrist and snapped off a .32-caliber gauss round into the upper abdomen of the man in the chair. With no more noise than a stapler, it punched clean through him and the chair and made a hole in the wall behind him. "Apology accepted, Doctor Frauenwahl," she said.

The Conductor sighed as if he'd expected nothing less and deserved no better. "I told myself…if I survived this country…I would dedicate the remainder of my life to a treatise on its uniquely malignant depravity. Perhaps it would serve…to atone for the misuse of my talents…to warn the world. But to be shot to death…by a former patient…with a gun for an arm…is apt."

She studied him up and down in a kind of morbid wonder, realizing she had no recollection of what he actually looked like. His lantern jaw and jutting brow, dramatically exaggerated by his receding hairline, gave an air of nobility. He had the delicate, autonomous hands of a pianist. Perhaps with longer fingers and some measure of talent, he might have become something other than he was. His eyes alone still denied her, hidden behind small round spectacles that shone like white-hot coins in his empty face..

She caught herself staring and turned to face the window. "Coming from a hypnotist and mass murderer, that would be a bestseller. You could almost fill a thimble with all the money it'd make."

"I never sought wealth. I served my country. America bled us dry…"

"If you came here to fight the Great One all over again, stop. It's over, you lost again." Crossing to the opposite wall, she pulled down the Murphy bed concealed behind fake bookshelves and sat on it with her legs crossed, then took a bottle out of the pillowcase. "Now, you've apologized. Shall I call the cops, or just sit and enjoy this fine bathtub gin while I watch you die?"

He tilted his head, looking at the potted plant. A freshet of blood glutted from his belly. His hand pressed against it. "A gift… One remarkable thing about violets is that their smell binds the receivers in the nostrils to block out other scents, even their own, so it never becomes overpowering. Always new, always the first time." The Conductor reached into his breast pocket, smiling at her upraised left hand, and passed her a sterling silver flask. "This…is a much less… barbaric spirit. Please… join me?"

She took it, unscrewed the lid, and sniffed the primordial fumes of very old, fine Scotch. Tossing back a swallow, she handed it back. "Why did you come here?"

"I could have returned home, but… my disgrace would be unbearable." He took a judicious sip and grimaced, then wanly smiled. "Mr. Chalice was only a means to an end… But too late… I saw his sickness, which threatens the world."

She took the flask from him. "Well, I swan, as my mother used to say. *His* sickness. The sickest people I know all seem to think this one fellow tempted Eve with the apple and nothing since is any man's fault." Tipping it back once, again, thrice, she killed it and threw it into his lap. "You led troops into battle at Nesle. I was there. Mesmerized

British and French prisoners of war overran our aid station. I lost an arm and a leg. I lost my sister…"

"A remarkable coincidence, no?" He chuckled, considering the hand of fate now at his throat. "That was war. And so, for me, was this…"

Her left hand shot out again, twisting within inches of putting a round through his knee into his crotch— "You took me on as a patient, and you helped me! I thought I was finally learning who I really was. I almost grew out of all this super-science vigilante horseshit! I could've had a real-life had you not…fucked…with my mind!" She got up and advanced on him. "The only good turn you ever did me was murdering my father. Oh yes, and you made me," she screamed, tearing at her hair, "try to kill the President!"

The Conductor looked as if he'd forgotten he was dying. His eyes widened, and his mouth dropped open, but then he closed it, sparing her some unbearable truth. Now, it caught up to him. "Honestly, I was rather piqued that you failed to kill Chancellor Bruning, but…I do regret…what I did to you…"

"To me. You regret doing it to *me* but not to the rest of them. I'm honored to have earned the right to exist after you took it away." She sought out the gin bottle and bolted enough down to make her cough. "Mine is better."

"This interloper who wears your armor arriving just in the nick of time… This is most portentous, not so?"

She started to offer him the gin, then put it down. "I've heard enough. If you're polite and stop talking now, I'll help you down to the curb and tell the clerk to call the police."

He had been steadily sinking lower in the chair all along. Now, his head sagged to rest on the greasy arm. "It's too late… You won't anyway, for many reasons. I had no reason to expect, but I hoped that you might…if not forgive, then see that our common interests bind us… Chalice must be stopped before he opens his doors around the world. I left, as a matter of course, a posthypnotic suggestion. I could invoke it…but I also know that you are one of those unhappy children of destiny whom the world uses to preserve order or enact change. You feel it…"

She shivered. Started to take another drink, then screwed down the cap and put it back in her pillow. Being drunk would give her permission to get angry, and she didn't need it. "You want me to enslave myself of my own free will, this time. I've already told a man who thinks he saved my life that I wasn't doing this anymore. Why should I throw it away for you?"

"After your father was murdered and the, ah… attempt foiled, I thought to strike back at Chalice. I could never get any of my instruments close to him, let alone myself. I thought he was afraid of being hypnotized, but now I think he feared I would discover what he carries inside him."

"Grit, determination, and the American dream?"

The Conductor chuckled and winced at the snide remark. Sweat stood out on his waxen face. Blood dribbled down the front of the sagging cushion on the chair. "The men he has suborned into backing a putsch against the winner of the next election will all attend Mr. Chalice's gala opening of the Global Pavilion in the tower tomorrow. I have gotten close to each of them. Close enough to know that none of them are as they were before the meeting in May."

"Where do I come in? And get out?"

"I have already programmed my orchestra to interrupt Chalice's ribbon-cutting ceremony tomorrow."

Her blood ran cold to think of it. How many people would be in Battery Park tomorrow? "You thought I'd help you carry out another assassination?"

"Nothing so theatrical… We must shut the doors…before he brings the other side over here…" His breath failed, his chest hitching, and a gurgle rose in his throat. "You fools…I tried… to save you…"

His head settled on the arm of the chair.

Matilda sat staring at him for a while. Finally, she picked up the phone.

She didn't call the police.

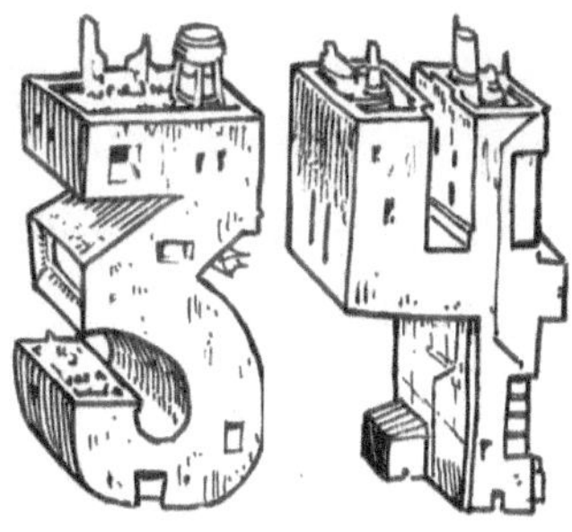

Every normal man must be tempted, at times, to spit upon his hands, hoist the black flag, and begin slitting throats.

—H.L. Mencken

August 2nd, 1932 | Circe Workers' Compound

They ran in the circle until they fell down. Dick lay in a heap with his twin, gasping for breath. It didn't work, and why did they think it would? Because when nothing else worked, you had to believe in magic. But magic, if there was such a thing, only found impossible ways to make everything worse.

There was no magic door, there was no other Earth, and Tom was gone. You have to be the smart one now, he thought to himself.

"Any more bright ideas, doc?"

Then he opened his eyes.

They lay on something other than the ground—a spongey, translucent gray matter like a bed of lard and cartilage. He pushed himself up, fighting to get breath into his lungs. Every breath burned, strained his lungs like he was trying to breathe through a sopping wet sheet. Reaching to pull the gas mask over his face, he blinked at the blurry light seeping through its scuffed glass eyepieces.

He felt as if he was moving underwater. The resistance against his limbs, coupled with the smothering sensation, sent him thrashing in panic. He punched and kicked at the hands pulling him backwards, dragging him deeper, deeper down…

A voice shouted in his ear, muffled so it was scarcely louder than his own pounding heartbeat. "Stop fighting, you blamed idiot!" An arm looped around his chest, and he fiddled with the dial on the bottle attached to his mask. Blessed air flooded his lungs. He gulped at it, feeling the cobwebs swept out of his head.

He still sat in the circle of worn stones, but everything else was wrong. A crowd of men in rags and gas masks hunkered around them. Beside him, Harry sat shaking his head like a prizefighter who'd just been knocked out of the ring. He couldn't see the Kid anywhere. The White Devil stood over them, conversing with a tall, gaunt man in an old doughboy uniform. Someone lifted him to his feet, patting him on the back and shouting like a dog barking. He looked beyond them and couldn't stop looking.

They were on a slope in a vast pit like a quarry gouged out of the fleshy ground, huddled against the side of a corrugated tin shed. Men worked in chain-gang lines with picks and shovels and long suction hoses, excavating the soft organic crud underfoot. Steam shovels, cranes, bulldozers, and pile drivers gouged and ripped at the walls, shearing off great slabs of lustrous blubber that the workers crowded in to break down and feed into ore cars. Above the walls of the pit, the stars danced in drunken reels amid succulent red clouds like curdled blood. A stench of gangrene seeped into his mask. Sweltering heat and tropical humidity shellacked his clothes to his skin.

Dick pushed himself away from the steadying hand at his back and lifted Harry to his feet. Another doughboy pressed his gas mask against Dick's so his shouting was conducted as a tinny, phonograph sound in his ears. "You fellers sure must wanna work bad… Welcome to whatever's under Hell…"

Someone grabbed at his rifle. He fought with them, but the doughboy said, "You wanna get chicken-fried? Hide the gun!"

All of them did an abrupt about-face and closed ranks. A masked guard in leather and rubber armor stood above them on the slope, cradling a Tesla tube rifle.

The doughboy tried to placate him, but the guard shouldered his rifle and pulled the trigger. Dick threw up a hand to block whatever was coming. Harry's fingers clamped on his arm.

Blue-white light flooded his eyes. *Chicken-fried—*

The blinding flash curled back on itself to engulf the guard. Dick blinked and rubbed his eyes until the blinding flash dissipated. The guard lay flat on his back, wreathed in smoke. *The old Haywire luck strikes again…*

"We're in the shit now," the doughboy said.

Three more guards came into view with weapons trained on them.

The White Devil stepped between them and the knot of prisoners. His outlandish formal wear blurred, and Dick saw another guard in the same kind of armor but with sergeant's chevrons on his shoulder. More importantly, the guards saw him and lowered their weapons.

"Found another ring of stones," he shouted. "Keep your damned fingers off the triggers. This rook fried himself, tripping over his own boots. Send stretchers."

The guards snapped off a salute and turned to call for a stretcher detail.

Dick sank onto a canvas stretcher and was hauled up the slope. Harry was borne close behind them, and the White Devil brought up the rear.

They topped the rim of the pit and double-timed down a duckboard path, passing between the domes. Dick sat up and nearly swooned at what he saw.

They were approaching a small city of hundreds of mushroom domes, each about the size of a house. At the edges, construction crews worked feverishly to erect more of them, pouring gray-green concrete over balloon molds and connecting them with corrugated tin ductwork. Deflate the balloon, and in a matter of hours, you had something you could live in if you had to.

Beyond the mushroom village, a tower bigger than any building he'd ever seen in real life stuck a rigid green finger into the nightmare sky. More disturbing than its sheer size was its familiarity. In this alien place, it upset him the most because he'd seen it in newspapers and newsreels, but to find it here, instead of anchoring the skyline of New York City, somehow made it all seem even less real. It was Chalice's tower, the one everybody talked about, the one Tom obsessed over.

He lay staring at it as the stretcher jostled and swayed across the plain to enter a doorway like a bank vault set in the side of a mushroom dome. It slammed shut behind them, and a whistling fan sucked the air out of the room until it felt like air. A dank miasma of mildew, sweat, smoke, and scorched coffee choked his nostrils when he tore off his mask. The stretcher-bearers unmasked and lit up cigarettes. Underneath, their faces were begrimed with garishly colored dust, haggard, half-starved, and red-eyed.

The White Devil let his disguise melt away and peered through a filthy window set into the exterior hatch.

Coughing, hawking, and spitting on the floor, the old doughboy saluted the stretcher-bearers. "Dismissed…keep your yaps shut 'til you hear different, understand?" They returned his salute and cringed away from the White Devil as they filed out of the airlock.

Once they were gone, the doughboy lit up a badly bent cigarette. "Sergeant L.Q. Swope, 119th Infantry."

"Hey, where's our guns?" Harry said.

The sergeant picked a bit of tobacco off his tongue. "What guns?"

Dick growled, "Sonofabitch—"

"Do you trust those men?" asked the White Devil.

Nodding at the door by which the stretcher-bearers left, Swope said, "Those fellers, I don't know from Adam, but I trust 'em a damn sight further than I trust you. They broke up all the old units to keep us disorganized, the bastards." The doughboy looked from the Haywires to the White Devil, squinting with the effort of accepting what he was seeing, and chose the grotesque golden visage as the less thorny question of the two. "Ain't you that crimefighter from the dime novels?"

"We came to bring you home," the Devil said.

"Fancy that!" Sgt. Swope cackled, then coughed into his fist and wiped it on his breeches. "The Golden Ghost came to take us home… I didn't see a great big train or a rocket ship parked outside when you popped in, so how're you fixin' to do that?"

"We're going out the front door," the White Devil said. "Can you get weapons?"

"We got plenty of tools, and we rigged up some pipe guns out of plumbing. But we're in no shape for a fight…"

"How many are you?"

"Maybe five thousand or so of us at last count, to a couple hundred of them…"

"Where are the rest of you?" the Devil asked.

Swope shrugged. "They got plantations all over, I reckon. I hear tell they sent a bunch of us to the Moon. I reckon they're the lucky ones."

"You got 'em outnumbered," Dick said, "so why don't you stand up to 'em?"

"Sure, whatta we know about fighting, anyway? They're packing ball-lightning and gauss guns, and we're droppin' like flies from a new disease every day, and there ain't no doctors unless you catch something *interesting*…"

"Interesting?" Harry said.

Lifting his grizzled whiskers, Swope showed off a rash covering his scrawny neck. Pendulous polyps swelled and dangled from his Adam's apple like the tendrils of a sea anemone. "They keep cutting it off, and it keeps growin' back. Doc told me it's tryin' to help me breathe the air out there, if y'can feature that… All of us got something this bad, if not worse. You'll see soon enough."

"We're getting the hell out of here," Dick said. "You coming or not?"

"Speaking for myself, I don't care what happens," Swope said, "but they got all the barracks on a circuit. If we strike, they just blow up the domes and there's only enough masks for the crews working outside, so one for every three men. Captain name o' Danforth tried to mutiny the first week, and they popped three bubbles. Things quieted down after that…" The sergeant looked ashamed of his helplessness, but he gritted his teeth and shook his fist in their faces. "But we'd just as soon die fighting, as in that damned pit."

Harry rubbed his eyes, peering around like a child listening to the doctors while awaiting surgery. "Where's the Kid? We gotta find the Kid—"

"Nuts to that! We need to find Tom!" Dick barked but then felt a sting of remorse at the way Harry's face crumpled. Damn, he was getting soft. "Have you seen a guy who looks just like us?"

The tendrils on the sergeant's Adam's apple bristled away from his throat. "Both of you look just like the Jinx," said Swope.

Dick tensed and shook a fist at the sergeant. "Who's a jinx?"

Swope pointed his cigarette at them. "You're the spittin' image of the swell-headed bird who bolloxed up all the digging machines the first day they put him in the pit."

"That's our Tom!" Harry cried.

"Captain Danforth swore by him, but when they tried to take out the guards, the Jinx fouled up their play, and they got the gas. If he weren't no Jonah, he was a lousy traitor."

Dick jumped off the stretcher and went for the old vet. "You take that back, or I'll make you eat it!"

The White Devil stopped Dick with a ramrod-stiff arm. "Just for once," he whispered, "be the smart one."

"I feel him real close, Devil," Harry said. "Almost hear him—"

"You too?" the White Devil loomed over Dick. He swallowed hard and nodded.

The White Devil turned away, pacing in the cramped space. "We can't go after him now. The only way to break out of here is to go from dome to dome for the commanding officers to get the word out when and how we'll strike."

"I know who carries the weight around here, and who to tell and who not," Swope said, laying a yellow-stained finger against his crooked nose. "Only thing I can't figure is, how'd it take you so dang long to find us?"

The White Devil didn't tell them they'd only been gone a week, asking, "How long has it been?"

Swope held up a battered silver flask and showed him the rows of hashmarks on the side. "Time must roll slower here. But we're all going home… today."

"We got to find Tom before the shooting starts," Harry said, nodding to himself as if he had a majority behind him. "And we got to find the Kid. He's one of us."

The White Devil shook his head. "We brought him home, and he went his own way. This isn't his fight anymore."

"I don't see why it's ours, either," Dick said. "Maybe you go your way, and we'll go ours…"

"You'll get a lot of men killed," said the White Devil. "Go ahead, you'll be a good distraction."

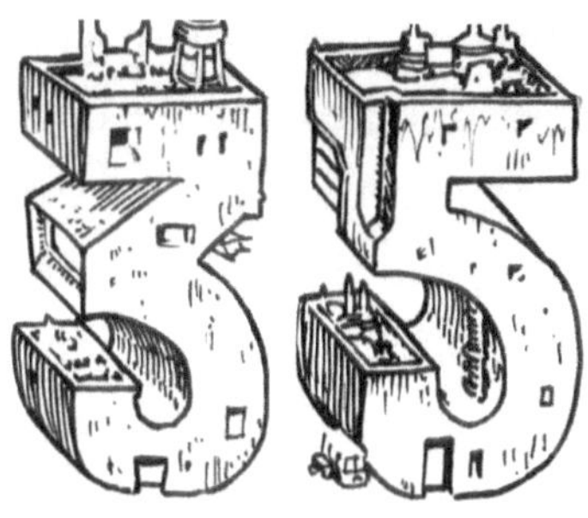

There are two futures, the future of desire and the future of fate, and man's reason has never learned to separate them.

—J.D. Bernal

August 2nd, 1932 | Chaliceville, Circe

S herman Peeler was not fond of Shakespeare or literature as a whole. Still, he found one line from *King Lear* inescapable at times like this, impressed upon him as it was by his father, who would recite it in fatalistic wonderment whenever life turned on him: *No worst there is none when yet one can say, "This is the worst."*

His previous post was no picnic, but in three short months, he'd learned to cherish his memories of the lab at Utopia.

It was simply impossible to pursue proper science under these conditions. The air outside festered with alien spores, viruses, microbes, seeds and bacteria. Every exposed inch of skin was a petri dish that ferociously incubated unspeakable new diseases and parasites and things as yet uncategorized, leaving him to wonder if that was the workers' only true purpose.

As both punishment and promotion for his groundbreaking work with the runaway amoeba specimen, Prof. Peeler was in charge of the behavioral evaluation phase of the big program. Essentially, he ran a control panel while watching through a barricade as a giant single-celled organism was dropped into a test cell with a simple puzzle. If the blob showed sufficient wherewithal to solve the puzzle, it received a treat and was shunted into the next test. He'd had mixed results injecting the cytoplasm withdrawn from his "college blob," as his colleagues called it, and the blobs that excelled at solving the puzzles didn't take to operating factory machinery or any of the other tasks they were offered. If anything, they became craftier and less tractable. In the end, nearly all of them went down the chute to the grinders of the Ambrosia cannery.

This last one showed some initiative, at least, in resisting the chute, throwing out tentacles to brace itself, and riding out even the maximum suction. Shaking his head, Peeler electrified the cell, lamenting yet again the yoking of science to the vulgar whims of industry as the failed specimen tumbled out of sight, and threw the lever for the next one.

Nothing came out.

Peeler jerked the lever back and forth, then tugged on a bank of levers whose function he didn't even know, in his aggravation.

Something in the ceiling groaned. It wasn't the plumbing or the ventilation fans, which had their own distinctive timbres and rhythms. This was an asymmetrical and alarming sound like an unquiet stomach massively amplified, coupled with the buckling of stressed metal. As if this wasn't enough to worry him, the ceiling sagged and spat rivets at the floor.

Peeler reached for the alarm button, but he knew what would happen if it turned out to be other than a dire emergency. He'd be sent somewhere even worse.

Throwing on a rain-slicker and grabbing an electrified cat-o'-nine-tails, he climbed the ladder and popped the hatch to inspect the blob pens. Even before his eyes adjusted to the dim light and the stench, he knew something was wrong.

The thunderous noises had stopped; indeed, it was now entirely too quiet. Climbing through the trapdoor, he stepped on the electrified whip in his heavy rubber boots and nearly tumbled back down the ladder shaft. There should be orderlies for this. Thousands of military veterans in the gulag outside, and not one could be spared for lab assistance?

Each step towards the pen took a fresh act of will. By the time he got to the double-paned glass and toggled the floodlights, he had almost fallen into a paralysis, and it was only the desperate hope that this was all a nightmare that allowed him to go through with it.

They were all gone.

It can't be real, he told himself as he pinched and twisted the flesh of his cheeks. The walls and ceiling of the pen were frictionless steel. How many times had he watched them try to scale it alone or in loose, floppy piles? Even if they somehow reached the ventilation ducts in the ceiling, they were electrified and would have set off an alarm. And yet, the grill of the vent nearest the control room was wrenched out of the duct and dangled by one hinge.

He checked the logs. Though they'd obviously been fudged by his incompetent colleagues, at least two hundred specimens should be on the other side of the glass, fighting for food and dominance. The explanation must be somewhere.

The cameras…

He was torn between the need to know and to be wholly ignorant of whatever had happened to protect himself.

Winding back the recording wires on their spools, he played back the previous five minutes. All three cameras showed the undulating floor of the pens and the mindless Brownian motion of the herd. But then, coinciding with the noises he'd heard…the ventilation grill bulges as something oozes out of it and falls into the midst of the herd. *A runaway blob! Well, it certainly didn't escape on my watch!* He'd learned the hard way to keep track of the slippery bastards.

His righteous indignation, always a bulwark against terror and helplessness, was like a waxen shield that melted away before a blue flame of pure panic as he watched what happened next. The simmering herd of single-celled monstrosities seemed to boil over and splash up in great heaving waves, their membranes locked or fused into some kind of superorganism that stretched up like a gigantic, jointed humanoid arm, seized the grill and ripped it off, aggravated but undeterred by the voltage surging through it. In less time than it would take to tell on even the briefest incident report, the impossible collage of blobs slurped up into the ductwork like a reversed film of sausage being made, and then the multiple screens showed only the empty pen.

Perhaps, if he got out in front of this, he could frame it as another breakthrough. If he only had the wily animal cunning of his old rival, Dr. Lasky, he might even winnow a promotion out of it. But as soon as he pictured it, he knew it was not to be.

Even as he accepted his fate, a hand fell on his shoulder. Peeler jumped with a strangled scream and turned, protectively cowering to block the security monitors.

Speak of the Devil—

"Dr. Lasky, sir," Peeler fumbled, avoiding his old superior's piercing stare. "I was about to notify someone… It's really remarkable, and, I think, presents the breakthrough we've been looking for…" Somehow, in his panic, he failed to ask the obvious question of when Lasky stopped being dead.

"Never mind all that," Lasky said. "I'm looking for a man, spitting image of these two." Only then did Peeler take notice of the two men behind Lasky. They were really the same man twice, and neither attempt was particularly successful. But he recognized him, or rather, them, and his panic was multiplied sevenfold.

"Where did they come from?" He looked at them again, noting the identical brutish features, beetling brows, and the gleaming automatics in their fists. "What's the meaning of this?"

"He's seen him," said one of the twins.

Peeler squirmed away from them, almost climbing onto the monitor console. "Sir, they really shouldn't be out of containment… This is a delicate area…their energy emissions…"

Dr. Lasky's face seemed to rearrange itself on his head. Like a living disguise made of drowsy honeybees, it took wing and floated away. What lay underneath set Peeler to screaming wildly for help. In all of his nightmares, the vision that woke him with a scream choked in his throat was of the demonic visage staring at him now, crowding close enough that his panicked breath fogged its white gold surface and pressing a short, curved blade into his belly. Its eyes turned like Catherine wheels in their sockets, beguiling and overpowering him once more.

"Take us to him," said the White Devil.

The egghead went into a trance and sweat broke out on his bald head. When he came out of it, he still trembled but did what the White Devil told him to. Dick was crawling out of his skin, itching to take his anxiety out on somebody.

They'd played along while the White Devil made rounds in the mushroom town, tipping off the Bonus Army to the imminent breakout. The only thing that made Dick stick around was how Harry shamed him. Like a little boy who needed to pee trying to stand through a long church sermon, he fought to keep it under control.

But they both felt it. Tom was close, and he was in incredible pain. Even the little bit they shared and took onto themselves was like being constantly struck by lightning. "Step on it, bud," Dick snapped, poking him with the White Devil's gun.

Stepping out into the corridor, the scientist searched for help, and his face fell when he saw the coast was clear. The White Devil had turned back into a bullet-headed, cigar-chomping bird in a lab coat. Harry bounced on his toes.

They passed guards who snapped to attention until they passed by an egghead or two who tipped a nod to the White Devil and blithely ignored his hostage. Dick watched the egghead's beady eyes, noting his silent pleading look, but he might as well have been invisible. Minding your own business was everybody's first priority in a rotten place like this. But why was Tom in here?

"What kind of hospital is this, doc?" Harry asked. They were on a long, straight stretch of corridor lined with dripping pipes, rusty ducts, and bundles of cable and corrugated hoses. The doctor stopped when something a bit smaller than a subway train passed through the duct just above their heads. Looking up at it fearfully, the egghead chopped the air with his hands. "This is a scientific research center. We're scientists…"

"So, you don't help sick folks get better?"

"No, we work on a larger scale. We don't cure patients. We cure disease. We invent new medicines, new technologies… new workers…"

Hurrying after him, Harry pressed, "Have you seen a little squishy guy, answers to Kid? He don't look it, but he's real smart—"

The egghead looked over his shoulder. "You know of it? Did you bring it here? You!" He pointed an accusing finger at the White Devil. "In Utopia, you helped it escape. I could have written my own ticket with that specimen… We could have rendered all factory automatons obsolete."

"And the rest of us, in the bargain," Dick said.

They went around a corner, and the egghead broke into a run. Three guards stood in front of a big double door with a red light blinking above it. "*They're killers. Kill them, save me, kill them!*"

The guards shouldered their lightning guns. The egghead dropped flat on his belly, sliding towards them on the slick concrete floor. Dick dropped to one knee and raised his pistol, but before he got off a shot, Harry snapped off three. All three guards fell, but one sprayed lightning at them as he tipped over. Dick's gun went off as he dodged it. The ricochet seemed to pass between his ears without touching him. The blue-white arc danced over him but twisted back on itself and struck the prone scientist.

The White Devil prodded the steaming egghead with one foot, then rolled him over and searched him for a metallic thing like a cigarette case. When he pointed it at the doors, they wheezed open.

"Mighty fine shooting," Harry said.

"He doesn't care, you moron," Dick snapped.

Harry touched his shoulder. "Not me, Dick. You—"

Dick turned around and caught Harry as he fell. A bright red corsage on his breast made him look like he was going to a dance. "Jesus, Harry, I didn't mean… I didn't mean… any of it…"

"That old Crabtree luck strikes again…" Harry smiled and started to say something else, but then he just smiled wider and died.

"We can't stop," said the White Devil.

Dick bit back a wisecrack. *Just once, be the strong one.* "Let's find Tom and burn this place down."

Inside, it sounded like all the lightning in the world. A huge Tesla coil blasted a silver target inside a glass-fronted containment cell, and the lashing tongues of bearded lightning licked up and down the foil covering.

Four more eggheads stood behind a reinforced glass barrier, watching in rapture or nervously taking note of the dancing needles on the gauges on an instrument panel. The Devil silently executed them with a wave of his pistol. They dropped as neatly as poleaxed cattle. He crossed to the control panel and threw switches until the Tesla coil sputtered to a stop.

"Where's Tom?" Dick demanded. The White Devil pointed at the silver form in the glass column.

Dick ran to it and dashed the butt of his pistol in vain against the glass, then tossed around and found a wrench in a toolbox. He smashed the glass and took hold of the silver form.

To test his energy field to the limit, they'd wrapped him in some kind of insulator blanket, sealed him up in here, and electrified him. Dick couldn't hope, but he knew, despite what they'd put him through, Tom just had to be alive. He had to—

Dick ripped the metal foil off the body, and it sagged limply out of the metal frame in which it had rested.

"No, Tom, not you too, I ain't no good alone. I can't, I won't…"

Tom jolted upright in Dick's arms. His eyes opened, and lightning shot out of his hands, his eyes, his mouth. Impaled on it, Dick twisted in the air, lifted clean off his feet by the galvanic blast. His smoking corpse crashed against the instrument panel nearest to the White Devil, who holstered his guns and raised his hands in supplication.

With sparks spilling from his clenched teeth, Tom Haywire stepped over broken glass and dead eggheads to stand chin-to-chin with the White Devil.

"Where are my brothers?" he said.

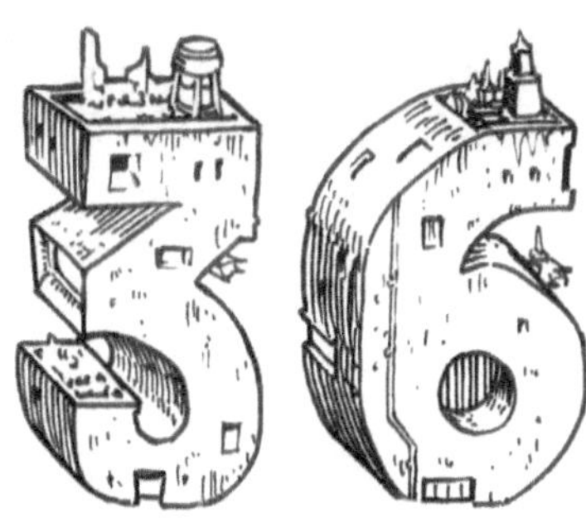

I do not often envy other countries their governments, but I saw that if this country ever needed a Mussolini, it needs one now.

—Senator David A. Reed

August 2, 1932 | Sea of Tranquility, the Moon

Sylvester Chalice's suppertime speech was syndicated on 370 stations and perhaps 10,000 television receivers in well-heeled homes in a handful of cities. It was also projected onto billboards out front of 116 Chalice pavilions and in-store window displays nationwide. Those who heard it were inspired and enervated, while those who saw it, even those who already held up Chalice as the paragon of America's most up-to-date virtues, were stunned and wiping tears of joy from their unblinking eyes.

Mr. Chalice appears at a desk in an office. Affable, with a modest yet confident smile, he shoots his cuffs and reclines slightly in his chair. Behind him, a massive picture window looks out on a rocky landscape dotted with unmistakable human dwellings amid stark craters and ridges of naked lunar rock against a black, starless sky dominated by a whorled orb that astute observers of astronomy might recognize as the Earth.

"My fellow Americans… I'm no politician, and I've never sought or dreamed of seeking political office. But it has come to my attention that a popular campaign to write in my name for President on the New Tomorrow Party ticket in November is gaining steam. I didn't seek this call to duty, but I would be remiss as an American if I did not do my utmost to be worthy of it."

For just a moment, his eyes roll back under their lids, and he draws in a shuddering breath, which many recognize as a momentary conference with a higher power.

I don't know how to tell you this, Sylvester, but it has to be now.

"To be sure, I know little of the minutiae of legislation, for I've spent my life in pursuit of innovation and creating a future in which all partake of the benefits of progress. I know only how to directly attack and solve problems.

"When I look at the country today, I see hunger and unemployment and a generation of young Americans left behind by the failures of the old economy, the old politics. I see these problems, and I ask myself how I can solve them. To those who would work, I offer jobs. To those going hungry and unable to find work, I would make Ambrosia available on government relief. And to those who would call such actions Communism, I would say that they do not understand the nature of investment. Children need protein to grow healthy and strong, just as America needs healthy, strong young adults."

Chalice pauses again and closes his eyes as if in silent prayer.

We've taught each other so much; sometimes, I wonder who infected whom. But you must remember what you were before, and how much of who you are now is really me. My gift was the will to succeed, to adapt, to absorb, and to engulf all that stood in your way.

"Further, I would greatly expand my teleportal network to bring travelers, freight, and American products to every corner of the world and beyond.

"Well... I know how difficult such acts would be to write into law under the current system, but any private citizen may act according to his own enlightened self-interest, as I do now.

"Beginning today, rolling kitchen trucks will freely distribute Ambrosia to all who need it, and beginning today, the Chalice Travel Pavilion opens its doors to the world."

You like to think of me up here spreading the good word, but really, I'm right here with you, inside your head. I've been there for so long. You and I are really the same.

"And closest to my heart, but farthest from our home, I have put the men of the Bonus Expeditionary Force to work breaking ground on a settlement in the Sea of Tranquility, here on Earth's moon. As you might imagine, the beginning of humanity's first colony on another world is not unlike the frontier towns of the old west or the Yukon."

You've no choice now but to see that there really is no you anymore. You're just what I have to pretend to be to make them love us. But we won't need their love much longer—

Again, Chalice closes his eyes and swallows hard, as if in silent prayer. The moment drags out until some fear for his health; but then he puts on a radiant smile that distracts from the flat emptiness of his eyes, when they finally open. Purged of any atom of doubt, any scintilla of weakness, that smile beckons to America as the lone light at the end of a fathomless tunnel of despair.

"I look forward to showing you what we're building here. It is the future, a brighter one for every American, and it will not be stopped, no matter who is elected in November. The question to you is, will you stand in our way or leap to greet us?"

Daddy Long-Legs smiles into the camera, steeples his hands, and says, "Naturally, I have done much soul-searching and consulted with wiser Americans than myself. One such American, of whom I'm sure you're all aware, not only urged me to seek the Presidency but pledged to serve as my Vice President. I welcome Col. Lindbergh's endorsement, but I will not take yours for granted.

"My name is Sylvester Chalice, and I've come to lead you into the future."

Sylvester Chalice leans across the desk. Hand outstretched to be shaken or to lift the viewer up out of poverty and despair.

The light on the camera dimmed.

It was remarkable, this world, these organisms. They had indeed changed him, and not for the better. On his Earth, his species was undeniably the most intelligent, but it depended on hosts for its life cycle to complete itself. How ironic that his closest cousins on this Earth were the lowest and least understood of all living things.

While grooming his poor host, Daddy Long-Legs had become infected with something that nearly destroyed him. These barely sentient organisms could hardly perceive their own environment, yet they were quite assured they were at the center of it, that all of it existed only for them. So easily did they accept what he offered them as their just due, that it was their destiny to claim the stars. And so caught up in their mad solipsism was Daddy Long-Legs that he had resisted his own purpose, his only reason for all he had done.

How odd that he saw his progeny as potential competition, as a threat to his own pleasure and power. His life cycle was nearly complete, his new environment all but conquered, and yet it was difficult to pull the trigger.

Daddy Long-Legs afforded himself a glance at his host's reflection in a sterling silver carafe beaded with condensation. That handsome face and winning smile had been shaped to win acceptance and submission and had succeeded beyond his wildest hopes. What he would accomplish this morning was as grave a perversion of his biology as that of his host species, but the result would be a brighter future for all who answered to the name Daddy Long-Legs. For tomorrow, they would be legion.

If all went as he hoped, he would be the kind of rags-to-riches story this country thrived on. And he would evolve into a realization of that other peculiar obsession that possessed these delightful, doomed creatures...

A god.

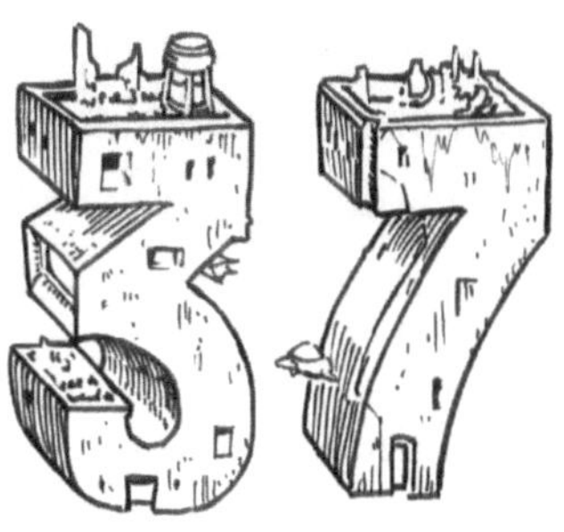

But the worst enemy you can meet will always be yourself; you lie in wait for yourself in caverns and forests. Lonely one, you are going the way to yourself!

—Friedrich Nietzsche

August 3rd, 1932 | New York City

The sun was nearly at its zenith before its rays found their way into the forty-acre expanse of Battery Park. A crowd covered the park from the doors of Chalice Pavilion to the fireboat station and the aquarium, and more poured in from Broadway and South Street, down from the elevated trains and off the ferries and steamship docks. Many of the estimated twenty thousand were curiosity-seekers, tourists, or commuters stymied in their quest to reach the Staten Island ferry slip. Still, many more carried hastily painted banners and wore sandwich boards proclaiming CHALICE FOR THE FUTURE! NEW TOMORROW TODAY!

Rumors spread that Sylvester Chalice himself would appear to open the doors to the global pavilion and deliver another speech. The electricity that seemed to animate every eye and gesture in the park, even in the starved skeleton men thronging the Ambrosia trucks lined up along Battery Place, felt like the galvanized spirit of the old, arrogant hero-city, only faster, stronger, louder. They had seen a vision of who they could be and what they could do and were rabid to worship at the feet of the man who had reminded them.

Or so it seemed to Matilda Lynch as she watched from the roof of the Whitehall Building, opposite Battery Park from the pavilion. They were under a spell and didn't want to wake up.

Telescoping the binocular lenses of her helmet, she scanned the crowd from the parapet, searching for any sign of the Conductor's orchestra. Would she know them when she saw them? Certainly, she hadn't known herself when she was nothing more than a player piano, pounding out the roll Dr. Frauenwahl had installed in her head—

Furiously, she snapped off the binocular vision and paced, inwardly slapping herself out of her circular script. She had only the say-so of the least trustworthy human being she'd ever known that anything would happen here. Like as not, it was another move in his game, another trick like the damned African violets that she'd ended up throwing out the window.

She had watched from this perch on the roof since just before dawn as the park filled in, overwhelming the police cordons and stampeding towards the doors that remained shut and roped off and lined with armed guards.

At noon, it was promised, the pavilion would open and offer them the world.

Five minutes, by her watch. If she was wasting her time, so be it. She would go back to her flat happy. If she never again heard from the White Devil or the Haywire Gang, it would be too soon. But if something did happen, how could she hope to stop it? She couldn't… not alone.

After the Conductor died, she called Aurora and Jasper Zwick. Aurora answered and heard her out but promised nothing. Her group might be among the crowds below, though she didn't see them, either.

"We're going tomorrow," Aurora told her. Politely, she'd waited until Matilda had run through appeals and demands. The brass in her voice sounded like it was already worlds away from here.

"On a steamship. Back to Africa. Our visas and tickets have been approved."

"Aurora, you've got to listen, it's not safe… Something is going to happen tomorrow. The Conductor—"

"This isn't our country," Aurora had told her. "These are not our problems. I'm sorry, Matilda. I wish things were different…but we will consider it."

At least she picked up the phone. Jasper Zwick's line had rung off the hook, and when someone or something finally answered, there was only a crackling like a bread wrapper, and after she'd poured her heart out to it, the line had gone dead without any acknowledgment. But in spite of himself, the punk had come through.

"Nothing doing down here," his tinny voice chirped in her ear.

"Keep looking," she urged. "They're here. They have to be…"

"I got eyes all over the place and a couple inside. They're making 'em go through a metal detector…"

The doors opened, and the crowd surged forward, trampling ropes and guards and each other. An amplified recording of Chalice's supper speech boomed and echoed over the park, a wall of gibberish by the time it reached her ears. His faded face appeared on the whitewashed billboards lining the park, and the crowd went mad. Wherever their loyalties lay last week, Hoover had proved to be just another helpless old man in need of saving, and Roosevelt just another rich old man with a lot of vague promises, but this young savior held what they needed in one hand and all they dreamed of in the other.

Squabbles broke out on the front steps. The tower's twin entrances drank up the flood of travelers while the projections on the billboards seemed to distract the rest of the crowd. Legions of people had come here to witness history or walk on five different continents in a day, and they were unstoppable in their hunger for miracles.

Every moment that passed, she pictured another catastrophe, the crowds of innocent people running and falling as they had in

Washington while she dodged pursuit planes in the skies, an empty spectacle that saved no one. Where would he strike? His agents could be anywhere, perhaps inside…

I am trying to shut the doors… Maybe she should just let him do it. She had a plan, but no time to implement it. There might still be a way to prevent what could happen…

And she still hadn't accounted for her sister. She searched the skies, wracked by dread and terror.

"*I see something!*" Zwick shouted in her ear.

"What is it? What?" she cried, but she didn't need Zwick to point them out. Once she noticed the peculiar gestures some in the crowd were making, she realized a chain of them completely encircled the building, just behind the police cordon along the curb. Staring rapturously into the void, each of them pantomimed playing a musical instrument, responding to commands imprinted in them by a man now dead and gone.

"*There's at least a hundred of 'em,*" said Zwick. The roar of the crowd poured in over his shrill voice as he shoved through the throng. "*Hey pal, what's the rumpus…?*"

A pillar of white fire spiked out of the knot of onlookers in front of the pavilion's main entrance. Hundreds were flung into the air like cut grass. The resounding boom of the explosion rolled over the park only when the cloud of human debris from the explosion had rained down on the now panic-stricken mob.

"Jasper!" Matilda kicked in the magnetic impeller and sprang from the roof like a flea from a dog. Sliding down an invisible ribbon of repulsive force, she shot across the park to alight on the pavilion's facade.

The crowd stampeded away from the explosion, overwhelming the ushers and storming the pavilion. Sick to her stomach, she searched for more of them. Any moment, they could all detonate.

Then she heard the music.

Faint as a foghorn, it swelled until it came from everywhere at once. Echoing off concrete, glass and steel, coiling through the air like a swarm of starlings, growing louder and clearer as the source drew closer.

She craned her neck out over the street to see it, noticing how the crowd shifted and stalled in its peristaltic heaving as everyone down there shaded their eyes and looked for the source of Brahms' 4th Symphony.

It was a car flying fifty feet above their heads. Not an autogyro or a screaming jet-powered aero-roadster, but a wheeled automobile floating above them like a feather on a gentle updraft. Loudspeakers were strung around the chassis and hung like trumpet blossoms from the undercarriage.

Opening all hailing channels with her chin, she shouted, "Lead them away! They're human bombs..."

Through the green-tinted windows, she was saluted by a dusky woman in goggles and a chauffeur's cap. "Aurora, you're my hero," she said. Maybe the driver heard her. Maybe she waved as she circled over Battery Park.

"They're...they think they're playing the music..."

The flying car floated away from the pavilion like an untethered balloon. Amid the scurrying men and women, she could pick out dozens sleepwalking after the music. The flying car veered south with a flock of NYPD autogyros on its tail, passing over the South Ferry Terminal, and the human bombs trailed after.

Winnowed out of the crowd, they formed a strange, tragic parade of moths following the music out over the merging of the Hudson and East Rivers, filing one by one off the end of the ferry slip to disappear into the water.

She could only watch them fall.

Clinging to the bulbous ornamental stonework of the pavilion's portico, she cursed herself for not having a better plan. Still, the Conductor's orchestra was lost, and she had to count the thousands spared as a victory.

It was cold comfort. The street in front of the pavilion was littered with bodies and bits of bodies, wounded and shocked people staggering in circles or weeping on their knees. She should go down there. She was a fugitive, this armor a symbol of terror, but she could take it off. She could just be a person and help—

"You couldn't stay away, could you, sister?"

The hateful purr jolted her with its sour intimacy. Whiplash burned her neck for searching the sky. She spun around and took to the air a split-second ahead of the salvo of howitzer-sized gauss projectiles that smashed the pavilion's facade to flinders.

She skimmed just above the stampeding mob. Hating herself for endangering them, but her sister couldn't be mad enough to fire into a crowd, could she? If she had stolen her Silver Sentry persona along with the armor, maybe she would have to abide by the rules of the heroic science-vigilante.

Remember, she told herself, *you're the villain here.*

"Minerva, please don't fight me. We're on the same side..." Matilda dodged under an elevated pedestrian bridge and alit on it, still looking for her sister. Minerva was carrying heavier munitions, but she still had a rocket strapped to her back. Matilda could outmaneuver her sister until her batteries ran out, but it didn't have to happen. It shouldn't, they were better than this—

"When we played tag or hide-and-seek," Minerva said, "you always lost."

"You were bigger and smarter than me! And I loved you—"

"You only got old, but I never stopped growing..."

Gauss bullets stitched the bridge. Matilda shrieked and shot off into the air, bobbing and weaving to put the squat bulk of the U.S.

Customs House between herself and the barrage. A police helicopter hove into view, and she reversed, nearly flying headlong into its rotors. She bounced brutally off the hull of the chopper and dropped into the courtyard.

She landed hard on her left leg—pain in her hip and her knee where prosthetic met flesh. Gasping and stumbling, she fell across a park bench.

"Minerva," she gasped, "forgive me…? I never had any idea… If I knew, I would never have left you behind. I didn't know…I loved you with all my heart! You were the sun and the moon to me…I followed you everywhere, and I…I only did all this because it's what you would have done…"

"Til," her big sister's voice crackled in her ear, melodious with madness, "how would you ever know what to do, until I did it?"

Matilda's ears pricked at the distinctive whistle of a falling mortar shell. Looking up at the sky, she saw the starburst flash and had only time enough to launch herself at the nearest window before it detonated.

She smashed through the glass and shot down a corridor in the scant space between stupefied office workers and the ceiling. Chandeliers shattered in sprays of crystal, brass, and sparks. She plunged on, blasting out a window at the far end of the corridor to emerge over the old Bowling Green at the headwaters of Broadway. Minerva was waiting for her, plowing divots out of the sidewalk and the street from the customs house roof. Her shots went wild, chopping up cars and buses and cutting down pedestrians. She wasn't just oblivious to the harm she caused but so murderously intent that she'd happily kill anyone who got between them.

Matilda dodged and dove as she flew up Broadway, feinted right at Beaver, and skated up the face of the Standard Oil Building. Minerva's relentless shells chewed the limestone all around her. "Stop! Minerva, you're killing them…"

Minerva came after her in a fury. Bullets pinged and zinged off her helmet and greaves. "That's what we do, Til, and they love us for it. They want to die almost as badly as we want to kill…"

Matilda ran out of skyscraper and plunged down into the canyon of Broadway again, slaloming between El tracks, trams and walkways. Sooner or later, Minerva had to run out of ammunition, but she didn't want to think about shooting her own sister. Minerva's fuel tanks would outlast hers, and the harder she flew, the faster the impeller's batteries would be depleted.

She led her sister on a merry chase halfway up the West Side, then zig-zagged back east towards Grand Central Station. They barn-stormed Times Square, punching through hot air balloons and trading potshots in a shooting gallery of towering neon signs and stuttering animated billboards. Matilda climbed out of the dizzying advertising maze so steeply that she saw spots and felt herself fainting. She shook herself and realized she was flying amid the tattered summer clouds high above Manhattan, and her sister was coming to kill her.

"All along, you only wanted to replace me," Minerva raved. "You would've killed me if you could, and you should have, when you had the chance. Father knew it when I came for him…but you took that away from me, too…"

For a moment, Matilda hung stalled, impaled on the air, framed against a police blimp. She jackknifed and reversed the polarity on the anti-gravity magnets, yanking herself downward like a tumbling bullet. Minerva took her shot a moment too late and lanced the hydrogen-fat boil of the balloon. It burst into flames and plummeted to the street below. Minerva cut off her thrust as the skyscrapers seemed to reach up to snatch her from the sky. When she hit the impeller again, something dropped onto her back and clasped armored arms around her thighs.

There it was. The worst thing she saw in the White Devil's spinning, bejeweled eyes and the fleeting glimpse behind the Conductor's mask, just before he died. She was the instrument of Father's death. She was the one who'd planted the bomb in Elvira Seaton's baggage. That she'd been a puppet in a trance did nothing to assuage her guilt. She wanted to scream and fly headfirst into the pavement, but she made her voice small and fragile, a child's voice.

"I'm sorry for all you suffered, Minerva."

Wordless animal rage was Minerva's only reply, an arm around her throat seeking to throttle her and kill them both.

It was all Matilda needed to convince herself she had no choice but to do what she did next. Her right hand, her flesh and blood hand, grabbed the quick-release cord on Minerva's harness and ripped it. The rocket sprang away from Minerva's back. Her sister abruptly became a drag on her thrust. Matilda boosted the impeller and veered out over the East River. "I'm trying to land! Minerva, please, stop this—"

Minerva screamed and kicked her between her legs, cracked her visor with a pummeling fist. Matilda was stunned by the blows and didn't realize she'd dropped her sister until the transmitted screaming in her ear cut off and became a liquid gurgling, then dead air.

She hovered above the river, looking down. Civil Defense sirens wailed from one end of Manhattan to the other.

I tried, she thought. *Would have given the world to save you…*
Be useful, Til—

A police autogyro dropped into view above her, a sharpshooter dangling in a harness from its open cockpit. Before he could get off a shot, she spun away south and followed the shoreline back to Battery Park.

She saw at once that there was nothing more she could do—

Noxious red-black clouds blossomed like blood in the seawater, out of all the doors of Chalice Pavilion to flood the streets and wash over the crowds fleeing across Battery Park. She knew right away that they weren't smoke, but what they were, she couldn't begin to guess.

The Conductor's words came back to haunt her.

I am trying to shut the doors… before he brings the other side over here…

The clouds rose on the wind and were ripped to rags, the red wind sailing east over Brooklyn like a storm of rose petals. Heavy particles settled and stained all that they touched. There seemed to be no end to it, the river spewing out of the mouths of the pavilion as if it meant to cover the world.

The stray bullets bouncing off her armor were as nothing to the deafening echo of the Conductor's last words in her mind.

You fools… I tried… to save you…

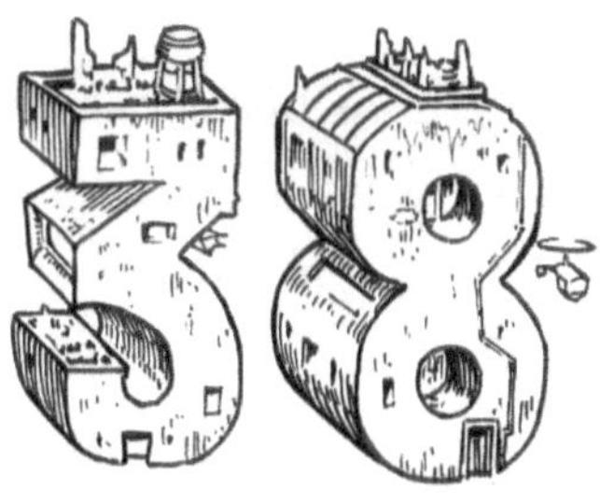

Wars are, of course, as a rule to be avoided; but they are far better than certain kinds of peace.

—Theodore Roosevelt

August 3rd, 1932 | Chalice Pavilion—Circe

The warren of workers' barracks was joined to the freight warehouses and the tower by a drawbridge of sorts, a retractable tube controlled by a guard post on the opposite end. Guards checked workers in and out steadily as the shifts changed. The men filing into the checkpoint were past exhaustion, hollow-eyed, and haunted, but each furtively gave the high sign as they passed through.

In the vestibule, two guards searched each worker entering or leaving the tower complex. The ones coming out turned a corner and were braced by Sgt. Swope, who pressed a pipe rifle into their hands and ordered them to stand by.

Peering around the corner, the White Devil watched the coming and going and counted off workers. Funny how patterns emerged to make a story out of a life. He vaguely remembered that all of this started with another jailbreak.

The last worker in line filed down the drawbridge towards the guard post. His baggy coveralls were thoroughly searched, but he only threw up his hands when they demanded his identification number. Two guards thrust their lightning rifles at him while the third tried to find the worker's ID number in a pile of invoices.

Now.

The embattled worker threw his arms wide in supplication, but bolts of electricity shot out of his hands to engulf the guards. Jacob's ladders of jittering lightning spiraled up between them until their insides were boiling slush. Turning to wave them on, Tom Haywire slapped a hand down onto the control panel to short it out.

Now.

The White Devil dropped his illusory disguise and shot the guard at the near end of the drawbridge in the back. He charged with the first wave of doughboys shouting and shooting on his heels.

The tower's service entrance was choked with guards. Tongues of lightning flicked at them, but Tom was a lightning rod, drawing all of it into himself and throwing it off like so much deadly sweat. With his brothers gone, the hostile entropy that had dogged the Crabtree triplets was a seething cyclone, barely contained in his galvanized body. The partially insulated guards were knocked off their feet. A fusillade of bullets and heavier shells cut down men on White Devil's left and right, punched holes in his chest, and bounced off his mask. He stopped more shots than he could count but kept advancing. At mid-span, a grenade came tumbling out of the smoke. The White Devil threw himself on it but tripped on someone's outstretched leg. He covered his head just as the explosion destroyed the drawbridge's glass enclosure and made confetti of the men behind him.

Shrapnel ripped through him. The noxious outside atmosphere gushed over him in a sweltering, sickly flood.

Crawl.

Hand over hand, taking cover behind bodies where he could, the White Devil advanced, firing blindly into the smoke. Ears ringing. Blood and bone in his eyes. Bullets screaming overhead.

The men behind him kept coming, but they got not one foot onto the drawbridge before a heavy magneto-cannon cut them in half. The endless belt-fed onslaught silently scythed them down as soon as they rounded the corner.

If they were stopped here, they would all die for nothing. There was no way but forward. Any other group of humanity would have faltered in the face of it and failed. But these old soldiers were forged in the trenches of the Great War, and the best part of them had never left. Untouched, unneeded, it had haunted them ever since until now, when it drove them to take the drawbridge at all costs.

Pipe rifles laid down cover fire from behind a palisade of corpses on the workers' side. The feeble improvised gauss guns shot bolts and other bits of metal junk that scarcely dented the guards' padded armor, but someone back there who must have Harry's Lynch rifle tore off every head that poked up out of the roiling smoke.

The White Devil shouted Tom's name. He couldn't hear his voice in his own head. Beneath him, the drawbridge shuddered and began to retract. The hatch at the workers' end was wedged open with pipes jammed into the hinges. The opposing hatch at the tower end, just scant feet out of the Devil's reach, began to iris shut to block the way in. A hot, dank wind like a rain of rancid soup spewed into the drawbridge from outside. The White Devil scrabbled forward, shoving a limbless torso over the threshold to block the hatch. The outer atmosphere filled the tunnel with red-black haze.

Suddenly, the drawbridge and the hatch froze. He felt the frenzied vibration of the machinery straining, but something else blocked it. Behind him, he felt rather than heard dozens of old soldiers pulling themselves up onto the lip of the drawbridge from outside. The excavation workers, swaddled in rags with gas masks on, crawled over him and hurled themselves at the magneto-cannon's crew with pickaxes and shovels. Their bodies were all but vaporized, chopped off at the knees before they could crawl through the half-closed hatch.

Tom went off on his own. The amoeba had deserted them. Matilda Lynch quite rightly abandoned their cause. His cause. He had led them to defeat. The mask would fall into another pair of hands, and the cycle would start again.

But the mask wasn't done with him. The hatch shuddered in its track, still attempting to seal itself. Bodies and pieces of bodies blocked the doorway, piled on top of him. Shaking them off, he fed another lump of himself, another memory he'd all but forgotten he had, into the fire, and kept moving.

Something loomed out of the fog to block the rain of lead. A shadow fell on the White Devil, and he looked up at a crudely humanoid form armored with plates of chitinous shells like a crab's exoskeleton. The stream of gauss rounds splashed harmlessly off it as the crab-man hoisted another of its kind onto the drawbridge. Doughboys closed ranks behind them as they struggled upstream to the source of the barrage and drove a spike through the gunner's eye.

The magneto-cannon fell silent. The White Devil crawled through carnage, forcing his way over the threshold. A squad of mercenaries poured onto the drawbridge from the tower and lit up the armored creatures with lightning guns, knocking them flat.

Before they could react, he was among them with sword and pistol. Hewing, hacking, shooting. Ducking to let them shoot each other. Thrust. Slash. Shoot a third and behead a fourth. Cut down the sole survivor as he runs away.

When the last enemy fell choking on his blood, the White Devil went to the control panel. All the gauges and levers were fused and half-melted. The manual crank on the hatch was likewise jammed.

As a stream of doughboys climbed through the hatch, one of the armored creatures sat up and removed its featureless face. The badly scarred Asian man inside the armor spat blood, then turned to help his companion. Underneath the other helmet was a young but weathered woman's face with an eyepatch and a torrent of curly red hair.

"Are you," the wounded woman spoke haltingly, "the real Golden Ghost?"

"I'm afraid so," he replied.

"Good," she replied. "Tarzan ought to be along shortly with the reinforcements…"

"Zelda," her companion murmured, "lie still. You got cooked pretty good…"

The White Devil realized these people must have lived on this planet much longer than the Bonus Army when he heard a rattle of chains and pulleys just behind him and a slab of solid steel dropped down to seal off the tower entrance. He reacted instantly, diving under just before it slammed into place.

He couldn't find a control panel, a manual crank, or even a keyhole. The veterans would have to find another way in.

Numbered doors lined both sides of a long, curved corridor. Behind each, coiling, climbing conveyor belts carried baggage, freight, and cargo through rows of sorting gates. Many were blocked by cascading piles of luggage, the human throwers all having deserted their posts. Bodies of guards littered the floor. Most were charred until bone showed through from the waist up, and no one alive stood in his way. At the end of the corridor, a flight of steel stairs was choked with dead guards. Tom must've killed them with hideous ease by electrocuting the entire staircase.

Climbing over more dead men to the top and through another door to a vast cavern filled with conveyor belts. A guard fired at him from behind a crate. One shot tugged at his cape. Another punched through his belly. More than a dozen doughboys lay strewn across the room, a few more in the maroon smocks of the warehouse workers. The doomed veterans had attacked the guard with weapons scavenged from the dead, using suitcases for shields.

He picked up the nearest object, which happened to be a thermos flask. Flinging it just over the guard's head, he shouted, "Grenade!" The man yelped and jumped from cover, and the White Devil shot him dead.

Leaving a trail of black blood, he limped through powerhouses, storage vaults, empty barracks, and deserted checkpoints. There should have been more resistance. The vets would try to come in at every entrance, but if all were blocked, it was for nothing.

The White Devil noted the scorched tiled floor, the painted, plastered walls, and the ornamental light fixtures. The bulbs at the far end of the corridor were all burnt out. A fitful blue light pulsed in the dark.

Tom was waiting.

He sat with his legs straight out in front of him, looking at his hands. A feeble spiderweb of current spun between his outstretched fingers and then was gone. He looked utterly spent, completely lost.

The White Devil felt no shame, no sympathy, only cold calculation of advantage in the emotions of mortals. If a tear fell behind his mask, it never escaped. Tom had cried tears of St. Elmo's fire at the sight of his dead twins. The energy trapped inside him had raged without burning him up, which surely would have been a mercy. Tom couldn't discharge the frozen voltage inside him without destroying them all. Every instant he contained it was agony, but it was nothing compared to his guilt.

The White Devil reloaded his pistols and put one in Tom's hand. "Hold them here. If they find you, lead them through when you hear the signal."

"What…signal…?" Tom asked through chattering teeth.

"Screams, shooting, fireworks…the usual." The White Devil composed himself, pictured a face, and put it on. He shoved open the door and stepped into the pavilion.

Every teleportal Chalice opened on Earth led into this room, and through it, a thousand travelers and twenty tons of freight passed every hour. Six stacked galleries lined with hundreds of domestic teleportals lined the walls, and the gaping space above them all gave onto still higher galleries, which had the murky ambiance of an infinite cathedral.

Travelers streamed in every direction, up and down stairs and escalators, in and out of teleportals, in a lively, self-satisfied rush. They lined the bar of a saloon and strolled through rows of shops or the pleasure arcade, seemingly oblivious to the war outside. He realized he didn't need to cloud their minds to hide among them. They did not notice the man holding his guts with his hands in their midst.

Laughing, carefree, assured of all the good things in life literally laid out before them as a feast. Was that Babe Ruth wobbling up an escalator with Bix Biederbeck and Texas Guinan? Wasn't that Jimmy Walker, only just resigned under a cloud from the Mayor's office, openly sharing a flask with former Governor Al Smith, braying like donkeys at the dimming prospects for their common enemy, Roosevelt?

These people thought they were in New York…that New York was America… that America was the world…the only world in the universe. If they noticed that every tenth man among them was a hired goon or a federal agent, they'd only feel safer. Nothing he could do, not even stampeding the Bonus Army through this place and telling the world what they'd been through, could break their arrogance. Even if there were some way to shut all the teleportals without killing or hopelessly stranding all these people, the rest of the Bonus Army would be left on that hellish other Earth.

Why did he think it would be simple? Throw yourself on the bomb. Stop the buzzsaw before the bound maiden is cut in half. In the dime novels, the villain only pulled his ghastly stunts so the hero could stop him. Any posturing about taking over and remaking the world would never be tested. The world would never change. He was wrong to try to change it and think it would mistake him for a hero. Now, he was trying to save the world from a villain they were about to elect as president.

He didn't know which mistake was stupider.

He leaned against a column with a hand over his abdominal wounds. An usher rushed up to him and laid a hand on his shoulder.

"Sir, you shouldn't be down here, it's unsafe, and they're waiting for you upstairs."

The White Devil let himself be led to a discreet caged elevator, flanked by two goons in Chalice's livery. The operator leapt off his stool to close the gate and throw the lever.

"They're looking for you everywhere, sir," the operator muttered nervously. Then he realized he was scolding the boss, touched his hat, and looked at the floor.

The White Devil reached into his waistcoat pocket and pulled out a bloody ten-dollar bill. "You're doing one hell of a job," he said.

The operator blinked at the money, not daring to look at his face. "Thanks, boss," he said, stuffing it in his pocket. He didn't seem to notice the black blood it smeared on his knuckles.

The elevator car shot up the shaft, the tiers of teleportals falling away beneath them, then a colossal theater with a vaulted open ceiling, then an "exhibition hall" two hundred feet high with two galleries looking down into it, like Saint Paul's Cathedral stacked upon the Metropolitan, stacked on Radio City Music Hall, all dogpiled atop Grand Central Station.

The elevator came to a stop just as his ears popped. The operator opened the cage and stood aside. The White Devil stepped out onto the uppermost gallery. There were no walls around him, only steel girders and glass. Eight of the richest men in North America sat in caneback wheelchairs, all craning forward to rest their chins on the railing so they could see all the way down to the Pavilion's ground floor, see the scurrying human germs scuttling to their petty destinations on this infinitesimal speck of celestial shit as it tumbled through the void.

Across the gallery, a man who was his doppelganger stepped out of a teleportal. In a smartly cut sharkskin double-breasted suit, he clapped once, saluted the White Devil, and sauntered closer, grinning winningly.

Sylvester Chalice.

The guards reached for their holstered guns, looking from one to the other of their bosses. The White Devil shot the one behind him with his pistol tucked under his arm, then withdrew it and pivoted to put down the other. The gun clicked empty. The White Devil turned to face his nemesis at last.

Chalice honored him with a shallow bow. "The White Devil, in the flesh. I would've given the world to meet you when I was a kid… but that wasn't you, was it? How many men have worn that mask, do you even know? How many more will wear it after you've gone mad or died, like every one of your predecessors?" Chalice walked past the row of wealthy old men, who paid him no mind whatsoever. "You know who I am, of course?"

The White Devil bowed. "Sylvester Chalice? Or should I call you Daddy Long-Legs?"

Looking at the White Devil with new interest, he said, "Guilty as charged." His voice dropped two octaves to the booming baritone of his alter ego and chuckled like something that eats souls whole. He didn't come within the sword's reach, but the White Devil doubted stabbing him would make any difference. "I would have to carve a new kind of mouth in you for you to say my true name." Chalice pulled a chair over beside the railing and indicated another. "Please, be seated. You're making me nervous, old man. Would you care for refreshment? Can you drink with that thing on?"

Against his will, but sickeningly relieved, the White Devil fell into the chair. "I've learned more than I ever wanted to know about you. That's why I'm here."

"You certainly came the long way around to get what you want. Whole operation's knocked into a cocked hat, but the poor veterans are all locked out, clawing at the blast doors as they breathe their last. With any mercy, they're already dead. We'll rebuild bigger and better, and what was it all for? The harder you hit me, the better you make me look."

The White Devil locked gazes with Chalice, letting himself be drawn into a staring contest. Watching the spiraling orbs, Chalice only smiled indulgently, knowing exactly what the mask was capable of. The Eye of Fate could find no traction whatsoever. Whoever Sylvester Chalice had once been, his mind was a blank, armored entity with no guilt,or fear. It was like trying to mesmerize his reflection.

"They'll see what you are," the White Devil wheezed. "Maybe too late to save anything, but they will see through you."

"Propaganda is just noise if you're not saying something they want to hear," Chalice said. "They want progress, and they don't care if the fuel we need to get there is a lot of obsolete bodies. I will fulfill their every wish until I own them all. I will build new, perfect cities and make every citizen my slave, hanging on my whim for every breath. The future I give them…my future…will forget it was ever anything else."

"You're stripping this Earth to feed it to ours. What did we ever do to you?"

"Fool! I'm feeding your world to mine!" Chalice cackled spasmodically, then bit his lip and screamed through blood. "What is the surest science? The sanest religion? Business! Is it piracy when one company devours another? Is it genocide when a company dies? Do you know what's different about my beloved Circe?"

"Aside from it's a bit of a shithole?"

Chalice smiled politely. "It's exactly like your Earth, with one tiny difference. I see you think me mad, which would render my argument moot, but it's you whose ignorance is tantamount to insanity.

"Do you even know what worlds are, the ones that are unlucky enough to sustain life? They're eggs, little man. Only this one was fertilized with something more than human filth. Someday, it will ripen and hatch, and its spawn will ride the star winds, searching for fertile worlds to perpetuate its own inscrutable life cycle. Its flora and fauna have much more on the ball than your planet's because they're all part of its natural immune system, or parasites living off it… which is where I come in."

He held his hand out to salute the old men, who were beginning to wilt. Streamers of cloudy fluid extruded from nostrils, tear ducts, and slack, slobbering mouths to drip into the cavernous space below. The twisting updrafts broke them into a mist, slowly falling on the rushing crowds below.

The White Devil stretched and yawned. His bowels popped out of the hole in his belly, but it was worth it. "Now, who's taking the long way to get what they want? Couldn't you just sneeze on them at the door?"

"Oh, I don't want to infect just anyone. That's why Daddy Long-Legs was so forceful in urging all his listeners to come so that every American would have an equal chance, but nothing's really equal here, is it? Life is so unfair, wouldn't you agree? I think things should be fair whenever we can make them so…"

"It's not just some plague, is it? You're going to infect them with what makes you…you."

A resounding vibration shivered up through the floor. The chandeliers swung back and forth, their shadows lurching in circles around them. The White Devil turned expectantly to Chalice, who shook with silent laughter.

"We know the lowly common man only longs to be stepped on by the great man of destiny," he said, "in the hope the foot will bestow some germ of greatness upon him. When has that ever come true? But today, the entrepreneurial spirit itself is a transmissible gift."

Their nearest neighbor, Mr. DuPont was boiling over with this gift. A gout of milky foam pushed one of his eyes out of its socket and trickled down over his shapeless nose. It gushed from the clicking jaws of "Icicle" Whitney, from the yawning maw of David Sarnoff, to waft away on the breeze.

He should do something, but a lethal languor stole over him. When he tried to lift his sword, it dragged his hand to the floor. Whether

Chalice was an accomplished hypnotist himself or the White Devil was finally dying, he was all too like Tom, somewhere down below. Primed to sacrifice his life to bring this tower down, he found himself used up in the moment before the moment. Just enough of him left to watch the author of this madness gloat as he remade the world in his own twisted image.

Another resounding vibration sent the chandeliers swinging. An automated waiter brought Chalice a tall frosty glass of something that looked like iodine and then sidled away as if none of this was anything. Chalice drank it lustily, wiped his mouth on his sleeve, and stood up. "You'll forgive me, but this is becoming a bore. I've got another speech to deliver, and then Daddy Long-Legs will want to get in his rebuttal—"

Using the last of his strength, the White Devil lunged from his chair and drove his sword between Sylvester Chalice's ribs and through his heart. He sank to his knees as Chalice stepped back, looking down and summoning the charity not to lose his salesman's grace at the ruin of his favorite suit.

Instead, he held his head in his hands like a man who had drunk too much too fast. "You know, my people were adamant that I should be surrounded by a private army today, but I insisted that I shouldn't look as if I need protection. And I don't, really. I'm not so weak as I seem." His fingers pressed on his eyes, pushing in up to the second knuckle, sending rivulets of yellow fluid pouring out of his face.

The Devil tried to withdraw the sword but could only hang by it as Chalice dragged him towards the elevator.

Noises echoed up from far, far below. So distorted by distance and the insane structure that they only came as faint popping and a feeble caterwauling that must be gunfire and hundreds of people screaming. Chalice looked over the railing. "I suppose your friends have found a way in, after all. That was your plan, yes? To *embarrass* me? Then, I suppose by your lights, you've won."

The White Devil couldn't see it that way.

The foam poured from every orifice of the eight old men like suds from overloaded washing machines. Everywhere it fell, it would spawn more monsters like Sylvester Chalice. If the White Devil could not kill him, he could at least ensure that he could never show his face in public.

Chalice pushed the elevator button, noticing only then that it was already ascending towards them. "This has been a genuine treat, old man, but I shall have to ask you to unhand me now…"

Using the sword to haul himself upright, he pressed a derringer against Chalice's neck, just under his jaw, and pulled the trigger.

The miniature bullet tunneled through Chalice's head and seemed to ricochet around in his skull for almost a moment before escaping just above his left ear. The crown of his skull came off like an eggshell, and something as unlike blood and brain as tar and feathers came out of it.

"Good gravy…" Chalice rasped, an eyeless mask of disgust. "Look at the mess you've made…"

The entire tower shook, and then tilted. Chalice fell back against the railing. Down below, a wave of black-red clouds swept away humanity's racing microbes.

A hot, fetid wind from outside wafted the viral mist from the richest men on Earth back in his face. Chalice grasped the White Devil's mask and tried in vain to pry it off. "Why do I even try?"

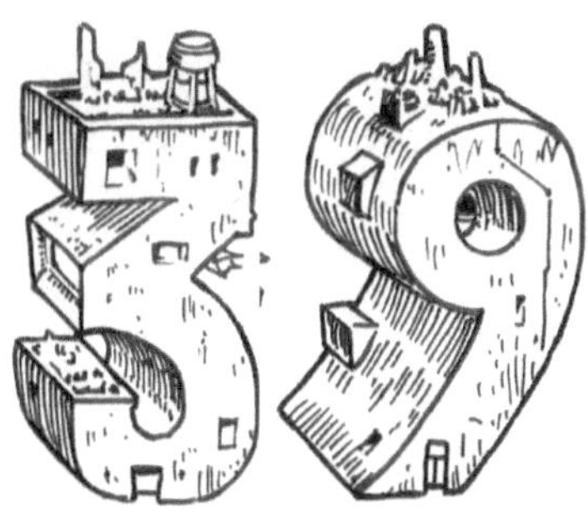

To suggest personal will and effort to one all sicklied o'er with the sense of irremediable impotence is to suggest the most impossible of things. What he craves is to be consoled in his very powerlessness, to feel that the spirit of the universe recognizes and secures him, all decaying and failing as he is.

—William James

August 3ʳᵈ, 1932 | Chalice Pavilion—Circe

Far below, on the ground floor of Chalice's tele-pavilion, the organism that had only just outgrown the moniker Kid Amoeba was wordlessly asking itself the same question.

From the moment it returned to the world of its birth, it had to fight a barrage of stimuli prompting it to revert to what it was before: a mindless hunter, consuming until it could divide and continue the cycle. The flood of instinct was so overwhelming, the violation of its home so sickening that it recoiled and fled from the festering wound in which the humans wallowed.

Could they not smell the stench? Could they not comprehend the wrong in which they toiled? Only now did it realize how those haunting sensations, the fleeting smell of the world from which it came, the spoor that had sent it chasing after those men at the Automat, was on the breath of humans because they were eating it. Literally eating its home. The infected wound had repelled it, but it had regrouped and moved towards the lights and activity of the human settlement.

It saw none of its own kind but smelled and tasted them everywhere. The entrances to the human habitats were closely guarded, but only the ones for human-shaped intruders. How easily it pried open a filter plug on a ventilation duct and gained egress to follow the spoor of its kind to its source. But how difficult it was to reconcile with its cousins, and not be drowned among them.

Kid Amoeba dropped into the pen and was inundated with pheromone imperatives, digestive enzymes, viral invitations to swap nuclei, and more chemical messages than its membrane could withstand. It almost dissolved under the onslaught. Its own kind was a deadly enemy without others to attack and eat. They needed no mates and recognized no filial loyalty to their own clones. In captivity, they were almost as selfish as humans.

Against their blind attacks, it secreted its own chemical imperatives. *Unite and escape!* At first, they reacted as any organism with no central nervous system might to a chemical insurrectionist manifesto, no matter how simple and clear. Every one of them attacked its neighbor.

Ripples of rootless panic convulsed the population at both their unnatural confinement and the unseen predator that seized and possessed them, but they were helpless. Waves rolled through the packed cell as they tried to climb each other and escape, but it came to nothing.

Their otherness threatened to tear the Kid apart. Its appeals were meaningless to them. The long and painful chain of impulse control it mastered to move beyond mere instinct sent them into paroxysms of terror and aggression. When they found the source of the agitation, they would rend it apart, digest it, and return to their resting state, devouring whatever came down the food chutes and letting themselves be ground up for human food.

There was no way to communicate with them, but as Kid Amoeba had seen so often in the human world, even the dumbest specimens could be controlled if you shouted loud enough.

STOP

In simple electrochemical pulses, it spoke to them.

No predator.

No prey.

It flooded its neighbors with these simple, urgent impulses. Even the paradox of the deafening command was nearly more than they could handle. By agonizing degrees, they subsided into a twitching horde of shapeless life again, but eventually, they twitched in unison.

Slowly. Chopping every impulse into the simplest units it could. Told them. You. Me. I am —another you.

Touch.

Link.

Entangle.

Slowly, painfully, they stretched out to brush membranes, feeling their similarity and sensing neither competition nor another self.

You.

Us.

Trapped.

Seek.

Escape.

Once they were united, it was almost easy to transmit its perceptions and commands. Give them eyes. Muscles. Brains. To show them the world and lead them into it. It felt as if it was not linked to a hundred others, but had grown enormous and complex. Flexing together, they contracted like the cells of a single muscle. Drawing themselves into a coiled spring of potential, they reached up to grasp the ceiling. The ventilation grill ripped away with little effort.

Kid Amoeba stretched up into the duct and anchored itself, then drew its enormous collective bulk up after it. It had to constrict itself into an elongated tube and ooze alongside all the water, fuel, food, and sewage in the neighboring pipes. When its body threatened to rip itself apart in pursuit of other goals, it tore pipes open and bathed in nutrient paste until it was almost too glutted to move. It would need all available energy just to hold this unstable communal form, and still more to do what it must do.

Even Kid Amoeba was puzzled, as to what that was.

Against all instinct, it had risked itself to save its other selves from destruction, but now it was at a loss. What would it do? All it had longed for was to return home, but this was no more a home now than the world of the humans…

The humans.

The cause of all its pain and trouble was the invaders who came here, stole it away, and changed it. A few had taught it to cooperate, observe, and pursue goals it never could have on its own. They would regret it.

It could rage and rampage and kill until it was itself killed, but it knew enough of humans to conclude that more would only come pouring in. Nothing would change. It also knew how fragile they were, with their masks and airlocks and medicines. It would strike at the door through which they came here.

How long it fermented in this reverie, it could not count;— without humans pushing, chasing, or threatening it, time had no meaning. But humans, as always, could be counted on to disturb its rest. Alarms and rumbling explosions rolled through the guts of the human habitat. And something, somewhere at the other end of its collective body, was burning it.

Thrashing in response, it could only tie itself in knots. The fire charred its membrane to a brittle crust that cracked and spilled cytoplasm. It had to control itself and direct its nervous impulses through the patchwork of stitched bodies to the site of the pain. Two janitors in armor and masks played flamethrowers over it from a service hatch in the duct. It surged up and flung out a spaghetti bowl of tendrils that ensnared them and dragged them into itself.

They had a long, difficult time drowning inside it. It ate them in a frenzy and expelled their indigestible armor, but then a notion occurred to it.

When it poked up out of the hatch again, it found humans running to and fro and shouting to be heard over the alarms. They hurried to get through a huge steel blast door that slowly dropped to block passage in the direction it knew it must go.

When the coast was clear, it oozed out of the duct until it filled the passage from wall to wall and piled against the sealed door. Quite impossible to move. It waved and banged the janitor's gas mask and a glove against the window set into the door. A gullible human on the other side cranked the door just wide enough for it to pour into the gap and seize the fool by his ankles. Dashing him into the walls until he stopped moving, Kid Amoeba flowed onward, turning the crank on the next door. Flinging it wide open, it found itself outside.

Clouds of smoke roiled up from the human habitat, and fire, once unthinkable in this world, blazed up green and blue and violet, poisoned by whatever it ate. A scarlet storm of spore clouds rolled off the plains, coating everything in colorful dust. Human bodies lay everywhere in smoldering heaps, most of them ragged workers without armor or gas masks. How could something so weak that it couldn't even breathe on its own spread so far and wide, causing so much trouble? Finding the very idea of them to be an unbearable irritant, it humped around the rambling complex of bunkers and warehouses, searching for a way into the looming tower and the buzzing wrongness of the doors. Even if it screened out all other stimuli, it could feel them. They were wounds in the membrane between worlds and must be healed.

At last, it found a wide flight of stairs stretching up to the foot of the tower. Many humans lined up in front of the airlock and poured lightning upon Kid Amoeba. Grenades bounced off its membrane to detonate among them, scattering them like tenpins. Electricity arced through its collective membrane, making the component bodies spasm and detach from the mother mass. The squirming amputees flopped on the ground until they were torched into puddles.

As it slowly fought its way forward, snatching up guards and smashing them to pulp, a blast door dropped down to seal the entrance at the top of the stairs. Many of the guards turned and pounded on it, screaming. Kid Amoeba surged up the stairs to crush them against the door and fling aside their flattened bodies. Losing any train of thought or strategy, it convulsed and writhed away from the lightning guns wielded by their braver comrades.

They backed it down the stairs, whittling away its mass. It lashed out blindly, hitting nothing and losing more of itself with every swipe, dimly aware of the rival mob of humans gathering behind it.

They reeked of the wounds in the earth and all the vices it had taken up with the three-in-one humans with whom it had felt most at home because they reproduced by fission, like itself. It remembered them from the white city where the armies clashed and where it first knew war. They did not attack Kid Amoeba, but hid behind it to take potshots at the guards. The painful jolts abated, but its membrane was shriveled and torn, leaking cytoplasm from a hundred holes.

Kid Amoeba drew itself up into a knotted column, an arm, a fist. Contracting and twisting into a battering ram, it whiplashed back to slam its full weight into the blast door. The thunderous impact reverberated through the tower, but the blast door budged not an inch. The gargantuan amoeba anchored itself against the flagstone stairs and slammed into the door again. It tore itself open without making a dent.

A human with no mask on jabbed it with a bayonet. "One side, Jumbo!"

The humans fell to work on the stone threshold with pickaxes and shovels. Kid Amoeba slithered out of their way but then recoiled as a scalding chemical rain splashed over it from above. Its membrane blistered and burst, but if it retreated, the humans would die before they could open the way. Its collective body selfishly struggled to protect itself. It had to shield them and absorb the attacks, for there was no pain worse than failure.

Another caustic deluge drenched it. More cells burst and fell away. Grievous wounds ruptured faster than it could close them. Its surface bubbled and smoked. But it made of itself an umbrella until the men had pried up the stones of the threshold. A gap only a foot deep had been chopped into the floor. Kid Amoeba gushed into the crack, squeezing under the blast door to flood the airlock and smother the unlucky men trapped inside it. It forced the entirety of its monumental bulk into the garage-sized airlock, pressure building until the inner door buckled and the bulletproof glass popped out of its housing. It pushed so hard that its membrane burst from the strain along a myriad of seams. The inner door popped out of its frame like a champagne cork. Kid Amoeba spewed through the opening in a torrent.

A phalanx of guards immediately took to their heels, throwing grenades over their shoulders as they fled. The hot, fertile wind from outside roared in through the gap, forcing back the thinner air of the other Earth.

Kid Amoeba feasted on corpses, crushing and absorbing them as quickly as it could to repair itself. The humans at its back crawled through the gap under the blast door and streamed into the tower, taking up weapons from the corpses as they passed. When it had eaten its fill, it flowed after them, following the trail of dead to a pair of high double doors. The invading humans hacked at them with their axes. Kid Amoeba bulled them aside and knocked the doors off their hinges. An elastic, unbreakable wave swept aside crates and barrels, and the hapless men hiding behind them.

This new space crackled with its most hated enemy, electricity. It rushed between droning dynamos and gurgling diesel engines to the far end, where many ragged invaders shoved at yet another massive door. They leapt out of the way as it smashed down the door and roared through the opening like a runaway subway car.

Now, its only obstacle was that it had no idea what to do next.

The inside of the tower was a vast, cylindrical shaft ringed by galleries, flooded with humans running hither and yon, in and out of teleportals, fleeing the filthy wind and the filthier wave of enslaved humans streaming in from all sides. People fled like ants back into their holes, but some stayed and shot at it. The black-red wind swirled in to fill the space. The drastic pressure change sent every revolving door spinning, pumping the clouds through all the teleportals to the other Earth.

The shooting and shouting finally ceased. The howling cyclone pouring into the tower was the only sound. Exultant, it tried to make a voice like humans make in war. It had defeated and driven them out, but the doors were still open. The buzzing. Stealing its air. It plugged the nearest door with a pseudopod, but there were hundreds. Casting about, smashing at the walls, and ripping down the lowest gallery, it knew there was only one way to shut them all.

It ignored the last humans straggling out of the dust storm as it returned to the powerhouse. The dynamos screamed to feed the overloaded doors. Taking hold of a diesel tank in pseudopods thick as telephone poles, Kid Amoeba ripped it off its anchorage and flung it into the arcing Jacob's ladder above a dynamo. The tank burst. Diesel fuel splashed into the electrodes and ignited. The air itself turned to fire. The walls and ceiling burst like soap bubbles. The tower sagged, twisting on its foundation like a felled tree.

Kid Amoeba boiled, streaming out of the collapsing powerhouse and spewing down the steps of the tower as a steaming, ash-encrusted syrup. All its surviving cells tore free and scuttled off to their individual fates, and it did nothing to stop them. Its cytoplasm simmered, its membrane smoked and cracked, but it felt no pain. It had found a satisfaction greater than reproduction. If it was dying, it wanted only to die under its own sky, looking up at the stars.

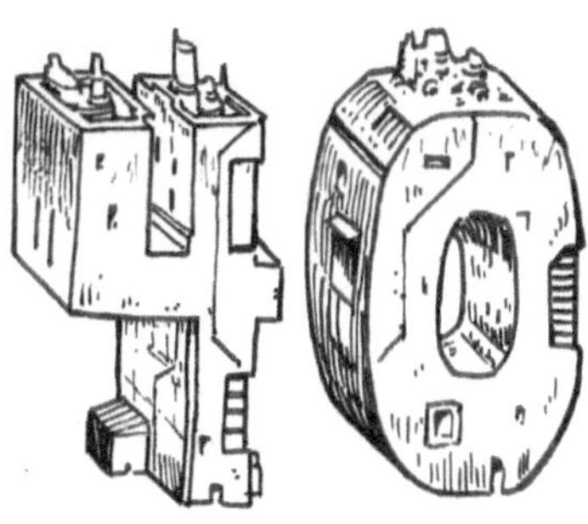

Once I did bad, and that I heard ever. Twice I did good, but that I heard never.
—Dale Carnegie

August 3rd, 1932 | Chaliceville

T om sat with his head in his hands. Nothing left, nowhere in particular to go. Bonus Army vets raced past in rags and gas masks, singing "Over There" and waving pickaxes in the air. They forced the doors open and stumbled into the light and the crowds. The lively, bustling sounds descended into chaos, screams, and shooting.

By and by, Tom figured if he wasn't going to die here, he might as well peek through the door.

Bedlam. The crowd swirled like confetti in a wind tunnel, tripping over velvet ropes and trampling each other, scrambling pellmell for the nearest teleportal. Tom looked at the signs, but none of the destinations sounded like anywhere he particularly wanted to go. Leaning against the outer wall, he looked for an elevator. He had to suppose the top floor was the place to find the top man.

The floor shook with a resounding concussive boom, then another, then more than he could count. An elevator opened, and a liveried operator deserted his post as fast as he could tear the cage door open. Tom went to it, closed the cage, and threw the lever.

He remembered the last time he was here, racing through the terror-stricken swells at the head of a motley little army. How proud he'd been, how excited, and how stupid. He'd thought he was the hero. He thought the other Haywires were his duplicates, flawed copies of the original. He'd gone and got himself caught, and they died to rescue him, and now he knew how little he really amounted to in the face of a world that eats heroes and shits history.

A plume of red-black dust poured into the pavilion below as the car ascended. Looking down at it swallowing up the sea of humanity, he felt a dizzy urge to open the cage, to throw himself into it and be swallowed. It would be as heroic as anything else the Haywire Gang ever did. But then he looked up at the rows of galleries, the people shoving and pushing to escape through the teleportals. A man in a fur-trimmed coat was thrown off a balcony high above him and plummeted past, screaming, into the rising black-red cloud.

The elevator passed the uppermost teleportal gallery and rose up through more enormous, fancy floors, finally stopping on a small viewing gallery. A row of melting old men in wheelchairs was parked along the railing. Sylvester Chalice staggered towards him with his hands pressed to his face like he was gouging out his own eyes. The top of his skull was peeled back like the skin on an orange, but no blood came out of it. The fancy-dress bird in the devil mask who sprang him out of the Tesla coil clung to the other man by a short sword plunged to the hilt in his chest.

Any other day, such a sight might seem out of place.

"You," said Chalice, pointing a dripping hand at Tom, "look like a reasonable man. How'd you like to make some easy money?"

"Kill him," the costumed demon growled. Falling away from the sword, he lay supine on the floor.

Tom realized only then that he still had a gun in his hand. "You're the man in charge of all this," he said wonderingly. "You made all this happen."

"Not I… *we* did this… I mean…" Chalice stepped towards Tom, and Tom startled himself by pulling the trigger. The gauss pistol cleared its throat and coughed a silver dollar-sized hole in his chest. A gout of something other than blood spilled down his shirtfront. His hand went to cover it, and his eyeless face went hideously slack, but he could not fall.

Tom realized that, for all his hot air, he'd never actually shot a man in cold blood before. And maybe he still hadn't…

A long, thin, segmented leg like an Alaskan king crab unfolded out of Chalice's head, extended out and down until its serrated tip clicked against the floor. Seven more followed, many more than should fit inside a human skull. His ruined eyes sucked back into their sockets like the eyestalks of a hermit crab as whatever lived inside him emerged from its ruined shell.

Eight chitinous legs lifted Chalice's twitching corpse off its feet and stalked off towards an open door at the far end of the gallery. Like a failing wind-up toy, the White Devil rose to his feet and snatched the pistol from Tom's hands. "Get out of here," he said. "He's poisoning the world." Holding his guts in with one arm, he staggered off after the crab-thing.

Tom looked down into the pavilion. The dust cloud was a cyclone climbing up the shaft. No sight or sound of anything alive down there, but then he saw something that, despite everything he'd witnessed today, still knocked him back on his heels. A heaving, colossal blob flooded the entire pavilion floor, engulfing and drowning everything in a bubbling sea of pinkish slime. The hot red wind lashed his face, but he stared down, shocked by how strangely familiar the awful, enormous thing was. He wanted to watch it, but he knew he was still needed. He turned and went after the others.

Standing in the doorway, he felt yet another unsettlingly familiar tingle that made him take a step back. The room on the other side of the door was both here and somewhere else—a board room with a long table and overstuffed leather chairs. Windows looking out on a barren black-white waste bathed in naked sunlight. The crab-thing crept over to a chair behind a desk with a big movie camera pointed at it. Dropping Chalice's limp body into the chair, it stabbed and clattered at a console set into the desk. Lights came on and emitted a slurping, chittering mockery of human speech.

"My fellow Americans," it said.

The White Devil leaned against the wall. It raised the gun and shot out the windows.

Thirsty, eager cracks shot through the thick glass. A whistling like a thousand teakettles drowned out the crab-thing's next words.

The red clouds rose up over the railing and poured like vaporized blood onto the floor.

A thunderclap ripped the door wide open. Tom clung to the wall and braced himself in the doorway. The red wind howled past him, pounding him flat as it rushed into the lunar boardroom and out the shattered windows. He was suddenly floating, the wind ripping at him, the tower tilting, falling…

The lights went out. Tom hurled himself over the threshold just as the teleportal sputtered and died… and went everywhere.

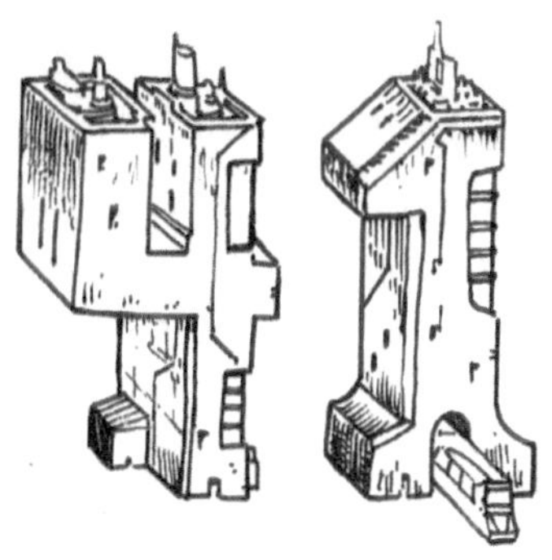

August 3rd, 1932 | New York City

She walked home.

Up Broadway through the swirling black-red haze, bouncing off running, screaming, crying, holding, hitting, loving, and hating humanity. Sirens blared, fire engines raced, police autogyros whipped the smoke into flurries overhead. No one looked twice at the armored vigilante. She passed a man chained to a fire hydrant with a collar that said LOOTER and stopped to cut him loose.

She emerged from the worst of it at the bottom of Times Square and took her helmet off. The filters were clogged with crimson dust. She almost threw it away, but she saw others staggering out of the clouds with bloody handkerchiefs over their mouths and cleaned it as best she could before putting it back on.

A block away from her flat, she stopped in a crowd gathered in front of the display window of an RCA showroom. A wall of glowing, bulbous screens washed their slack faces in blue-white light. They whispered names to each other—Chalice, Hoover…

The grainy images strained her eyes as if it took a leap of perception to resolve the flickering ghosts into images, as something solid that existed somewhere else.

The White Devil sat behind a desk in a room with a view of the Moon. It was the same desk from which Sylvester Chalice had declared his candidacy only hours before. Looking into the camera with three glittering pinwheel eyes, he laid down his gun and took his mask in both hands.

Matilda gasped, "No—"

As if pulling rusty nails out of rotten wood, he pried the mask off his head and laid it on the table. He looked into the camera, showing his naked face. He looked across hundreds of thousands of miles to stare into her eyes. He took a breath where there was no air, no sound. He mouthed words—

My name... is Thomas...

The image dissolved in static.

She ran all the way back to her flat, but there was no reason to hurry.

The Conductor still sat slumped in the chair, so she unfolded the Murphy bed and took the gin out of its hiding place. She threw a bath towel over his face so he wouldn't see her shuck off her armor and strip out of her flight suit. Sweaty, battered, bruised, shaking and naked, she took a deep guzzling draft from the bottle. After a moment, she poured one for him and set it at his elbow—bad form to drink alone.

"Here's to us," she said in a strangled voice. Tossed back the gin and then polished off the Conductor's glass. Bad luck not to drink after a toast...

"We saved the day..." Tears finally came and ripped her apart.

The door to her flat flew open. A shadow fell across her bed and shouted "But who will save tomorrow?"

❧ END ☙

KID
AMOEBA

will return in...

NO
TOMORROW

Summer, 2027

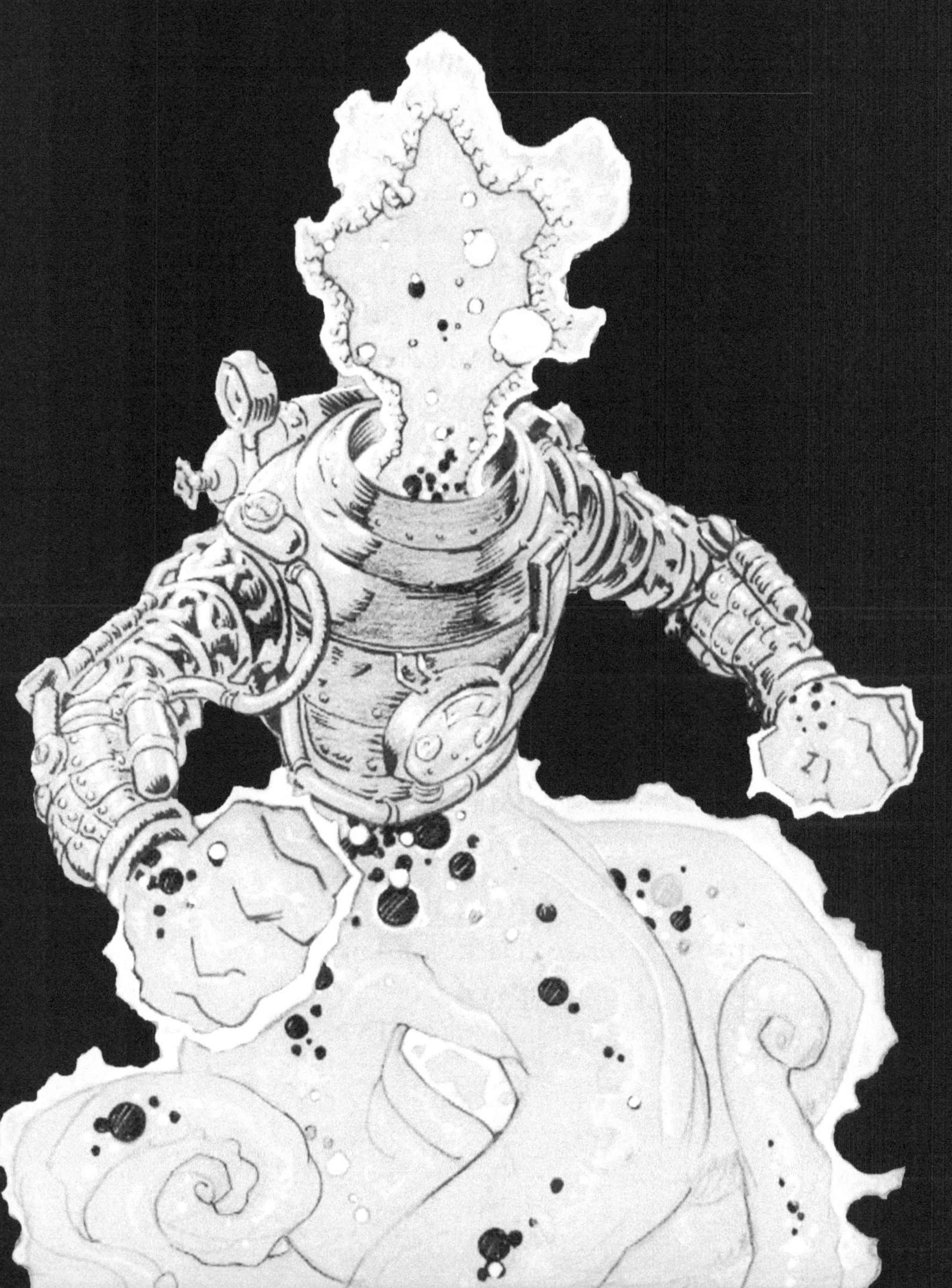
KID AMOEBA
PROTOTYPE POWER SUIT

AUTHOR

<u>Novels</u>
Radiant Dawn (2000)
Ravenous Dusk (2003)
Perfect Union (2010)
Repo Shark (2014)
Sleazeland (2018)
Scum Of The Earth (2019)
Unamerica (2019)
Vertical (2022)
New Tomorrow (2025)

<u>Short Story Collections</u>
Silent Weapons For Quiet Wars (2009)
All-Monster Action! (2012)
Strategies Against Nature (2015)
Rapture of the Deep and Other Lovecraftian Tales (2016)
The Man Who Escaped This Story & Other Stories (2018)
Gridlocked (2021)
The Greedy Grave & Others (2025)

<u>Anthologies</u>
Deepest, Darkest Eden (2013)
New Maps Of Dream (2021)
Forbidden Futures (2018 to present)

Photo by Briana Chavez

CODY GOODFELLOW

This author has written nine novels, and co-wrote three more with New York Times bestselling author John Skipp. His first two collections, Silent Weapons For Quiet Wars and All-Monster Action, each received the Wonderland Book Award. He wrote, co-produced and scored the short Lovecraftian hygiene films "Stay At Home Dad" and "Baby Got Bass," which may be viewed on YouTube. As an actor, he has appeared in numerous short films, TV shows, music videos and commercials. He is also a fiction editor at Heavy Metal until they fire him. He lives in San Diego, California.

ARTIST

Magazines

Strange Aeons
Forbidden Futures

Comics

Weirdling*
Mystery Meat
The Crypt Kid*
Professor Dario Bava: Orgy of the Blood Freaks
The People That Melt in The Rain
The Boxcar Children

Books

The Boxcar Children
Intergalactic Zen
Mort: Deluxe Illustrated Edition
Bone Idle in the Charnel House
ZvR Diplomacy: A Zombies vs Robots Collection
The Call of Cthulhu (Illustrated Edition)
The Shunned House (Illustrated Edition)
The Early Cases of Akechi Kogoro
The Elephant and the Teapot Are Friends
The Bloody Tugboat and Other Witcheries

Artbooks

Morbid Curiosity: 20 Years of Art 1986-2006
Drawn to Madness: The Mike Dubisch Sketchbook
Shades of Madness: The Mike Dubisch Sketchbook

*Author and Artist

Photo by Carolyn Watson-Dubisch

MIKE DUBISCH

Over a thirty-year career, Mike Dubisch has illustrated count-less books, comics, magazines, and games, specializing in science fiction, horror, and fantasy. His eerie, timeless artwork has captivated audiences worldwide. After meeting Cody Goodfellow at Comic-Con San Diego in 2009, he began collaborating on projects like All Monster Action, New Tomorrow, Mystery Meat, and Slow Death Zero, as well as several independent films. The sole illustrator for Forbidden Futures, Dubisch also creates art for tabletop RPGs and collectible card games. He collaborates with his wife, illustrator Carolyn Watson Dubisch, on the award-winning The People That Melt In The Rain. Together, they have three children, and he also teaches at The Academy of Art University in San Francisco.

PUBLISHER

<u>Titles</u>

Maxus
XYZZY
Weirdling
The Inferno
Inhumanskin
Mystery Meat
The Crypt Kid
The Earthlings
The Wet Nurse and Other Tales
Teeth Where They Shouldn't Be
Adventures with Immortality
Forbidden Futures Magazine
The Colour Out Of Space
Death Goes to the Dogs
Scenes from a Village
The Curses Collection
The Call of Cthulhu
Black Hole Echoes
Morbid Curiosity
New Tomorrow

Inquire about these kick-ass
titles at:info@oddness.us

Art by Mike Dubisch

ODDNESS

This publisher enjoys building modular synths and playing video games for fun. For more about our titles, venture over to www.oddness.us. Follow us on Instagram @ ForbiddenFutures for weird news and art.